ADD MAGIC TO TASTE

A SPELLBINDING (AND SCRUMPTIOUS!) COLLECTION OF

HEARTWARMING QUEER STORIES

Duck Prints Press, LLC
Schenectady, NY

The stories in this anthology are works of fiction. The characters and events portrayed are a product of the authors' imaginations. Businesses, places, and incidents pulled from the real world or history are used in a fictional manner. Any resemblance to real people or events is coincidental.

Add Magic to Taste © 2024, Duck Prints Press, LLC

"Harmony" © 2024 I. A. Ashcroft
"A Family Thing," "A Family Thing Excerpt," and "A Family Thing Coda" © 2024 Jessica Black
"Something in the Water" and "Homecoming Dance" © 2024 Willa Blythe
"Unusual Blends" © 2024 Scarlett Gale
"The Tasty Crumpet" and "The Tasty Crumpet Coda" © 2024 A. L. Heard
"A Leap Worth Taking," "Ten Minutes to Closing," and "In Favor of Tomorrow" © 2024 T. S. Knight
"Dreaming of Pines," "Sustenance" and "Waiting to Breathe" © 2024 Tris Lawrence
"Rain and Moonlight" and "Rain and Moonlight Coda" © 2024 Lex T. Lindsay
"Breaking Bread" and "Breaking Bread Prequel" © 2024 Beth Lumen
"The Ballad of Yggdrasil" © 2024 Kristi Mae
"Confluence" and "Confluence Poems" © 2024 Puck Malamud
"In Like Flynn" and "In Like Flynn Prequel" © 2024 Jo Mathieson
"The Magic Kin Know" and "Rebellious Daughter" © 2024 Owl Outerbridge
"Herald of Love" and "Herald of Love Coda" © 2024 Maggie Page
"Tomb Many Cooks" © 2024 Em Rowntree
"Sea Salt and Caramel" and "Chocolate and Roses" © 2024 Shea Sullivan
"Bånd" © 2024 Florence Vale
"Knishes and Noshes" and "Angel" © 2024 Nina Waters

Front and back cover art © 2024 Liz Lee Illustration

Edited by A. L. Heard, A. Reilly, Nina Waters, and Rachael L. Young.
Print manuscript formatting by Hermit Writes.
E-book formatting by Nina Waters.

Published by Duck Prints Press, LLC
Schenectady, New York
duckprintspress.com
ISBN: 978-1-962488-07-5 (Paperback)
ISBN: 978-1-962488-14-3 (ePub)
ISBN: 978-1-962488-13-6 (PDF)

TABLE OF CONTENTS

More Magical Morsels

Sea Salt and Caramel

SHEA SULLIVAN

bipoc, coffee shop, creature transformation (fish), customer service representative, customer/employee, first kiss, interspecies relationship, m/m, meet cute, new england, present tense, the beach, third person limited point of view, united states of america

One of the few advantages Kyle has, being the only Amp in town, is that he's got the bathhouse to himself in the aftermath.

He's been shedding his skin for a decade, now, Sunday through Thursday, 1 p.m. sharp. Every single time, it *hurts*. Not just his thick, dry skin, or the sudden limitations of bones and gravity. There's pain in the harshness of the fish sellers' calls on the dock above him, the piercing screams of the gulls, the light that scalds through the window.

The minutes it takes to recover feel like an eternity, and even then his legs are weak. They're the last part of his body to acclimate; until they do, they're ready to split back into tentacles and drag him back into the ocean.

The streets are still festooned with blue-striped flags and tropical-ocean-themed balloons. Clearly, everyone thoroughly enjoyed the Treaty Day celebrations. Everyone but Kyle, anyway. He'd had the holiday off, but it was hard to celebrate with his family. They brought him crabs from the farm, pulled him out of his den to play, surprised him with gifts of kelp and urchins for his garden, and it all felt like a lie.

They still think he's some sort of hero because he was with the Amp delegation when they negotiated the Treaty. They think he's important Above because providing food Below is so prestigious. Nothing he says can convince them otherwise.

But the delegation he trained with six years ago moved on to more important diplomatic work without him, and his "vital role" in food provision is actually second shift as a barista at Opal's Café, so…

Kyle's irritation is more than the typical residue of the shed as he walks into town to do the world-saving work of stocking baked goods and steaming milk for lattes.

The grating of skateboard wheels stokes his anger into a tsunami, dark and crushing, as he emerges from the cross street. "Hey!" he yells, his dark, human skin screaming a warning yellow and making the cobalt around his eyes and mouth glow. "Can't you read? No skateboarding!" The scarf around his neck—the skin he sheds every day to come to this ridiculous job—ripples with warning patterns triggered by the adrenaline rush as he pins the culprit with his black-eyed gaze. He thrusts out his hand to point at the wooden sign on the coffee shop wall:

NO LOITERING, LITTERING, SHIFTING, SKATEBOARDING, HIGH MAGIC

His anger drains away as he actually *looks* at the skateboarder. He'd expected a punk kid, but this boarder is Kyle's age, as thin as Kyle is stocky, and he moves on the board like he was born there. He flashes silver-quick along the packed earth like a porpoise riding the surf, skids along the stone curb, then flips the board with one foot as he goes airborne, lands lightly, and spins to a halt. Finally, he turns to give Kyle his attention as he levers the board into his waiting hand. His face is nearly as dark as Kyle's, flushed ruddy with exertion. He grins broadly, but it wilts into a sheepish smile under Kyle's glare.

"I'm sorry," he says. "I was in the groove." He taps the board on the ground. "I just got it; it's been forever since I rode."

Kyle swallows. His human skin has gone darker, calmer, but the skin around his neck is now working through a mortifying courtship display. He wishes desperately he'd stayed in his den this morning.

"Yeah," he manages. "Good. Don't let Opal catch you out here. She hoards those." He nods at the board and gestures at the eaves of the shop, then forces himself into his curated "leave me alone" posture.

The boarder's eyes flick up and widen when he sees Opal's confiscated boards layered over each other like shingles. His knuckles go white as he grips his board tightly.

"Thanks," the boarder says. "I appreciate the heads-up. Guess I'll stick to the boardwalk." He steps forward and sticks out his hand. "I'm Clovis."

Kyle freezes, staring at Clovis's hand for a long moment before taking it. The taste is immediate—not as strong as it would be if he were wearing his true skin, but still striking and intimate.

Kelp. Salt. *Home.*

"I...I'm Kyle," he says finally, dropping Clovis's hand.

He's still reeling when Clovis opens the door for him with a sweeping "after you" gesture, then follows him inside.

Kyle knows, in his bones, in his skin, in his blood, there's something different about Clovis. And Clovis—as far as Kyle can tell, Clovis is blissfully, frustratingly, *completely* unaware.

Kyle doles out change and bares his teeth in a facsimile of a smile before looking up to greet the next customer.

His smile falters; the skin around his neck ripples blue and green. "Clovis."

"Hi, Kyle." Clovis's smile curves wide, indenting dimples into his dark cheeks and nearly hiding his eyes. It's more natural and captivating than any facial configuration Kyle has ever managed.

"Hey. What can I get you?" he asks as he tries to cover his skin's latest display.

Clovis scans the board. "What do you recommend?"

"Uh." The more Kyle grasps for a reply, the more his mind goes blank. "The sea-salt caramel latte? That's the one I like."

Clovis tips his head in consideration. "Yeah? Awesome. Make it a big one!"

"You got it." Kyle puts in the order. "Three-fifty."

Clovis hands the coins over and throws another in the tip jar as Kyle points down the counter to where Vestain is handing out drinks.

"Thanks." Clovis waves.

Kyle nods and takes a deep breath, turning to help the next customer.

At the end of their shift, Vestain hands him a latte in his favorite mug. "What's this?"

"Your friend bought it for you. He asked me to deliver it when you were done for the day. 'A "thank you" for the recommendation,' he said. It seems it made an impression." Vestain's zen smile carries a hint of humor.

"Oh," Kyle says.

Your friend.
"Thanks."

Kyle doesn't make friends Above, and he certainly doesn't go out after work. But when Clovis asks, it doesn't feel like a choice, it feels inevitable.

Like the push-pull of the tide.

"Why skateboarding?" Kyle asks as Clovis rolls up beside him, returning from a series of tricks along the boardwalk. The air is heavy with humidity and the smell of the ocean, and for once Kyle isn't desperate to pull his skin on and slip back into the water.

"Why not?" Clovis shrugs. "It feels good. It can be easy, just the smooth ride of the road, or challenging, like when I'm learning a new trick. And it feels *powerful*, you know? Free, like flying." He laughs. "I used to think I was a Viv, I loved it so much. Then a bunch of my friends had their first shift, and I realized...I just like it, I guess."

Kyle looks at the long blue marks that run parallel to Clovis's collarbones. He considers saying something about how swimming feels like that—like freedom and weightlessness. He's silent. Everyone finds their way in their own time, and he doesn't *know*, not really. He just senses it, like the warning tingle of a barracuda cresting the reef behind him.

"A Viv, huh?" he teases instead. "I'd like to see one of *them* do that triple-flip thing. Even with wings, that'd be tough."

Clovis laughs. "Right? I was always better at skating than they were." He shrugs. "Guess everybody's got something, huh?"

"Yeah, they do," Kyle agrees vaguely.

"You're gonna try it, right?" Clovis asks.

Kyle snaps his head around in alarm. "Try what?"

"The board. I'll show you. C'mon!"

"No, no, I'm good," Kyle protests while Clovis tugs his arm and makes dubious promises that he'll keep Kyle in one piece.

In the end, Clovis's a pretty good teacher, and Kyle's a terrible skateboarder, but for every bruise, there's a bout of laughter.

Secretly, Kyle considers the day a success.

Clovis points, tacitly inviting Kyle to lean closer. "Ursa Major—the bear. And that one? That's Orion, the hunter."

"In the ocean, we just draw them ourselves," Kyle says, trying not to be distracted by Clovis's shoulder touching his, tasting temptingly of kelp and sea salt. "The algae in the Deep, it glows like that. My siblings and I played in it when we were young."

"That sounds incredible," Clovis says. Then, he goes quiet—one of those long silences Kyle has learned not to take personally—and tension grows slowly, coiling in Clovis's body where they touch. "Can you tell me...?" Clovis's voice wavers with uncertainty. "What's it like Below?"

Kyle stiffens, his skin going pale. It's a charged question to ask anyone. Most people, you can't tell their other form on sight. Of course, everyone knows Kyle's an Amp because of all the fanfare that came with the delegation's arrival and the start of his training.

But most people have the decency to pretend they don't.

Kyle trusts that Clovis doesn't mean to be invasive or rude. If anything, he sounds desperate. But, even with the best of intentions, Kyle's experiences are hard to explain. The way his family celebrated him on Treaty Day is the kindest example of how his existence is misunderstood.

Kyle sighs. Whether Clovis realizes it or not, he should probably know what's out there and, while Kyle may not be the *best* option to tell him, he is the only one here right now.

"It's quieter," he says finally. "Meditative, almost. But the language, the priorities—the entire structure of everyday life—they're different. It's hard to explain. Like, try to imagine describing *here* to someone who's never even...taken a breath. You can't! There's no *context* to understand, no frame of reference. So, it's hard to say. If you experienced it for the first time, it would be completely new. You can't try to map your life Above to it, you have to just...feel it when you're there. Go with what your body tells you. I guess, well, it's slower and sharper, somehow. More in focus. Simpler and more immediate. You're more...embedded in it; not just on it, but *part* of it, the landscape and the water and the other creatures...it's beautiful, too; there are forests and canyons and colors you can't imagine." He smiles softly, thinking of bringing Clovis Below.

"You like it better there, huh? With your family?" Clovis asks. His voice is quiet. Reflective.

"I used to hate it here," Kyle admits with a sigh. "It's so *intense*. The shed is hard. I'm so clumsy. Everything is loud and bright, and my body is dull. It doesn't feel the world the way it should." He swallows, reluctant and nervous. "But lately...hanging out with you, I'm starting to see the good. I never watched the sun set from Above before."

Clovis looks at him, eyebrows in his hairline. "Never?"

Kyle shrugs, glad his skin's colors are muted in the moonlight. "After the delegation left, I didn't bother with things like that. What's the point of trying to make a life Above if I'm no good as an Amp?"

"Seriously?"

Kyle shrugs uncomfortably. "Yeah. I mean, they'd know, right? Amps, if they do it right, they help people. Change lives. So, if I'm not good enough for that, what's the point?"

Clovis tips his head. "Wait. But...from what you've told me, you negotiated for your family's farm, right? Like, the prices and the space, and the import of the initial stock?"

"Yeah, but the delegation arranged for the shark protection detail. They coordinated the purchase of the land and fair payment to the temperate sentients."

"With your help."

"It was more like an apprenticeship kind of thing."

"But didn't you set up Opal's salt-sourcing with the porpoises?"

Kyle sighs. "That was her idea."

"You drew it up and made sure it was fair, right?"

"It wasn't like that!" Kyle flushes. "I'm not a diplomat. I just try to help out when I can."

Clovis chuckles. "You really don't see the difference you've made?"

"I *haven't*—" Kyle protests.

"You *have*. You're an Amp, Kyle—a good one—and there's so much to do here. I'll bet that's why you didn't get assigned when the delegation left."

"No. They *told* me—"

"We think this is the best place for you," Demia had said.

"Did they say you weren't good enough?"

"Not...not in so many words..." Kyle's caught in a tumbling wave of memories and forgotten kindnesses.

"I think you're right where you need to be," Clovis says.

"Oh," Kyle whispers, stunned. "Thanks."

Clovis settles back with a sigh and stares at the stars until Kyle relaxes and joins him, seeing them in a whole new way.

Kyle finds his instinctual crush complicated by their friendship, established despite his initial reluctance. More than the antics of his skin in Clovis's presence, he thrills at Clovis's compliments and challenges, at his haphazard approach to conversation. Kyle never knows what's coming, and he actually likes that. But Clovis still seems blissfully unaware that he might belong to the ocean as much as to the land, and it's starting to feel like something Kyle is *keeping* from him.

Vestain is quietly watering plants when Kyle finally seeks advice.

"Hey," he says, trying to sound casual as he stocks the bakery case.

Vestain looks up, their pale face serene as always. "Yes?"

"I…" he trails off. "Have you ever met anyone that didn't know they had another form? Like, they *did* have one, but they just…didn't *know*? They'd never shifted?"

Vestain smiles and croons at a palm tree. "Sometimes, the heart knows things before the mind does. But they come into alignment with patience."

Kyle sighs. Vestain is wise, and old. The downside is that they can be *incredibly* cryptic.

"Uh, thanks. I think."

"You're welcome," Vestain laughs softly. "Patience will serve you, Kyle. Everything will find its place." They glance out the broad window fronting the store. "I believe I need to put some things in the back." They smile as they head into the storage closet, and then the bell over the door rings as Clovis walks in.

"Hey," Clovis says, voice cracking. It sets off Kyle's markings, which flare in warning to an unknown threat.

"Are you okay? What's wrong?"

With a shake of his head, Clovis answers vaguely, "Yeah, yeah, of course. I just…I wanted…" He stares up at the drink board.

Something is *wrong*.

"Clovis—" Kyle tries again.

"Can I get…can you give me that drink you suggested? The salt one?"

"Yeah, of course."

Clovis digs for change with shaking hands, and Kyle waves him off. "On the house."

Oblivious, Clovis keeps searching.

Kyle touches his arm. "Seriously. I got it."

"Yeah." The digging finally stops. Clovis looks up at Kyle like he's waking from a dream. "Yeah, okay. Thanks."

The café stays quiet as Kyle brews the espresso. He calls to Vestain on his way to Clovis's table, "Taking my break!" Then, he passes the coffee over and sits. "What happened? You all right?"

After a long sip of the latte, Clovis barks a laugh that verges on hysterical. "Yeah? Yeah, I'm good. I'm...I'm good."

Kyle waits. Under the table, his hands worry against each other, the self-soothing of wrapping his tentacles together.

Clovis looks at his mug, the wide-mouthed one Kyle knows he likes. He tips it one way, then the other. "I should have known," he says. "The first time I had this drink, I knew where the salt was from. Not just...not just that it was from the ocean, but that it was *this* ocean, this bay, *specifically*. I could taste it. That's..." He looks up. "Most people can't do that, can they?"

Kyle smiles gently. "I don't think so."

"I lost my dad when I was a kid. Did I tell you?"

"You didn't. I'm sorry."

"The only thing my mom would tell me was that the sea took him. *Took* him. Weird way to say it, right? I..." He laughs again, high-pitched and frantic. "I thought he drowned. I thought that was why we moved inland."

Kyle covers Clovis's hand with his and tastes the sour taint of fear. "What happened?"

"I've always been afraid of the ocean." Clovis looks out the window, voice quiet. "But I've always been fascinated by it, too. The waves and the sand and...and what's underneath. And I thought...you're there every day, right? It can't be *that* bad."

Clovis turns his hand under Kyle's and holds on like he's afraid of being ripped away. "I didn't swim, I just...I barely got wet, but I...I couldn't breathe. Something happened. Something changed. I couldn't see. I..." His free hand goes to his chest, to the blue markings there.

"You started to shift," Kyle says quietly.

Clovis nods, over and over, like he's forgotten how to stop. "Yeah." He looks at Kyle. "Did you know?"

"I suspected." Kyle steels himself for anger, but Clovis just keeps nodding.

"Oh." Clovis looks around them, restless. "Well, thanks."

"For what?"

"For talking to me. About your life there. I know I shouldn't have asked, but I just…it felt important, and you talked to me, and you didn't rush me, and I…I appreciate that."

"Yeah, of course. I just thought…I wanted to help. If I could."

"Well, you did." Clovis gives him a wan smile. "Can I…" He shakes his head. "Never mind."

"Ask me. Anything. What do you need?" Kyle asks urgently.

"Can you come with me? Tonight? Can you…can you show me?"

A warmth grows in Kyle's chest. Clovis *trusts* him. Even at his most vulnerable, Clovis wants Kyle *with* him Below. Just as Clovis has been his guide Above.

"Absolutely!" Kyle squeezes his hand reassuringly.

Clovis closes his eyes and takes a shuddering breath. "Thank you."

"Gimme one minute," Kyle says, then steps away to knock on the closet door. "Vestain? I'm sorry, would it be all right if—"

The door opens, and Vestain is already nodding as they emerge. "Go ahead. Don't keep your friend waiting."

Kyle stares, then smiles. Somehow, Vestain can still surprise him. "I owe you one," he says, pulling his apron over his head before heading back to Clovis. "Whenever you're ready. There's no rush, okay? I'm here as long as you need me."

Clovis's face goes tight, and he rubs his cheeks briskly. "That…wow. Thanks. Can we just walk?"

"Sure."

Kyle holds the door.

"I thought these were birthmarks," Clovis says. He rubs a finger along one of the blue lines that jut above his collar.

"Gills, I think," Kyle says, gauging Clovis's reaction. There's not even a hitch in his stride. "They should open when you go into the water. That might be what you felt when you went in earlier. If your gills opened above the water, that would feel…really scary."

"Yeah." Clovis shivers. "It did."

"My first shed was when I was thirteen, and we lived in the Deep. If we hadn't been hunting in the shallows, I probably wouldn't have made it to the surface. I know how you feel. I'll make sure you're safe."

"I know you will."

They walk along the beach, Kyle closest to the waves.

"What if I don't come back?" Clovis asks.

"Nothing hunts near town; we won't go into the Deep. You'll be safe."

Laughing nervously, Clovis says, "That's not…I meant, what if I go in, and I never *want* to come back? That happens, right?"

Kyle thinks back. "Maybe? But you won't be a different person down there. You'll still be yourself, still want the same things you want now."

Clovis looks at him sidelong. Looks away.

"Think about what's here, Above. What's important?"

"My mom."

"What else?"

There's an odd intensity when Clovis looks over again. "I don't know."

"Skateboarding?"

Clovis shrugs. "What if it's just a poor substitute for swimming?"

"What if swimming's a poor substitute for boarding?" Kyle smiles gently. "Anything else?"

"The lattes at Opal's," Clovis says, sly.

"We have amazing omelettes, too," Kyle laughs. "Have you tried them?"

Shaking his head, Clovis huffs a laugh.

"So, you'll have to come back at least once."

A grudging smile. "Yeah."

"You're gonna be fine. I'll be with you the whole time."

Nodding, Clovis edges closer to the water. "I…can we try?"

"Let's start in the bathhouse, okay? We'll get you a locker."

Kyle brings Clovis to the residents' side—the lockers there are larger, for long-term use. Clovis chooses one next to Kyle's, and they strip carefully, hanging their clothes up before Kyle leads Clovis into the alcove. The water laps up from under the dock, and Kyle steps into it first, resisting the stretch of the skin around his neck as it strains to cover him. He turns to watch as Clovis enters the water and gasps, his expression hovering between fear and awe.

"Kyle?" he says, voice wavering.

"You're doing great," Kyle assures him, moving closer.

"It feels…it *pulls*, I can't describe it."

"You don't have to," Kyle assures him.

Clovis smiles tightly. "Right. Of course."

Moving into thigh-deep water, Kyle waits for Clovis, waves rising and falling around them. Clovis wades deeper and reaches a hand toward Kyle; Kyle accepts it gladly.

By the time they're waist-deep, the fear on Clovis's face is fading, but he still clings to Kyle like a barnacle.

"You'll be all right," Kyle reminds him, letting Clovis take the lead.

"I know. I know."

"When you're ready, you'll know what to do. We won't be able to talk after the shift, but I'll be there, okay? My family'll spread the word, and someone—someone like you—will come and show you around."

Clovis's grip tightens. "You said you'd stay with me!"

"I will! But you'll need someone like you to help with questions I can't answer—about your form and your group, where you can stay and get food, what's protected. The one who comes, you two will understand each other. You and I won't—different forms, different languages."

"Okay. I guess…okay."

Clovis is just starting to relax when his gills flutter open: first, the long ones that lie along his collarbones, then smaller ones that gape along the line of his neck. "Kyle?" His eyes are panicked.

"Easy now…slide down." He helps Clovis float so his gills move rhythmically underwater. "It's okay. Relax, now."

"You'll stay?" Clovis pleads.

"No matter what," Kyle promises.

The change begins, and Clovis gets heavier in his arms. Pectoral fins flow out from his sides, incorporating hands and arms and unfurling majestically; his legs stretch into a beautiful whiptail. Kyle walks him deeper, until they're both submerged; Clovis flaps experimentally, drifting out of Kyle's arms. The world is a strange combination of color and vibration; only when his lungs begin to burn does Kyle pull on his skin.

Clovis swims a tentative circle, then returns, his form—a manta ray—dwarfing Kyle as he glides overhead. Kyle stretches a tentacle out to touch him, and the powerful flavor triggers his skin into a full-fledged courtship display. The shallows are clear water, sand and stone. Knowing his siblings watch from the edges of the kelp forest, Kyle freezes with embarrassment. He'll be fielding a lot of questions later.

A nudge from Clovis brings Kyle back; he shakes off his self-consciousness even as his skin continues to broadcast his feelings through the shallows.

He leads Clovis deeper, into the kelp forests where his family lives. Their dens are hidden among the outcroppings of sand and stone, camouflaged with lush growth.

A shape from the deeper water resolves into another ray: the ambassador Kyle has been expecting. He's halfway to greet them when Kyle finds Clovis frozen behind him. Kyle reassures him with gentle strokes along one pectoral fin as the ray approaches more slowly.

Kyle stays close as Clovis relaxes. The rays talk, first with slow undulations of their pectoral fins, then with more animated, deliberate gestures of their bodies, tails, and cephalic fins. They seem to come to an understanding, and then the ambassador swims off toward the coral canyons. Clovis follows, and they move together with an ease that has Kyle forcing back a burst of jealousy.

Just as he's convincing himself not to wallow in self-pity, Clovis circles back and slides underneath him playfully, lifting Kyle briefly on his broad back and then spinning around when Kyle slides off. He dives again, swirling Kyle into a whirlpool before veering away. It feels joyful, free, the way Clovis had described skateboarding, the way Kyle had felt years ago when it was just him and his siblings in the Deep.

The third time Clovis comes around, Kyle gives in and joins in the fun, snagging a tentacle on Clovis's back so he's pulled along, flattening his body so they glide easily through the water together. Clovis leaps above the ocean skin, and Kyle clings fast.

Teasingly, Kyle lifts his tentacles to create a rudder and send Clovis off course. Clovis responds by leaping high, forcing Kyle flat and close. They can't speak, but they're beginning to understand each other; this is a language Kyle looks forward to learning.

The other ray joins them and leads Clovis in increasingly complex flips and acrobatics until Kyle releases his hold to watch from Below, marveling as the rays' huge bodies slide under the water then thrust back above it.

It's beautiful. Where Kyle's own skills lie in subtlety and camouflage, the rays' are in strength and agility. He's never dared to imagine *sharing* this with someone. Knowing someone, Above and Below. Being known, completely, by another being. The enormity of the moment tugs at him like the jet stream—he's helpless, bursting, overcome with emotion.

Eventually, the other ray talks with Clovis and swims off, and then Clovis nudges Kyle into leading them back through the kelp forests, where Kyle shows him how to swim near the ocean skin so the fronds slide along his belly. Clovis flips effortlessly so they dance along his back, and Kyle catches a ride with two tentacles hooked over his fins.

They explore the forests together, chasing each other through the tangled leaves until Clovis is moving smoothly, quickly, without snagging his fins or getting caught on the shelves of rock that hide eels and urchins.

The glow of the sunrise is just piercing the shallows when Kyle leads them, exhausted and ecstatic, back to shore. He laughs when Clovis finds a burst of energy to race him to the dock. Kyle sheds his skin while he's still swimming and catches Clovis as he crests the waves, raising his gills above the water in frustration.

"Easy," Kyle soothes, hoping Clovis understands the tone if not the words. "Take it slow, it'll come. I'm not going anywhere." Clovis pushes out of the water again, then slides lower to wet his gills. "Good. Don't drown yourself."

Slowly, Clovis's shape narrows.

"There you go! Take your time, you've got it."

For a few minutes, Clovis is stuck between, his whiptail churning in the sand.

"Easy, now. I've got you. Don't worry, now, just a minute."

One second, Kyle is holding a narrow ray in his arms; the next, Clovis slides into his human form with a shudder, grinning ear to ear.

"That was *amazing*!" Clovis stumbles as he remembers how to stand, and then he spins, whoops, grips Kyle's arms and leans in. "I never imagined— That felt *incredible*, better than I could even—! And everything is gorgeous, I mean—wow. Kyle. I couldn't have done it without you."

Heart bursting, Kyle schools his voice. "I've…that was really something." He laughs. "Your first time out—you were swimming circles around me!"

Clovis laughs, loud and bright. "Guess my skateboarding really did come in handy."

"You're a natural down there!" He moves toward shore, and they clamber into the bathhouse together.

Kyle hands Clovis a towel and grabs one for himself.

"So, the ray we met?" Clovis offers nonchalantly. "He said your skin…it…you were flirting with me?"

Kyle flushes.

"Were you?" Clovis asks incredulously.

Kyle's heart pounds in his ears. "Was I…well, it's not…it's actually…yes?"

Clovis grins. "Really? Oh, that's…*awesome*."

"Yeah?"

"Oh, yeah," Clovis nods, pulling on his pants. He gives Kyle a sly smile. "Not to be forward or anything, but…ah…you want to get some breakfast?"

"Are you asking me on a *date*?" Kyle laughs. His legs shake as he fights his way into his clothes.

"I can't do the flirty skin thing! This is all I've got! *But*," he says enticingly, "I *do* know a nice coffee shop. I hear great things about their omelettes."

Giddy, Kyle laughs again. "That sounds…perfect." He waits for Clovis to pull on his shirt before he offers his hand.

The world shrinks, silent and still, as Clovis pulls him close. Raising a hand tentatively, he whispers, "Can I?"

Kyle nods, his skin rippling.

There's a hint of kelp, the mineral tang of the deep sea in Clovis's fingers against his cheek, and then their lips meet, intimate and uniquely human.

"Thank you," Clovis whispers against Kyle's mouth. Stunned and breathless, Kyle stares at his radiant smile as they drift apart.

Clovis clears his throat and looks away, then steps back and opens the door, guiding Kyle through with a hand on his back.

There's something about the way the world looks, now, Above. There's a depth of color only his human eyes can see. Sunlight sparkles on the sand. He can imagine exploring Above with Clovis and finding *joy* in it. There are so many things he wants to show Clovis, Below.

Something inside him has been split open. Everything is new.

"Ready?" Clovis asks, reaching out.

Their fingers tangle together as they fall into step, and the breeze off the water is fresh and full of possibilities.

CHOCOLATE AND ROSES

SHEA SULLIVAN

Opal hops in through the upstairs window, wings and lungs still burning from her flight. She'd pushed herself hard, eager to get home before dark.

"You made it!" Vestain greets her with a kiss as she stumbles into the kitchen. "How was your trip?"

Opal sighs, leaning into their tall form. "It was good! Really productive. Nothing signed yet, but the terms are based on the porpoise contract Kyle put together. I think it covers everything. The ambassador's bringing it to the Civets next week."

Vestain smiles, broad and fond, holding her with one long arm and pouring hot water into a waiting cup with the other. "You're doing amazing things."

Opal sighs as they press a cup of tea into her hands. "Thank you."

"Come into the garden," Vestain urges her gently, a supportive hand at her back.

She takes a whiff of the tea—rose and chocolate, the perfect amount of cream—and lets Vestain guide her onto the patio.

She takes a pillow from the pile under the awning and folds onto it, Vestain sitting behind her. "Rest with me," they say, stretching into their other form. Their arms are now branches that hold her, their chest a broad, supportive trunk. She strokes through their oak leaves in thanks and sips her tea.

Soon, she'll become an oriole again and nestle into the nook they've made for her, safe and snug for a much-needed nap.

"It's good to be home," she murmurs.

The wind through Vestain's branches agrees.

UNUSUAL BLENDS

SCARLETT GALE

bipoc, customer/employee, f/f, first kiss, getting together, the grumpy one is soft for the sunshine one, magic use, meet cute, miscommunication, pining (mutual), present tense, tea shop, third person limited point of view, witch, witches have familiars

At 6:00 a.m. precisely, Vivian wakes up to the prism-refracted sunrise, the crystals in her window throwing rainbows across her clean white bedroom. She takes a moment to appreciate the familiar splashes of color and the warm, pink-toned light.

Marshmallow, her familiar, stretches, and a particularly large patch of rainbow paints her fluffy, white fur opalescent. She yawns in that cat way that turns her adorable face into a gaping, spiky maw. Vivian scritches her ears and gets out of bed before the clock switches over to 6:01 a.m., falling into the comfort of her finely tuned routine.

First: a run, pavement flowing by under her shoes as the town wakes up. Afterward, she stretches and has breakfast. She tends her houseplants, showers, and dries her blue-black hair with a wave of her fingers. Vivian dresses for the day in a white dress, a white apron, and white ergonomic shoes. Her hair gets twisted up in a braided bun tied with a white ribbon. Vivian likes white. She likes its simplicity, how it makes her golden-brown skin glow, and *especially* how Marshmallow's fur doesn't show up on it.

Unusual Blends Tea and Herbs is below Vivian's apartment; she and Marshmallow arrive there at 7:30 a.m. The space is pristine: shelves of neatly labeled teas on the two customer-facing walls; raw ingredients in containers behind the counter; white paint, pale wood, and blue accents. Vivian knows how her day will go, which locals will come in for their favorite blends, and which will need refills on their prescriptions.

Today's Monday. Mrs. Sullivan will pick up poultices for her knees. Old Man Charlie (who is at *most* thirty) will show up at eight, tell her the day's squirrel gossip as she pours him four ounces of the Earl Grey he likes, and disappear back into the woods. Later in the day the tourists will come, because the town is small enough to be quaint and large enough to have vacation rentals, and therefore there's no avoiding them.

Vivian doesn't like tourists. She tolerates the conversation of the locals who understand her silences. Tourists talk and talk and *talk* and, worse, expect her to respond. Vivian has never been good with words like she is with herbs. If someone wants a blend that tastes like childhood evenings warm by the fire with grandma knitting in her armchair, she can do it, and the look on their face when they smell her work is enough. That's the reason she opened Unusual Blends in the first place: to help people, not—*ugh*—to *talk* to them.

Vivian knows her sister worries about her non-existent social life, but Vivian has her cat, her work, and her bi-weekly dinners where Veronica fusses over her. She doesn't need more than that. It's a quiet, predictable life, and Vivian likes it that way.

It's 10:48 a.m. on a Monday when Vivian's life changes, wholly without her permission.

It starts with the door opening, as customer interactions generally do. Vivian glances up from the catmint she's sorting (Marshmallow lazes nearby on the counter, pretending she's not planning to steal some), expecting to see a tourist. Instead, she looks directly into a smile so brilliant it sears itself onto her retinas.

"Hi!" says the smile's owner, sunlight making her brown skin gleam and gilding the edges of her puffy pigtails. "Wow, this place smells *amazing*! I kinda expected it to, since it's a tea shop and all, but *dang*."

She steps inside, all red plaid flannel and ripped black jeans. Her eyeliner is messy, her red lipstick perfect, and even if her magic wasn't fizzing over Vivian's skin, the crow on her shoulder would mark her as a witch. She stands out like a weed in a flowerbed, and looks just as determined to stay.

"Can I help you?" Vivian asks, belatedly. Perhaps this loud, messy, beautiful witch is a customer, and she can sell her something and go back to working in silence.

"No!" the witch says, delighted eyes roaming the shop. She wanders to a shelf, pulls down the jar of "Dreams Where You Can Fly," and pops the lid to sniff it. Vivian watches in mild horror. "I mean, yes! I mean, hi!" She puts the jar back on the shelf off-center and bounces over to the counter. Vivian has never bounced in her life. She's never considered bouncing as a form of locomotion, and now she can think of nothing else.

The witch leans her elbows on the clean wooden countertop, that megawatt smile on her face. It's like standing in a sunbeam.

"I'm Gwendolyn!" the witch says as her crow flutters over to investigate Marshmallow. "I just moved in across the street, and I'm making the rounds, dazzling everyone with my wonderful personality, trying to make some new friends!" Her honey-warm brown eyes dart to the side, and her smile somehow grows wider. "Looks like Quoth has me beat on that front. What's your familiar's name?"

Vivian tracks Gwendolyn's gaze to find Marshmallow purring loudly as Quoth preens the ruff around her neck. "Quoth?"

Gwendolyn's eyes glitter. "Yeah. You know. Quoth the raven."

Vivian quirks an eyebrow. "That's a crow."

Gwendolyn bursts into laughter, as loud, uncontrolled, and brilliant as the rest of her. "I know!" she cackles. "That's why it's funny!"

Vivian rocks back on her heels, her desire to retreat from this uninvited bundle of chaos at war with her desire to make sure Gwendolyn's chaos doesn't spill out into the shop and de-alphabetize her shelves.

"My name is Vivian," she says matter-of-factly. "My familiar is Marshmallow. Did you need anything?"

Gwendolyn's eyes crinkle at the corners. "Vivian," she says, curling her tongue around it like an incantation. "What a great name! Can I call you Vivi? You can call me Gwen!"

No one has *ever* called Vivian by a nickname before, and she doesn't have time to decide how she feels about it, because Gwendolyn— Gwen?—*Gwendolyn* barrels on.

"Are you an earth witch? Do you grow all the herbs yourself? I mean, I know you don't *have* to be an earth witch to do herbology. I dabble a little; whatever I need for my jinxes."

Vivian blinks, her composure sanded away under the onslaught of Hurricane Gwendolyn. "No," she says, technically an answer to both questions, and braces for the inevitable follow-ups.

"Neat," Gwendolyn says, nodding like Vivian had explained her magical practices in detail. "You didn't feel like an earth witch. I bet you specialize in dreams and memories, right? That's half of your stock." She waves a hand around and barely avoids smacking her own familiar in the beak. Quoth pecks at her, squawking, but seems resigned to her witch's antics. Vivian is abruptly, viscerally, envious of a bird.

"Can I get a cup of something?" Gwendolyn asks, peering behind the counter. Vivian prepares to explain that she doesn't brew on demand until Gwendolyn interrupts with, "Oh, you have stuff ready to go! Awesome! Is it different every day?"

Vivian shuts her mouth with a click and nods stiffly.

"Cool!" Gwendolyn's smile widens. "I'll have an excuse to come back, then!"

Gwendolyn leaves with a wave of her fingers, a to-go cup of "The Feeling of Looking Up at Clouds in the Blue Sky," and the fluttering of black feathers. Vivian stares after her in the sudden silence and feels her entire life shift a few degrees off-center.

True to her word, Gwendolyn comes back. In fact, she comes back every day with questions about and reviews of Vivian's teas. She leans on the counter and talks about the customers at You Owe Me a Coke, the closet of a shop across the street where she sells custom jinxes and curses.

"Don't look at me like that, Vivi!" she says, laughing at Vivian's stern glare. "They're not *bad*. They're mostly pranks, with the odd self-defense jinx thrown in when someone needs it."

"Pranks," Vivian says, voice flat. She doesn't look up from the scale where she's measuring out burdock root.

"Pranks," Gwendolyn confirms. "And good ones! The kind where *everyone* laughs. Making someone's slippers run away from them is pretty freaking funny, and it only lasts thirty seconds." She pokes Vivian in the shoulder, chin propped on her other hand, elbow on the counter. "C'mon." She tugs at Vivian's sleeve. "Admit it, Vivi, that's funny."

Vivian moves her arm out of Gwendolyn's grip and pours the burdock into her mortar. She doesn't respond. She *can't*. Words always tangle up on her tongue, and it's worse around Gwendolyn than anyone else, because Gwendolyn doesn't stick to a script. She flutters around unpredictably, like a butterfly on the breeze, beautiful, glimmering…but absolutely, positively *infuriating*.

"You'll see," Gwendolyn says, unconcerned by Vivian's silence. "One of these days, I'll prank you, and you'll laugh and admit I was right, and I'll brag about it forever." Her necklace chimes, flashing red, and Gwendolyn lifts the crystal to check the notification. "Crap, a customer. I'll see you tomorrow, Vivi! C'mon, Quoth!"

Bird and woman flutter away, and when Vivian is sure she's alone, she bends in half to press her forehead against the countertop. Gwendolyn is so *loud*. She *hates* it.

She wonders what time Gwendolyn will come tomorrow.

It takes a month, but Gwendolyn manages to sample all of Vivian's standard teas. Vivian thought, naïvely, that this achievement would mean she'd have respite from Gwendolyn's loud, glowing presence in her shop every day (and sometimes twice on Sundays).

She was wrong.

"So," Gwendolyn says at 1:43 p.m. on a Tuesday, "can you make a blend that's 'The Quiet Feeling of Looking Out a Window on a Rainy Day When You're Safe at Home'?" She leans against a shelf, scritching Quoth under the chin and always, always smiling.

"Vivi," Gwendolyn wheedles at 10:27 a.m. on a Friday, laying halfway across the counter to tug at Vivian's sleeve, "can you make a blend for 'Help Me I Just Want to Sleep Instead of Thinking About a TV Show I Don't Even Like'?" She bats her eyes, her braided hair falling over them in an uncomfortably appealing way. "I need your help!"

"I want a blend," Gwendolyn muses at 4:32 p.m. on a Monday, leaning against the counter, "that tastes like the first bite of a meal you haven't had in years and thought you'd forgotten about but now you remember in vivid detail." She tips her head back, catching Vivian's gaze with those sparkling eyes. "Can you make that?"

Vivian can. Vivian does. Vivian makes every outlandish blend Gwendolyn asks for, because she's very good at her job. It's professional pride, nothing more, that flares up in her rib cage when Gwendolyn takes her first sip of her latest ridiculous request and her smile blooms like a flower.

"It's perfect, Vivi," she always says. "One of these days I'll stump you!"

"She sounds friendly," Veronica says over dinner.

"She is *infuriating,*" Vivian replies tightly. It's true. Gwendolyn is loud, distracting, disruptive, and annoying. She's always *there,* talking talking *talking,* without even the encouragement of an answer. Vivian has mismeasured ingredients at least twice a week since Gwendolyn started showing up. *Unacceptable.*

The frustrating icing on the intrusive cake is that Marshmallow is utterly enamored of Gwendolyn and Quoth. She happily trots to the door to greet them and spends the entirety of each visit getting groomed or petted. Vivian glares at her familiar, currently sprawled out on the empty side of the table.

Traitor.

"If you say so," Veronica says, in the "smug older sister" way that means she definitely disagrees but isn't going to *say* it.

Vivian considers throwing her salad into her sister's face. She refrains, but it's a pleasant mental image while it lasts.

It all goes wrong on a Tuesday afternoon.

Restless dreams plague Vivian all night, dreams that couldn't be dispelled with tea or a charm. Sleep deprivation has teamed up with a familiar migraine to ruin Vivian's mood. She can sense an oncoming storm, the intensity of it overpowering her strongest painkilling tisane. It would be nice if her meteorological powers were less *annoying.* She drags herself to work on time by the skin of her teeth and brews a cup of "Please Let Me Get Through This Day."

Tuesdays are usually quiet, at least, with none of the early urgency of Mondays or the procrastination panic of Fridays. Vivian handles a few regular orders and a couple of tourists while the approaching storm weighs on her sinuses and stabs like an ice pick behind her eye. Vivian mixes some warming draughts and refills the blends that evoke coziness, sure there'll be a run on them. This storm is going to last a while.

She's finishing a full jar of "The Feeling of Waking Up and Knowing

You Don't Have to Get Out of Bed" when the door swings open. A customer stumbles in through the wind and fights the door shut before pushing their hood back, and ah. Of course. It's Gwendolyn.

Vivian's headache gets worse.

"Wow, it is *miserable* out there," Gwendolyn says, unzipping her hoodie and extracting a rumpled crow. "Quoth tried to fly over and got blown into my face, poor thing, I put her in my cleavage for safekeeping."

Vivian, who is acutely aware that Gwendolyn also keeps her *wallet* in her cleavage for safekeeping, says nothing. Checking the time, she realizes that she's overdue for another tisane for the throbbing pain, and pulls down the appropriate jar.

"Anyway," Gwendolyn says, "I was talking to Mrs. Sullivan, and she was praising the poultice you make her, which, *obviously* anything you made would be great, because you're *amazing*—"

Vivian concentrates on measuring the tisane into her teapot with steady hands, ignoring the way her chest clenches at the compliment.

"—and she was saying her knees ache more when a big storm is coming in, so we complained about weather magic, since it's absolutely the *worst*, no one likes having weather magic unless you *only* have weather magic at, like, sorceress level—"

This is true. Major weather magic is rare, and the few specialist weather witches she knows have all the benefits and none of the downsides that come with being only a *little* weather-touched. *They* don't get migraines warning them of weather changes that are as easily predicted by meteorologists. Vivian isn't given to envy, but she allows herself a little as she fills her teapot.

"—and then she said *you* had weather magic, which I had no idea about—you never tell me anything—I gotta learn it from everyone else—and I realized that if Mrs. Sullivan's knees were bad, you had to be *way* worse off—"

Vivian watches sidelong as Gwendolyn wanders, leaving Quoth to have her feathers carefully groomed by Marshmallow (the traitor). It's hard enough to look at Gwendolyn's brightness on a *good* day. Today, even a glance makes Vivian's head pound. She grits her teeth. The painkilling tea will be done soon, and Gwendolyn will leave, and Vivian will be alone in her quiet shop and feel slightly less miserable.

"—so I figured I'd come over and check on you, and then I remembered I worked up a new item for the shop, so I brought you a prototype so you could test it! I think it's gonna be a good seller. Like, obviously there's prank potential, but it has a lot of uses—"

Gwendolyn digs in her sequined fanny pack, arm going much deeper than it should in a way that would startle non-witches. Not that Vivian's *watching*. She's *definitely* not watching. Vivian's studiously pouring the finished painkilling tisane into her mug.

"—tampon, tampon, *magic* tampon, bandages…" Gwendolyn mutters, and then her expression transforms triumphantly. "Yes!" she crows. "Found it!"

She whirls around, takes a victorious step toward Vivian, and trips on her own perpetually untied shoelaces. She unbalances *spectacularly* (later, Vivian will admit she respects the theatricality) and takes three wildly stumbling steps toward the counter. She avoids smashing her face, but in so doing sweeps the full jar of "Waking Up on a Weekend," the jar of painkilling tisane, Vivian's teapot, and Vivian's mug off the counter. Vivian watches them tumble through the air with detached horror, vaguely hoping that the inevitable won't occur.

The inevitable occurs.

The jar of tea shatters in an explosion of glass and herbs, closely followed by the jar of painkiller, guaranteeing a mess that will take hours to salvage. Vivian could do it. She'd have to summon out the glass and then each herb, spice, and tea leaf. It'd be painstaking, but she *can*—

The teapot and mug hit the ground with a splash. All the tea, all the tisane, every single leaf, seed, and dried flower are soaked in the painkilling tisane Vivian was about to drink. It's ruined, her shoes and her work both. There's no saving a blend once it's steeped, and that's certainly one way to describe the pile of wet leaves at Vivian's feet.

"Oh *no*," Gwendolyn says, stricken. "Oh, Vivi, I'm so—"

"*Inconsiderate*," Vivian snaps, her composure shattering as spectacularly as the jars. Gwendolyn goes silent, her eyes wide, and Vivian can't control her mouth. "You invade my space and take up my time with your constant *talking*. Why can't you leave well enough alone?"

"I—" Gwendolyn tries, her face doing something Vivian's never seen before. It isn't enough to stop the flood, though.

"That was the last of my nettles," Vivian hisses. "An hour's work you ruined that now I can't get back, and for *what*? More of your chatter?" Vivian's fists clench, the headache jabbing her temple, and she ignores Gwendolyn's crumpled expression.

"Vivi," Gwendolyn says, wavering, "I didn't mean—"

"My name," Vivian says, icy cold, "is *Vivian*. Now, did you actually *need* something? Because, if not, I'll ask you to please *leave me alone*."

Silence rings in the shop, marred only by the whistling wind. Gwendolyn slowly pushes upright, avoiding Vivian's gaze.

"I wanted to give you this," she whispers, setting whatever she'd been holding on the counter with a *clink*. "I'm sorry about the tea." Her dark eyes glance up and away, wet at the corners. Vivian tells herself she doesn't care about the tremble in Gwendolyn's lower lip. "Come on, Quoth."

The crow flutters over and gives Vivian a baleful look as Gwendolyn walks to the door. "Vivian," she says to the wood, "I'm sorry. I'll fix this. I promise."

And then she's gone into the storm as raindrops pelt the pavement, leaving Vivian alone in the silence she asked for. She takes a deep breath and goes to find her second-best painkilling tisane. When she can move her head without wincing, she starts cleaning. Peace eludes her, even with the shop empty, and Vivian sweeps up broken glass, unsettled.

It's the storm, she tells herself, dumping wet leaf-mud into the trash. *I'll feel better once it breaks*. Except the storm *has* broken, rain clattering in the downspouts, and Vivian still feels awful.

I don't like messes, she tries, casting a final cleansing spell. It's true, except that the mess is gone, and the ill feeling in her stomach remains.

Gwendolyn's crumpled face haunts her vision. She'd been *hurt*, Vivian realizes. Vivian had hurt her, had spat angry words born of frustration and pain. Gwendolyn could have injured herself running into the counter, and Vivian had snapped at her for keeping herself safe at the expense of a couple of jars? Some dried herbs?

Vivian swipes at the counter and only registers having hit something by the sound. She picks up what appears to be a leaf-shaped wooden brooch decorated with a few rhinestones, the whole thing tingling with friendly magic. Vivian blinks and affixes it to the collar of her dress. The dregs of her headache disappear as the brooch shields her from outside magic, and Vivian staggers with relief.

Gwendolyn brought this for her, Vivian remembers with a sharp jolt. Vivian has been frigid for months, and Gwendolyn has been nothing but warm and friendly. Gwendolyn brought her a *gift*, one specifically tailored to help her, and what did Vivian give her? Cruelty.

"Hell," she swears, regret a cold fist around her heart. Marshmallow headbutts her arm, and Vivian pets her absently. "I messed up," she admits, and Marshmallow doesn't say, "I told you so," but she does pointedly bite her wrist, which Vivian deserves. Vivian allows herself precisely one minute of wallowing and squares her shoulders.

Twenty minutes later, Vivian closes Unusual Blends early, sends Marshmallow upstairs to their apartment, and struggles through the vicious wind to knock on the door of You Owe Me a Coke. She has a four-ounce bag of "Sincere Apologies" in her pocket, along with a small bag of the freshly invented "I'm Very Glad You Didn't Break Your Nose." Hopefully, between the two, Vivian's intentions will be clear, but she's been rehearsing her actual apology since she started blending the tea.

Now, if Gwendolyn would open the door.

Vivian knocks again. And again. She peers through the door into the darkened shop and knocks harder. She presses her hand to the brick and casts a minor detection charm, seeking any life inside; she finds nothing. Out of ideas, she staggers into the fortune teller's shop next door.

"Vivian? What are you doing out in this weather?" Iris, the local diviner, looks surprised to be interrupted, an unfinished sandwich in their hands.

"I'm looking for Gwendolyn," Vivian says, trying not to drip everywhere. "Do you have any idea where she is?"

Iris frowns. "No. She stopped by earlier and asked me to keep an eye on the shop. She said she was running an errand for *you*." Vivian's face does something, and Iris quirks an eyebrow. "I'm guessing you didn't ask her to."

"No." Worry crawls up Vivian's spine. Where could Gwendolyn have gone in this storm? "If you see her, would you tell her I'm looking for her?"

"Sure thing," Iris promises, and Vivian gives them a nod before struggling out into the alley. She presses her hand to the door of Gwendolyn's shop, imbuing it with a "When you get back, come find me," message, and goes home.

Marshmallow rushes to meet her, realizes she's soaking wet, and skids to a dignified halt a few feet away. It's objectively hilarious, but Vivian's too anxious to notice.

Where did Gwendolyn *go*?

Vivian tries fruitlessly to cast tracking spells, but between the storm and the brooch's magic shielding, all she gets for her trouble is a renewed headache. She eats dinner on autopilot and goes to bed early, exhausted by the anxiety prickling over her skin.

I hope Gwendolyn's safe, she thinks, and promptly drops off.

Furious knocking drags Vivian out of a fitful sleep, and she's so groggy she struggles to comprehend the sound. Someone's...at the door? It's almost ten. Who would come see her so late, and during a thunderstorm? She staggers upright and bangs into the table on her way through the apartment, so when she opens the door, she's *very* awake, mildly in pain, and grumpy about it.

"What—"

"Hi, Vivian," says a sopping Gwendolyn, a bedraggled Quoth peeking out of her hoodie. "S-s-sorry for coming over so late, I just..." She shivers violently, water splattering off her body with the force of it. "I wanted to make it up to you as quickly as p-p-possible."

Vivian shuts her mouth, blinks, and opens her mouth again, though she has no idea what she wants to *say*. Gwendolyn, as usual, keeps talking.

"I d-d-don't know how much you needed, and maybe they're not the best quality, but here. I think I got it mostly right?"

Gwendolyn pulls a messy bundle of nettles out of her fanny pack, still mostly dry. Vivian tries to process this tableau.

"You—" Vivian starts, scrabbling for words like dropped coins. "What did you *do*?"

"You s-s-said you were out, and I spilled them, and I said I would f-f-fix it, so I fixed it." Gwendolyn waves the bundle, shivering so hard the leaves rustle. "Did I do okay?"

This is where Gwendolyn went, Vivian realizes. She went out into a freezing thunderstorm to gather *nettles*, as an apology for something that wasn't her fault, after Vivian's cruelty, after months of Vivian's rejection. Gwendolyn's hands are covered in nettle rash, her jeans are muddy, she's soaked and shivering, and Vivian *loves her*. The depth of her feelings hit Vivian like a slap, and she's helpless against the knowledge, helpless to do anything but grab Gwendolyn's collar and reel her in to kiss that rain-chilled mouth.

Gwendolyn makes a surprised sound, and Vivian freezes, jerking backward.

"Um—" she tries.

Gwendolyn says, "No, no, I'm—" and pushes back in, fitting their lips together.

Something hits the floor with a botanical *splat*, and then Gwendolyn's arms are around Vivian's waist, her soaked hoodie drenching Vivian's nightgown. Vivian has just discovered that Gwendolyn's mouth tastes like cinnamon chewing gum when Quoth squawks a very valid protest. They startle apart, and the crow climbs out of Gwendolyn's cleavage to flutter off into the apartment.

"Uh," Gwendolyn says, shivering and dazed. "Were the nettles that good?"

"I am actually very upset with you for endangering your personal safety for something as silly as *nettles*," Vivian says. This is absurd. Why are they still in her doorway? Why is Gwendolyn still wet? Vivian pulls her into the apartment, casting a charm as they go, and between one step and the next Gwendolyn is dry.

"Sorry?" Gwendolyn says, tripping on the stack of damp nettles as Vivian leads her to a chair. "And oh my god, thank you. I forgot what it was like to be dry. Turns out it's nice!"

"Ridiculous," Vivian says, finally allowing herself to sound fond. She summons the salve she wants from her bathroom in a total waste of magical energy. "Foolish." She rubs ointment into Gwendolyn's cold hands, watching the rash disappear under her touch. "Reckless."

"Sorry," Gwendolyn says, again pulling in on herself. "I guess—I guess it was pretty silly—"

"Shush," Vivian says firmly, working on Gwendolyn's other hand. "I didn't say I didn't like it." She dares a glance up, and Gwendolyn's ever-smiling mouth is an "O" of shock. It's cute. Vivian drops her eyes again, heat rolling across her face. "I need to apologize," she says to Gwendolyn's left palm. "I was cruel to you earlier. I had a migraine from the weather, but that's no excuse." She takes a deep breath, making herself meet Gwendolyn's eyes. "I don't think you're inconsiderate," she forces out. "I enjoy it when you come talk to me."

"Oh," Gwendolyn whispers. "Oh, Vivian—"

"Vivi," Vivian cuts in. She's still holding Gwendolyn's hand. They kissed earlier, but this seems more intimate. "I like it when you call me

Vivi. No one ever gave me a nickname before." Another deep breath, the silence broken by the pounding rain outside. "No one's ever talked to me like you do. You're so bright and friendly and *alive*. I didn't know how to handle it."

"I have such a crush on you," Gwendolyn blurts, fingers tangling with Vivian's. "I knew I was being annoying, but I couldn't stay away. That's why I kept asking for custom blends. You're so *pretty* when you work, Vivian—*Vivi*—I just wanted to watch you all the time." She swallows, her eyes gleaming. "I just wanted you to like me."

"I did," Vivian admits. "I do. It scared me." She runs her thumb over the back of Gwendolyn's knuckles. "Gwen," she says, warmth pooling in her belly from the way Gwendolyn's eyes light up at the nickname, "I like you so much. I'm sorry I pretended I didn't." She fights the second confession pressing up her throat and finally finishes, "I've never felt this way before, and I—I have no idea what I'm *doing*."

"That's okay," Gwendolyn says. "We're pretty smart. We can figure it out, yeah?"

Vivian kisses her again instead of answering. Gwendolyn makes a pleased sound, swaying closer. They kiss in the stormy quiet of Vivian's kitchen while rain pounds the windows, kiss and kiss and kiss until—

"Mrow."

In unison, they turn to the table where Marshmallow and Quoth are watching them with inescapably smug expressions. Vivian hadn't even known a crow could *look* smug, but Quoth is doing it.

"Rude of you to interrupt," Gwendolyn tells Marshmallow, "but you're right. It's late." She gives Vivian a mournful look, hands still tangled in her braid. "I should go home and let you sleep."

Lightning flashes outside, followed by a roll of thunder. It's like a theater tech hitting a cue. "Stay the night," Vivian blurts. "Going out in this weather once is enough."

"Vivi." Gwendolyn's mouth quirks. "I live across the street."

Another flash of light and peal of thunder. Vivian gives Gwendolyn her most commanding look. "As your personal apothecary, it would be irresponsible of me to send you out there. You should stay the night." She pauses, swallows, and adds quietly, "With me."

Gwendolyn smiles like sunlight. "Okay," she says. "Okay, Vivian. I'll stay."

Vivian can't help it; she smiles. "Good," she says, and kisses

Gwendolyn again.

The next morning, Vivian wakes up at 6:00 a.m. with Gwendolyn's warmth pressed against her side. Sunlight swathes the room in prism-reflected rainbows, one painting Gwendolyn's cheek in a swipe of color. Vivian smiles, kisses that jewel-bright cheek, and gets out of bed, at which point her slippers come alive and run away from her.

Vivian laughs so hard she wakes up Gwendolyn, who pulls her back down into bed to kiss the laughter out of her mouth. Her morning routine ends up thoroughly ruined, but for the first time in Vivian's life, she doesn't mind at all.

THE TASTY CRUMPET

A. L. HEARD

age difference, bipoc, coffee shop, customer service representative,
customer/employee, fae and fairy folk, flirting, interspecies relationship, m/m,
misunderstandings, oblivious, past tense, pining (mutual), speciesim (mentions of),
third person limited point of view, vampire

Stay out of the magic quarter.

It was the one rule Danny's great-grandma had for the family. Mamie
Mari was deeply superstitious, the living embodiment of the phrase "old
wives' tale." She might not be the matriarch she once was—most of her
authority had ebbed away, and now she spent her days knitting and baking rather than poking her nose into everyone's business—but she could
be downright scary. His cousins were more adventurous, but Danny followed the rule rather than expose himself to Mamie's wrath.

That was why, when Bus 42B turned toward the magic end of town
instead of going around its borders, Danny sighed forlornly and got off
five stops early.

It was raining. Because of course it was.

He pulled up the hood of his sweatshirt, tucked his hands into his
pockets, and barely avoided the puddle between the curb and sidewalk.

Maybe he could wait out the rain? Another bus would come along
soon, right?

Considering his luck had stranded him ten blocks from his job interview in the middle of a rainstorm, he didn't hold out much hope of his
luck magically improving.

Resigned to looking—and feeling—like a drowned cat, Danny raised his chin and marched in what he hoped was the right direction.

It turned out luck *was* on his side.

Near the end of the street was a shop with an old-fashioned wooden sign straight out of a Renaissance Festival. It read "The Tasty Crumpet" in an elegant navy script that glittered with gold flecks, a baker's cap and wooden spoon bracketing the words. The light cast through the windows was soft and inviting—a sharp contrast to the dreary weather—promising warmth and tasty treats.

All of that was tempting enough, but the "HELP WANTED" sign taped to the front window sealed the deal. The sign was old and battered, like it'd seen its fair share of use, but the words "AVAILABLE IMMEDIATELY INQUIRE WITHIN" at the bottom caught his eye. How could he say no to *that*?

The door chimed as he stepped inside, a bell that tinkled more than rang, and the sound made him smile despite the water dripping off his nose. He shook out his hair and stepped toward the counter.

The shop had a homey vibe. There was a stone fireplace at one end, a fire casting dancing shadows across the floor. Along the walls, shelf after shelf was lined with battered editions of books Danny'd been forced to read in high school, and a fair number he'd never even *heard* of, like *The Tales of Ghatotkacha* and *The Harrowing Story of the Spirit of St. Clair*. The shop's furniture was mismatched, a mess of shapes and colors that shouldn't have looked as inviting as it did, each piece tempting him to run a finger along its edges and learn its history.

And then there was the smell: coffee and spices, chocolate and bread. His mouth watered; even if he didn't leave with a job, he was definitely leaving with a latte, some muffins, and a chocolate croissant.

Danny loved the quaint comfort of the place; something about it spread through his chest and chased away the chill from the rain.

"Greetings, weary traveler," said the petite woman behind the counter. Her ears were lined with so many piercings, they looked like they ended in points. "What may I offer you today?" Her smile promised that she would highly recommend everything and would force free samples on him to prove just how tasty the crumpets were.

"Uhm," Danny said, jerking his thumb toward the front window. "I was actually hoping for a job?"

The woman's eyes went wide, and she clapped in delight. "Really?

You'd like to join the dwindling number of baristas supporting my small establishment?"

Danny frowned, hearing a hint of Mamie's accent in the woman's lilting voice. "Sure? If you don't mind someone with no experience and—"

"Pssh." She waved a hand like she was clearing away his words as easily as smoke. "Experience is a wonderful thing: you get it in the doing. I'm Siobhan." She held her hand out palm-down as though she expected him to kiss it.

He shook it awkwardly instead. "Danny. When can I start?"

"I would say immediately, but you're soaked through. Take a seat by the fire, and I'll bring you some tea. Once the bleakness of the storm is lost from your eyes, we can talk business."

Arguing with Siobhan seemed pointless, so he did as he was told. Soon, he found himself in an oversized armchair holding a floral-smelling tea in a handmade mug dotted with ladybugs. He didn't recognize the flavor, but he was too damp to care; what mattered was that it was hot. Stretching his feet toward the fire, he sipped at the drink and decided that, job or no job, being here was *way* better than going to some random interview across town.

"You're in my seat."

He looked up into granite eyes framed by tight, dark curls. Words like "Adonis" and "Vitruvian man" came to mind, and Danny got lost tracing the perfect lines of his perfect jaw. The longer Danny stared, the more the man's lips quirked into an amused frown, until Danny belatedly remembered, *Oh yeah, he said something.*

"Oh." The absurdity of reserved seating in a café occurred to him, but he wasn't rude enough to challenge the man over a chair. "Sorry. I didn't know. Let me—"

Danny started to get up only to have the man gently poke him with the end of his umbrella, pushing him back into place.

"Sit. You're new, and it's not my place to scare you off. But…it *is* my seat, so do you mind if I join you?"

"Be my guest." He wasn't going to say no to a handsome stranger, even one who was bossy about seating. "Let me just…" Danny compulsively tried to tidy up, found only his drink and someone's abandoned newspaper, and sank farther into the armchair, wishing he could make a better first impression.

The man took a seat in a beautifully upholstered antique chair. It didn't look as comfortable as Danny's seat (though Danny's selection had been driven by fear of ruining the embroidery with his wet hoodie and khakis), but it suited the man's blazer and tie.

"I'm Azad El Bachir." There was an air of hesitant expectancy as he said it, like he was afraid of Danny's response. Danny couldn't understand why. It was a nice enough name, and Azad's subtle accent made it sound particularly good, dripping like honey, heavy but sweet. Nothing about it suggested Danny should react to it…yet Azad seemed to expect him to.

"Danny." He offered his hand and ignored the chill when their grips joined for a cursory shake.

"It's a pleasure, Danny." A pause. "Do you truly mean you've never heard of me?"

Danny blinked. Had he? He was pretty sure he'd remember someone like Azad.

"Should I have? Are you a famous model or something?"

A deep laugh startled from Azad, filling the cozy space between them.

"I'm certainly not a model, and I'm apparently not as famous as I thought."

"Then why—?"

"Just my ego, I suppose," Azad said with an apologetic smile. "Admittedly, I may prefer obscurity. What brings you to this side of town, Danny? It's not often this lovely place sees a fresh face."

"Well, I'm here completely by accident, but I just got hired as a barista," Danny said, marveling at the changes in his fortune. Then, he curled his toes, realized his socks were still drenched, and wasn't sure the job alone balanced things out. Talking to Azad, though… "I think my first shift starts whenever I finish my tea? Siobhan told me to warm up and find her when I'd 'lost the rain.' " He smiled conspiratorially, sure that a regular like Azad would know Siobhan well enough to find her as delightfully strange as Danny did.

But Azad nodded sagely and said, "That'll take at least another cup of tea. I can still see rain clouds rattling around in your head. What are you drinking? I'll get you a second cup."

"No, I couldn't impose. I work here—or, *will* work here—" Would this disaster of a first meeting ever end? Gods, he could only imagine how flustered he'd be as Azad's barista after this debacle.

"I'm aware, and I offered all the same."

"All right, then, another of…" He looked at his cup. "Whatever this is."

Azad stood and patted his shoulder. "I'll ask Siobhan," he said, then left, navigating the café's strange layout with practiced ease. Danny tried not to watch as Azad talked to Siobhan, a friendly familiarity in their interactions that Danny longed for. A place to belong, where he fit in.

Azad returned with a small smile (more evident in his eyes than on his lips) and two steaming mugs. "I've secured you another cup of freedom. I think you owe me some conversation."

Danny gladly took the drink and breathed it in. It was spicier than the last brew but just as appealing. "I already owed you one for stealing your chair."

"Then I suppose you'll owe me a second chat later," Azad said, his voice like velvet. Danny couldn't help but lean in. "So, Danny." Goosebumps sprang up on Danny's arms. "Tell me about yourself. However much you can fit in a cup of tea…"

Danny looked over the cappuccino machine, saw Azad with his nose in a book, smiled—then caught himself smiling and overcompensated by glaring at the hot-water spigot.

Why was he looking at Azad *again*? And why did he *care* that he was looking?

Why did he want Azad to catch him and smile back?

Having a crush on a customer was inconvenient, especially an unfailingly regular one. The guy was handsome and nice—the worst combo in the world, really. Danny hoped he could will his feelings out of existence before things got awkward.

Busy staring *again*, he accidentally knocked over a dark container with an even darker, molasses-thick substance inside.

"Shit," he hissed, rushing to grab a dish towel from the sink, but by the time he returned to mop up the mess, it was too late. The stain from the container's mysterious goo wouldn't go away no matter how hard Danny scrubbed at it. He gave up and went to apologize to Siobhan for ruining her counter on his second day, hoping she wouldn't be too hard on him.

"You burnt the edges," Siobhan said as she bent down to inspect the pastries. "*But...* the rest is good."

Danny perked up. "Good enough to put in the display case?"

Siobhan hummed in consideration, gently removing one of the tarts from the pan. She breathed in the aroma, then nibbled an edge. Danny rocked on his heels as he waited for the verdict.

"You have much to learn, but these are quite scrumptious. They taste sweet from the joy you put into your baking. Customers will enjoy the pieces of your aura that come across in the smell."

"Awesome," Danny said, because what else *could* he say? The bell rang out front—the just-opened shop welcoming the first customer of the day—and he started toward the door separating the kitchen from the café proper. "Will you bring them out when they cool down?"

Siobhan was already preoccupied with the oven. "Yes," she managed before she was lost in the next tray of baked goods.

He was surprised and pleased to see Azad sitting at his favorite seat, too occupied with the morning paper to need Danny just yet. Azad always finished reading the headlines before ordering a drink.

Trying to distract himself, Danny pulled out his phone.

> **Gina**
> does your granny know you work so close to magic town?
> i saw a *gargoyle* on my commute over!!

> **Danny**
> no she doesn't pls don't tell her
> it's far enough away, i'm not breaking any rules!

> **Gina**
> where is this place??
> you said corner of 5th and main?

> **Danny**
> yeah it's easy to find
> it's across from an antique store and next to a bank

> **Gina**
> i'm at the bank. there's no cafe??
> ugh, i have to head to work. can't be late again ☹

"What's wrong?"

Danny flashed Azad a smile before continuing his text message. "Sorry, gimme a second. Trying to get a friend to visit me on her way to work, but she's having trouble finding the place."

"Friend?" Azad asked with a polite curiosity at odds with his gloomy expression.

"Yeah, she lived across the street from me when we were kids. I gave her a GPS coordinate; I don't get why she can't find it."

"Maybe her blood's too thin."

Danny looked up. Too thin? Like anemia? What the heck did *that* have to do with anything?

Gina
sry bb g2g maybe next week???
bring me a pastry you made pls

"Did she give up?" Azad asked sympathetically, though there was a smug glint in his eyes.

"Yeah." He tried to wipe the disappointment from his face as he pocketed his phone. "Ugh. I'm being super rude. What can I get you?"

"I'm in no hurry," Azad assured him. "Can I have one of the tarts you made? They smell delightful."

Danny grinned, then narrowed his eyes suspiciously. "How do you know about that?"

"Sooner or later, Siobhan has all her baristas try their hand at baking."

"Oh." Why was Azad's answer disheartening? What had Danny expected him—*wanted* him—to say?

"It doesn't smell like smoke, Siobhan's not shouting, and you're not crying, so I assume the attempt was moderately successful. I don't mind being your first test subject."

Mollified, Danny chewed the inside of his cheek. "I don't see you eat much."

"I don't," Azad agreed solemnly, "but I'm willing to make an exception. What did you make?"

"Blood-orange tarts."

Azad blinked at him. "Blood-orange tarts?"

"It was Siobhan's idea. Strange choice, but *all* her food's a little strange—" He frowned as he took in Azad's grimace. He was either holding in a laugh or trying not to scowl, and Danny wasn't sure which would be worse. "What's wrong with blood orange?"

"Nothing," Azad reassured him. "It's merely a joke at my expense. I'll have one of the tarts and my usual tea, please."

"Weird how much that guy likes the cucumber bread," Danny mumbled as he closed the display case. "*Cucumber* bread? Where does Siobhan even *get* these ideas?"

When he stood up, he was greeted by Azad leaning on the counter and looking over the day's specials.

"He's a kappa," Azad said. When he saw Danny's blank face, he added, "That man with the cucumber bread. He's a kappa."

Danny frowned. "He's in a fraternity?"

Azad gave him a puzzled look. "No. I mean he's—"

"Stop flirting," Siobhan teased as she pushed out of the kitchen with a tray of cookies fresh from the oven.

"I wasn't flirting," Danny said defensively. He really hadn't been, even if Azad was unfairly attractive. He knew better. Azad was *way* out of his league.

"Not you," she said, giving him a gentle smile before eyeing Azad. "I've no interest in finding another barista after you steal him from me."

Danny couldn't help but laugh.

Azad gave him a strange look.

"Sorry," Danny said reflexively. "What can I get you?"

"A refill." He slid a mug across the counter, empty save for the dregs floating in a tacky, red residue. Danny frowned; that didn't look like any of the drinks Siobhan had taught him to make.

"I'm impressed, you know," Azad said, fingers drumming against the counter while he waited. "You've been doing so well."

Danny preened. "Thanks."

"You were so good with that kappa, despite their reputation, and not many of Siobhan's baristas have earned a smile from that grump Gerry, never mind a tip."

"Grump?" Danny bristled with the need to defend a regular. "That old man who always orders porridge and warm milk? He's a sweetheart. Siobhan is better off without baristas that make her customers grumpy. It's not a hard order to get right."

Amusement sparkled in Azad's eyes, like he could never have anticipated Danny's answer but was delighted by it all the same. "You're right, of course," he said. "Am I not allowed to be impressed? I meant what I said—you do wonders making everyone feel comfortable here. Your presence is soothing."

"Oh." He stared at Azad's hands on the counter until his cheeks weren't on fire anymore, then he looked up into stony eyes and gave a shy smile. "Thanks."

The weeks blurred together, in a good way. Danny woke up ready for the day, worked hard, and left The Tasty Crumpet tired but content.

It was the little moments that stood out.

A gangly teenager with unkempt hair had been bashful about asking for a different spoon (because he was allergic to the silver one). Azad had been wearing a pale-purple scarf that perfectly complemented the rich sepia tones of his complexion.

A man with a preposterously large nose that somehow fit with his small eyes and long ears had asked for a drink with coarse, stinky powder sprinkled on top. Azad came late that day, no books in hand, and perused the store's shelves before giving up and talking to Danny while he swept.

A pair of twins with auburn hair and a fox-like tilt to their eyes had stared at him like they guarded secrets he'd never know; they ordered tofu in matching high-pitched voices, then skipped away. Siobhan and Azad had argued about new menu items, Siobhan taking Azad far too seriously as he teased her with suggestions of blood sausages.

Then, there was the time he really started to wonder about the clientele at The Tasty Crumpet.

Danny's eyes traced the line of a strong jaw, lingered on plush lips, and got absolutely *lost* in granite eyes. He'd been stunned the first time he'd looked into Azad's gaze, and it made him dizzy to meet someone else whose were the exact same hue.

"What lovely skin you have." The man reached across the counter, ignoring the espresso he'd ordered, and took Danny's hand. He traced the line of freckles up Danny's forearm and left goosebumps in his wake.

A blush crept up Danny's neck, his cheeks, all the way to his forehead. "Uh…thank you?" He'd never felt so tongue-tied in his life; it wasn't a pleasant feeling. "Would you like anything else?"

Disappointment flashed in the man's eyes; he sighed wistfully and released his hold on Danny. "I suppose not. I'm sorry, darling. I didn't realize your heart was spoken for."

"My— *What?*" Danny'd had a lot of strange conversations since he started working there, but he couldn't wrap his head around this one.

"They're lucky, whoever they are. I've heard wonderful things about you. I can tell you're a good one. Definitely a keeper."

"What? Sir, I, uh…I don't—"

The man waved his hand dismissively. "It's all right. I'd have to sing to reel you in, and Siobhan would disapprove."

"You sing?" Danny asked, leaning in to hear him better. His voice *was* sweet; Danny imagined he had a wonderful singing voice, the type that really drew people in.

The man took his drink and laughed like Danny had told a joke. Danny stood there long after the man left, ignoring the tightness in his chest.

Danny rushed in, wincing as the bell announced his late arrival. Siobhan would understand, but he was mortified. Hurrying toward the counter to grab his apron and get to work, something caught his eye; stopping short, he backtracked to a high-top by the door.

"Why are you sitting over here?" Danny asked, pointing accusingly at Azad.

Azad didn't look up from his book. "My chair is taken."

Danny looked to Azad's usual spot. The seats by the fire were occupied by two stone-faced men so large Danny was surprised their chairs didn't break and their porcelain teacups didn't shatter.

"It's been taken frequently of late," Azad said. "Seems this place is getting popular."

It was true; most of the seats were filled, and there was a line at the counter. But the café was *always* busy. If anything, the quiet days when he'd first started working seemed unusual (though at the time, he'd been thankful he could get into the swing of his new job without much pressure).

"It's because of you," Azad said with a fond eye roll. He put the book down. "They like *you*."

"Me?" Danny squeaked.

"Everyone thought Siobhan was crazy for opening a café in this part of town—"

"This is a lovely part of town!"

"—and few people were willing to make the trip—"

"Why? It's only a block and a half from the bus!"

"—but word spread about how good *you* were, and now people are flocking over to give it a try. Once they're here, Siobhan's baking seals the deal."

"But— But what's it got to do with *me*?" he sputtered. Danny had always been unremarkable at anything and everything he did. That he might be *good* at something? Impossible. "I mean, that's flattering, but I'm nothing special—literally the world's most average barista."

"I wouldn't say that."

Danny blushed and managed to choke out, "Am I a slightly-above-average barista, then?"

"You're superb. *Definitely* something special."

A handsome guy—and Azad *especially*—saying he was special short-circuited Danny's brain. Without any conscious thought, he muttered what was hopefully "Thanks" and went behind the counter to help Siobhan.

And made sure to drop by and top off Azad's tea at every opportunity he got, enjoying Azad's amused and smug attention.

"Thank you, lad," said the woman in a thick Scottish accent. "This smells divine."

"Anytime!" Danny sprinkled seaweed flakes onto her latte, careful not to spill any as he then handed it over. Nori and coffee would usually rank up there on the weirdness scale, but plenty of people here asked for weird things. Probably some new nutrition fad.

The woman took the drink and offered him a warm smile before downing it in a single gulp. It was way too hot to drink that fast; Danny tried not to gawk. Okay, probably *not* a fad—she was wearing a fur coat that matched her dark eyes, so maybe she just liked heat.

The bell over the door rang, and Danny looked over. When he saw Azad with a few books tucked under his arm, he licked his lips and wondered if it'd be too obvious how smitten he was if he started preparing Azad's usual drink now.

"Wonderful." The woman held up the cup and batted her eyelashes. "Could I trouble you for more seaweed…?"

"Sure," Danny said. And what the hell, yeah, he could start some tea for Azad while he got her refill. There was a fresh batch of blood-orange tarts, so he grabbed one of those as well. He wasn't sure if Azad actually *liked* them, beyond whatever inside joke Siobhan was making, but it was the only food Azad ever ordered. He gave the woman her drink, then rushed over to Azad's usual spot.

"Glad you got your chair back," he said breathily. He cleared the abandoned cups from the last patrons to make room. The pleased smile Azad shot his way made it worth the risk of revealing his crush. "What're you reading?"

Azad closed the book, his thumb holding his place as he turned the cover for Danny to read: *The Rise and Fall of Vampiric Cults in Northern Africa.*

"Oh," he said, feeling terribly uncultured. He barely read fiction, and here Azad was, casually reading through some history book.

"You can take a look, if you'd like." Azad offered him the book.

Danny leaned forward, suddenly aware of how close they were. His eyes drifted to Azad's lips; he diverted them back to the book. When he reached out to take it, their fingers brushed. He suppressed a shudder, unsure where the sudden chill had come from.

"Thanks," he mumbled, and skimmed the back cover with unfocused eyes. He couldn't concentrate, not while imagining soft lips whispering promises and offering him the world, if he'd only listen *properly.*

When he felt he'd dutifully fake-read enough of the summary, he handed it back. Azad licked his stupidly kissable lips and opened his mouth—no doubt to ask Danny his opinion on a topic he knew less than nothing about—and Danny had to distract them both.

"You into that sort of thing?" Danny blurted out, realized he wasn't sure if he meant the book or the half-formed idea of the two of them making out by the fire in Azad's favorite chair, and added, "Vampires, I mean. History of magic. Er, magical…transpirings…"

Azad raised an eyebrow, granite eyes shining. "Magical transpirings are an interest of mine, yes. Vampires, too." The corners of his lips twitched like he was holding back a grin. "Are you not interested?"

"No," Danny said before he could stop himself.

"No?" Azad sounded confused, and his eyebrow raised. "Not at all?"

Danny shrugged self-consciously and busied himself with bussing the dishes. "I don't know much about magic, and my family's not…we're very…well, if any of us ended up in the magic quarter, we'd spontane- ously combust."

"...I assume you don't mean that literally," Azad said slowly. "Are you saying there are absolutely no magical members of your family *at all?*"

It was hard not to snort. "Definitely not. I don't think there's a more un-magical group. And that doesn't excuse my not knowing about magic, but I've never felt the inclination," he added in a rush, because he did *not* want Azad to think less of him.

Azad didn't seem to be listening anymore. There was a distinctly glassy look to his eyes, and his expression was so lax it made the laugh lines around his mouth disappear.

"Is something wrong?" Danny asked nervously, fearing he'd ruined things.

"Your family isn't magical," Azad repeated, then burst into laughter. "That is...perfect, actually. Adorably perfect. And it explains *everything.*"

Danny's cheeks heated up, and he reminded himself that Azad was just nice. He was polite, and a friend of Siobhan's, and he was definitely *not* flirting.

"Thanks?" And then, with what little dignity he had left, Danny hugged the cluttered tray to his chest and rushed back to the counter.

To his surprise, Azad followed him.

"Wha—?"

"Siobhan," Azad called with a devilish smirk. "Are you busy?"

Siobhan's head poked through the bakery door. She looked around suspiciously and wrinkled her nose. "Is something on fire?"

"Merely a few questions, I promise." Azad waited; Siobhan stepped fully into the café, dusting flour off her hands. "Are the wards on the shop working?"

Danny's head whipped around, a misplaced sense of betrayal welling up inside him. "Wards?!"

"Of course," Siobhan said. "I check them every morning."

"So it would be completely outside the realm of possibility for a human to find their way in?" Azad asked with mock innocence.

"No one gets past the wards unless they've got magical blood," she said. "Humans can't even see this place—there's nothing but a brick wall when they look. Very tastefully graffitied. My magic's not the best, but I can manage *that* much."

"You're magical?" Danny squeaked.

Siobhan quirked her head and gave Danny a once-over. "Fae. Same as you, judging by the way your aura shines." She turned back to Azad.

"Anything else?"

"Well, if you'll finally share that blood tea recipe—"

Siobhan twirled on her foot and danced back into the kitchen, a tinny laugh fading in her wake.

"I've got magic blood? That's imposs—" Realization dawning on him, he rounded on Azad. "You're not human."

"Not for some time, no." Again he offered Danny his book, this time open to a page with a glossy reproduction of a medieval portrait.

The man in the portrait looked suspiciously like Azad, wearing a deep-burgundy tunic lined with gold-and-pearl beads, embroidery so detailed that Danny wondered how the artist had captured it. He squinted at the caption.

LORD AZAD EL BACHIR, MOROCCO, 1691

"You're a vampire?" Why didn't that worry him as much as it would have a month ago? "Wait, you're a *lord*?"

Azad held out his hand. "I think it's time we meet properly. I'm Azad, vampire. I've known Siobhan for a century. I'm unfortunately rather well-known in the magical community. And I've been flirting with you for the past seven weeks and getting nowhere, so I'd concluded you weren't interested because of my background."

Stunned, Danny hesitated before accepting and shaking Azad's hand, the chill of it now familiar and welcoming.

"I wish I'd known about the flirting. And the magic. And the 'I'm not fully human'…thing."

Azad's eyebrows rose. "Well, not-quite-human Danny, now that we're on the same page about who we are…and about the flirting…may I take you out for dinner?"

Danny had no idea what he was.

Danny had no idea what was going on.

Danny had no idea where his life was headed…but he knew one thing: he wanted Azad along for the ride.

"Absolutely. Just…maybe not in the magic quarter? When Mamie Mari finds out I've been accidentally working in a magical café this whole time, she's gonna flip. Don't want to make things worse until she's forgiven me for that."

Azad took Danny's hand in his, waiting for Danny's nod before pressing a featherlight kiss to a knuckle. "As you wish."

THE TASTY CRUMPET CODA

A. L. HEARD

Danny leaned against the counter, giddy. "After Mamie Mari explains everything, and I'm allowed in the Magic Quarter, where will you take me?"

Azad's smile froze. "Mamie Mari? Your grandmother isn't *the* Mari Dubois, is she?"

"I mean, that's her name. Why?"

"Oh, dear." A pause, then a reluctant, "I might know her."

"You know my Mamie!?" How many life-altering reveals was Danny in for today?

"I knew *a* Mari Dubois, half-fae, with eyes not unlike yours." Azad leaned forward and caressed Danny's temple; Danny shivered. "She vanished."

"What happened?" he asked in a daze.

"It was in Arcadia. One night, we were playing poker; the next moment she was gone. I thought it was because she owed me money, but after the British expulsion, I worried. Never did find out what happened to her."

"Oh," Danny managed, then brightened. "You should come over for dinner, then. You two can catch up. Maybe I won't get in trouble for the magic stuff, because *you'll* be there."

Azad raised an eyebrow. "You want me to protect you from your own grandmother?"

"She's very scary!" he insisted, pointing an accusing finger at Azad. "You oughta know—you said you'd met her!"

With a moment's consideration, Azad nodded. "I have. She is. Yes, perhaps family dinner is our wisest course. I'd best ask for her permission before taking you on a proper date, anyway…"

BÅND

FLORENCE VALE

asexual, biromantic, break-up (past), coffee shop, customer/employee,
curses (accidental), gender non-conforming, interspecies relationship, f/m (past),
m/m, magic use, magical mishap, norway, past tense, reaper, third person limited point
of view, witch

The door squeaked when it opened, letting in a gust of cold autumn air. The smell of watery asphalt and wet leaves rolled into the room and curled about the counter, bright and vibrant and rotting beneath.

Thomas was cleaning up after the afternoon rush, such as it was, loading plates and cups into the dishwasher. "Be right with you," he called, aiming for cheerful.

It had been a weird day, emotionally speaking. Amanda had called around lunchtime about a CD he had left behind when he moved out—

"Keep it," he'd said into the phone, speaking quietly so the old ladies from the poker club wouldn't overhear. He and Amanda had barely talked since he moved out. It was strange to realize that they were both still out in the world, existing independently in their separate spaces.

It wasn't that he still loved her.

He *did* still love her, and she still loved him, but their feelings were out of proportion and at the wrong angles, a story you read over and over until the sentences went stale.

Thinking about her listening to Postgirobygget in her Bergen apartment was almost nice. It still stung, but he liked to imagine that there was something left from the past six years—even after how everything shook out—that was worth keeping.

But Amanda had laughed, soft and warm. "You're the only one who owns anything that'll play it, Thomas."

"Not true," he said, though it was mostly true. "Some computers—"

"When can you pick it up?"

"Uh." He glanced at the calendar over the counter, tapping his fingers against the back of his phone. He worked most days, but if he wanted to take a weekend off, it wasn't like anyone could stop him: he owned the place. "Schedule's pretty packed. We've got the last of the summer tourists driving though, and then the traffic safety charm rush…"

There was a pop of static on the line and then a crackle.

"Is that—" Amanda said, half laughing. "Are you spelling the line?"

"I'm. No," Thomas said. He pressed his fingers against the hard plastic of his phone case, forcing them still, but it was too late—the spell was tapped out and set loose, and now the connection was breaking up, squealing in his ear.

"—better—e on your end and not mine," Amanda said.

"I really didn't mean to this time," Thomas had said. With a final, *spark-pop* and *crackle-shriek*, the phone had gone dead.

The whole thing had left him off-balance; it sat in his gut like a bad meal, heavy and unpleasant and hard to digest. His phone hadn't been able to find a signal after the call, either. God only knew when that would show back up. It had been a while since he'd had a spell mishap.

"Mishap" might be the wrong word. Usually, whatever spell he was tapping out helped solve the problem he was thinking about at the time, even if the solution was unorthodox.

Take, for example, the broken cell phone. It kept him from talking to Amanda for a while, and that was fine by him.

He washed his hands, tapped the screen to check if the signal had come back (it hadn't), and turned to greet the new customer.

Eikehuset got a steady stream of visitors. Some passed through on their way to Bergen or Stavanger, or, if they were taking the long way around, Oslo. Others were locals, or next-to-locals from other towns-that-weren't-really-big-enough-to-be-called-towns nearby: artsy city types living out their cottagecore dreams on newly bought småbruk; older people meeting for cake and companionship; parents rewarding their children with cinnamon buns and hot chocolate after a walk; workers stopping by for coffee or lunch or after late shifts that ran until sunrise.

And then there was the final type of customer: those who needed a spell.

Running the food-service aspects of the shop was enjoyable, but even if it hadn't been, his spellwork would have kept Eikehuset in business. State-authorized and state-subsidized, Eikehuset was part of a network of stores that doubled as spell suppliers. Travelling without up-to-date safety charms was dangerous, so every community needed someone who could make them. After his years-long Bergen detour with Amanda, Thomas was happy to fill that niche someplace out of the way.

He'd seen a bit of everything when it came to customers, so he expected a bit of everything when he turned to meet the stranger at the counter.

The stranger, who was—

Thomas blinked.

Who was—

The man standing in front of him was—

He had—

He was so nondescript it was difficult to look at him.

It wasn't that he looked average, exactly, or that Thomas couldn't take in his appearance. Part of his brain didn't *want* to look at him. The visual input scanned as something as profound as wallpaper, as exciting as drying paint. And the second Thomas's eyes slid away from him—which they did immediately, like water off a non-stick pan—it was impossible to recall how he looked, even though Thomas had just seen him.

"Hello," said the man.

"Uh, yeah," said Thomas, blinking. He had a headache coming on. "Sorry. How can I help you?"

The man looked at him and then at the counter between them. His expression—what little had been on his face in the first place—didn't change. "What would you recommend?"

That, at least, was a question Thomas could answer. He forced his arms to stay straight at his sides to keep from tapping on the edge of the counter—there had been enough of that today, thanks—and smiled. "Depends what you're looking for! We've got a selection of teas, coffees, and hot chocolates, as well as assorted pastries, muffins, pies, sandwiches, and the soup of the day. If you're *really* jonesing for a meal, though, you might want to check out the pub down the street."

The stranger frowned at him. "Here is fine."

"…right," Thomas said. This was so far shaping up to be a lot like playing charades. "So…any of those options sound interesting, or should I…just…choose something for you?"

The stranger did a little blink-and-head-twitch combo. Thomas just had the time to think his eyelashes were pretty long before the memory that gave the thought context was washed out of his brain. It was unpleasant, having a piece of himself come apart like wet tissue paper.

"Please," the stranger said.

Thomas pushed the nail of his thumb into the pad of his pointer finger and held it there. Whatever was up with the guy, he seemed willing to experiment, and far be it for Thomas to keep a man from experiencing the luxury of indecision. As long as he could pay, everything would be fine.

"Where are you from?" Thomas asked.

"Not here," said the stranger, and didn't elaborate.

"Right," Thomas said, because what else could he say? Instead, he got to work. He put a cheese melt (mushroom and red onion) on the grill. He filled a bowl with the soup of the day (tomato) and poured a mug of hot chocolate with marshmallows. The stranger watched him put everything on a tray—Thomas added a marvpostei for dessert and a glass of water for free—and said nothing.

"That'll be two hundred and ninety kroner," Thomas said, expecting a wince, but the guy's expression didn't change. He fished a card from his black leather wallet. It was also black, with a raven sketched onto the surface in bright silver ink.

Thomas stared at it.

"You have that specially designed?" he asked. "Or, uh, did you draw it yourself?"

The stranger looked at him and to the card and back again. "No," he said, his voice as bland and nondescript as his appearance. "It's a company card."

"Yeah?" Thomas asked. "What's the company?"

"Private," the guy said, and then fumbled his way through paying. It was embarrassing to watch, but like everything else about the man, Thomas found it hard to make himself care. It took a good three minutes of the man failing to find the right approach to defeating the card terminal before Thomas managed to cut through the fog of disinterest.

"Let me help you," he said, and reached out.

Their fingers brushed.

There was a loud crack and the smell of burning gasoline—

The air shuddered and shifted like a heat haze, thick as an emulsion on the edge of breaking—

The other guy tore his hand back.

The card clattered onto the counter.

This memory stuck, too jarring to slip away like his thoughts about the stranger's appearance had.

"Ah," Thomas said. "Sorry."

He wasn't sorry.

But he might be having a stroke. He'd read something on the internet once about smelling things that weren't there and oncoming strokes. He wasn't sure if it was true, but it sure came to the forefront of his brain at moments like this.

He wasn't having a stroke. Probably.

There was just something about this man, standing here in his café despite the wards Thomas had painstakingly tapped out and carved and whispered into every corner of the building.

The sensible thing to do would be to let it go and not ask questions. Maybe offer the guy a bit of rice porridge for good fortune, just in case he turned out to be a tusse or some other cryptid.

Thomas picked up the card. It was strangely greasy to the touch, like it had been smeared with oil. He glanced down, expecting the soapy, rainbow sheen of an oil slick, but it was just—normal, everyday plastic.

Carefully, he pressed the card against the reader and then slid it back across the counter.

This time, their fingers didn't touch.

The stranger took his tray and sat down at a table in the corner. He pulled out a thick, softcover book. Thomas watched him leaf through the pages with an intensity that had him leaning over almost double, and then he watched him eat, trying not to be too obvious about staring…and failing.

On the bright side, the stranger didn't appear to have noticed. He was eating with the kind of singular focus Thomas had rarely seen outside of a monster movie.

But it was probably fine. Thomas tapped his fingers on the countertop, unable to stop, needing to get some energy out *somehow* without pacing. The stranger had never been here before and was probably just passing through—it was unlikely that he'd come again. And even if he did—well.

Hopefully, he'd be a bit easier to pin down next time.

The stranger finished his meal. He left the dishes on the table, and, without looking back, he walked out of the door and out of Thomas's life.

And that's where it might have ended, if it hadn't been for the spell.

Three days later saw the first properly miserable autumn storm of the year. The rain came down in sheets. The wind tore into any patch of exposed skin, digging in deep and sour. The sky stayed dark even in the middle of the day, the colour of coffee stains. Even the café was affected: the lights dimmed and brightened and dimmed again at random; cold seeped under the door and through the windows; and the wind shrieked through the glass. Thomas tried to combat it by peddling out a couple of space heaters and cranking the temperature up, but the heat refused to spread out into the rest of the room. Instead, it hung around the counter like a listless ghost.

Maybe it was lucky that any potential customer was staying home today.

As he thought it, the door to the café swung open.

The stranger with the weird credit card stepped inside.

Thomas wasn't sure how he recognised him, but he did—the moment the guy came in, there was this shift in the air, a shiver that made him think: *oh. It's you.*

The guy was wearing a cherry-red, all-weather jacket today, its edges lined with silver high-visibility stripes. Everything above his neck was soaked, and his hair was dark with water; it ran down his forehead and temples in lazy little rivulets.

"How can I help you?" Thomas asked.

The stranger marched up to the counter, leaving mud in his wake.

"You cursed me," he said. His eyelashes were clumped together with rainwater, spiky and long like the legs of a spider, and his eyes were dark and very, very wide.

Scared, Thomas's mind supplied.

"Sorry?" he managed. He hadn't—

But he remembered tapping his fingers against the grain of the wood. With a sinking feeling, he remembered thinking, idly, that he hoped the guy would be easier to pin down next time.

He hadn't meant to curse him.

But he had.

"I'm so sorry," he said again, more sincerely.

The stranger's mouth thinned. He drew in a short, shaky breath. It sounded like he was breathing through a straw.

"You need to reverse it," he said. "I can't do my job like this. I'm useless. I'll—I'll give you anything you want."

"I, uh," Thomas said. "It was an accident."

"That doesn't help," the stranger snapped, and then went pale. "Not...that...you're obligated to help, of course, but I promise the compensation will be worth it."

"Okay," Thomas said, trying to calm him down. "Why don't you come behind the counter and sit down, and I'll get us both some tea."

"I don't want tea," the stranger said, bleak as bones. "I want you to fix this."

"Right, well," Thomas said. "That's good and all, but I need to figure out what the spell did before I can fix it, and that'll take a hot minute, so I suggest you send your boss a message and settle down with a cup of something."

The stranger crossed his arms.

"Fine," he said. "But I want hot chocolate."

"You look...different," Thomas said. "Than last time, I mean."

The stranger was perched by the same table he had sat at his previous visit, staring into the depths of his mug with an unnerving intensity.

"Part of the job is to not be noticed," he said into his hot chocolate. "You took that away from me, so now you're noticing."

As he talked, he seemed to fill out more, taking up space like a drop of ink spreading through a glass of milk. Every minute, Thomas noticed new details about him—the soft curve of his chin, and the way his hair curled with the rain. Or had it always curled like that?

He cleared his throat. "I really am sorry."

"Me too," the stranger muttered, then winced. His mouth moved soundlessly, like he was rehearsing, and then he said, "Sorry. Please don't change your mind on this."

"On what? Helping you?" Thomas asked, bewildered. "Why would I? It's my fault."

"Affective magic," the stranger said. "You must have thought I was a threat in some way."

"No," Thomas lied. The stranger levelled him with a stare. "Okay, mostly no. I just"—he tapped the table twice before he could stop himself—"you didn't feel right."

The look the stranger gave him was flat, and the tone of his voice was worse. "Didn't I."

"When something messes with my thoughts, that's a bad sign, typically," Thomas said.

"You weren't supposed to notice!" the stranger snapped. "I'm"—and his hands came up to hide his face, fingers pressing against his eyelids— "I'm a ferryman. When someone dies on the road, I pick up their spirit and drive them to the other side. If everyone can see me, that's not the kind of thing I can get away with for long."

Thomas stared at him. His brain felt like a staircase with steps missing. "When you say 'drive'...?"

"I have a company car," the stranger said miserably.

"Right," Thomas said. Then, gently teasing, "And does it have ravens on it too?"

The stranger blinked up at him. His head twitched to the side. Then he snorted. "I wish."

"Maybe suggest it at the next employee meeting?"

The stranger lowered his hands, placing them flat on the table. His fingernails were painted turquoise except for a small part on his thumbnail; he must have touched it before it could dry. The sight of it—that tiny gap in the blueish-green—made Thomas feel...something. Fondness, maybe. It was this mark of being a person, of being someone who carefully filled in the blank space and then ruined it just a little, stamped into this guy's nail. Thomas couldn't look away.

"I'm Thomas, by the way," he said. "And my powers have been a bit out of whack since I, ah. Well. They've been unreliable lately."

The stranger shot him another long look, though this one was less flat. His head did that little twitch again. "…you can call me Jay."

"Right," Thomas said, smiling. "Sorry again, Jay. Let's break you of that curse."

And he meant to.

He hadn't had to undo one of his own curses before. Mostly, he steered clear of casting them; it seemed like bad luck to bring misfortune on someone else. The Jay Debacle (as he called it quietly in his own head) was proof of *that*.

Curses came in all shapes and sizes, some thin like a spider's web and others spiky like barbed wire, some sharp like glass and others soft and suffocating like a living and particularly malicious blanket. They were invisible unless one knew how to look, and Thomas pulled out his quartz glasses from the back office, just to be sure.

Jay was sitting with his knees up in one of the booths. He looked up from his plasticky guidebook—the cover read "NAF VEIBOK" in large, golden letters—and startled. "What are *those?*"

Thomas's face heated. "They help—"

"—your uniform?" Jay asked, grinning.

"The curse-finding." Thomas put the glasses on. The light in the room shifted. Jay looked the same, but what resembled a thick, rose-coloured rope came out of his chest, right between the ribs. It hung lazily in the air between them, and—

Oh.

Oh, great.

It was tethered to Thomas's sternum. The sight of it coming out of his own chest, solid in every way but the tangible, made him light-headed. He sat down next to Jay with a heavy *thump*. The tether between them shrank to fit their closeness. Experimentally, Thomas leaned away; the tether lengthened again.

"Thank God," he said under his breath.

"What?" Jay asked, frowning. When Thomas told him about the tether, he winced and then tucked his book into the depths of his bright-red jacket. "That's not ideal."

"It could be worse?"

Jay frowned harder. "My boss would disagree."

After some testing, they managed to get a better feeling for how the tether worked. They were tied together, but there didn't seem to be a limit to how far from each other they could go. Disguise spells and potions refused to stick to either of them. Now that he knew the tether was there, Thomas could *feel* it. It sat in his chest like the soft hum of the motor in an expensive car, or the sound of the café refrigerator kicking on, blending into the background noise of his body.

It was harder to work out how to *break* the curse. That first week, they tried verbal and somatic approaches, a bottled curse-dispeller, and a pair of enchanted silver scissors, but to no avail. The thread between them refused to be broken.

"I really thought this would do it." Thomas sighed, stabbing listlessly at the tether between them with the scissors.

"It would have been nice," said Jay. "As a metaphor."

"Yeah, no luck there." Thomas sighed. "I'll try calling in a favour."

"And get me some hot chocolate?"

"Sure."

"Oh," Jay said, like he hadn't expected Thomas to agree. He jerked his head down, mouth a sharp, unhappy line. "I can't really pay?"

Don't worry, I can take care of you.

Thomas cleared his throat. He tried to clear the thought away, too, but it stuck. It was just—

He felt bad about cursing him, of course, but in the days since Jay returned to the café, Thomas had increasingly come to like the guy. Maybe it was the laser-sharp intensity of his focus, or how he treated every task like it was the most important thing he would ever do, or how he could never just sit like a normal person, or the sharp way he smiled, or the way he wore nail polish but never neatly—

It was just. God help him, he liked having Jay around.

"You get the 'friends and family' discount," Thomas said.

"We're friends?" Jay asked, like he wanted to be sarcastic, but he was smiling, still looking down at his shoes.

"You get free hot chocolate regardless," Thomas said, and went to make a cup. Over his shoulder he said, "The 'friend' part is up to you."

"We'll see," Jay called after him. Thomas grabbed a mug from the rack, hiding a smile in his free hand.

After the scissors failed, Thomas called a potioneer from Andøya, who rolled in with a small army of tiny crystal bottles and succeeded solely in turning both of their hair bright purple.

Jay called in a friend of a friend who covered them head to toe in red ink and made them stand back to back in a circle of pine trees for the final two hours before dawn, shivering.

"Is this some kind of reaper hazing?" Thomas had hissed. It was very dark and very cold. The trees around them were lined with perching ravens. "I *know* that species of raven isn't endemic to this region."

"Ferryman, not reaper," Jay said. Thomas could practically feel him rolling his eyes. "And I don't know what hazing is."

"*What?*"

Jay went stiff. "I've been a bit busy! What is it?"

Thomas grinned into the darkness, grateful that Jay couldn't see him. It was just—he just felt—

Fondness.

You're a person, he thought. *And I'm a person. And we're standing back to back in the woods, and it sucks, but we're here, together, in this moment.*

"Well," he said, "hazing is…"

Five months later, Jay still didn't get hazing, and they still hadn't found a way to break the curse. Jay camped out at Eikehuset, coming in every morning to sit with his knees up in one of the booths, feet planted firmly on the upholstery. It had started as passive aggression, but now it was…nice. Familiar.

"My boss is still angry," Jay reported, leaning his chin against his knees. "So, nothing new there. And reaping is pretty much my whole life, so. This is an adjustment."

"Enjoying your extended vacation?" Thomas asked, handing him a mug of hot chocolate.

Jay looked at the mug and then at him. For a moment, his eyes seemed huge. The bright light of the sun reflecting off of the snow outside lit them up, gave them the colours of a forest pond in the middle of summer. Out of nowhere, Thomas was struck with the urge to hug him. He didn't know why, but he *felt* it, all the way down to his bones—like he was already watching a future version of himself do it and feeling jealous.

"I'm a bit restless," Jay said quietly. He unfolded himself like a letter and took a sip of cocoa. "Thank you for this."

"No problem. Never a problem," Thomas said. "And I'm sorry. Again. I really didn't mean to do this to you."

"To us. And I know. You're making up for it."

Thomas sighed. "Trying to, anyway."

"What's next?"

"I'm following some leads. There's a guy in Finland who might be willing to take a trip down to take a look. He does—what was it?—spectral analytics."

Jay did his little blink-and-head-twitch thing. It was really—

Cute, Thomas realised. It was incredibly cute.

"Ghosts?" Jay asked. He put down the mug and dug into his pockets, pulling out a bottle of nail polish.

"Apparently, he's working on a method to apply it to all intangible phenomena."

Jay gave a small, judgmental "hmm" as he unscrewed the nail polish. "Good luck to him."

Thomas laughed. "You don't think we should ask him?"

"No," Jay said, applying an uneven streak of turquoise to his thumbnail. He was practically allergic to straight lines and it showed. "But we might as well try."

Without any input from his brain, Thomas asked: "Do you—Do you want me to do that for you? The nail polish?"

Jay blinked at him, iceberg slow. "I— Sure."

Which was how Thomas found himself holding Jay's hand in one of his own and applying nail polish with the other.

"It's a good colour," he said. "It suits you."

"Thank you," Jay said with a small smile, not quite looking at him.

"Did you…were you wearing it the first time you came in?" Thomas asked, because his mind was blank, and they were practically holding hands, and he couldn't think of what else to say.

"Yeah," Jay said. "Even if no one else could see it, I still could, you know? It's nice to have a thing that's mine."

Thomas squeezed his hand gently, careful not to mess up the nail polish. For a moment, he'd thought that holding hands would feel strange.

Like touching some forbidden, magical artefact that might break beneath his fingers. Instead, it just felt nice. Familiar.

"I guess I won't be able to see it anymore once the curse is broken," Thomas said.

"It'll be different," Jay said. They were sitting very close. "You know me now."

His thumb stroked up the line of Thomas's palm. Thomas couldn't look away from the motion. It was a light touch, but it was grounding, settling him inside himself. When he looked up, Jay was smiling, bright enough to steal the breath right out of his lungs, and—

Oh.

In the end, Thomas called a curse breaker. She came into the café six months after the curse had set in, heels clicking on the floor tiles, and put a small paper bag onto the counter.

"First of all," she said, "here's your CD back."

Thomas gave Amanda an awkward smile. She leaned up to kiss his cheek. At the other end of the café, Jay stood up so fast his chair fell over.

Amanda looked at him and then back at Thomas. "Thomas," she said, half laughing. "That's not a curse. It's a soul bond."

"A *what?*"

"Once in a blue moon, two people meet and their souls catch—like, hook onto each other and spin out like a tether. A soul bond spells out unrealised potential, romantic or platonic. It's like…a need for connection so strong it ties two people together until the connection becomes real and internalised."

As Amanda broke it down for them, Jay kept looking at him, eyes unreadable and bright like copper.

"What does that mean, '*internalised*'?" Jay asked.

"It means that you have to come over here and hold hands. Whatever is at the core of your connection, you both need to say it out loud," Amanda said. "And you both need to believe it. Then you won't need an outside link anymore."

Jay came over, moving like a spooked animal.

Thomas took his hand and squeezed it. "Hey," he said. "You okay?"

Jay nodded jerkily. "I'm good."

"I…" Thomas said. Now they were *both* looking at him. "I think I came here because it felt safe. After Amanda…that felt like that was *it* for me. I couldn't imagine caring for anyone else like that again. I couldn't touch that part of myself without it hurting, but I couldn't let go of it, either, so I was holding on and trying not to at the same time. And then you came in the door, and even when I couldn't keep my eyes on you I wanted to know you. And now that I know you, how could I do anything but love you?" His vision blurred with tears. "How could I do anything but let go?"

"Are you crying?" Jay asked, teasing, but he was looking misty, too. "I. Me too. Without the ex, sorry Amanda—"

"It's fine."

Jay smiled at her and took a deep breath. He turned back to Thomas. "I hated being seen, in the beginning. And then I hated that I didn't hate it, when it was you looking at me. You were kind to me when I was a stranger. You gave me hot chocolate, you fixed my nail polish, you're—you're *good*. And I love you. Clearly."

"Clearly?" Thomas laughed. His blood was singing like an electrical current. There was a rushing sound, growing louder.

"Yeah," Jay said, squeezing his hand. The noise around them was deafening, but Thomas could still hear Jay clearly.

There was a loud *crack!*, then silence. Amanda gave them a sly smile and went outside without another word.

"Did it work?" Thomas asked.

"I think so," Jay said. "I feel different."

Thomas looked at him. His dark eyes were huge in the fluorescent lights of the café. "You look the same."

"I'm not the same," Jay said. His appearance rippled like water, turning nondescript and then back again. "And you aren't, either."

"I'm not what?" Thomas asked. He felt a smile coming on, unstoppable, filling his mouth like sunlight. Jay was smiling, too, baring a sharp little slice of teeth.

"You're not the same," he said. "You look settled."

"Yeah?" Thomas said, but he wasn't really asking. As Jay said it, he felt it; in his bones, in his body, right between the ribs.

A FAMILY THING

JESSICA BLACK

angst (minor), coffee shop, college setting, curses, customer service representative, customer/employee, m/m, miscommunication, present tense, soulmates, the nature of free will, third person limited point of view, united states of america

"You're gonna burn the espresso."

Connor is *not* going to burn the espresso. He's been working at Firehouse Roast for three years now and has never once burnt the espresso. "Don't you have paperwork or something? Go do manager stuff somewhere else."

"I'm managing perfectly fine right here."

"You're impeding my ability to serve paying customers."

There's a twinkle in Seo's calculating gaze, the kind that signals she's about to make him wish he still worked the morning shift instead of the afternoon one that better fits his current class schedule. "The only paying customer I see is the one whose drink you're about to ruin."

Connor sighs and throws his arms up in defeat, backing away from the espresso machine to let her take over. If it were anyone else, he'd dig his heels in. But Seo has knowledge of a certain secret Connor would rather keep buried and absolutely no remorse when bringing it up.

He'd really thought that moving a couple thousand miles away from his hometown for grad school would put some distance between himself and this stupid family "curse."

"I'm doing you a favor," Seo says with a smirk, directing the foam to form the shape of a heart.

Connor's eyes narrow at her, and he glances sideways at the customer waiting for his drink. The guy's young, handsome in a way that looks like he put some effort into it, and not-so-subtly checking out Connor's ass.

Shit.

"If you put my phone number on that cup, I'm quitting," Connor hisses.

Seo leans toward him and whispers, "If I don't try to make up for your complete lack of game, Mackenzie, you'll never meet 'The One.' "

It's an ongoing argument between them, and the only one Connor refuses to back down on. "I don't need 'The One.' There *is no* 'The One,' and even if there were, I wouldn't need any help finding them."

Seo rolls her eyes. "Your love life is too depressing for me not to intervene."

"I don't have a love life!"

"Exactly."

She makes her way over to the guy who she apparently thinks is Connor's Goddamn soulmate, but Connor manages to snatch the permanent marker from her hand on the way, so at least she doesn't actually get to share his contact info.

Of all the problems Connor thought he'd have at this point in his life, the manager at his part-time job continually pestering him into looking for the love of his life was not one of them. But then, Seo happened to catch him video chatting with his mom during a break. The two of them immediately hit it off, and now Seo is practically Mrs. Mackenzie's stand-in for everything related to Connor's relationship status.

Connor doesn't want a relationship status. Or, rather, he *would*…if it didn't come with the crushing weight of his family's—and now Seo's—expectations.

It's a family legend going back generations, one that Connor has no intention of ever taking seriously: every second son has another half—a soulmate—and is cursed to "wander the earth in despair" until he finds them.

Connor's older brother used to tease him about it when they were growing up, and his mother used to sigh wistfully while imagining how Connor might eventually meet this mythical person. But Connor's mom is an incurable romantic, and his brother is kind of a dick.

Curses aren't real. Soulmates aren't real. Connor is perfectly happy working on his bioengineering degree and slinging espresso part-time at the local coffee shop.

He's told Seo this several times over the past couple months, to no avail. "Are you kidding me, Mackenzie?" is her standard response. "Your face is stuck in permanent brooding mode, and the only thing you ever say about your classes is how much you hate them."

So maybe he really only chose his Master's based on the expectation he'd settle into a "sensible" career, and maybe working customer service in the meantime isn't exactly a dream come true, and *maybe* the last time he went on a date was too long ago to be worth talking about. But this doesn't mean his resting face "evokes the pain of a thousand Greek tragedies." He *smiles*. Occasionally.

Connor scowls down at the register until Seo places a gentle hand on his forearm.

"Hey," she says, without the usual clip to her tone. "I'm never gonna actually force you to do anything, I hope you know that. Like anyone could even make Connor Mackenzie do something he wasn't already set on doing!"

He rolls his eyes, though quirks his lips with something like fondness.

"But *damn* if you haven't been wound tighter than anyone I've ever met since the day you got here. And it's getting worse. If I knew how to soften your edges a little, I'd do it, but actually talking about shit is kind of your kryptonite, so I'm flying blind here."

"I talk about shit," he grumbles, petulant, even though he knows it's a lie.

The day proceeds like every other. Connor greets customers with his usual grumpiness; the regulars no longer seem to mind, since he makes a mean cup of coffee. He studies for his midterms whenever things slow down. He avoids catching glimpses of his reflection in the glass display case of croissants and muffins.

It's just his face. It's not stuck in "permanent brooding mode." Brown hair, brown eyes, a handful of freckles…nothing to suggest he's unhappy, other than the few times Seo points out that he's frowning without realizing it.

Connor spends the week with "permanent brooding mode" perpetually in the back of his head. Every time he sighs at the dirty dishes his roommate leaves out, or contemplates hitting snooze a couple more times instead of trudging to class, or pauses over his phone when he realizes the only person he could text about his issues is his mom, thousands of miles away, and he knows she wouldn't get it…every time, he wonders if he's even marginally happy.

And what if he isn't? What could he possibly do to change that?

A potential answer comes in the form of one of the most beautiful men Connor has ever met.

"Do you guys do the frap thing, or is that just for chain stores?"

Connor lifts his head from restocking cups to come face to face with…some kind of male model, if he were to hazard a guess. Dark curly hair gone just wild enough that Connor can't tell if it's intentional or not, broad shoulders that narrow into a trim waist, grey-blue eyes that stand out in contrast to his dark complexion, a hint of stubble along his sharp jawline. His jeans and T-shirt look the kind of expensive that's both well-tailored and slightly askew. Tattoos peek out from beneath the shirt sleeves encircling his biceps.

"Do we what?" Connor asks, blinking and feeling a bit dazed. He's never had a reaction like this to someone before. Sure, beautiful people exist, and he's admired his fair share of them, but they've always felt distant. People who look like *that* might as well be a different species.

"Like, the blended shit or whatever," the man says. "Do you guys do that here?"

Blended shit? Connor mouths with obvious disdain.

"Yeah. You know. Caffeine, but actually palatable."

"…so you don't like coffee?"

The guy pulls a face that should make him look ridiculous, but somehow his cheekbones make it work. "I like things that taste good."

Connor pinches the bridge of his nose, huffing a sigh. "This is a coffee shop."

The professional underwear model in front of him smirks. "That's a no on the frap, huh?"

What the hell is even happening right now? Most people, especially customers, don't bother engaging with Connor once they see his furrowed brow and pursed lips. How is the man in front of him so unaffected that the smirk on his face gives the impression that he thinks he's winning whatever weird debate they're currently having?

Because he is definitely *not* winning. Connor will be damned if he lets this douchebag come out of this interaction victorious.

Connor grabs a marker and a cup with sudden determination. "Caramel or chocolate?"

For the first time, the man looks hesitant. "Uh. I mean. I don't see a blender back there."

Connor shrugs a shoulder. He's always been stubborn and competitive, and he feels more so right now; it makes putting up a mask of disinterest even easier. "Caramel or chocolate," he repeats.

"…caramel?"

"Got it. Name?"

The guy stares at him like Connor's speaking a different language. But then he shakes it off, takes a half-step back, and gives Connor a considering once-over. Connor's ears grow hot, but he feels like he won their contest. And then feels like he's won another when the man finally meets his eyes and says, "Ish."

"Ish?" The name rings in Connor's ears strangely. Like it was supposed to take up more room than it does, and like Connor's the one who inadvertently decided not to pay enough attention to it.

Or, no. Not inadvertently. Connor usually decides not to pay attention to outlying emotions and reactions, but this feels like something he's *supposed* to notice.

"It's a nickname." Ish's tone goes a touch defensive and a touch bored, like he's had to explain this a lot.

"It's not even a whole word," Connor mutters, feeling strangely defensive as well.

"I'm not sure, but I don't think customer service is supposed to include so many insults."

"Those are on the house."

Connor turns away, in part to begin making the drink, in part to better ignore the smile on Ish's face, as well as the one threatening to break out on his own. He grabs the cold brew and the caramel sauce, and he does his own version of magic with an added bit of cinnamon and whipped cream. Connor would never drink it—he's strictly an extra-dry cappuccino guy—but he thinks it'll win over Ish.

"I'm not paying for a drink I didn't order," Ish responds as Connor hands it over, but his lips keep tilting up at the corners like he's more amused than he wants to let on.

"You'll love this drink, or I will buy you some Goddamn *'blended shit'* from somewhere else."

Ish grins and takes a sip. His eyes widen, and Connor feels a smug look settle across his face.

"Did you just make coffee palatable?" Ish asks, staring at his drink like he doesn't understand how it exists.

"That barely counts as coffee, but if by 'palatable' you mean 'ninety-percent sugar,' then sure."

There's a beat of silence as Ish takes another sip, stares at his cup, then at Connor. Connor shifts his weight from foot to foot awkwardly, feeling suddenly self-conscious.

"I'm still not paying for it," Ish says, even as he's reaching for his wallet.

"You will next time." And Connor doesn't know how he's absolutely certain that there will be a next time, or why he hopes that there will be despite how confusing this guy's presence is, but the statement still falls from his lips like truth.

Ish stuffs a twenty into the tip jar and heads out. Connor does *not* watch him go the entire way to the door, and definitely doesn't jump about a foot in the air and splash almond milk all over himself when Seo returns.

"What the hell is your face doing right now?" she asks.

Connor startles. He scowls and reaches for a towel to clean himself up. "I don't need another lecture about my general grumpiness."

Seo rolls her eyes. "Your grumpiness is not in question here. Whatever made your facial features momentarily lose about ten years of dire apathy is."

Connor doesn't know the answer to that. Doesn't *want* to know. Because there's no way, no reason, to think…

There is, indeed, a next time. The very next day, in fact. Ish walks in, and Connor's stomach does this strange little somersault that he decides to attribute to frustration. Because who the hell goes to a coffee shop to order something that barely resembles coffee? And who the hell is named *Ish?*

"All right, let's see if you can pull off that coffee hocus-pocus a second time," Ish says as he approaches the counter.

"There isn't anything magical about it, unless you consider it miraculous that I'm even considering making another drink for you when you didn't pay for the last one."

"Well, I didn't order the last one."

"Is this a scam you've run before? Should I already know about the most notorious food-and-drink grifter this side of the Rockies?"

Ish leans forward with both elbows on the countertop, a shit-eating grin perfectly center on his extremely symmetrical and aesthetically pleasing face. The blue hoodie he's wearing is too baggy, but open enough to reveal the tank top underneath (that is *definitely* too tight). His jeans have strategic holes in them, but also a few very not-strategic stains.

Connor can't make heads or tails of this guy. Ish moves through a room like he owns it, but also as if he has no idea that he does.

There is a glimpse of another tattoo—close enough to Ish's exposed collarbone to be partially visible—that leaves Connor with one more mystery he itches to solve. First: the nickname. Now: half a sentence in Morse code.

"Nah, you're just special," Ish says. And then *winks*, damn it.

Connor pinches the bridge of his nose and huffs a breath. This is *not* an interaction he's equipped to handle. "You want the same as last time? Or something new?"

There's a moment's crack in Ish's confident-and-carefree armor that floors Connor enough that he doesn't have time to analyze it before it's gone. "You really think you could whip up something completely different for me? Just like that?"

"As long as you're willing to suffer the consequences, sure."

Ish leans away, like a bow being pulled backward and taut, and laughs in a way that stretches out the defined lines of his body even more. "Okay, on with it, then. Surprise me…" he trails off with an expectant raise of his eyebrows.

Connor has never once given a customer his name. He's had honest-to-God roommates who didn't know his first name. Yet, for some reason, it comes out now without a second thought. "Connor. Connor Mackenzie."

The answering smile is blinding. "All right, Mackenzie. Let's see what you got for round two."

Connor knows he's blushing as he works. How is this happening to him? He can hear his mother's voice in his head reminding him about destiny and leaps of faith. He can hear his brother's voice taunting him for entertaining the idea at all. But Connor's already giving himself enough grief for that, and he's pretty sure that leaps of faith require actual faith.

Still. Something about the turn of the Earth feels steadier lately. Something in Connor's chest feels looser and better able to draw in breath.

And when Ish takes his first sip of this new drink, the way his eyes light up in delight is more captivating than it has any right to be. "Marry me," he says, tone so serious that Connor is taken aback.

Until Ish smirks and takes another sip, leaning sideways against the countertop like he has nowhere else in the world to be.

Ish shows up every day, though never at the same time. And every day, Connor attempts to create some new beverage for him that will impress as much as the day before. It's…fun? He's never applied any creativity to his job (or to anything else in life) before, and he finds he enjoys it. Not just the challenge of it, but also the small unknown: the moment when he grabs a cup and writes Ish's name on it, Ish's amused expression front and center in his mind, and Connor has no idea what's going to come next, just that he'll be the one to set it into motion.

If he's being honest with himself, Ish makes him feel that way in general. Like the moment the guy walks through that door anything could happen, but it's not scary or aggravating. In those moments, it feels like Connor's been granted freedom from all the expectations in his life.

The expectation that he'd graduate with a serious degree and go on to work a serious job. The expectation that he'd one day meet and marry his perfect other half…when Ish is grumbling about coffee, or teasing Connor for his taste in music ("Dad Rock" is a perfectly acceptable genre for a twenty-something to listen to!), Connor doesn't feel any of that weight.

For once, Connor can just…create a sugary drink that wins a smile. He can have a conversation with a pretty man who seems to enjoy his company. He can let himself breathe.

"You could switch majors."

Connor's head snaps up to stare at Ish, draped across the countertop awaiting his mystery order. Ish's tone is casual, but his words are precise. Connor starts to wonder how much of himself he's let slip over a dozen of these brief encounters that always border on flirting.

Ish hasn't let slip a whole lot, but Connor's hoarded every bit of it. Day job: freelance editor. Favorite color: purple. Closest relative: a sister in San Diego. Top item on his bucket list: play the piano for someone other than himself.

"It's a Master's, Ish" Connor says stiffly. "I'm kinda locked in."

"You don't have to be."

It sounds so easy when Ish says it, and for the first time in his entire academic career, Connor wonders if that's true. Maybe he "doesn't have to be" stuck. Maybe, this entire time…he didn't "have to be" anything.

"And it's Ismael, by the way."

There's a record scratch in Connor's head at the non sequitur. He blinks dumbly for a second, holding an empty coffee cup in one hand and a bottle of gourmet dark chocolate syrup that he brought from home in the other.

"What?"

"My name. It's Ismael. I hate it, so please don't call me that, ever. I have no idea why I'm even telling you, but…yeah. Mystery solved. Guy who has issues with his father also has issues with the name his father gave him. I'd write a book about it, but there are already so many others to choose from."

Ish seems like the type to foster mysteries rather than reveal them, and so this confession is either very out of character or very meaningful.

Or both.

Connor really wants it to be both. Connor, with a sudden intensity that completely snuck up on him, *wants* something, and it's exhilarating.

That want doesn't go away. It intensifies every time Ish stops by the shop, casual as anything, with a smirk and an irreverent turn of phrase. It makes Connor look forward to picking another argument with him, has him excited for the next day: what it might bring, what it might mean.

Ish hesitantly sips on the coffee-adjacent concoction he's just been handed, and Connor holds his breath.

"Wow." It's a strange word coming from Ish's mouth, who's so far only ever said it sarcastically, but his tone is utterly sincere now.

Connor laughs. "Again, why are you here if you don't like coffee? The sign out front is pretty clear about what we serve."

Ish tugs at his bottom lip with his teeth. It's the most vulnerable Connor's seen him. His eyes dart across the floor as though he's internally debating with himself, then he looks back up and meets Connor's gaze with a seriousness that leaves Connor a little winded. "Do you believe in fate?"

The bottom drops out of Connor's stomach.

"I don't really talk about it," Ish continues before Connor can do more than gape at him, "but I've got this…thing. A family thing. More interesting than the 'daddy issues' bullshit, I promise, but infinitely crazier. You're gonna laugh at me, but I swear this is legit. Once every other generation, the only son of—"

"Stop," Connor interrupts.

"I know it sounds absurd, but—"

"No. Seriously. Stop. Are you here to make fun of me?"

Ish's big grey-blue eyes grow even bigger. "…no?"

Connor can't breathe. For the first time in his adult life, he thought he was getting somewhere in a relationship on his own. Sure, Ish is completely out of his league, and it probably wouldn't have gone anywhere beyond what it is now. But Ish still comes in every day, still lights up at Connor's prickliness like it's somehow charming, and that's something. That had been enough.

And it's all, what? A joke? Or, worse, there's a ring of truth to the magic-soulmate-destiny bullshit he's heard all his life, and Connor never actually had a say in his love life at all?

"Did Seo put you up to this?"

"Is she the mean one who works here?" Ish smirks, though it's forced, like he's attempting to lighten the mood. "The *other* mean one, that is."

The mood does not lighten. Connor can barely hear Ish over the ringing in his ears. He stumbles back a step and drops whatever he was holding. A spoon? A dish cloth? He can't remember.

"Hey, Mackenzie, are you okay? I didn't mean to…" Ish trails off uncertainly. Connor sways on his feet and grips the counter with one hand.

And then Ish is in front of him, expression bordering on panicked, looking like he has no idea what to do with his hands. Which is ridiculous. Ish is the epitome of "always knowing what to do with his hands."

They're good hands. Connor likes staring at the long fingers wrapped around a coffee cup. Likes to imagine what would happen if he let his own hand linger in the cup exchange, what that brush of skin might feel like.

"Please tell me Seo put you up to this," Connor manages.

"I honestly don't know what 'this' is." Ish finally settles on reaching a hand out to gently squeeze Connor's forearm. It feels stupidly good. How long has it been since another person touched him? Too long, probably.

"Connor?" Ish tries, hushed. It's strange to hear his first name in Ish's voice. It sounds right in a way that neither logic nor reason can explain.

"I, uh." He pauses and wets his lips, chuckles breathlessly, the sound a little sad and a little disbelieving. "I might also have a, uh, 'family thing.'"

Ish's grip on Connor's forearm tightens. He leans in slowly, until they're sharing the same air. "Wait. So, you believe me? Because I think...I mean, the moment I saw you, I sort of *knew*, but I didn't want to get my hopes up. God knows I've been wrong before and gotten burned for it. But...it's really you, isn't it?"

"No." Connor shakes his head and swallows. "No. It's not real."

"What?" Ish pulls his hand away and takes a step back, looking like Connor's slapped him. "Of course it is. You think I'd ever come into a coffee shop for the coffee? It happened, just like my grandmother said it would. The signs appeared, and they led me here. To you."

Connor shakes his head again. "Listen, it's a romantic notion, but I don't...that's not how..." That's not how Connor's life works. Just because his mother wants it to—just because his family history tells him it does—Connor knows himself. The romantic ending is not the one he gets; he's all but made sure of it over the years.

Ish is frowning at him now, thick eyebrows furrowed inward, broad shoulders so tense Connor thinks something inside Ish might snap. "You really don't feel it?"

The messed-up part of it is that yes, he does. He *does* feel it.

And it scares the shit out of him.

When Connor's silence has gone on long enough to be its own answer, Ish backs away farther. Each step feels like a new loss, but what is Connor really losing? A regular customer and a few minutes a day of entertaining banter? He'll live.

"All right. Well, guess this is me getting burned again." Ish laughs humorlessly. The sound sends a lightning bolt of pain through Connor's chest. "If you change your mind..." he starts, then trails off. He shrugs, pulls a business card out of his back pocket, sets it on the counter, then heads for the door.

He leaves his unfinished drink behind.

Connor takes the days that follow to unpack his last conversation with Ish. It's the first week in a while now that he doesn't see Ish every day, and time seems to move slower as a result. He goes to class and does his homework and goes in for his shifts, but it all happens through a kind of brain fog. He starts hitting snooze more often, hands in assignments at the last possible minute, scares off more than a few customers with the force of his scowl and his judgmental tone when they try to order anything even vaguely resembling "blended shit."

It's not until these bad habits have returned that Connor realizes they'd been gone. For some time now, he's been happy to come into work. He's approached his schoolwork as though it were an interesting problem to solve instead of a chore. He hasn't needed his alarm to get up, let alone the snooze button, in a long time.

He doesn't want to attribute it all to Ish. It doesn't seem fair for one man to hold the entirety of another's happiness in his possession. But maybe Ish was, at the very least, a wake-up call.

And maybe if Connor is so dead set on not letting the supposed family curse dictate who he falls in love with, he also shouldn't let it decide who he *doesn't* fall in love with, either.

"Are you happier since you met him? Before you ruined it all, I mean," Seo asks with her usual unfettered directness.

Connor rolls his eyes with a huff but answers the question. "Yes." At this point it would be impossible to lie, even to himself.

"Then who cares what mystical forces nudged it into being? For Pete's sake, Mackenzie, let yourself be happy."

A phone call doesn't seem like enough; Ish works from home, his address neatly printed on his business card. Is showing up unannounced romantic or presumptuous? Connor has no idea. He's never cared about a relationship enough to bother with understanding romance.

He tries to prepare a speech, but feels silly. There's not a whole lot to say other than the obvious.

"I'm sorry."

Ish stares at him from his open door, and it's unfair how good he looks in sweatpants and a threadbare T-shirt. His bare feet and slightly-thicker-than-usual stubble project a softness that he so often hides in public. Connor feels desperately grateful to be able to witness it now and desperately hopeful that he'll get to see it again.

Maybe even call it his own one day.

"You didn't do anything wrong," Ish says, matter-of-fact. "*I'm* sorry if I made you uncomfortable."

"You didn't," Connor is quick to assure him. "It's just, my family. They call it a curse. Like the only kind of life I'd ever get to have without you was too miserable to consider. I've spent so long fighting that idea, trying to prove them wrong, that when faced with the possibility that they might be right..."

Ish's features screw up in indignation. "Screw that. You don't need someone else to be happy."

Connor doesn't bother fighting back the smile that blooms on his face. "But you *do* make me happy."

A half-smile quirks one side of Ish's mouth up. He shrugs a shoulder. "Bonus perk."

It feels too easy, and too good to be true, but for once Connor allows himself the indulgence of unabashedly staring into Ish's eyes and letting all of his want show plainly on his face.

"How does this curse of yours work, then?" Ish asks, stepping forward onto the landing and into Connor's space. "How did you know I was 'The One'?"

"I just did. I just *do*."

One of Ish's hands rises up to rest on Connor's chest as Connor's heart tries to beat itself straight out of his rib cage to meet it.

"How does yours work?" he asks.

Ish huffs a laugh. "Oh, it's all very dramatic. My grandmother tells it well. First, there's a bird song, and then a forced left turn. A missed step, a crying baby, the sun peeking out from behind a cloud to shine right onto my final destination."

"That all sounds very specific."

"You'd be surprised. Like I said, I've gotten it wrong more than once."

"So how do you know you're right this time?"

"Well, see, there's a second part to it." Ish smirks, leaning in, and Connor is more than happy to meet him halfway.

Ish kisses him like his life depends on it, like everything is on the line with this one act. And maybe it is, because the lightning now coursing through Connor's veins is nothing like he's ever felt. If he hadn't already been convinced that something fateful had occurred between them, he certainly is now. Because this kiss…it feels like joy, and possibility, and something else too big to name.

It feels like magic.

A FAMILY THING
EXCERPT
JESSICA BLACK

"The usual, please," Ish says with a smirk as he saunters up to the counter.

Connor rolls his eyes. "You don't have a 'usual.' "

"Of course I do. Have you not been paying attention this entire time?" Ish scoffs exaggeratedly, playing up how unimpressed he is, and leans against the display case of Danishes. His biceps look so good in this pose that he's either doing it on purpose, or the universe has it out for Connor. "I swear, the customer service in this place is abysmal. I don't know why I keep coming back."

"Because you're a masochist who thinks he's being funny when he says completely incorrect things about coffee?"

One corner of Ish's mouth starts to pull up in a smile, and even though he quickly aborts into a serious moue, he's already given away the genuine amusement beneath his façade.

"My usual," Ish repeats in a bored tone but with a teasing glint in his eyes.

Connor sighs. "And what the hell is that?"

"You."

There's no hiding the blush that blooms across Connor's ears, cheeks, and nose. He mutters some offhanded expletives while turning to make Ish's drink and ignore Ish's laughter.

The blush doesn't fade until a full hour after Ish leaves the shop.

A FAMILY THING
CODA

JESSICA BLACK

"Is this braille?" Connor runs the pads of his fingers along the tattoo he once thought was Morse code.

Ish smiles, easy. "Yeah. That grandmother who spins a good story about destiny? Blind as a bat. She taught me a little."

"What does it say?"

" 'Amor fati.' "

"…Latin?" Connor hazards a guess.

Ish nods. " 'Love of one's fate.' "

Connor raises himself up on one elbow to stare down at Ish. The man is more beautiful than ever, laid out and tangled up in warm cotton sheets, with his tattoos and his abs on full display. Connor wants to memorize him.

"You're kidding," he says flatly.

"It was never a curse for me," Ish shrugs, and then says sincerely, "I'm sorry it was for you."

But that's not what has Connor suddenly nervous. "It isn't just the magic that you love, right?"

Ish smirks, a devastating little twist of his lips made all the more infuriating (and hot) by his lack of dress. "Is there something else you'd rather I direct my devotion toward?"

"I'm just saying—you've fallen for random strangers before simply because you love the idea of fate—"

Connor doesn't have the chance to finish as he's rolled over onto his back in a soft tackle. Ish pins his wrists to the pillow and traps Connor's thighs between his own.

"I didn't fall for them," Ish says in a no-nonsense tone. "I was led to them. Or, I thought I was. And then I…I hoped. When I was led to you, I didn't just hope. I knew." Ish draws a shaky breath. "And, with you, it wasn't about asking the universe to make this the ending to the fairy tale I'd been told. Instead, it was me pleading to all the gods I could think of that I wasn't wrong."

They stare at each other for a long time, breaths held.

"You weren't wrong," Connor finally says.

THE MAGIC KIN KNOW

OWL OUTERBRIDGE

accidental baby acquisition, coffee shop, f/f, fae and fairy folk, fostering, handfasting, lesbian, magic use, parenthood, past tense, pining (mutual), reunion, second chances, star-crossed lovers, witch

The mists hung over the forest like a shroud, wending and weaving through the conifers and half-barren oaks like chiffon. This close to Samhain, it was easy to believe the veil between this world and the spirit world was an actual, physical thing brushing against Isla's skin. She shivered and tied her cardigan tighter. Perhaps it hadn't been a great idea to travel so deep into the forest alone.

This forest was one of the kindest she'd ever wandered in, and generous, too. The wicker basket that bounced against her leg as her rain boots crunched over twigs and fallen leaves was almost full. King Bolete mushrooms, chanterelles, and a handful of Oregon truffles would make a rich soup; rose hips and hawthorn berries would make a tasty dessert. But, in the early morning, the forest belonged to the Fair Folk and the night creatures. She had an understanding with the fae—a silent pact they'd agreed to long ago. She could intrude upon their hours to share the forest's bounty with the other Magic Kin as long as she abided by their rules.

In a world of smartphones and freeways, they each did their part to keep the ancient ways. She had no enemies here, but that didn't mean there was no danger.

This morning, the air carried more aromas than the usual sea salt, damp moss, and humus. Anise and clove itched Isla's nose. Beneath the orchestra of crickets staging their final performance and the calls of the morning birds was a persistent hum, as if the forest itself sang. Not the creatures, or the wind, or the trickling of a steam—it was the ferns and the flowers, the stones and the branches. They were alive with ancient magic, and not of the human variety.

Time to get away from the things mortals shouldn't meddle in. Isla turned to leave.

A breeze rustled her hair and caressed her cheek the way a parent might. As if compelled, she stopped at the edge of a babbling creek.

"*Shhh.*" The wind picked up and whispered in a woman's voice. The mists grew more dense. The hum of magic flooded Isla's heart until it tightened in her chest, near to bursting. "*Stay.*"

Everything stilled and fell silent. Even the ever-present roar of distant waves disappeared until it was just Isla, the quickening of her breath, and the thunderous beating of her heart. She grew roots and became one with the towering pines.

The Magic Kin knew when the Fair Folk gave an order, one listened.

Her ears strained. She needed something, anything: a voice; a whisper; an answer. This silence was unnatural, like a grave.

Who would run the Bubble and Brew if the Fair Folk took her prisoner for breaking their laws? Who would infuse Mrs. Patel's morning coffee with the spells to ease her arthritic pain? Who would take over her hearth and provide the Magic Kin with their gathering place, tucked away from the mundane world?

Just as she imagined her life without her in it, a powerful cry, full of righteousness and fury, ripped through the silence.

An infant's cry.

The wind wrapped her in a cocoon of nutmeg and anise with swirling leaves the color of flames. "*Stay.*"

On the other side of the creek, half-hidden by foliage, the silhouette of a woman rushed through the trees, familiar like a forgotten dream. The figure ducked down and, moments later, the infant's cries settled.

"There you are. They sent me across an ocean and an entire continent to find you, my love," a gentle voice spoke, transformed into something ethereal by the magic, but carrying notes of the Scottish Highlands. That, too, was familiar, and Isla's spirit drifted toward warm memories of a country far away and a life she'd left behind. "You're home now."

Isla sank to the ground and tried to ignore the moisture soaking into her jeans. She focused on breathing and allowed the memories to fill her so her mind wouldn't flood with thoughts of fairie children and the complicated relationship between the Magic Kin and the Fair Folk.

Those days in Scotland were spent in carefree roaming, in mentorship, and in learning magical forest stewardship.

The other things that happened, she didn't dwell on.

Gradually, the singing of the morning birds and the buzz of insects returned. The stream and the ocean added their rhythm and harmony to the chorus. The sun was above the horizon now, the skies brightening from navy to gray. The first of her customers would be looking for their morning coffee, but she couldn't leave the forest yet.

Water splashed around her boots as she crossed the stream. Nothing seemed out of the ordinary on the tree trunks around her or the branches above. She continued deeper until she found an ovular clearing. In the center stood a perfect fairie circle of flat, white mushrooms. The circle beckoned, and despite hundreds of warnings never to enter the ritual spaces of fairies, she stepped inside.

The magic was new and strong; Isla had felt something like it only once. Back then, it hadn't tasted so fresh, nor had it filled her with warmth as she drank it in like mulled apple cider. It rolled over her skin and sank into her pores.

It felt like love.

It felt like belonging.

It was hard to tear herself away.

"Good morning, Isla! Blessed be!" Gordon Bailey's voice boomed as he stepped in the doorway three days after Isla's morning adventures. "What a beautiful day for our Samhain celebration."

Isla jumped and turned on a heel, her hands covered in flour and her counters covered in sea-salt-and-rosemary sourdough. "You scared me!"

She took a deep breath to calm her runaway heart. If she didn't, it'd probably flee back into the forest, to the fairie circle with its mushrooms laid out like children's toys arranged for some forgotten game.

"Lost in thought?"

"You could say that." She moved to the sink and washed her hands.

Truth was, since then, she'd been a ghost in her own home, too full of questions to be truly present. Why had the Fair Folk let her see such a sacred ritual as the gifting of a non-magical fairie child to their human foster mother? Why had they let her step into their circle without punishment and allowed their magic to infect her?

"Well, today *is* a day for reflection." His smile took up half his face and brought out the wrinkles in his brown skin. "It's for new beginnings, too, if you're open to them."

"Would you like your usual, or is it too late for caffeine?" This conversation was heading down a familiar path.

"Yes, please. If I don't, Miss Elsie's cider will put me to sleep in the middle of the harvest feast."

"That's true." She set about filling a teapot with hot water, scooped her strongest black tea, and selected a seal-shaped tea infuser—Gordon's favorite—from her varied collection, which included everything from magical runes to a replica of a space shuttle. Every tea drinker in the community had a favorite, and she remembered each person's.

"Running this place and hosting these community celebrations is too much for one person," Gordon said. There it was. "How long are you going to live in this big house and handle all the cooking, brewing, spelling, and event planning yourself?"

She placed a milk jug and sugar bowl on his tray along with a salal berry Danish to hold him over until the feast. "As long as I must, I suppose. I'm not like my father—my magic doesn't call me anywhere. I prefer a single hearth and deep roots."

"All the more reason you shouldn't be alone." Gordon's eyes held kindness overlaying concern. She coaxed her magic awake and whispered a blessing for good health over his food, then passed the tray to him.

Once, she'd thought she'd found someone to share her hearth—a beautiful woman to love forever. It hadn't been meant to be. She'd never tell him how much she envied the women who flitted through their community, minds free from dreams of wives, swaddling blankets, and cradles. She longed for that freedom.

Nor would she tell him she was in love with a woman whose address she didn't know—couldn't know—who spoke to her through ink on thick paper in letters that fell from open flames.

"I've met all the women here. None of them suit, and I won't move.

I'll be blessed when the time is right," she said firmly, more for her benefit than his. He handed her cash, and she made his change. "Besides, I'm not too lonely, and my coven helps with the festivities." She gave him a conspiratorial wink. "You know how efficient they are."

He chuckled and shook his head. "Sometimes I think people need to get out and help their blessings along, if you know what I mean." He wrinkled his nose, deepening the crevices around his eyes, then took a huge sniff of the air around her. "Unless someone else has decided to intervene. I wondered when they were going to get involved, given who your mother was." He shook his head. "Never mind, forget I said anything. Just an old man rambling. You get back to your rolls, and I'll see you later."

Isla stared after him as he took a seat in a corner of the empty coffee shop. What did he know of the fairies getting involved in her life, and what did it have to do with her long-dead mother?

"Me next, me next!" little Talia Hernandez shouted, or perhaps it was Gracie Lin? Isla had trouble telling the girls' squeaky voices apart. She scanned the bouncing, frenetic crowd of children surrounding the caramel-apple bar, saw it *was* Talia, nodded to acknowledge her, and dipped her chin toward Talia's toddler brother, Gabriel, with his wide brown eyes. She smiled at him, and smiled wider when he returned it.

"I'll give you both yours and Gabe's. You can help him put toppings on his before getting your own."

Isla handed Talia two caramel apples; Talia gave a solemn nod, as if she were being entrusted with a valuable artifact. Gabe jumped up and down beside her, little hands reaching.

"I want. Gimme!"

"Shall I take over?" asked Elbe, a member of her coven who was as thin and tall as a willow. "You should walk around."

"You know, maybe I should." Isla smiled and wiped her hands on a rag. "Thank you."

Isla's coffee shop of crystal, sea stones, driftwood, and shells had been transformed into a magical realm of twinkling lights and jack-o'-lanterns carved with fairy-tale scenes. The community's harvest overflowed the back counter: a cake here; a farm-fresh ham there; a round of cheese aged for almost a year; a pound of butter made just yesterday;

and so much more. Magic Kin had poured out of their isolated homes, left their small, distant communities, and piled their city covens into rented vans to come out and celebrate as they did every year.

Their laughter and joy filled Isla with a buzzing, excitable energy.

"Beautiful, as usual," Mrs. Patel said as Isla passed by the elders grouped in a corner. Gordon's laughter roared above the crowd, and when Isla turned to look, Miss Elsie seemed pleased with herself. "Won't you sit with us for a bit, Isla?"

"Maybe later."

"At least take some cider." Miss Elsie pressed a stein into her hand, and Isla wouldn't dream of refusing it. She took a large draft of the crisp and spicy brew.

"Even better than last year," she said before she wandered off, leaving Miss Elsie beaming behind her.

"Isla, come, rest a moment," Maria called, gesturing for Isla to join her at a table in the center of the room. She was as lovely and round as a mother goddess, and favored by one as well: Talia and Gabriel belonged to her, and, in another month, there'd be a third Hernandez. Along with the newborn that Starla, with her rosy cheeks and pearly smile, nursed beside Maria, it'd bring their coven's brood up to eight. All those who'd wanted to become mothers had done so.

All but her.

"There's a seat next to me," Starla said.

Isla gave her a smile and spared another for the tiny bundle in her arms. "I'm making my rounds."

She should join in the fun. Samhain usually filled her energy well for months, but her heart was in the forest. She'd be less lonely if she told them what had happened, but the fostering of a fairie child was something the Magic Kin only knew of because they were taught. How could she explain what she'd witnessed through the mist?

Gordon's laughter peaked again. Isla spared a look in his direction as she stepped behind her counter. He knew something about all this.

"Excuse me," an accented voice asked in a Highlands lilt. "I was wondering if you have any warm water I could use for formula. My daughter's about to start wailing like a banshee."

Caught while lost in her thoughts—for the second time that day!—Isla started and jerked around.

"I'm so sorry, I didn't mean to frighten—" The woman cut off as her mouth fell open. The newborn, wrapped in a sling around her chest, grunted and rooted while shaking her perfect little fist.

Isla's breath caught. Time froze, like a spell had been cast on the café, like a scene from a movie. The woman before Isla was also in her thirties and long, brown hair hung in waves down to her collarbone, framing a face with tired, obsidian eyes.

Hers was the voice that had haunted Isla for three days. In silent, sleepy moments, the memory of her had hummed like the wind through the trees. In the dark of the night, she'd danced through the exposed eaves of Isla's bedroom like a sprite causing mischief. She'd reverberated between the folds of Isla's brain, twisting and shifting, so familiar, but her identity had remained out of reach.

Oh, how had Isla not realized?

This voice was beloved—the voice of warm summers and chilly falls and first love whispered under the pale moonlight while laying on pillows of meadow grasses, the voice of blood oaths whispered at midnight while passion and power coursed through hot veins. The magic had been too strong for twenty-two-year-old girls drunk on romance novels.

This was the voice of broken hearts and partings, of longings and regrets.

This was the voice Isla had imagined as she'd read a hundred letters over the last decade.

And here it was—here *she* was. The veil between the worlds must have been thin indeed.

What were the Fair Folk getting at, bringing her here after—

Now wasn't the time to dwell on that.

"Aven." Isla's whisper was almost inaudible over the din of the party.

Aven's round face had aged, narrow lines sculpted into her fair skin. Her freckled cheeks were more bone than fat, now. The painter of years had enhanced her beauty: turned a girl into a maiden into a mother. Aven's allure raised goosebumps on Isla's arms.

Aven didn't respond. She only blinked, as surprised to find Isla here as Isla was surprised to find her.

The little one let out a whine and shook her head with its wisps of straight, black hair. Isla studied her. Under the padding of her cheeks was a bone structure far more similar to Isla's than to Aven's. Isla frowned. At her side, her fingers twitched. She wanted to touch the baby, to hold her, to feel the essence of her new life and understand why she'd been brought here.

"Right, water. You need warm water, and I have plenty." Isla attempted to smile, but it came out stretched and lopsided, uncertain of what expression it wanted to be. The baby began to cry, and Aven's attention shifted. She bounced and shushed and hummed as Isla hurried to fill a pitcher.

"Let me," she offered with her arms open as Aven dug through her diaper bag. Aven didn't hesitate, and moments later Isla held a squirming, red-faced fury.

"Hush, wee one. Your mama will have food in a second," she murmured. Her power came to life of its own accord, awakened by the baby. The child calmed, dark eyes fixed on Isla's face, as the magic in Isla sang to something inside her. Almost like blood magic. But that was impossible. Isla had no brothers and sisters. Her mother was dead, and her father was "chilling" in Sussex, per his last phone call, a widower studying the impact of mushroom moods on spell work.

None of them were fae.

Aven reached to take the baby back, and Isla gave her up reluctantly. "What's her name?"

"Shaela." A beautiful name. "She's—"

"Let's talk tomorrow, when there are fewer people around." Isla nodded toward the crowd and hoped Aven would catch on to her body language, because Isla could feel Gordon's eyes on her back. The emotions they were projecting had probably caught the attention of every empath in the room, and Shaela's cries had caught the attention of the elders. A new member of the community, and with a baby no less. No better siren's call. "I'll open the door when I wake. Come by anytime."

Isla's dreams were of moonlight and blood-smeared hands bound with a golden cord. There were whispered vows and breezes of swirling flower petals. There was the scent of butterscotch magic and laughter that carried in the midnight sky over crag and creek. Aven was warm beside Isla, and her kisses were sweet. Soft hands traveled over bodies freely shared. Their magic sang, woven together like the knotted cord at their feet.

One knot. *These are the hands of the one who loves you most. Your best friend who promises to love you forever as maiden, mother, and crone.*

Two knots. *These are the hands that will help build your future, stone by stone, in any weather and through every storm.*

Three knots. *These are the hands that will show you passion...*

Isla's dreams turned. Anise and clove singed her nose. The breeze's gentle caresses turned to sharp lashes, and a whisper in the wind said:

"She has given you what she cannot give. It's no fault of her own. She didn't know."

There was danger in the air, intangible, like an electric current—safe as long as she didn't touch it. The voices carried no malice, only a too-human blend of sorrow, regret, and resignation.

"This bond, we must break."

Isla found herself alone in the center of a fairie circle in a field of blooming heather and mountain thyme. There was no laughter, no wind, no whispers. No sound at all.

The breaking of a heart, it turned out, was a silent affair.

She woke with heavy eyes and a dry mouth. Her heart pounded against her rib cage with the force of a timpani drum. Despite the autumn chill, she was warm, so she opened the window and gazed at the cliffside behind the café and at the sea beyond it, white-capped waves catching the pre-dawn light. The ocean's perfume washed away the spice of fairie magic.

Pulling her gaze away, Isla's eyes traveled to the necklace of hag stones hanging from the curtain rod. Aven had collected them for her over the years of their relationship. Isla reached up and ran her fingers along them. They were for luck, Aven had said.

Down, she moved, until she hit the row of wishing stones on the windowsill. Aven had gifted her those, too, so her dreams would always come true.

How little they'd known then.

Some of the stones were the size of table tennis balls, others as large as baseballs. Some were dark, others light. Each had a single, unbroken ring of quartz around their circumference. Her father had balked when she insisted all forty-two needed to make the journey back to the United States with her.

There were only a couple dozen left now. Many had carried her wishes into the sea over the last eleven years. Some of those wishes had come true. Others, well...maybe Aven's arrival was a good sign.

She touched each one until she landed on the first Aven had given her the day they'd met as awkward fourteen-year-olds with limbs too long and dreams too big.

"I hope you're not boring. It's been naught but my brothers and me for ages," Aven had said in an accent so thick Isla had squinted as she struggled to understand.

Isla picked up the stone and held it between her hands, then poured the only true wish she'd had for eleven years into it.

"Please, give her back to me."

The bells on the door rang when Isla was halfway through her triple-shot Americano. She caught a whiff of butterscotch and set down the singed page she'd been reading—Aven's first letter, sent in defiance of the Fair Folk. When it had fallen through the flames of Isla's fireplace, she'd been so surprised that it'd caught fire before she could retrieve it.

Don't tell me where you are. Don't tempt me that way. But tell me how you are. I can't stand not knowing. This spell will find me wherever I am.

They'd tried to schedule their letters after that.

When she turned, she found Aven in the doorway, face pale and eyes framed by shadows. She wore a simple sweater dress over leggings; a möbius wrap held the infant against her chest. Judging by the waxiness of her skin, she couldn't have slept more than a couple of hours.

She was breathtaking.

Isla wove her way through mismatched tables and chairs until she stood before Aven. Uncertainty flashed in Aven's eyes. Amazement and disbelief, too.

"It's not a dream?" Her accent was thick in her exhaustion. Good thing Isla had learned to understand long ago.

"Not unless we're dreaming together." Isla's hand floated to Aven's cheek until they touched, and she felt warmth and energy beneath her fingertips. She snatched her hand back. Aven hadn't given Isla permission to touch her so intimately, and it'd been eleven years since they were together. Isla's body remembered the shape of her, but both their shapes had changed.

Aven frowned.

"Isla…" The name was spoken like a prayer, like hope for water on a scorching day.

"Come in. Sit down. You must be exhausted." Isla's Pacific Coast non-accent sounded flat to her ears. How could Aven see her as anything but inelegant and lumbering? Her hands were rough from a decade of washing dishes and foraging in the forest. Fine lines stretched out from her eyes and lips. It wouldn't be too many years until those fine lines turned to canyons. They weren't so young anymore.

Yet, Aven's gaze remained on her. She showed no interest in Isla's driftwood or jasper art, nor in the apothecary jars filled with tumbled agates, glowing orange with witch-light.

She was intent solely on Isla.

"Coffee or tea?" It was a safe question. Conversations like these were easier with a drink in hand.

Aven took a seat. "I'd love some tea."

Heading behind the counter, Isla assembled Aven's breakfast. Odd how she remembered Aven's favorite blend. She picked out the owl tea infuser, because she'd never forgotten that Aven loved owls. She knew Aven preferred fruity breakfast pastries over spicy ones. Aven took the tray with a smile, checked on the baby sleeping against her chest, then poured water from the pot over the infuser. Each move was calculated, almost ritualistic.

Before Aven's tea finished steeping, Shaela woke.

"I came prepared." Weariness suffused Aven's words. She pulled a full bottle from her diaper bag. "Not like last night."

"May I?" Isla reached out, drawn to the baby, eager to hold her again.

Aven nodded, relieved, and handed the child gently across the table, then passed the bottle, already warm—she must have heated it before coming over.

"I was in the forest four days ago," Isla said as she slipped the bottle into Shaela's mouth. It took effort to tear her eyes away from the girl's intense stare. Her magic stirred again, but she was alert to it now, and she convinced it to rest. "I didn't know you were a fae-chosen foster mother."

Aven didn't look surprised that she'd guessed.

"I thought we'd be together, and I'd have time to tell you," Aven said, fiddling with the diffuser. The owl swam in and out of murky tea waves. "Ma never told me the rules—that the Fair Folk had to approve my lover, that they'd only allow me to be with someone they trusted."

It made sense. Hundreds of years ago, or so the stories went, the

Fair Folk had selected families to care for the children born to them who showed no fairie magic as infants. Such youths were better off in the mundane world. If they developed powers as teenagers, they transitioned back. If not, they continued to live among the Magic Kin.

"I've not found anyone since. No one is…" she trailed off, eyes growing cloudy.

The same? Adequate? As beautiful and wonderful? Isla's heart knew how to finish the sentence.

How awful to know the Fair Folk had found Isla so wanting that they'd broken a blood oath and ripped two hearts to shreds.

But…

"They've brought you here, after they tore us apart? They never do anything without a reason."

"I was told to be in your forest, at that moment, and not to be late. I thought it was absurd, but it was an order."

Aven dug in her bag and produced something which she slid across the table. "I found her swaddled in a basket with this resting atop her."

A golden cord lay between them, stained dark brown in places. The aroma of butterscotch and mulling spices were thick around it. Isla reached out and touched it, and Aven did too. A hum rose from the cord and a wave of power washed over them, then moved beyond them, stronger than anything Isla had felt since the night their bond had broken.

Gordon arrived first. At Isla's raised brow, he shrugged. "We know to come when the Fair Folk call."

Within twenty minutes the café was full. People had dressed in simple clothing and brought coins, stones, and flowers from their homes. They spoke quietly. Isla's coven surrounded her, the children unusually subdued; even Talia and Gracie. Miss Elsie tossed Isla a questioning glance, but she had no answers, only the same humming, tugging energy that'd drawn everyone to come together.

They marched into the forest with Isla and Aven leading the way. Isla cradled Shaela in one arm and held Aven's hand with her free hand.

They came to the clearing with the fairie circle. Without even a look between them, she and Aven stepped into the center.

Driven by the ancient magic that lived in their souls and bones, each member of the community placed their gift inside the circle one by one, then took position around it. They didn't know the ritual, but their magic did.

The breeze picked up after the last gift was placed. *"Have you ever wondered, child, why we let you in during our times?"* It lifted Isla's hair and twisted around her. She pulled Shaela closer. *"Did your father ever tell you he stole a rebellious daughter from a nobleman's house?"*

The voice was familiar. The same speaker had broken their blood oath eleven years ago. She'd held such regret and sadness when she'd done so; her feelings were harder to read now.

"It angered our father, so he wanted nothing to do with you." The wind felt like a hand on her cheek. The air shimmered, and a woman with skin as pale as a seashell and hair dark as midnight appeared in a gown of rainbow mists, hand placed where Isla had felt the touch to her face. "I was against it. We don't abandon our children, even those born without fairie magic. I've watched over your entire life."

She gazed down.

"Now I ask you to watch over my daughter. I trust no one more. Raise her with love. Raise her to know her blood." She smiled and winked. "Raise her with a hint of rebellion." She kissed her daughter's forehead and stepped back. "Do so *together*. I know of your letters and your dedication to each other; your bond will be stronger than before. When you're ready, we'll require an offering."

They'd been ready for eleven years.

The wishing stone warmed in Isla's pocket. She took her hand from Aven's, withdrew it, and held it between them. The stone held a decade of hopes and dreams for this moment. What better offering?

"I've grown boring these last few years. I hope you don't mind." Tears fell as Isla passed the stone to Aven.

"I know. I've read your letters. It's the right kind of boring, I think." Aven pulled a piece of burnt paper covered in Isla's handwriting from her diaper bag. Isla folded it around the stone, pressed the package between her palms, closed her eyes, then gave it to the fairie woman—gave it to her aunt.

"This will do." The woman faded away, leaving the clearing buzzing with power. Isla gently laid Shaela on the ground between them. Their foster daughter was alert, as fascinated by the magic as everyone else. Around them, the Magic Kin reached out to take each other's hands.

Aven sliced her palm with a small athemé, also from her bag. Isla took it and sliced her own palm, wincing at the sting. They clasped hands with the community as their witnesses. Aven placed the cord over their hands and wrapped it around their wrists once.

"These are the hands that..."

REBELLIOUS DAUGHTER

OWL OUTERBRIDGE

The breeze giggled. Purple and white wildflowers waved and tall grasses bent like supplicants before their queen around the baby's hand-knit blanket. Carrying the perfume of a spring forest blended with anise and nutmeg, the wind flipped Einsley's hair then folded a corner of the baby's blanket. A stream of cherry blossoms fell like snow from a tall, old tree abandoned by a homesteader long ago. A single petal landed on the bridge of the baby's nose.

Einsley laughed. "Okay, Lyra." She looked to the space above her sleeping daughter's head. "I know it's you."

The air rippled, and a teenage girl with black hair and a sweet face appeared. Her opalescent gown created a halo on the ground where she crouched. "She's lovely. What's her name?"

"Isla."

Lyra plucked the petal from Isla's nose. "Fitting, given the circumstances."

"Father's not coming?" Lyra's smile fell. "No. He's still livid you married that human. Maybe it'd be different if Isla had fae magic, but..."

"She still might when she grows—she does have Kin magic. Will he deny her birthright and keep her from the forests during our times?"

"He will." There should have been finality in those words, but Lyra's eyes sparkled with mischief. "I disagree, and so do the other noble children."

Lyra scooped Isla up and cradled her, kissing her forehead. The mischief trickled into her smile as she looked back to Einsley. "Rebellious daughter, don't worry. There's still room for you in our forests. We'll make sure of it."

HERALD OF LOVE

MAGGIE PAGE

bilingual, bipoc, bisexual, coffee shop, curses, customer service representative, customer/employee, dragon, f/nb, f/f/nb, flirting, found family, genderqueer character, getting together, magic use, non-binary, oblivious, past tense, pining, polyamorous relationship negotiation, polyamory, tarot, texas, third person limited point of view, united states of america

The woman—perhaps Lauren or Lorelai?—examined the jar of loose-leaf tea. "Where are the blue bits?"

"Leaving the cornflower petals out won't change the taste," Trina said. "They're decorative."

"I have tea parties with my granddaughter, and she likes this blend because it's pretty. Would you have any in the back?"

"I could grow some extra." Trina tightened the sagging bow of her apron strings. "It'll take a few minutes."

"That's fine. I'll wait."

Trina nodded and held out her hand for the jar. A long beat passed before the woman returned her tea selection. "I'll be right back."

Forcing their awkward interaction from her thoughts, Trina skirted around the island which housed the shop's biggest machines to reach her planting supplies. Depositing a few cornflower seeds into a waiting pot, Trina rolled her neck, shaking off the stress of the morning rush. She'd always been in tune with nature—much more so than with people. When she closed her eyes, she could sense the potential in the seeds, as effortless as breathing, and she let her exhalations direct her intent, imagining a sprout emerging, then blooming. Once she felt centered, she pushed her will outward.

When Trina opened her eyes, shoots of the indigo blossoms she'd pictured stood between her hands. She picked several flowers, sent another burst of magic through the stems to dry them, and mixed the petals into the tea blend.

With a solicitous expression fixed on her face, she returned and set the tea on the counter again. "Can I get you anything else?"

"No, that's it."

"That'll be $10.96."

Maybe-Lorelai paid, slotted her card back into her wallet, and walked away.

"Thanks for shopping at the Mellow Meadow!" Trina chirped at maybe-Lorelai's back. "Have a nice day."

Trina's shoulders relaxed as the next customer approached...and it was Eloddie. "Before you go on break, could I have the apple-cinnamon tea with honey, please?"

"Of course." Trina dropped her vacantly cordial customer service mask to flash Eloddie a genuine, fond smile. "Though, you know, Christa is perfectly capable of making drinks."

"Darren's getting there, too, but there's something about the way you do it."

Trina's stomach flopped with contentment; she hoped her cheeks hadn't flushed.

"Javi'll be down in a few, so add their usual to my order. While you're at it, make yourself something—on me."

Trina fiddled with her sleeve as she glanced up from the register. "You don't have to do that." They'd had the same conversation a million times in the last six months, but Eloddie always insisted that she pay for Trina—owner or not—as a show of support for the shop. As if she hadn't already done more than enough to help the business flourish! Trina's first regular customers had come in when Eloddie rented the incongruent nook formed by the gap between the storage room and the storefront as a space to offer tarot and tasseomancy readings.

"I want to." Eloddie's voice was firm but amused. Trina wished—not for the first time—she could sink into it like a warm bath and never leave.

Sorting their drinks allowed Trina to muse over Eloddie's order. A recurring theme had appeared in her recent beverage requests. Today's drink supported Trina's suspicion: apple and honey aided rituals for love, while cinnamon bolstered success. Eloddie was aware of Trina's specialization in nature-based magic. Trina also knew Eloddie had learned the foundations of magic from her mother, the leader of the largest local coven, and had mastered precognition at her side. Recalling the magical properties of herbs was child's play to them both. So, Trina had to wonder if Eloddie's drinks were merely personal preference or if they carried a deeper message.

She emerged from her musings to watch Eloddie deftly shuffling a tarot deck, commencing their daily tradition for Trina's morning break. She set down Eloddie's order and took a seat across from her.

Eloddie cut the deck, drew one card, and hummed thoughtfully as she reached for her drink.

"What's the news today?" Trina asked.

Eloddie laid the card on the table. "The Two of Pentacles signifies changes that will elevate and balance domestic life or business."

"Changes to what?"

"Good question. Let's ask for clarification." Eloddie drew the next card and set it beside the first. The Four of Wands. "That's interesting. The—" Eloddie paused and lit up as she glanced across the room.

Trina followed her gaze to see Javi coming down the stairs from their shared loft above the shop. Their long, cyan cardigan stood out against the oak panels and slate tile on the wall. They trailed their fingertips over the moss Trina grew between the stones, then skipped off the bottom step and made a beeline for their table.

Javi greeted Eloddie with a kiss.

Trina averted her eyes until Javi sat beside Eloddie. Could they feel the strange tension in the air, or had her imagination conjured it to torment her? She'd developed a crush on the couple not long after Javi introduced her to Eloddie, but they were together, and not with her. Trina's yearning wasn't their problem. She cleared her throat and gestured to the iced coffee she'd prepared.

"Your heart palpitations await."

Javi chuckled. "Thank you, Trina darling." They set down their phone, the case boasting a genderqueer flag and their preferred pronouns: he/they. "I can't believe you started the daily draw without me!"

Eloddie rolled her eyes but bumped Javi's shoulder companionably.

"Only just." She explained what she'd told Trina, then picked up where she'd left off. "So, that indicates the coming change is the culmination of a desire, and will bring a sense of completion and contentment."

"Completion, huh?" Javi winked. "Sounds promising."

Wow. Desperate for a safer topic, Trina's eyes fell on Javi's necklace. At a glance, it looked like a figurine of a dragon, with silver accentuating the fine scales, claws, and webbing on the wings. She'd always wondered about it, so she asked, "I've never seen you take that off. Does it have some special significance?"

Javi hooked their thumbs through the necklace's chain as they glanced down at the figurine. "My abuelita gave me this. It's supposedly a charm for 'luck in love,' though I'm not sure there's a legit enchantment on it." Their fingers snagged in the chain as they reached for their coffee.

A hollow, wet *plop* and a faint *clink* sounded in the quiet shop as the necklace came undone, plunging the pendant into Eloddie's teacup and tumbling it on its side.

"Shit!" Javi jerked away from the table as Eloddie shoved her chair back to avoid the spilling tea.

Trina plucked napkins until she had a handful to pass over. "It's no big deal. A splash of tea's not gonna damage rose quartz, and the spill is an easy fix."

While Trina and Javi patted at the mess, Eloddie's eyes stayed riveted on the overturned cup. A teasing remark was on the tip of Trina's tongue, but Eloddie's distraction gave her pause and prompted her to take a closer look.

The tiny figurine had grown to the size of a hamster and radiated magic like heat emanating from asphalt. It stepped out of the puddle sinuously, shaking itself off and unfurling thin, opalescent wings. With a squeak, it reared, flared its wings, and took flight.

Trina caught the necklace chain still running through one of the silver spikes on the dragon's neck. It hissed, soft and distressed, and struggled against the taut length. Tiny jaws opened and spewed forth bubbles, their delicate sheen matching the dragon's scales and bearing the same aura of magic.

"It's casting!" Javi warned, their demeanor sobering.

Trina's grip on the chain faltered; the unclasped end whipped toward her, and the dragon zipped free. She barely had time to raise her arms to protect her eyes as the bubbles sped toward her face. Most of them popped against the back of her hand, but one burst against her chin, spattering honeyed moisture along her bottom lip. Within seconds, her skin tingled as magic seeped into her.

Countenance serious and resolute, Javi conjured a shield. The barrier crackled as Javi stretched it with an ease born of repetition—such protective measures came with the territory for a professional cursebreaker. Some of the tension in Trina's body faded as she took in Javi's calm. They knew what they were doing. With their help, she'd get through whatever symptoms the dragon's breath might trigger.

"I haven't got an anchor on me, so this won't hold for long," Javi warned. "Since we're dealing with an unknown enchantment, containment is our first goal. We should close the shop."

"Okay," Trina began, uncertain how to proceed with the evacuation. Most of the other customers had turned their way, watching the spectacle with expressions ranging from curious to confused to fearful. "Whatever we have to do."

"Can you two maintain the shield while I get them out of here?" Javi asked.

Eloddie shot Trina a nervous glance and raised one eyebrow. Eloddie's skill with divination neared prodigious, but her grasp on common magic? Iffy.

Trina straightened, finding courage in the face of Eloddie's hesitation. "Of course we can."

"Here." Javi held both hands out. Violet sparks—the energy fueling the spell—hovered over each of their palms.

Eloddie and Trina scooped up the light in concert, transferring their energy to the barrier. The shield shimmered, wavering, but it didn't buckle. Above them, the dragon bumped against the barrier again and again, seeking a way out.

With an authoritative air, Javi waved the other customers toward the door. "Okay, everyone—nothing to see here!" Reaching into their pocket, they withdrew their badge. "Licensed cursebreaker. Everything's under control. Make your way out in an orderly fashion, please."

Relieved that Javi had handled the challenge of commanding strangers, Trina turned to her baristas, who lingered behind the counter, unsure if Javi's order applied to them. "You heard them. I'll text you when it's safe to come back."

"Will y'all be okay?" Christa asked, reluctantly removing her name tag. "Do you need anything? Should we call someone?"

"Javi knows their stuff. We'll be fine," Trina assured her.

Christa tucked away her apron as Darren and Marcus emerged from the storeroom. "You're not docking our pay for this, right?" Darren asked.

"Magical hazards happen." With her free hand, Trina motioned for them to join the people filing out of the shop. Out of the corner of her eye, she saw Eloddie's jaw clench with strain. "I'll cover the hours you're losing."

As the door jangled closed after the last person, Eloddie and Trina dropped the shield. The release of magic left Eloddie's fingers shaking, and she sat down heavily.

"Are you okay?" Javi and Trina asked simultaneously.

"I'll be fine in a few minutes," she said.

The three of them eyed their flying guest as the dragon wended its way toward the flower beds lining the storefront display windows and disappeared into the chamomile.

"How do we handle this?" Eloddie asked.

"First—" Javi tossed their badge upward, caught it decisively, and stowed it back in their pocket. "We need supplies."

Eloddie adjusted the headband framing the coiffed curve of her afro, reached into the bag beside her feet, and drew out a butterfly net. "Something told me this might come in handy today."

"Perfect! Let's see what else we can find," Trina said.

Together, they made short work of gathering everything on hand that might prove useful. Along with the net, they had a broom, glass jars, and every set of oven mitts Trina owned, including the fancy high-heat pair that Eloddie had bought her for Yule.

Bemitted and poised, they nodded, silently acknowledging their readiness.

"I'll try to grab it again, since it's already gotten me once," Trina said, heading toward the flower beds.

Rustling mint leaves betrayed the dragon's current location, and bite marks on several jasmine flowers showed where it had been. She nestled her covered hands between the mint and lavender, hoping to snatch the dragon as it wandered by.

It stilled.

To provoke further movement, she skimmed her hand over the leaves, and the dragon reversed direction, hopping between the tall leaves of lemongrass. Trina sighed, sidestepped, and created another oven mitt blockade. The dragon launched into the air over her shoulder. She spun and almost collided with Javi as they swiped a jar at the dragon, missing by inches, and the dragon glided, uninhibited, toward the high shelves behind the bar.

"Oh, no," Trina whispered. A collision between the dragon and the jars of ingredients displayed beneath the menu boards would be dreadful.

"Go after it!" Eloddie urged, rushing back to their table and sweeping up her deck. "I'm going to try something."

Javi and Trina dashed down the center aisle, skidding to a halt as the dragon swooped up and landed on a ceiling fan blade.

Annoying, but the jars were safe.

"What are you thinking?" Javi asked.

"I'm going to assign directions to the cards—Swords for right, Pentacles for left, and all that." Eloddie's deck was a blur in her hands as she prepared to guide them. "To keep you ahead of the dragon."

As Eloddie spoke, Trina climbed onto a chair beneath the dragon. Broom in one hand, oven mitt on the other, she stretched toward the fan and tapped the dragon. Knocked off-balance, it fluttered its wings indignantly, yet didn't leave its perch. Trina nudged it again. Unfortunately, she wasn't tall enough to sweep the broom along the fan blade, so she angled the handle and pushed with the bristles.

The dragon chirped, took off, and dived toward her, silver claws keen and glinting. Alarmed, Trina jumped from the chair, only to be surprised when it neared her, sniffed…and wheeled away.

Eloddie flipped a card over. "Go forward!"

The dragon landed on a porcelain pestle resting in its matching mortar. As the creature's full weight settled, the pestle pivoted, then dipped.

"Javi, go left. Trina, to the right." Eloddie kept drawing cards. "It's going—" Flailing its wings, the dragon tried to rebalance—too late. Pestle and dragon toppled to the ground with an ominous *thunk*. "—down."

If they were lucky, the pestle would have incapacitated it…

Trina crept over to peer behind the bar. No such luck: the dragon had landed on its feet. She put a finger to her lips as she met Javi's eyes and gestured to the opposite side of the room—she should go right, and Javi should go left, as Eloddie had instructed.

Javi, jar still in hand, mirrored Trina's slow approach, attempting to stalk toward the dragon noiselessly. After painstaking seconds, their cautious footsteps brought Javi and Trina within feet of the creature.

Holding their breath, Javi crouched, gingerly set the open jar on the ground, and waited with the lid in hand.

From the bar, Eloddie whispered encouragement as she consulted the tarot. "That's it. Forward."

Trina took another step, holding the broom steady before her. The edge of the bristles brushed against the curl of a spiked tail; the dragon bobbed away. Another inch forward…Trina prodded the dragon again. Again, the dragon moved a short distance and resettled. They repeated the process—poke, shuffle, poke, shuffle—until the dragon had only two options: enter the jar or take wing.

Hoping to propel the dragon into the jar, Trina pushed harder.

"Come on. *Come on*," Javi whispered.

The creature bounced onto the rim of the jar, ignoring the opening.

"Up! It's going to fly!" Eloddie warned.

"No, no, no!" Trina hoisted the broom, struggling to press the dragon back to the floor, into the jar, but it skittered on the glass and evaded her. With a croak, it propelled itself into the air, weaving around their legs, then circling their heads, seeming to taunt their failure.

Pinning it down again proved harder.

Dealing and reading rapidly, Eloddie called out a stream of predictions, yet barely kept pace with the creature. Nothing they did worked. The dragon was too fast, too alert, too opposed to confinement.

"Back, left, back. Heading down again…oh, no!"

Finally, the dragon dipped low and alit amidst the curated chaos of Javi's dark curls, wriggling as if to arrange the locks into a more comfortable nest. Ridiculous that Javi still looked incredible. The stubble on Javi's slack jaw appeared more pronounced than usual, accentuating the full, lush pink of their lips. The want of a kiss had never felt so out of Trina's control before.

Javi closed their mouth as they raised tentative hands toward their head. The dragon shied away, teetered, slid, and blew another stream of bubbles down the side of Javi's neck. Seeking purchase, it clawed at Javi's face; one talon scraped their cheek, leaving three thin lines of red behind. They gasped at the unexpected pain and jerked toward the wound, startling the dragon away.

Tension pooled through Trina again, and the sight of blood motivated her to tear her gaze from Javi's mouth. Nothing good could come from Javi's exposure to the dragon's breath. Panic wouldn't help. She relaxed her shoulders and let out a long breath.

Javi's face scrunched with concern. They drew close, cupped Trina's arms, and rubbed soothing circles with their thumbs. "We're going to be okay."

The sudden rush of desire was strange.

She'd wanted to press her lips to Javi's many times, but she usually controlled herself better. Javi's show of physical comfort seemed stranger still. They were quick with banter and never hesitated to flirt, but they rarely touched her, much less hugged her.

Could this...sensual overload...come from the dragon's magic?

A magnetic drive to steal a kiss pulled at Trina, but a mellifluous voice registered, seeping into her brain like light fighting through a fog.

Eloddie.

"...either of you, I could use a hand here!"

While they'd been distracted, the dragon had honed in on Eloddie, who was weaving between tables to avoid it, her cards clutched to her chest.

Javi grabbed the net from the lineup of supplies and bounded down the center aisle. "Run toward Trina!"

Eloddie obeyed.

Trina tracked the dragon as it pursued Eloddie; Eloddie sped past, and Trina wielded the broom like an overlarge tennis racket, batting the dragon into Javi's range.

With a graceful swing, Javi caught it. The dragon dangled in an undignified heap at the tip of the net. Hissing, it twitched, redoubling its efforts to no avail.

Eloddie arrived with a jar.

Javi dumped the dragon inside, and Eloddie slammed the jar's basket-weave lid into place.

Eloddie grinned as she screwed the lid on securely. "Looks like I was right about the net after all."

Trina laughed. "You always are."

Trina came downstairs with her first aid kit. Chest tight, she paused at the head of the stairs and watched, guiltily, a moment of intimacy between Eloddie and Javi.

Eloddie yawned and stretched. As she went to her tiptoes, her hem rode up.

"You're beautiful." Javi circled their arms around Eloddie and dropped a brief kiss on her lips. Their gaze drifted over Eloddie's shoulder and a slow, sly smile bloomed on their face. "I want to take you and Trina dancing. She'd be shy, but once she starts to enjoy herself...I'd stop just to watch you two move together."

Javi winked.

Heat flooded Trina's cheeks. Her thoughts raced; her tongue lay heavy and useless in her mouth. She could imagine the low music, Eloddie's gentle touch, Javi's appreciative gaze, the feeling of connection.

"Javi," Eloddie admonished softly. "We shouldn't push her."

Trina couldn't be sure she'd been meant to hear. The two of them had dropped flirtatious hints before, but fear and doubt had kept her from finding out if they were serious.

The first aid kit dropped from her numb fingers, clattering on the floor.

Eloddie pulled free from Javi's embrace, turned, and gave her an apologetic smile. Her sleeve had slipped down her arm, baring her shoulder, and Trina's eyes traced the path of rich, umber skin up the swoop of her neck. El and Javi were both so attractive and funny and talented.

Trina heard herself reply, "You'll never know unless you ask me."

Javi and Eloddie looked taken aback. Usually, Trina brushed off their insinuations, so any response—let alone one so bold—must have seemed out of character. They gave each other a searching glance before facing her again.

Javi took a confident step toward Trina, but Eloddie curled her fingers in a restraining grip around their wrist. "I'm not saying I'm complaining, but what's gotten into you two?"

"I'm not sure." Javi squinted, befuddled. They inclined their head and felt behind their ear as if to check for fever.

"I didn't mean to say that," Trina admitted. "I'd thought the way I'm feeling might be linked to the dragon's breath, and now Javi, too..."

Eloddie's suspicious expression melted into understanding. "We can add 'loss of filter' to the list of symptoms. Anything else feel off?"

Trina hesitated, struggling against the tug of magic as she sat down.

"My thoughts are less restrained. I can't sway my focus from things I normally wouldn't dwell on."

"The distraction is intense," Javi added. "You know my attention span isn't great on a good day, but..."

"It's a lot," Trina agreed.

She didn't have the luxury of stewing in her embarrassment, so she ignored it, suppressing the voice begging her to confess her feelings. Unclasping her first aid kit, she took a seat at one of the shop's empty tables and set the kit before her.

"Enchantment or not, we should see to your actual injuries," Trina said, taking out several items and beckoning Javi closer.

They took a seat, scooting their chair close enough to bump knees with Trina. Trina tilted Javi's face toward her and cleaned the scratches on their cheek with an antiseptic wipe. The dragon's tail and claws tinkling against the interior of the jar was the only sound disrupting their companionable silence while Trina worked. Eloddie picked the creature up and examined it; it hissed at her, talons scrambling uselessly.

"It's kinda cute, isn't it?" Eloddie asked.

"I suppose." Trina returned the salve to her kit and shut the box. "What do we do next?"

"I might be able to fix this." Javi shifted to study the dragon too. "If not, we research."

While Javi ran through the common reversal spells in their arsenal, Eloddie rifled through her tarot deck.

Trina texted her workers an update on the shop's closure, then, unable to resist the dragon's magic, leaned forward and twirled a lock of hair. She peered through her lashes when Eloddie looked at her, tilted her head, and smiled coyly. "Would you do a reading for me, El?"

Eloddie raised an eyebrow but played along. "Sure. What do you want to ask about?"

"My love life."

Eloddie concealed a hint of shock. "I'll need you to shuffle the cards so they pick up your energy for the reading." She pushed her deck across the table. "Think of your question and pass the cards back when it feels right."

The cards were large and unwieldy in Trina's hands, but she sensed an aura of comfort and invitation from their sleek faces. The feeling increased into a golden rightness that told her: it was time. Her fingers brushed over Eloddie's knuckles as she passed the deck over; the touch sparked warmth up her arm, spread through her skin, and left her engulfed in a pleasant haze.

Javi rocked their chair onto its back legs. "Nothing's working." They raked their fingers through their hair, heaved a sigh, and plonked their head on their hand—then gasped and jolted upright. "Wait, there's an entry about the pendant in my book!"

Bolting up the stairs, Javi disappeared into the loft and returned in a flash, flipping through the pages of their family's heirloom *Libro de Secretos*. They set the book on the table and continued perusing the headings until they stopped abruptly to page back a few entries. "Here we go! Let's see if this is useful."

A likeness of the pendant was drawn in intricate, crosshatched ink above an ornate title: Heraldo de Amor. Javi skimmed the text, then translated the relevant sections aloud.

"Wake the dragon, and it will bestow an enchantment to lower participants' inhibitions, allowing for open, honest communication. If no feelings are present, no effects will manifest." Javi paused to give Eloddie and Trina a meaningful look. "To end the spell, soak the pendant in an infusion of agrimony, lavender, and sandalwood. There's also an accompanying ritual—El, we can use your cards as a focus for it."

"I have most of those ingredients." Trina moved to gather the listed supplies. "I'll just need to grow some agrimony."

While Trina took care of the infusion, Javi and Eloddie set up the ritual space. A triangle of candles waited, unlit. In front of each one lay a tarot card. Javi and Eloddie were already in position, each with a candle before them, when Trina stepped into place. Completing the circle, she poured the herb mixture through the wired lid caging the dragon. Sloshing in the water littered with flowers and sandalwood chips, it turned to face each of them, then lifted its neck with an imperious, expectant air.

Javi held back a chuckle.

Eloddie cleared her throat and struck a long match. "We entreat the cards we bring here to lend power to our intent," she intoned. "We call on the Ace of Swords to help us keep an open mind." She lit her candle and passed the match to Trina. As Trina set her own candle alight, Eloddie continued, "We call on the Ace of Wands to guide us to follow our hearts." Trina held out the match for Javi. With all three candles burning, Eloddie completed the invocation. "We call on the Ace of Cups to encourage us to welcome new connections. Let these qualities drive our ritual and actions."

Nothing visible changed, but the space between them quivered with potential. Javi's and Eloddie's eyes were bright with the swell of their combined power. They each rolled up a rose petal and dropped them in the jar in tandem.

The dragon's head snapped up, and it caught one of the petals as it drifted down, then the next, then the next. Once it had munched all three offerings, the dragon adjusted its limbs and stilled.

The pose was the same one the pendant had always displayed when Javi had worn it. Trina glanced up questioningly; Javi nodded, and Eloddie held out her hands. The candlelight surged as their fingers intertwined.

Javi squeezed their palms, and together they commanded, "¡Duerme!"

The water at the bottom of the jar fizzed. As the bubbles popped, a mist formed and coalesced into coils that swirled around the dragon, then disappeared.

"I think it's done," Javi said.

Trina knew it was true. The odd warmth and compulsion that had pricked at her all afternoon had faded. The weight of what had passed between them descended on her, and her heart sank like a stone in her belly. "Oh, gods." She let go of their hands and stepped back. "I can't believe I said those things. I'm sorry I acted so—so foolish."

Unconsciously, Trina drifted toward the bar, distancing herself from them.

Eloddie took deliberate steps to block her retreat. "Trina, nothing you did was foolish, and you've done nothing that requires an apology. Unless you think loving us is wrong?"

"You don't believe that, do you?" Javi asked.

"No, of course not!"

"Then what are you afraid of?" Eloddie pressed, but Trina could only shake her head; she had no answer. Eloddie gestured to the table where her deck lay undisturbed after Trina's interrupted reading. "You wanted to know about your love life. Why don't we finish what we started?"

Trina straightened up in response to Eloddie's no-nonsense tone. She wanted them. They seemed to be suggesting...they wanted her too? So why should she shy away from the truth?

"Fine."

Trina's pulse fluttered in her throat as they all settled at the table, and Eloddie dealt three cards. Javi looked between them with quiet curiosity. The corner of Eloddie's lip quirked up as she revealed them. "In the simplest terms, the Two of Cups indicates an affectionate connection, the Three of Pentacles symbolizes solid, effective teamwork, and the Nine of Cups promises granted wishes. Together, these cards tell of a meeting of hearts that, when working as one, can achieve anything together. If the connection is nurtured with mutual effort, communication, and trust, the people will find success and bliss."

Javi wet their lips. "If I were you, I don't think I'd argue with that."

Eloddie leaned forward. "Trina, I want you to know as explicitly as possible: we both want you."

"It's true."

"I want you, too, but I'm afraid," Trina said. "I don't want to lose either of you."

"Is fear a good reason not to try?" Javi asked. "Imagine how wonderful it could be if we take the chance."

Javi's cajoling drew a smile out of Trina despite her nerves. "You're right. You're both worth it."

"So, you'll be with us?" Eloddie asked.

"Yes," Trina confirmed. "I want to do this."

"Yes!" Javi bounced on their toes, beaming big enough to dimple their cheeks and crinkle the corners of their eyes. "You know, we'd been planning to talk to you soon. I've been daydreaming about visiting the Artisan Fair together for a date."

"We should," Trina said.

"Absolutely," Eloddie said. "But we should relax tonight. Order in. Watch a movie, maybe."

"My bed is big enough to accommodate cuddles for three," Javi added. "What do you think?"

"I'd love to," Trina said. "Especially if we get Gigi's Pizza."

Eloddie hummed in agreement. "Mmm, yes."

"Let's do that." Javi kissed each of their cheeks and spun toward the stairs, leading the way to the first of what Trina hoped would be many quiet evenings together.

HERALD OF LOVE
CODA
MAGGIE PAGE

As Trina set the pizza boxes in the back seat, Aunt Joyce's attention fell on the fountain in the center of the square. The water feature boasted three tiers topped with a sculpture depicting a woman pouring out the contents of two basins. Over her stone shoulder, a kinetic star spun with the breeze.

"Beautiful, isn't it?" Trina asked.

"It's all lovely." Joyce scanned the streets they'd toured with a small smile and turned to Trina. "I've been worried about you out on your own, but you seem happy here."

"I am." Trina tucked her hair behind her ear and ducked her head, unable to keep a telling grin off her face.

"I'm glad." Joyce squeezed Trina's shoulder. "Now, show me this shop of yours."

"Before we do that…" Trina leaned against the trunk. "There's something I need to tell you."

"Okay," Joyce agreed with concern as she settled against the car next to Trina. "I'm all ears."

"I want to introduce you to a lot of people. My partners, most of all."

"Partners?" Joyce echoed, elongating the "S."

Trina bit her lip and nodded. "I've talked about Javi and El before."

Joyce chuckled. "I feel like I know them already. I'm excited to meet them."

"We're together. The three of us," Trina clarified.

Joyce stilled Trina's hand-wringing with a touch. When Trina looked up, Joyce met her gaze head-on and repeated, "I'm excited to meet them."

KNISHES AND NOSHES

NINA WATERS

ableism (mentions of), baker, bakery, blind, customer/employee, dragon, interspecies relationship, jewish, m/nb, magic use, meet cute, mute, non-binary, past tense, pining (mutual), third person limited point of view, united states of america

"Order up for Anton," Benjamin called. On mornings this busy, Benjamin regretted running the shop with both counter and table service. Thermal signatures moved chaotically amidst the closely packed tables, passed through the door in rushes of frigid nearly black winter air, and waited in a knot by the pickup window.

No one answered his call for "Anton."

He raised his voice. "I've got a tall cinnamon-caramel cappuccino with oat whipped cream?" The coffee mug steamed, an incandescent 55 degrees except where the whipped cream made an oil-slick rainbow gradient to a cool, blue nine degrees. "Anton?" If they didn't answer, Benjamin would leave the order for Esteban—wherever they were, trying to wait tables amidst the crowd—but no, a waving blur of 37-degree-yellow caught his eye, silhouetted against the iridescent light playing over the chill exterior window.

Benjamin raised a thumbs-up of acknowledgement and looked again for Esteban. There: their silhouette was distinct thanks to the glowing baubles that secured their braids and the special 30-degree thread sewn into their yarmulke. They were making small talk—an inescapable task for a server—with someone person-shaped but 8 degrees too yellow-white (a were, they ran hot), and a cat whose tail lashed whenever someone bumped their chair. Too busy to deliver the tray themself. Benjamin would have to bring it.

Most customers moved out of his way—they recognized either his face, his name tag, or his official "Benjamin's Knishes and Noshes" T-shirt—and he wove through the press. Around a table—not where it should be, thank G-d for the heat-reactive tape that marked the corners at a steady blue-pink 15 degrees—and past an aisle, around a chatting group of…harpies, maybe? They weren't human-shaped, and they sounded like birds…and into a mercifully clear space. Anton was only a couple meters away, and—

The contents of the tray shifted as Benjamin's foot caught on something. His free arm windmilled in a vain attempt to catch his balance, and the cappuccino went flying as he tumbled to his knees, a hand glancing off something smooth, maybe 5 or 6 degrees. Scalding coffee puddled on the floor and formed a luminous, flowing veil over whatever Benjamin had tripped over. A…cylinder? No, it tapered, thin at one end, thicker on the other…a tail. And the smooth texture…must be scales.

A dragon. Of course. Their thick hides protected them, and those around them, from their magical breath…and made them invisible to the heat-detection spell Benjamin had invented to help him see.

Oy vey.

"Apologies, honored guest! I didn't…" What could Benjamin say? "Allow me to…" Anger and embarrassment surged, intensified by the need to maintain a customer-appropriate veneer.

The dragon answered with a soft rumble; when they opened their mouth, their breath made a diaphanous orange fog that limned their wedge-shaped face, long neck, and torso until its temperature equalized with the surrounding air. Three powerful fingers grasped Benjamin's upper arm, long talons poking through the fabric of his shirt, but despite their strength the dragon was gentle when they helped him to his feet.

"Thank you," he said to the apparently thin air beside him. No…the air of the café was a steady purple; where the dragon stood was blank and black. Benjamin should have realized. He shouldn't have tripped. He should have—

"Are you all right?" Esteban's voice was at his side; Benjamin had been so focused on his mishap, and his invisible customer, and his frustration, that he hadn't noticed them.

"I'm fine." Benjamin shook off Esteban, the dragon, and his irritation. "Towel?" Esteban tugged one from the front of their apron and handed it over. He dropped it onto the wet spot and used a foot to push it around; color and heat diffused in a weird pattern as the terry cloth absorbed the spill. "Ask Ridwana to remake Anton's order."

"Of course!" They moved as they spoke, heading toward the front counter.

"And bring the mop over!" he called after them, then turned toward the void that was his first dragon customer. "Good dragon, your order's on us today—get whatever you'd like."

Another sound vibrated from the dragon, a declining glissando that Benjamin interpreted as polite disagreement. Their hums had a pleasant lilt that reminded Benjamin of afternoons in Bubbe's kitchen when she sang wordlessly while she baked, the smell of baking apple and honey wafting through her small apartment.

"Of course—if you'd prefer to leave, I understand. I'm sorry for the inconvenience. I hope you'll return so we at Knishes and Noshes can make it up to you!"

The dragon huffed. The air before them eddied as if something was rapidly moving, and Benjamin concentrated, trying to interpret the thermal information he could see. Dragons could usually talk, Benjamin thought, and if this one wouldn't, or couldn't…sign language, maybe?

Invisible sign language. Signed by the invisible dragon. Aaargh.

"I'm sorry…I don't…" When someone with discernible body temperature signed, Benjamin *could* understand. He wouldn't lie and say he didn't know sign—he'd worked too hard, for too long, to sell himself short—but even most of his staff didn't know he was blind. He didn't owe anyone, even an offended customer, a disclosure.

"They say they'll stay, and they'll pay—no harm done, and you shouldn't worry," a customer amidst the onlookers translated.

Benjamin ground his teeth. Not giving free food to a customer on whom he'd spilled cappuccino was anathema. Arguing with a customer when they were wrong was *not* anathema; when someone behaved unreasonably, they'd hear it from him. But the dragon *wasn't* being unreasonable, and Benjamin didn't *want* to argue with them…*and* he wanted to give them a free meal.

Maybe he should offer to take them out to dinner?

Shaking his head, Benjamin leaned down to pick up the sopping towel as Esteban returned, pulling the mop and bucket behind them. What was he thinking? Flirting? *Now?*

"As you say," he lied. Do *nothing?* No way. He'd upsize the dragon's order, minimum. "Thank you for understanding!" Maybe surreptitiously slip a gift card onto the dragon's tray. "Sorry about the delay, everyone!"

Bonus: the dragon would have to return to use the gift card. Benjamin would get to see them again.

Wait…no…Benjamin definitely *wouldn't* see them again.

But he would *encounter* them again.

The waiting customers murmured their understanding that accidents happened, and Benjamin shouldn't trouble himself, the usual niceties.

"I'll finish cleaning this," Esteban offered.

As near-disasters went, this could have gone *much* worse.

("Kein ayin hara!" he could imagine Bubbe admonishing.)

Superstitious nonsense…but Benjamin still knocked on the counter as he returned to the register and resumed taking orders.

Usually by midafternoon, Benjamin would be in the kitchen preparing knishes, meat pies, and bialys for the after-work crowd, but *nothing* had gone right today. Four employees had called out sick—even Esteban, who *never* missed work. His milk frother had broken. The kitchen stank of char because a batch of babka had burnt. The only employee who *had* come used the dairy can opener for tuna fish; Benjamin had fired him on the spot. Between working the counter helping walk-ins, preparing to-go orders, making drinks, delivering trays to tables, and bussing dirty dishes, Benjamin was *exhausted.*

At least his evening staff would arrive within the hour. If none of them called out. He just had to stick it out until then.

The door opened and closed; Benjamin glanced over but saw only blackness. No…wait…Benjamin *could* see something. A golden halo floated about two meters above the floor. That couldn't be right. Seraphim were long gone from earth and, besides, they'd not *actually* had haloes. That was Christian hooey. Benjamin *had* read "seraphim" translated as "dragon" in some English texts, but surely that was a misnomer.

Well. Whether it was a seraph, or a dragon, or something else…it had a halo, which meant he could see them approaching the counter. Nifty!

The halo stopped before him. A burst of heat blew over Benjamin and swirled a rainbow temperature gradient through the purple-cool air.

"Welcome to Knishes and Noshes." Benjamin forced a semblance of brightness and looked in the direction of what he hoped was the customer's…it had to be a dragon, *the* dragon, right?…face. "What can I get you?"

Something tapped against the counter, and then a glowing red rectangle—a Knishes and Noshes gift card, ensorcelled to give off a heat signature—appeared and floated down to rest beside the tip jar.

It told him nothing. This *could* be the dragon from before…their silence and the gift card were suggestive…but that dragon might have given the card away, and while dragons *weren't* usually mute—Benjamin had checked—*some* were. It wasn't certain…

…but Benjamin *hoped* it was the same dragon.

Taking up the card, Benjamin scanned it with the register. "You have $15 remaining on your gift card," the programmed voice announced.

That *was* the amount he'd given the dragon.

It *still* wasn't certain, but… "Welcome back." He was surprised to find cheer easier to come by. It was nice to have even *one* not-shitty thing happen. "Same order as last time?"

The dragon hummed.

"You had a jumbo hot coffee with two sugars and a half dozen blueberry sufganiyot, right?"

A second hum suggested impressed confirmation.

"I'll get right—"

The dragon interrupted with a grunt.

"You'd like a change? Okay—one tap for yes, two for no. Any changes to your coffee order?"

Tap, tap.

"Do you still want blueberry sufganiyot?"

Tap, tap.

"A different pastry, then?"

Tap, tap.

Confused, Benjamin frowned, then realized— "You want a different sufganiyot flavor?"

Tap.

"We've got four. I'll number them. One tap, blueberry; two, apple; three, chocolate-and-nocciolata; and…" Drat, he *knew* there were four. "…right. Four: halva. What's your pleasure?"

Tap, tap, tap, tap.

"Got it: a jumbo hot coffee and six halva sufganiyot. Yeah?"

Tap.

"Anything else?"

Tap, tap.

"Your total is $15.03. I'll charge $15 to the gift card and grab the three cents from the coin tray."

Tap—followed by a nails-on-chalkboard sound…no, a talons-on-leave-a-coin-take-a-coin-tray sound…and the dragon daintily, laboriously scooped out three pennies and pushed them across the counter. Had the dragon realized Benjamin was blind—did they think that Benjamin wouldn't be able to pick out the change himself? Had the dragon thought that *Benjamin* thought the *dragon* couldn't get the pennies, and wanted to prove that they could? Either the dragon was being ableist, or the dragon thought Benjamin was being ableist.

Or he was reading way too much into three pennies.

It was probably that one, but Benjamin wished he could be sure.

Regardless, he was sure that each of them was trying to accommodate and understand the other.

"For here or to…" Benjamin shook his head. *Yes or no questions, schlemiel.* "For here?"

Tap.

"Okay, in-house, awesome. I'll bring your order out when it's ready. Make yourself at home!"

The halo bobbled off; when the dragon turned from him, two additional glowing loops encircled their tail.

They were both *succeeding*, despite the obstacles.

Maybe Benjamin's day wasn't going so poorly after all.

Benjamin wasn't sure when he developed a crush on the dragon.

It might have been when he realized that the halo over the dragon's head was the size and shape of a yarmulke with a heat-generating band inserted within it.

It might have been when the dragon special-ordered three of Benjamin's Tu B'shevat platters, then tried to stuff a crumpled-up handful of bills into the International Tree Foundation collection box without Benjamin noticing.

It might have been when, on a snowy Tevet midmorning, the dragon stayed for over an hour, laboriously tapping their way through a one-sided conversation with Benjamin.

He couldn't have said, really—but he could say when he realized that the dragon maybe returned his feelings.

Shevat 22. A cold and windy Thursday, with the forecast promising overnight ice storms.

The dragon came in and approached the counter. They set down a sheet of paper and a jar, the contents of which sloshed turbidly, turquoise, 16 degrees. Something—a talon, Benjamin assumed—dipped into the jar and emerged coated with liquid. The paper's location shifted, the tip of the talon swept lightly over the page, and letters formed in its wake.

I'm Eli, the dragon wrote. Eli. What a lovely name.

"I'm...I'm Benjamin," he replied, oddly breathless. The flutter in Benjamin's chest and the butterflies in his stomach were ridiculous.

I know, said Eli. *You're the owner.*

Right. This was his bakery. The shop was called "Benjamin's Knishes and Noshes." He wore a work shirt. And a name tag. Off to an awesome start, this conversation. "So, um. Ink, huh?" Benjamin asked, desperate to change the topic. "Your work?"

Tap.

"That's *awesome*. I tried to bespell something similar for years, all through school—it would have saved me *so much time* if I could've read assignments instead of using TTS for everything." Aaaand he'd just admitted he couldn't see. Whatever. Eli must have realized long ago, or else he wouldn't have come in with a halo, wouldn't have borne Benjamin's inability to understand Eli's sign language, wouldn't have brought in— *invented?*—this ink. "I never succeeded. How'd you do it?"

Eli had written him a *note*, using this ink casually like it wasn't the most remarkable thing Benjamin had ever seen. Ever. *Seen.*

It's mercury-based, Eli explained in loopy script. *Toxic to humans, but—*

"—you're not human," Benjamin finished with a slow nod. "You should patent that! You'd make bank."

There was a rustle of scales, a soft disgruntled snort, then— *Whatever. As long as I can talk with you.*

The flutter in Benjamin's chest took flight.

The butterflies in Benjamin's stomach stampeded. "Oh."

But I don't wish to be a bother, Eli added hastily. *I understand this is your job, and I'm a customer. We don't have to talk now, or ever. I'd not want to intrude.*

"It's no intrusion," said Benjamin. "With the storm coming, I won't get more than a handful of customers the rest of the night anyway."

You should close early. Your commute will be dangerous. I could help lock up and clean, if you wanted.

"I live next door—no commute," Benjamin waved dismissively.

Oh. Somehow, disappointment was palpable in those two neatly written letters. What was Benjamin *doing?* Eli seemed to want to stay. Benjamin *definitely* wanted Eli to stay. They could finally communicate. This was his chance!

What was the worst that could happen?

A sexual harassment lawsuit, probably.

But compared to the *best* that could happen? Was there a not-flirty, not-interested interpretation of *as long as I can talk with you?*

There really wasn't.

"My problem is," Benjamin ventured with feigned nonchalance, "I baked for the day thinking the rain wouldn't start until after midnight. If I'm lucky, I'll sell a fraction of this stock. It's hardly worth keeping the lights on for that. So, you're right...I *could* shut down early...but after I do, why don't you stay and help me eat these knishes?"

Are you asking me to dinner? Eli wrote, hesitance in every talon-stroke.

Benjamin's anxiety flared, those dratted rampaging butterflies stealing his brief confidence. "If I were?"

I'd say yes. And I'm paying.

"Absolutely not! Don't be absurd. If we don't eat them, they'll go to waste."

This is a business!

"And I'm offering you free surplus, from that business, while the business is closed."

But—

"You're still arguing with me?" asked Benjamin archly. "Why?"

Because— I don't know.

"That's what I thought," Benjamin laughed. "Come on—one night only, free all-you-can-eat—how's that for an offer you can't turn down?"

Spending the evening with you was already an offer I couldn't turn down, Eli replied, and Benjamin's fluttering heart flitted and sang like a bird. *Free food is a bonus. Be careful with that 'all-you-can-eat' offer. I can eat a lot.*

"I said what I meant, and I meant what I said," Benjamin promised.

I'll hold you to that.

"You can hold me to more than that, if you want," Benjamin replied, suggestively, hopefully.

There was a pause, Eli's talon unmoving, Benjamin's nerves a mess. Then—

I'll hold you to that, too.

Exhilarated, Benjamin grinned. "Okay—yeah—uh. Wow. I've gotta…um…" There'd been something…

Lock up?

"Right. That—but I'll be back soon, okay?"

Y… Eli scratched out the letter. *No hur…* They scratched out what they'd written again. *I'm glad,* they finally wrote.

A delighted frisson shivered through Benjamin.

"Me too," he replied warmly. "Me too."

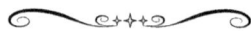

"Someone here for you, boss," Esteban announced from the kitchen doorway.

"Unless it's the oven fairy—not now," Benjamin answered tersely, getting a hand behind the oven and tugging it away from the wall. The side of it was cold. The back of it was cold. The entire room was cold.

His ovens were broken.

Benjamin wasn't even sure *why* he was tugging the oven away from the wall. He couldn't fix it. His usual mechanic wasn't available until Monday, which on a normal Friday morning would be fine. Normally, he could run the bakery until sundown with what he'd already baked. Normally, he'd close for Shabbat. Normally, he'd put a note on the door Sunday to explain why they were closed, and open Monday morning after the mechanic finished the repairs.

Normally, everything would be fine.

"There's an oven fairy?"

This was not a normal Friday morning.

Purim started Saturday at dusk.

"If there were an oven fairy, we wouldn't be in this mess," he snarled. He hated getting angry at them—this wasn't Esteban's fault—but Benjamin had pre-orders for *thousands* of hamantaschen in eight different flavors.

The dough was prepared. The fillings were reduced to thick, goopy sweetness. The first twenty trays were on a speed rack ready to fire.

"Oh."

He'd hardly slept for two days to prepare for today's great bake-off.

"What do you *want?*"

The cookies *had* to be done before Shabbat started.

"I'm sorry…it's nothing…I mean—"

And the *fucking ovens* weren't working.

A metallic tap interrupted Esteban, and they startled, their yellow mass bright against the deep black of the doorway behind them.

Wait…the doorway was black?

No—it wasn't. A swirl of blue air made a dusky line along one edge and a brilliant white halo nearly bumped the top jamb.

"Eli." Benjamin clenched his hands and swallowed his ire.

He didn't want Eli to see him like this, and he didn't want to feel like this, and he didn't want to act like this, and he really, *really* didn't want the ovens busted!

"Yeah. Them." Esteban offered apologetically. "I thought…"

With a whooshed exhale, Benjamin slumped, exhausted, against the chill tiled wall. "It's fine," he muttered, as if anything was fine. "Thanks, Esteban. You're doing great. I'm sorry. This is…"

"…the worst-timed bullshit that's happened since opening day?" they suggested.

"Bingo."

With a sympathetic nod, Esteban slipped past Eli and out to the café floor. The dragon sidled into the room; the kitchen door closed behind them, the ink pot appeared, and Eli wrote on a countertop.

Esteban told me what happened. I want to help.

"Help?" asked Benjamin blankly.

Eli's inky talon rose, stopped centimeters below their yarmulke halo, and was enveloped by sun-bright air swirls as Eli coughed suggestively.

Benjamin had no idea what the suggestion was.

But he'd never seen Eli's breath so *hot* before.

Wait…what was literally the most well-known dragon ability in the world? Benjamin was an *idiot*. "You can breathe fire?"

Tap.

"You can control the temperature?"

To within a few degrees.

"For how long?"

As long as you need. Eli's certainty radiated from their writing. Benjamin wished he shared their confidence. *We'll need a contained, fire-resistant space to trap the heat.*

"Right." Hurrying across the room, Benjamin threw the kitchen door open. "Esteban—grab a screwdriver!"

"80 proof vodka, or higher?" they called back.

"Phillips-head." Benjamin laughed. A *?* appeared on the counter in glowing ink. "We'll take the back off the oven. You stand behind it and, ya know, breathe. I'll load it from the front."

That'll work. Are you ready?

Benjamin grimaced. "I can't pay you."

And?

"It'll take hours."

So?

"Maybe past dusk…" Benjamin forced himself to acknowledge.

And it won't take you through the start of Shabbat if you're alone?

"I know…I don't know…I'm not Orthodox, so it wouldn't be so bad…are you…? I mean…I can't…but these orders…I mustn't—"

Powerful forelimbs encircled Benjamin's shoulders, a scaled torso pressed to his chest, and a serpentine neck curled around his head. Orange-tinged breath gusted past Benjamin's ear, and his fears dissipated into a sense of profound security. Eli was so solid, so present, so real, so steady. Benjamin had no idea what he'd done to earn Eli's trust, but he was beyond grateful for it.

"Thank you," Benjamin whispered.

Eli's answering hum was the most comforting sound Benjamin had heard since Bubbe passed.

3 sides to Haman's hat, and 3 folds to hold the filling in the center of a hamantaschen. 6 cookies in a row, and 4 rows on each baking sheet. 3 sheets per ovenful, and 15 minutes for each ovenful to bake. 72 hamantaschen every 15 minutes, or 288 hamantaschen per hour. It'd take over 12 hours to bake the 3,497 hamantaschen Benjamin needed.

If nothing went wrong. If nothing burned. If they didn't stop to eat or rest, if Eli hardly drew breath, and G-d help them if they needed a bathroom break.

And if either of them worked past 7:03…they had no excuse.

Amends might be made after, but the guilt and recrimination would last.

Benjamin tried not to think about how screwed they were as he measured fillings, folded hamantaschen, and arranged cookies on pans. He tried not to think about it when he spilled a bowl of prune filling, nor when he rolled the shells out too thick three times in a row, nor when he forgot to don oven mitts and grabbed a scorching tray barehanded, nor when he fumbled his way through assembling further hamantaschen one-handed.

He mustn't fail.

Customers expected the absolute best from him, but they respected him enough that they wouldn't ask him to violate the Sabbath over a few dozen Purim cookies. It would be all right if he couldn't finish. He could pick the customer least likely to be offended to call and say, "Sorry, no cookies this year." That would be fine.

Except it wouldn't be, because this was his business, and he'd taken deposits, and he relied on Knishes and Noshes' reputation to bring in customers and orders, and, and, and.

He couldn't afford to fail.

Winters, the bakery operated on thin margins. If he had to refund all of his Purim preorders, *any* of his Purim pre-orders... even thinking about it made him panicky.

He couldn't afford to panic, either.

He had too much to do.

But he didn't think they were going to make it.

He wouldn't say it aloud. He and Eli and his staff had tried so hard. The others were gone now—they'd run the shop throughout the day, locked the door at 6:00, left at 6:30, even Esteban, despite their protests that they could stay and help.

It wasn't hopeless. If they could get the hamantaschen baked, Benjamin could bundle and deliver them on Saturday night after dusk. As long as they were baked...

...but they wouldn't be, because they weren't going to make it.

The oven timer went off. Benjamin hurried to remove the latest batch, blistered hand cramping with pain. He removed them—placed them on the speed rack—leaned down—got the next set of trays—slammed the oven shut—set the timer again.

They weren't going to make it.

There was no more prep to do, unless one of the remaining batches burned—the leftover ingredients Benjamin had left were surplus. Unless he'd miscalculated. Unless he dropped a tray. Unless…it didn't matter. If something went wrong now, there'd be no time to rectify it.

"What time is it?" Benjamin hardly recognized his own voice, it was so colorless.

"The current time is 6:51 p.m.," his phone announced.

"Eli, you should stop."

Eli grunted a disagreeing rumble, and the color of their flames intensified by 4 degrees.

"I mean it."

Another grunt, 2 degrees hotter.

"That's too ho…actually…keep doing that."

Eli didn't respond, but the flame didn't cool. It wasn't ideal to cook the hamantaschen at a higher temperature—they'd be over-brown, the jam too caramelized—but it was only one batch. At least they'd be cooked through, and Benjamin wouldn't be ashamed to sell them.

"Maybe we *can* make it…" he breathed. Something tingled beneath his skin, like anticipation, like destiny, full-on beshert like Bubbe used to talk about when something went *just* right.

It made no sense—*nothing* had gone right that day. Except—

Eli's answering hum communicated an impressive amount of sardonic *duh, told you so.*

One thing had gone wonderfully, gloriously right that day.

Eli was with him.

With a burst of energy, Benjamin rolled the last speed rack into the fridge, wrapped the leftovers, and wiped the counters. Benjamin's emergency straightening wouldn't pass a surprise health inspection, but it would tide the kitchen over until Saturday night.

Maybe, just maybe, they'd make it.

Eli's flames burned bright.

The hamantaschen glowed as heat penetrated them, the jam warming faster than the dough, bubbling and thickening.

The timer ticked, ticked, ticked, the minutes away.

Impatience had Benjamin bouncing on his heels and staring at the oven. The cookies were 76 degrees…77…77.5…when they were 80 degrees through, they'd be done. Oh, his eyes *hurt*, from fatigue, from dryness, from magical backlash. He'd never run his thermal-vision spell this long…but he could stop soon.

They *might* make—

A cough interrupted the flow of fire, raspy and dry, and Benjamin's heart ached.

"You've done enough," he murmured, walking to the side of the oven and setting a hand on Eli's back. Scales, smooth and cool as glass, slid beneath his fingers.

Eli shook their head, and hot flames licked from their mouth only to sputter out in a cloud of stinky pink smoke.

"Stop. Trust me." Reaching down, Benjamin grabbed the oven back and shoved it over the opening, holding it in place with his uninjured hand. "That'll hold the heat in. Go drink. Go eat. Go to Synagogue. I've got things here."

Heat permeated the backing plate, and Benjamin hissed, switching to his other hand—ow—and back hastily.

There was a judgmental edge to Eli's silence.

"Or. Don't go." It'd be nice if Eli stayed.

The judgmental edge grew sharper as Eli shouldered him aside, taloned hands securing the oven back.

Circling to the front, Benjamin checked the hamantaschen…79 degrees, maybe a bissel over. Another minute, and they'd be done.

He was afraid to check if they had another minute.

The cookies brightened…brightened…brightened…

"They're done!" he cheered.

Grabbing mitts, Benjamin pulled the oven open and took out the last two trays. Steam and the sweet smell of baked strawberry jam filled the air. Hurrying to the fridge, he yanked the door open, slid the tray onto the speed rack he'd left within, and let the door slam shut behind him.

He took a deep breath, felt a swell of victorious satisfaction…

…and realized his phone alarm was going off.

"What time is it?" he asked, rubbing a hand over his face. His thermal vision dissipated in a cascade of colorful sparks that faded into black.

"It is 7:04 p.m. Shabbat shalom."

Benjamin had no idea if they'd finished on time.

Bull. In his head, in his heart, from his aching palm down to his sore feet, he was *sure*. They had. As Bubbe would have said, beshert wouldn't play him like that. Nonsense, his head suggested. *Fate*, his heart replied.

Yawning, Benjamin knuckled at his cheek and made his way back onto the bakery floor. He couldn't see, but he didn't need to, not for this.

This kitchen was his home. He knew where every table was, every counter, every proof box, every shelving unit, every stove. He knew where—

His foot caught on something, and he'd have pitched onto his face if not for someone catching him effortlessly.

Eli. He'd tripped on Eli. *Again.*

"Sorry," Benjamin mumbled. "I—" Eli silenced him with a talon over his lips. "Thank you. For everything."

Light breezes suggested Eli shifting, one hand still supporting Benjamin, and silence stretched out…and then Eli took his uninjured hand. A talon teased gently at his palm, tracing letters.

Can't see?

Benjamin shook his head. "I'm sorry, the spell duration…and now it's Shabbat, and I shouldn't…you know, no spells…sorry…even if I could, and I don't think I…I…I'm sorry."

Stop apologizing.

"But—"

I'm not sorry. About anything.

Benjamin didn't know what Eli meant.

But Benjamin knew what he *hoped* Eli meant.

Oh, who was he fooling? Benjamin knew *exactly* what Eli meant.

"Besherter?" he whispered.

Silence.

Maybe he should try besherte? Was there a gender-neutral version he wasn't familiar with? Had his tired heart run away with him? Had—

—and then Eli grabbed him, hugged him close, nuzzled his face, and drew him down, down, until they lay on the kitchen floor, and Benjamin reclined in the curl of Eli's torso. The warmth of Eli's yarmulke halo felt like sunshine on Benjamin's cheek.

Resting on the bakery floor violated at least four health codes, but leaving Eli's side, moving even a step, was inconceivable.

"I love you."

Eli had stayed with him. Eli had helped him. Eli's answering hum sounded like, felt like, adoration.

Replete, Benjamin let his eyes slip shut. They'd achieved the impossible. What else could it be but beshert?

And, on the seventh day, finally, Benjamin and Eli rested. Together.

HARMONY

I. A. ASHCROFT

be gay do crimes, bipoc, coffee shop, customer/employee, customer service representative, first kiss, homosexual, m/m, magic use, meet cute, past tense, sexual content (non-graphic descriptions), third person limited point of view, trans male

4 a.m. felt like the witching hour to Toby. Nothing seemed entirely real, as if the divide between the mundane and arcane was brittle, and the world had yet to settle on a choice.

"Good morning," he yawned into his headset, straightening his star-print apron. "Order whenever you're ready." Lightly, he scratched his short beard, waiting.

Waiting.

"Mrm," came a grunt in return: a man's raspy baritone laced with some hard-to-pin trace of Eastern Europe. "Large latte. *Three* espresso shots."

Toby froze. Then, as he gave the total, washed his hands, and rushed to get the drink poured, his ears began to ring. Caleb the Red? How? *Why*? Trouble must have been brewing nearby if the mage was here— some robbery, some scam, something that was going to bring the Guild's investigators sniffing…!

Stiffly turning toward the pickup window, Toby desperately tried to pour faster. Good gods. The truck waiting there was surely only running as the result of necromancy. Toby couldn't tell if it was painted brown or if that was just rust, and its engine bled a pneumatic rattle. From its window, Caleb's handsome, high-cheekboned face parted shadows that were as dark as his short, kinked black hair, his clever, *irritated* gaze piercing right into Toby's soul.

Okay! Don't panic! If he did, his chest binder would make it harder to breathe—*damn it!* Where were the lid refills? Finally, *finally*, Toby clicked a cap over the cup and passed it over, praying he wouldn't be recognized. Their magic community had never been large, but he'd never risen beyond being a lowly apprentice before leaving. Even so...

Wordlessly, the man examined him, then paid in cash—with exact change. However, he didn't pull forward. He just peered, sipping his coffee, his umber fingers smoothing down his white button-up shirt and leather jacket. Must have gotten wrinkled during all this excessive staring.

Toby said the only thing he could. "Is everything all right?"

The cup was placed back on the sill. Slowly. Precisely. "Only two shots. I ordered three."

"Oh!" Ha, yes, Caleb could level the building and make it look like an unlucky electrical fire, and this barista genius had screwed up his order. Perfect. On-brand. "My sincerest apologies. I'll re-make it. Just a moment." *Okay: scurry back. Get the cup. Coffee. Draw the steamed milk. All right. Let it settle and turn a soft brown. Add the shots. Mix. Three? Yes, three.*

Those dark eyes dissected his back the entire time.

Okay. Okay.

Magic wasn't something to be flung about: it could weave in ways unpredictable. But what Toby called on now was a simple, harmless sigil. Quick! Discreet! Nothing that would call the attention of the Guild. *Harmony*, he traced over the paper cup with his forefinger and thumb, so the flavors within would meld *precisely* the way they were meant to.

A glimmer flared from the paper's surface. Then it was gone, and the casting was done. Caleb would love his coffee and forgive all...hopefully.

"Here you are," Toby said with his most friendly smile. "Sorry for the extra wait."

The proffered beverage was taken. Caleb closed his lips carefully around the edge, sampling the brew so smote with caffeine it might launch another soul into space. "Mm," he said neutrally, nodding with what might have been approval.

Then his expressive eyebrow rose. Pearly teeth glimmered in a smile. Toby's stomach dropped somewhere near the vicinity of his ankles, and he could only smile back like enthusiasm would make the sun rise faster to save him.

"Thank you," Caleb said, popping a dollar in the tip jar. His eyes peeled away *ever* so slowly as he drove off.

It took Toby a full ten seconds to hear another throat clearing inside his headset, heart pounding in his ears. "Hello?" a woman said gruffly. "Ah…I want a double-shot mint-mocha. Large. With soy milk—no. Almond milk. No! *Soy*."

"Good morning. We also have coconut," Toby said faintly.

It was fine. Everything was fine. The mage was…gone.

There was an old sorrow bubbling in Toby's chest, but he pressed it down deep and returned to his mundane day in his mundane world. He pulled down chairs from tables. He turned on the lights. He waited for dawn, and he unlocked the doors, letting in the manager and two impatient customers lounging on the curb. They all demanded things from him and gave no thanks or gladness in return. No one smiled so early, he supposed—no one but Caleb. That was how the man was: all cocky, lean, and slinky flow, flaunting his leather jacket as if this city was a runway and not humble Dorchester.

Mages were often like that, even ones on the outs with the Guild.

The exception was Toby, of course, drab in his button-up and khakis, sporting a haircut so standard it had its own number on the barbershop wall. An unwillingness to attract attention was a good habit for a former whistleblower, though—once on the rise up the magical ranks with a highly respected mentor, now he brewed coffee to make ends meet.

Quiet. Hidden. That was his life now. It couldn't be helped.

He swept his mind of it. He swept the floors. He pushed through his shift to midafternoon: there were bills to pay, regrets to nurse, and a studio apartment to go to for a nap at the end. Finally, all that was left for Toby to do as time spun on was to hang up his apron, notching one more day off his life.

He turned to make for the back.

He nearly collided with stars-cursed Caleb the Red.

Caleb was leaning over the front counter, smiling at him the way orcas looked at baby seals. What? Wasn't Martha manning the…?

"Hello there," he purred.

"How can I help you?" Toby's customer service recording switched on, a half-octave too high, his blindsided gape too wide.

"Just need a medium caramel latte. Whipped cream. Wrapping up the afternoon."

"Coming right up," Toby agreed, engaging his mechanical memory as Caleb kept up that eerie peering. Cup. Coffee. *Don't look back.* But he did anyway; long, articulate fingers were turning counter items over for examination and putting shirt wrinkles to rights again.

Draw the steamed milk. Careful.

Really, Caleb had the most…limber hands. A delicate touch. A keen, exacting sense of control. One could see how he could draw such beautiful rune-circles.

Toby pumped caramel syrup all over his fingers instead of into the cup. Caleb's lips twitched.

"I'm so sorry," Toby croaked a rusty laugh. "Long day. I'll do this over for you."

"No rush." That little smile wouldn't fade. "Your do-overs are worthwhile." Caleb leaned further over the counter—he'd taken a regrettable curiosity in how everything worked beyond the invisible line separating customer from caffeine bombs. Slowly, that gaze shifted, cataloging every last topping and packet of tea. "You've worked here long?" came the drawl.

"Just three months." Toby couched this with the same upbeat tone he'd have used to comment on sunny weather—though gray, dismal rain pattered the glass—and he drew another cup from the stack.

"Paying your way through college, or…?"

His ears warmed. It was a surprising question; Toby didn't think he looked young enough—his facial hair was streaked with stress-white. "No, no," he said, keeping his smile chipper. "Just needed a change of pace."

"Mm. I understand that."

"Oh?"

"I…freelance. Have to be adaptable." That gaze had a delightfully cheeky glimmer, the exact same one from Caleb's many questionings at the Guild. Not his fault, he'd always say, that his crimson-inked scrolls kept turning up at crime scenes. Surely it was a problem with vendor background checks.

"What do you do?" Toby certainly did *not* mean to pry.

"Writing and calligraphy." Articulate fingers danced a complicated pattern over the counter surface—Caleb had *better* not have laid down some minor sigil for his own amusement…

"How interesting." The brew was drawn with a hiss of steam. "What do you write?"

"Whatever the clients want. Nothing noteworthy."

"I'm sure you're underselling it."

"…maybe…hm. I suppose I have a few exciting pieces. I do *love* a good mystery." Shiny teeth flashed oddly sharp.

This conversation was too dangerous. In went shot one of caramel. There went shot two. "Sorry for the wait," Toby found himself saying for the second time. Featherlight fingertips brushed his as Caleb took the drink.

…warmer than the cup, somehow…

Caleb the Red didn't pay with an information-revealing credit card; once more, he had exact change. While Toby dropped quarters into their drawer, Caleb went to the corner of the shop and curled up in a chair, knees to his chest, a small roost—an odd and pensive posture for such a man. His eyes scanned the street, the other patrons, the walls…never lighting back on the baristas, though he also didn't pull out a phone or other distraction.

There he remained until Toby, stalling, couldn't put off ending his shift any longer. So slowly, he pressed by Caleb, heading out the door.

"Oh. Right," his personal time bomb breezily said as if he'd remembered something at the last minute. "Take this." A fiver was pressed forward, precisely bent in half. "As a tip."

Cautiously, Toby accepted. "Thank you, sir."

"You're quite welcome." That raspy rumble thrummed softly. "You know, I'd like to talk with you again sometime."

"You…would?"

Caleb's nod was gravity-heavy despite the grin. "I also think," he said, "the Guild should have treated you better, Tobias Caldwell."

Toby forgot every word he'd learned in his thirty years on the planet.

"Consider it. I can't help but imagine…maybe we'd get along. Your hands…when you pay attention, anyway…they're *precise*. You know your work." Warmth bloomed in Toby's stomach, up his neck. "Also…" Caleb rose. "I like how you smile at me."

And then he strode on out.

Gone again.

Toby walked home in the opposite direction. Walked *fast*. He was going to have to get a new job, wasn't he? Damn. Damn! It was only as he got inside, put his things down, and pulled Caleb's money from his pocket that he realized a slip of paper had been folded into his tip. Slowly, he unbundled the message.

A…phone number…? Beside it lay a small harmony sigil in the most careful, exacting penmanship, a smiley face etched beneath.

Toby's heart thudded. …*oh*! Slowly, he laid back on his bed, listening to the mad drumming in his chest, hypnotized by the white popcorn ceiling.

He didn't call Caleb that night. He didn't.

But he fell asleep with his phone over his heart, a new contact saved, a question on his lips.

Morning came: another day, another shift, another tally on the calendar. The previous afternoon seemed a dream, an irrational longing for connection with the old days made real…with someone who understood. Toby had to let it go. But after he showered, he unthinkingly traced a sigil in his bathroom mirror's steam, right across his sandy-brown chest:

Harmony.

He sighed. There hadn't been any magic in the gesture, his intentions too wide and scattered. Yet, it gleamed damp against his reflection, almost hopeful.

A misplaced hope.

A few hours later, a Guild investigator came into view through the café window. Toby knew her marble-white skin and long, silver braids, knew her wool coat of swirled orange hues. He watched her pacing in the bleak smattering of rain, pretending to check her phone under the eaves. A cold pain thudded in his chest.

Mrs. Agatha Pinne.

The Pinnes were wealthy and dangerous; they'd kept enchanted silkworms and sheep herds for generations along the Eastern seaboard, selling fibercraft extraordinary and rare. But none of them ever laughed…or smiled…or *blinked*. Everyone knew something was very wrong with the Pinnes, but no one ever dared talk about what.

The investigator's piercing gaze flickered through the window, and Toby whirled, pretending to shuffle inventory, praying to the gods that she didn't know he was there. But she had to. She had to! Nothing Mrs. Pinne ever did was an accident; everything followed the weave of her design…

He turned back around—oh, thank the gods, she was facing away.

Unfortunately, Pinne placed a casual hand to the window frame behind her back, where no customers sat or could observe. Strings snaked out of her sleeve—glimmers, almost like mirages. Tiny bundles of threads wafted up the building's side, little poofs of fuzz floating on an unseen breeze, easily missed by the untrained eye. They settled in subtle gutters and nooks out of view, where they could wrap themselves tightly—the hell…? Were those artifice servants? Fibercraft *spying* constructs?

Pinne spun and walked off like she had somewhere else to be.

Toby's phone was up to his ear by the time the edge of her coat whipped out of view. It rang twice before silence filled the breach. "Hello?" Toby tried. "Hello? It's—"

"*Tobias Caldwell.*" How dare Caleb sound positively delighted. "I admit, I hadn't expected you to call so soon. Did you want to meet?"

"Er…I…" Toby rallied. "Agatha Pinne was just at the café."

"Oh? What did that old spider want?"

The flippancy nearly made Toby stall out again. "I don't know; she's done some enchantment. I think she might have gotten wind you were in the area. Or she's here for me. Either way, you probably won't want to come back."

"Hm. Odd!" Was he put out about this *at all*? "Circled the perimeter, I take it? Deployed some threads?"

"Yes! She—"

"When is your shift over?"

"Two hours?"

"Perfect. I can fix the matter and buy you a drink for the trouble. Hold things down until I get there. But don't go outside—I'll see you and your smile after you hang that apron up."

"…uh…but…?"

The line had already gone dead. Toby stared at his phone, flummoxed. What? *What?* All the coiled gray tension of Pinne's intrusion evaporated, and his brain wasn't sure what to *do*.

Had Caleb just arranged an after-work date with him?

Maybe?

What?

Still floundering, Toby carried out the remainder of his shift.

Several times, he considered sending a questioning text, but pulling up the app made his thumbs feel stupid. A trip to the restroom made him feel worse. He was in no condition to meet and converse with anyone; his beard was uneven and his shirt was getting a hole in the armpit. Great. Under the unflattering fluorescent glow, he wondered if it might not be smarter to run out the back, pack his things, and drive to some other city.

As if he'd been anywhere else in his life.

Toby slapped his face a few times, remembering nothing could be built on panic. He had to slow down. *Think*. Breathe, before anxiety made his chest ache again.

Slowly, his fingers traced meditative runic drills on the edge of the sink. Forward. Left. Back. *Ush. Kratyl. Sensho.* He'd written them ten thousand times each—it was expected that every mage-in-training be capable of perfect rune-writing blindfolded and drunk. And now, even without power behind them, they soothed. Channeled his stress.

Okay. He could loosen one or two buttons at his throat, right? Change up the work look a hair. Then, he could borrow a sharpie from his manager and scribble some sigils of danger-warding in discreet places. He had to remember he wasn't powerless, even if the first spell he'd done in three years had been last night. He could still feel the memory in his hands: the warmth, the connection, the sheer, laser-focused, beautiful intent to make the world a little better, a little more harmonious, even if it was just by creating a perfect cup of coffee.

Caleb arrived promptly as the shift ended, as Toby stayed fixated on the west-side glass. Like Pinne, he was dressed warmly in a wooly coat against the cold patter of rain; unlike her, he wasn't the least covert about his oddities. He gawked at the roof while adjusting his bright-red scarf, then traced in the air with his fingers like a man on some sort of drug.

And yet people kept walking by, forgiving his strangeness as just one more day in the city.

Suddenly, in the brief catches of light drifting between the clouds, Toby saw them: Pinne's silken creatures falling dreamlike and thick. Caleb kept chanting. Unspooling, shimmering, they melted around his face like strange snow—and he beamed up high, his smile almost child-like, bright and wondering. The passersby probably only saw something like wayward dandelion puffs on the wind. Toby's heart skipped a note.

Then, the constructs were gone. All that remained was a man bouncing backward around the shop, fingers waving as if conducting some invisible symphony. The warm undertones of his cheeks were bright from the cold air as he finally entered the store.

"It's taken care of," he said simply. "You done for today? Come sit."

"...are you sure it's okay?"

"Of course. And besides, I have a tattoo of Morton's Greater Scrying Ward. While you're near me, even Pinne's creatures couldn't get a good look at you."

Toby's brow furrowed. "That...that's a complex...you have it *tattooed*...?"

"Yes, and I've been known to let those I particularly like sometimes have a peek." Caleb winked and sat.

The hot flush haunting Toby's ear-tips set up permanent residence. He sat, too, not knowing what else to do. "I, uh...don't suppose you need more caffeine?"

"Always. And, as I promised, I'm going to buy you something. Wait here."

"Okay?" Toby wasn't sure he wanted anything, but Caleb didn't ask. When he returned with two orders—one a whipped-cream-and-sprinkle-topped monstrosity for himself, the other a far less flashy Americano roast—Toby was too perplexed to pick the gesture apart. Plain coffee? Nothing in it?

Cheap, if this was a date.

So he fidgeted with the cup, though he nodded his thanks. It wasn't easy for him to fight back his social awkwardness; he'd been trapped in a box of paranoia for years and hadn't tried making a friend in a very long time. "I...well...I'm sorry. I'm bad at this. Caleb...may I call you Caleb?"

"I have no idea what else you'd call me."

"It's just..." Toby's lips twitched up in spite of his mood. "You really want to get to know me better?"

Caleb shifted in his seat. "I suspect you're a man who can weave a damn fine bit of transformational arts. Of course I'm interested. And you know...Pinne's sort aren't the only kind of mages in the world—or even this city. Truly, I mean you no harm. I say this because I'm wondering how many temporary wards you've put on yourself today."

Another flush. "Not *that* many."

"You're almost buzzing!"

Toby deflated somewhat.

"Tobias... *if* I may call you *Tobias*." Those teeth flashed merrily once more.

"...just Toby..."

"Toby—if I make you uncomfortable, I can leave." Caleb's thumbs started to fidget, then his middle and index finger followed suit, tracing patterns in the table.

Runic drills. Forward. Left. Back. *Ush. Kratyl. Sensho.*

Oh! He was...nervous? Somehow, that filled Toby's chest with unexpected warmth. Caleb seemed so untouchable. For him to be nervous...

"It's okay. Really. I just...if you can't be scryed, then what was Pinne doing here?"

Caleb stared ruefully into his sprinkles. "My fault. Someone I'd given a lift to snatched my lucky charm from under my truck's passenger seat, and with it gone, the Guild's locators could get a sense of what region I was in. Very rude. I fixed it."

Toby sighed gratefully: he remained safe. They hadn't found him. The soothing clink and bustle of the coffeehouse was a fine balm to his nerves, too; there was security in its familiar rhythm. "I'm sorry. Something's also killing me: do you really have Morton's Greater Ward tattooed—"

"You only get to ask *where* if I'm also allowed a personal question."

A feathery flutter lit up Toby's chest. "All right."

Caleb leaned in, crossing his arms, and whispered intensely, "Very well. Yes, I do. It's on my ass, so I can invite those Guild bastards to kiss it when they get too nosy." He erupted in infectious snickers, and Toby croaked out something startled and scandalized and dangerously amused. He hadn't expected this glimmer of down-to-earth humor to exist alongside all Caleb's dangerous slinking about, and he didn't know what to *do* with that revelation. "My turn. You obviously have some talent for magic. Truly. Best coffee I've ever had. But you never made it out of an apprenticeship—the Guild shut you out *hard* for making them look a little awkward."

Awkward. That was...one word for it. Two of the Elders had been using mind spells on local politicians, and Toby had sort of...loudly insisted they not.

"I think they knew there was something special to you. So tell me…what was it you wanted to study most? What did they stop you from achieving?"

"…I…don't know if I have a good answer…"

"It's magic. There aren't wrong answers."

Sipping his coffee, Toby winced. Urgh. Bitter. "I don't know; I mean, my most memorable assignment was modifying a car exhaust pipe so it could shoot birds."

"Not quite what I asked," Caleb said with a soft laugh.

Toby curled in on himself.

"You know…I've got this old friend, Dorokhov. He liked fusing pigs and pigeons into half-ton chimeras." Caleb's nose scrunched in merry disapproval. "I'm pretty sure one or two of his train wrecks are still trundling around in Siberia, forging local legends. So you can see I won't judge you. Go ahead. Tell me what you wanted to do."

"Ah. Well. I…I mean, I was still an apprentice when I left. My mentor was an investigator for magical crimes, and wanted me to follow suit, but…"

"No wonder you're so cautious! Trained to be a magic cop."

"No!"

"Magic cop!"

"I…" Toby huffed a chuckle, then stared down at his feet, embarrassed. "Maybe the coffee gives it away. I wanted to *specialize* in transformative arts," he admitted.

Caleb considered this answer a long moment—Toby understood; most people made assumptions about why he was interested in transformation the moment they noticed the binder straps on his shoulder and too-patchy beard still growing in on his chin. But magic to enact such complicated and delicate changes on the human body was no small thing, and Toby hadn't wanted to endure thirty years of study to figure it out. He'd gone the way of mundane doctors, as most had before him.

"Transformation's not a cash-cow field," Caleb finally said, tilting his head.

He was right; most applications were too noticeable for the Guild to allow them in non-magical society. "Well…I actually wanted to…" Toby swallowed. "…to see if it could quietly be applied to gene editing. I have part of a biochem degree under my belt."

"Good gods…that's more than I expected. Medical therapies?"

"Yes, by altering small groups of cells that propagate. Manageable!

Theoretically. I never got far; I mean, things went down at the Guild well before I had a proof of concept."

An awkward quiet bloomed: a moment of silence for a dead dream.

"You know," Caleb whispered. "It's for the best."

"Hard to feel that way most days." The crack of loneliness was impossible to bury.

"But you're free." Caleb reached out then, took his hands. It was warm, shockingly intimate, even though it was only a light cradle. And somehow, inside it…Toby felt the flicker of the sigil he'd cast…like it had absorbed into Caleb's blood from that coffee, a spark of magic he'd gifted that was now gifted back to him in turn. His tight chest eased. The stinging beginning in his eyes faded.

He'd stood on his own without the Guild every day since that wrong. The hurt mattered, but it was old news, and it didn't define him.

"Imagine being under the thumb of people like that for the rest of your life," Caleb continued. "It's more dangerous out here, sure. It's harder. But one can get by." He released his friendly grasp. "Promise."

"Do you…" Toby felt out, "…have your own suppliers? Independent of Guild contacts…? How is it that you just…?"

"Of course; I have some friends who can hook you up if you'd still like to tinker! And I can bring you into the circle. Psh. You don't even need to ask. I just had to be sure you had the backbone to do something with it." Caleb waved a dismissive hand like this was all expected.

But it wasn't. It was offering water to a man dying of thirst.

"What's the catch…?" Toby said. "There has to be a catch. I'd never find the black markets on my own."

"No catch! I mean—yes, I *will* try to persuade you to enjoy a quiet *discussion* about it with me in one of our private homes, eventually. But that's entirely separate." Caleb rolled his eyebrows in a charming wave.

"I…maybe I…wow. I think I need to think…"

And those eyebrows just kept going! Wouldn't quit! *"Please do.* Now…may I offer a lift? You seem tired from your work."

Toby straightened—Caleb really had just wanted to get to know him a little today? Just…flirt and offer genuine help, then give him space to think about it?

Truly nothing like the mages of the Guild!

"I'd like that," Toby rasped. "Thank you."

A warm hand of solidarity grasped his shoulder for a moment.

"Come on."

Together, they walked toward Caleb's old truck, its large presence almost bullying the cars parked beside. Toby realized, to his surprise, that he felt relaxed, a crisp drizzle lighting on his brow. He felt safe around Caleb, a man who could be playful and decent despite his reputation—and they were safe from scrying eyes, too.

Maybe Caleb...maybe he had his reasons for being on the outs with the Guild. Maybe it was more complicated than Toby knew, or that he had the right to ask about...yet he wanted to, eventually.

He wanted to truly get to know Caleb too.

Before either of them could peel away for the vehicle doors, Caleb poked the plain coffee Toby cradled still. "Actually, I'll need a quick payment. I'd like you to show me that spell you did last night." Toby nearly fumbled the cup into the gutter. "Go on. No one's watching!"

Was he serious? Apparently...yes. He pressed closer, until Toby could feel the warmth of the drink inside his palms and of the chest against his knuckles. Their foreheads nearly touched. *Okay*, Toby suddenly agreed. Despite his nerves, he already felt the magic fizzing at the base of his brain stem and in his fingertips, lightheaded and wild. Heck, if Caleb had asked him to do a bank heist, he might have nodded. And this task, it was everything he wanted to do anyway. That last spell had been like breathing. It had been what he was born for, a shot of lightning in his blood: magic, joy, creation. He didn't even have to think; its light was the smallest burst of sunshine in his hands, tracing itself into the cup and sparking fires in Caleb's dark eyes.

The light faded, and Toby found he was giggling like a child with a secret. The sigil disappeared after searing itself into his gaze, memory, and heart.

Caleb took the cup, smiling too, broad and proud—and after he sipped, when those eyes fluttered in pleasure again, Toby's joy soared. "Oh, goodness. Perfect. You want to try...?"

"Yes! Of course I—"

Caleb leaned in and softly pressed their lips tight. It was so sudden, so brash and breathless, that Toby nearly jumped. That kiss, that tongue, that breath...it was all sweet cinnamon and rich sandalwood, perfectly melded, spiced by a question and a taste of arcana that sizzled into Toby's blood and made him feel like he could fly.

Not a single bitter note.

His eyes fluttered shut. He wanted to drown in this cologne and this promise that he wasn't entirely alone in this world.

But Caleb drew back, smiling in that devil's way of his. "See? It's good." Quietly, his knuckle edged against Toby's hand: another question. An offer.

Toby took it. The world seemed balanced and perfect and right…even if it was an impulsive decision…he wanted to let his walls down just a little longer. He wanted to enjoy this.

They finished their drinks, and he invited Caleb up his apartment's rickety, old stairs, those agile steps seeming to dance behind him. Toby traced a ward of silence on his door, and that night, he traced *harmony* onto Caleb's back, into his hair—onto both of them, and his guilt and fear of the past years were gone. And in the morning, he pulled Caleb close, heart beating slow and steady and true.

The apartment was warm in a way it never had felt before, like an entirely new space. Maybe that's what the transformational arts were. Today, Toby didn't feel like the same man he'd been yesterday, not at all.

"If you're off work…would you be up to meeting some of my connections?" Caleb whispered. "No pressure. I just think you shouldn't waste your talent going forward."

Somehow, Caleb still tasted of sugar and medium roast. Toby marveled at it before pulling away from his lips again. "Yeah. I'd like that."

"Mm." Caleb's smile glittered again, and this it seemed so genuine and lazy-happy. As he stretched, working out the cricks in his back, he was beautiful. "All right. But first, I'll need some coffee."

"No worries," Toby whispered, kissing his brow. "You relax. I'll make some."

(ONFLUENCE

PUCK MALAMUD

bipoc, coffee shop, creature transformation (animal), daoist, death of a child (mentions of), f/f, harm to animals, interspecies relationship, magic use, modern with cultivation, murderer, mythology (chinese), mythology (slavic), nature spirit, reunion, restaurant, russia, third person limited (alternating) point of view

"Oh, I'm so sorry!"

Alisa Rusakova groaned at the coffee stain sinking into her blouse, turning the embroidered pink-and-green flowers beige. She lifted her head, mouth opening with an invective before she met her inadvertent assailant's eyes.

In front of her was a round-faced Asian woman, looking at Alisa with a stricken gaze. She was about Alisa's height, wearing a soft-looking purple sweater; the front-most tresses of her long black hair, sleek and shining in the café's overhead lights, were pulled back into a mal'vinka[1] hairstyle. Alisa would think her beautiful if not for the confusion of emotions on her face.

"Are...you all right?" Alisa asked, caught by that inexplicable expression—grief? shock? sorrow?

Then, just as inexplicably, her face transformed, eyes and mouth forming arcs of open delight.

"It's you!" she exclaimed. "You're alive!" Her free hand lifted toward Alisa's face and then faltered. "But I thought you were human."

---

1 мальвинка (mal'vinka): a hairstyle for long hair, where the front tresses are tied together behind the head while the rest of the hair hangs loose

"Wh—?" Alisa spluttered. She grabbed the other woman's hand where it had frozen centimetres from her face and dragged her out of the way of the other customers. "Keep your voice down," she hissed. "Who the fuck are you?"

"Oh, uh, Liran," she said. Her accent was Russian, but not her name. Chinese, if Alisa ventured a guess. "Liran Yan. I'm— You saved my life! It was, well, it was a hundred years ago, and I look pretty different now, but—"

She must. Alisa would *definitely* remember saving the life of a girl this vivacious, even with a hundred years distance.

Liran was *still* talking, words pouring over themselves with the kind of nervous energy Alisa most associated with the youngest rusalki, the ones who lived in young mountain springs, deer-swift and hungry. Alisa had once had many sisters quite as beautiful as Liran, the better to lure landfolk into the river.

"Look," she said, cutting Liran off. It was too late to deny anything, her reaction too compromising, but she could still do damage control. "We can't talk about this here. Why don't I buy us some coffees and we can start over?"

"Oh!" Liran exclaimed. "I can't let you do that. I ruined your pretty blouse. Let me at least buy your drink."

Alisa pursed her lips. Well, nothing ventured, nothing gained. "How about I replace your coffee, and in exchange, you clean my shirt?" Luckily, she always kept spare clothes in her messenger bag, just in case. "I'm Alisa, by the way."

"Alisa," Liran repeated, brightening. "Sure, sounds great."

Liran watched Alisa head to the washroom, pulling a blue T-shirt out of her bag as she went.

She tried to ease the flickers of doubt running through her now that her initial excitement had faded. Fox eyes and human eyes perceived very differently, and it had been so long ago…Liran couldn't be sure she remembered correctly. So she looked again, filling in details that had faded with the years or that she'd never known.

Alisa had fair hair—that strange intermediate colour between blonde and chestnut—and pale, lightly freckled skin. She was of a height with Liran but gave the impression of being taller, with her long, narrow limbs, like the hooded cranes that used to alight for a rest in Shifu's garden[2]. (In the early days of her cultivation training, Shifu had a senior disciple supervise her meditation in that garden. It must have made quite the picture—the fox and the cranes and the stern-faced Daoist.) Alisa's face was angular—high cheekbones, sharp jaw. Her mouth was wide, though, made for laughing, for all that she'd been grim during their whole exchange.

But Liran remembered the laughter that long-ago day, one that had started out as the worst of her life.

Liran still dreamed of it sometimes, could still hear the baying of dogs, those long-nosed Borzoi hounds with their persistence and pack instincts and sharp teeth. And behind the dogs were the men with their rifles. The shots sounded like trees exploding in the too-cold Siberian winter, and the bullets, when they connected, hurt worse than anything she'd experienced before or since.

When she came upon a narrow brook, she leapt in without hesitation. She paddled through the freezing water with her wounded leg, hoping against hope that it would be enough to escape. That hope was rewarded, for the moment her back paws touched the far bank, she heard a canine yelp, abruptly stifled, and turned to see the brook had risen behind her, the lead dog pulled under by a sudden current. The others stopped short, not wanting to risk the treacherous waters.

Liran kept moving, relieved that the pursuit was stalled but knowing she was not yet safe. She limped through the underbrush, slower now as relief stole her strength.

It was then that she came upon the girl. She wore a light sarafan[3] in bright colours and was laughing as she leapt down from a tree branch. Her laughter rang through the woods like chimes, carefree, at odds with Liran's terror and pain.

"There, little fox!" she said in Russian. Then her expression changed, her mouth shaping into a near-perfect "O." "But you're hurt!"

Liran had ignored the pain as best she could, too focused on her escape, but with the girl's words, she felt it again, stronger than ever. She

---

2 师父 (shifu): teacher

3 сарафан (sarafan): a long jumper dress that forms part of the Russian folk costume

stumbled, and then growled warily as the girl stepped closer.

The human held her hands up placatingly. "Let me help you," she said. "I can hide you from those men and their dogs."

Liran hesitated—torn between the promise of safety and the wary mistrust that had been her watchword for five years—but she could feel the pain of her wounds, the bullet in her leg. She kept up the low rumble in her throat, unwilling to express surrender, but she didn't try to bite the girl. The girl's arms were surprisingly strong; she picked Liran up and carried her to a place where the trees grew close together. They hid a clearing with their intertwined branches, beyond which Liran could still hear the brook.

"You'll be safe here," the girl murmured as she set Liran down.

In the weeks that followed, as Liran healed in that little clearing, an ember of determination lit inside her. Before, all Liran had known of humans was anger and hurt. This human girl taught her that there was kindness, too—hiding her from predators, binding her wounds with gentle hands, bringing her food.

Liran swore that she would find a way to take human form and repay that gift.

Alisa took her mocha from Liran, exchanging it for her stained blouse. Alisa could take the water out of it herself—easy, even with no waterway to fuel her power—but removing the coffee residue required mundane skill rather than rusalka magic. She was happy to hand that task off to someone else, even someone who…knew her from Russia? Knew what she was?

But no. *I thought you were human.*

Liran had been *surprised* to see her, surprised to find her still alive a hundred years after their supposed first meeting.

If nothing else, Alisa was curious. She hadn't met another non-human person in decades. The mermaids here in the West lived far out to sea. The rusalki back home were tied to their rivers and streams, those who still lived. Alisa had spent a long time hiding what she was, blending in among humans, making up for centuries of mischief with a century of better deeds.

She wondered what Liran was, *who* she was.

They found a spot in the park a few blocks away from the café. Alisa sat down, resting her elbows on the table, cradling her disposable cup in both hands as the chocolatey steam wafted toward her.

"All right, then," Alisa said once she was certain there weren't any humans within earshot. She spoke in Russian, too, for added security. "Explain."

"What's there to explain?" Liran asked, shrugging. "It's as I said—you saved my life. I owe you a debt of gratitude, one I never thought I could repay, thinking you a mortal girl. But look at you! Here now, all these years later and kilometres away—you look and sound just the same." She tilted her head consideringly. "Except you smile less."

Alisa froze at that, a hot wash of anger rushing through her body. She had no idea what her face was doing, but her expression wiped the easy smile off of Liran's face. She set her cup down carefully before she crushed it.

What did this strange girl think she knew about Alisa's smile? What right did she have to comment on her affect?

"Did I say something wrong?" Liran ventured after a moment of tense silence.

Alisa shook her head sharply and took a sip of her mocha, buying time. "Forget it," she said, unable to soften the harshness of her tone. "It's a good story, but I've never seen you before in my life."

"I did say I look different, didn't I?" Liran spread her arms wide; Alisa winced in anticipation of another coffee mishap, but this time Liran managed to gesture broadly without spilling a drop.

Alisa raised a challenging eyebrow. "Then what *did* you look like a hundred years ago, Miss Yan?"

The corner of Liran's mouth tipped up into a smirk. "It might be better to show you," she said.

Alisa found herself leaning forward across the table, as if Liran were about to dispel a glamour. Anticipation coiled in her belly; it didn't help that Liran's smirk was quite attractive. She had this strange mix of nervousness and confidence, compelling in its contradiction.

"Do you know the park at the north end of the city?" Liran asked. "With the triumphal arch at the entrance?"

Alisa leaned back in her seat again, frowning. "What about it?"

"There's a wood, deeper in the park."

"I know it."

"Let's meet there tonight." Liran leaned forward, mimicking Alisa's earlier posture. Her gaze was direct, her smile inviting. "I'll give you back your blouse—clean, I promise—and you can see exactly what I am."

Alisa toyed with the little plastic tab on her coffee lid as she thought it over. There was no denying the pull in her heart toward Liran: this supposed connection to her past, the secrets they both held…and, well, her attraction, too.

"All right," she said. "I'll meet you there."

Liran beamed. "You won't regret it! Nine tonight, all right? There'll be fewer people around after dusk."

Liran sat on the bench in the fading light, Alisa's freshly cleaned blouse folded neatly beside her as she watched the path into this section of the park, jiggling her legs impatiently. She tried to wait calmly, but the minutes until their meeting dragged. She jumped to her feet, the nervous energy driving her into motion. This would be the first time since leaving North Wudang Mountain that she would show someone her native form.

What would Alisa think?

Would she remember Liran and their time together?

Was she even going to come?

Liran paced worriedly, alternately making a circuit of the benches and zigzagging between them.

When she had first arrived at North Wudang Mountain, she'd already had her second tail, proof that her untutored attempts at cultivation were going in the right direction. The old daoshi[4] had recognized from the beginning that she was more than a normal fox. It had taken time to convince him to take her on as a disciple, but the flame of her life debt had burned in her heart, spurring her on through his trials. Shifu understood jiuming zhi'en[5], but he'd warned her that she might never have a chance to repay it.

Will you be satisfied with your cultivation if the only result is living a worthy life? he'd asked.

Liran had thought she would, but when she went down the mountain after attaining the human form she'd coveted, she went back to Russia

---

4 道士 (daoshi): daoist priest

5 救命之恩 (jiuming zhi'en): the debt for saving a life

first. Some part of her had always been searching for Alisa.

She shook off the recollections and sprang onto the back of her bench. Walking back and forth along it like a balance beam took up enough of her concentration that she missed Alisa's arrival.

"I didn't think coming out as a gymnast required this much secrecy." Her enren's[6] voice rang across the path, as clear and high as that first "little fox," though the dry amusement was new.

Liran wobbled before she caught herself, scooping up the blouse as she hopped off the bench and came to a stop in front of Alisa.

"You came!" she exclaimed. "I wasn't sure you would." She felt herself smile, too wide, too eager, entirely out of her control. "Here." She held the blouse flat across her palms like an offering. "Before I forget."

"Thank you." Alisa accepted the blouse and put it in her messenger bag. She didn't check for the stain. Liran wondered what that meant—a show of trust?

"Shall we?" Liran asked, tilting her head toward the trees.

"Let's." Alisa's eyes—green, Liran remembered from that morning, and wasn't *that* a benefit of having a human shape? Learning the colour of her enren's eyes—narrowed, and she walked down the paved path into the denser wood.

Liran hurried after and quickly overtook her. Once they were farther in, she led the way off the path into the trees. Alisa followed wordlessly.

After traversing the forest after Liran for a while, Alisa spoke up. "I'm beginning to think that I wronged rather than helped you in the past, and that you've lured me out here for revenge."

Liran laughed. "I have not lured you out into the woods to find a secluded place to strangle you."

"Have you heard of the Suspiciously Specific Denial trope?" Alisa retorted.

"No," Liran said, and then, apparently judging that they were far enough off the path, stopped and turned to Alisa. "I guess I haven't been human long enough yet."

"Not human—?" Alisa broke off as Liran transformed before her.

The light of the moon above collected around Liran, soaked into

---

6　恩人 (enren): the person to whom one owes a debt

her. Between one breath and the next, where a woman had stood, there was now a fox—silver fur shading to black on her muzzle, so that in the moonlight-dappled woods, she seemed almost a ghost. Five tails waved behind her like riverweed in an invisible current.

"Oh," Alisa breathed. "It's *you*."

Alisa remembered the fox, of course. Though she'd only had the one tail, then.

Rescuing the fox had been a whim, as so many of her decisions were in those days. She had been dangling upside down from the branch of a favourite tree when she heard the sounds of a hunt, felt fox feet splashing in her water, and decided to cause some trouble. Humans seldom came out as far as her little brook—a tributary of a tributary of a tributary of the Amur—so Alisa usually had to travel downstream to one of her sisters' waterways if she wanted to do them mischief.

It was the work of a thought to melt enough snow farther upstream to turn her brook into a deluge. The lead hound was swept away by it, and she laughed at the men's consternation.

She was still laughing when she slid off her branch, flipping neatly to her feet before the fox. She hadn't expected the concern that washed over her when she saw the fox's limping steps, the blood matting its fur.

She cradled the fox to her chest, ignoring the bloodstains on her sarafan—she'd stolen it off a clothesline and could steal another if need be. The bower where she hid the fox was her particular secret. Her brook ran near it but not through it, and few other rusalki came this far.

The fox snapped at her when she dug the bullet out of its leg, but weakly. She tore the sleeves off her sarafan for bandages and wrapped the fox's leg and side, working more from instinct than experience.

Thus began a strange period of Alisa's life. She gathered wild berries and snapped small animals' necks. She lay on her belly in the bower for hours, watching the fox eat and take halting steps on its healing leg. She didn't meet her sisters for weeks. Alisa had never been so invested in another creature's well-being. But having rescued the fox, she wanted to know that her efforts were not in vain.

The first time the fox touched her, bumping its forehead against her hand, Alisa squeaked in surprise. The fox shoved its muzzle into Alisa's hand more insistently, and Alisa tentatively stroked the black fur nearest its nose. After that, the fox would take the berries directly from Alisa's hand, and Alisa would bury her fingers in its fur, relishing the soft, fluffy texture.

The day the fox left, it twined around Alisa's ankles, rubbing its silky fur against Alisa's bare calves, before turning to face her. It chattered at Alisa, the way foxes do when fighting, but Alisa had the distinct sense that the fox was trying to tell her something.

"It's time for you to move on, isn't it?" she asked. She crouched down to stroke the fox's silvery head and scratched the brown patch behind its right ear. "Be safe," she said. "Stay away from humans from now on, all right?"

The fox barked at her, licked the tips of her fingers, and leapt away. Alisa watched it go until it disappeared beyond the trees. Then, she walked into her stream.

"Where've you been hiding these weeks?" Nastya asked when Alisa swam down to the confluence of their streams where they turned into Dina's river. Alisa smiled, sly and secretive, the kind of smile she knew infuriated her sisters.

Dina shoved her hard until Alisa stumbled into a tangle of roots. "Don't be a brat, Liska."

Alisa scrabbled among the roots and threw a clod of wet earth in retaliation, and amid the scuffle that followed, Nastya's question was forgotten.

It would be years before Alisa understood how the fox had opened her heart.

Once again, Alisa squatted down, getting to eye level with the fox—with Liran. "You really did recognize me," she murmured.

Liran took three steps forward and bumped her muzzle into Alisa's hand. Alisa laughed at the familiar gesture and stroked the soft fur around her nose.

"You don't owe me anything, you know," she said quietly. "Or, I owe you as much, in a way."

Liran barked sharply, and then there was that light, coalescing around a fox-shaped shadow. Alisa watched raptly as the shadow twisted and lengthened, shifting into human form. Then Liran was before her, her cheek cradled in Alisa's palm.

Alisa snatched her hand back, blushing.

"What do you mean?" Liran asked, tilting her head just as she had in her fox form.

Alisa gripped her right wrist with her left hand; her fingertips tingled with the phantom sensation of Liran's skin. "Why did you think I was a mortal human?" she asked in turn.

"You looked, smelled, and moved like one." Liran shrugged. "What else was I to think?"

"*Smelled* like one?" Alisa exclaimed. For some reason, this, of all things, affronted her. "How on earth—"

"It was a hundred years ago!" Liran pitched forward, startling a yelp out of Alisa before she realized it was intentional. A moment later, Liran sprawled on the ground, grinning up into Alisa's face. "I was wounded! *I* don't remember the specifics. Have pity on me, sestrichka[7]. The impression I went away with was that a beautiful human girl saved my life."

Alisa huffed and shook her head, smiling despite herself. She set her hand on Liran's forehead, letting the shape of her skull curve her palm. "All right," she conceded. "It was a reasonable assumption."

Liran pressed her head into Alisa's hand, exactly the way she had as a fox a century ago. "So what *are* you?" she asked. "How did you survive 'til now?"

The smile dropped off Alisa's face. It was the logical next question, of course, but she still wasn't prepared to answer it. She'd kept her secret for so long—thirty years among humans, away from her own kind— that it stuck in her throat now.

Liran's grin faded slowly as the silence stretched out between them. She opened her mouth to say something, and then her stomach growled.

Alisa smiled again, wryly this time. "Perhaps it would be easier to show you," she said. She rose and held out her hand. "The park café should still be open."

Liran took her hand.

The park café *was* open. Liran followed Alisa back through the woods to the main road and into the centre of the park, where old-fashioned streetlamps lit an array of tables and chairs around a central structure.

---

7   сестричка (sestrichka): sister, diminutive

Running water flowed through a man-made channel, winding around the tables on the south side of the café before disappearing elsewhere into the park.

The gnawing hunger in Liran's stomach shouldn't have surprised her—her first time in years changing shape *would* take a toll. She tried to think past it, though, to figure out what Alisa was thinking.

The girl she remembered from those weeks in the forest had been carefree, generous with her time and her gifts, lighthearted even when she struggled. Liran had kept the memory of that girl in her heart as she toiled her way through unfamiliar practices that took her closer to humanity.

That playful girl was still somewhere inside Alisa, but now she was wary and skittish—teasing and defensive by turns. Liran wondered what had happened.

They ordered coffee and sandwiches—Liran ordered two—and then Alisa led them to a table near the artificial stream. She pulled out a chair for Liran.

Liran sat, blushing, and set her coffee down. "Thank you."

Alisa nodded and sat across from her, her back to the water. "Watch closely," she said.

She closed her eyes and took a sip of her ristretto. Liran leaned her chin on her hand and watched as instructed. For a long time, nothing happened. Alisa sat with the ceramic cup cradled in her palms, eyes closed. The streetlamps glowed above them. Customers chattered at the other tables over coffee and wine and food. The stream flowed merrily along.

Then, so gradually that Liran didn't notice it at first, the stream rose. The flow of water past their table slowed, and the buildup from upstream caused a wave to grow—rising, cresting, but not breaking. Liran's breath caught; she flashed back to the brook betraying the pursuing hounds. She'd thought nothing of it at the time, too focused on her own pain, but this—Alisa had done it.

Liran owed her more than she'd realized.

Alisa let out a sigh and set her cup down. Her eyes opened. Behind her, the wave broke at last, crashing against the sides of its bed before rushing on downstream. The lamplight glinted off foaming rapids. Alisa sagged, resting her elbows on the table between them.

"I'm—" she began. Her eyes were distant, fixed on a point *beyond*

Liran. "I was—I am a rusalka. That stream you crossed was my stream. I heard the shouts, felt your paws in it, and came to see."

"Felt my paws," Liran echoed. "But you were in a tree when I saw you!"

"Everything that happens in a rusalka's stream, from spring to mouth, she feels." Alisa broke off as a waiter brought their food.

Liran's hunger, momentarily distracted by the revelations about Alisa's nature, came back full-force, and she bit into her first sandwich with gusto, forgetting to thank the waiter.

"Your home stream—" Liran said with her mouth full, then swallowed when Alisa snickered. "Sorry. Your home stream is far from here, though."

Alisa laughed again, a hard, bitter sound this time. "My home stream no longer exists."

Liran froze halfway through another bite.

"It was a little more than thirty years ago." Alisa waved a hand, and Liran remembered herself and began chewing again. "I started losing touch with rusalki in nearby streams. When my downriver sisters and I looked for them… Well, the humans were dredging and damming and digging out new waterways, killing all the spirits in their way. The leshiye[8] were dying too. When it happened to me… What can you do? The machinery they have…it doesn't matter how old you are, how strong your magic." She gestured to the artificial stream behind her. "My stream died just as my sisters' did."

Liran grew cold at this recitation. Alisa's voice was full of old hurt. No wonder she didn't laugh as she used to. "But you survived?" It came out a question.

"This I owe you for, I think." Alisa's hands came back to rest around her half-empty cup.

Liran blinked and set aside her food, focusing on Alisa. "How—? What do you mean? I was long gone by then."

"I can't explain it," Alisa said, "but I am different, after you." She spoke haltingly, trying to explain something she had plainly never articulated before. "I came to think—that fox, she was a person with her own wants, and I began to notice—not only the spirits of the forest, but perhaps the mortal creatures were people, too. You drown a boy, it's funny

---

8   лешие (leshiye) (sing. леший (leshiy)): Eastern Slavic forest spirit

while he thrashes, but after—that's a person gone." Alisa shrugged; Liran hoped she hadn't flinched at that last bit. "Nobody thinks like that, you understand," Alisa continued. "No rusalka. We aren't—*weren't*—creatures who worried about others so much as the pleasure of the hour." She drained the last of her ristretto and set the cup down with exaggerated care. She hadn't touched her food. "I think, perhaps, by the end, I was not rusalka enough to die."

"Alisa, I—" Lost for words, Liran reached across the table to take Alisa's hand in hers. Alisa stiffened but didn't pull away.

"You asked what I am," Alisa said. Liran's heart clenched at the ache in her voice. "What's a rusalka without her stream?"

"Maybe," Liran said slowly, feeling out the idea as the words left her mouth, "you're not entirely rusalka, the same way I'm no longer entirely fox. Perhaps…you've been cultivating to a human shape." She said the phrase first in her teacher's Jin dialect, then translated to Russian as best she could.

Alisa blinked, brows furrowing. "How's that? I've been human-shaped all along."

"Perhaps not all of you." The more Liran thought about it, the more it made sense; she felt the excitement of discovery rushing through her. "Think about it!" she exclaimed, leaning toward Alisa. "When we were younger, we had no notion of past or future, of any concerns beside our own. But now—we think, we plan, we empathize. Rusalka streams must have strong natural spiritual energy or else you couldn't arise in them! It takes conscious effort to cultivate, of course, but isn't that what you described? You may not have known that's what you were doing, but you made it so you could survive the death of your stream."

"I'm glad this is so exciting for you," Alisa said snidely, straightening in her seat and pulling her hand free of Liran's.

Liran didn't know what she'd said wrong this time. "I spent a hundred years studying cultivation," she said, trying to sound placating. "Of course I find it interesting."

"Why did you?" Alisa asked. "You didn't have a—a stream."

"I wanted to take a human shape because I wanted to thank you personally. I didn't know then what it would take, or I might have found the prospect too daunting." Liran smiled at her own past naïveté. "You need time for it, time and lots of spiritual energy. The energy in your stream was all tied up with you, so I couldn't even sense it. But there's lots of places with strong natural spiritual energy between Siberia and Shanxi. I didn't know the first thing about cultivation, but these were enough to sustain me until I found a teacher."

"So you...taught me"—Alisa stumbled over the unfamiliar term—"cultivation without knowing it. Is that what you think?"

"Do you have a better idea?" Liran raised her eyebrows challengingly.

Alisa shook her head. "I have *no* idea. All I know is that after a while, it became too painful to be around the rusalki who still had their streams, so I went west, and for almost three decades I have been entirely alone. Until tonight, in all that time, nobody has called me sestrichka."

Liran swallowed and reached for Alisa's hand again; this time, Alisa gripped it tight.

"You're not alone anymore," Liran said. "I took this shape not knowing you were still in this world. Now that I've found you, I'm sticking around."

Alisa laughed, startled, disbelieving. "That's a hell of a declaration."

"You don't honestly think we're going to have two coffees and then never talk again, do you?" Liran ran her thumb along Alisa's knuckles. "After a hundred years and thousands of kilometres, we meet again—tell me it means nothing."

Alisa's mouth shut. She looked at Liran for long enough that Liran began to fidget, sure she'd overstepped again.

Then, Alisa shook her head. "Well, why not?" She squeezed Liran's hand, a smile growing on her face. "Liran, lovely fox, shall we traverse the forest path of life together for a time?"

Liran felt her face splitting into an answering grin. "That would be wonderful."

CONFLUENCE POEMS
PUCK MALAMUD

i.
my nam's rusalka,
and at nite,
i hear a hunt,
some beaste in flite,
and hounds' feet fall
upon the rocks—
i call the flood;
i sayve the fox.

ii.
my nam is fox,
and wen I see
the prettye girl
who rescued me,
and we goe out
on moonlit trailes—
i change my shaype,
show off my tails.

iii.
Я хочу быть такой, как Рони,
И бегать по дикому лесу.
Познакомлюсь я с северным троллем,
И в горную реку залезу.
Буду лазать как козлик по скалам,
Станут крепкими пальцы и ноги.
Подружусь с лисой и шакалом,
Буду спать у медведя в берлоги.
Буду красть у белок орехи,
И водой ручьевой наслаждаться;
Из скорлуп сошью я доспехи—
В чём ещё же я буду нуждаться?

⟨BREAKING BREAD⟩

BETH LUMEN

agender, angst (minor), baker, bakery, flirting, death of a parent (off-screen), f/nb,
fraught family dynamics, iceland, interspecies relationship, merpeople, past tense,
pining (mutual), politics speciesism, third person limited point of view

The summons arrived on an unceremonious Tuesday at dawn. Pale light
was only just starting to filter down through the water, but Adla could
already tell the sun wouldn't break through the thick cloud cover domi-
nating the sky. The water would stay murky, the dark corners of the sea
bottomless. The waves were choppy, churning with the power of viru-
lent wind and the spray of salt. Adla could practically hear Lilja's teasing:
"Stop frowning, love. We'll never get any customers with your cranky
waves splashing up over the tables!" But Adla couldn't help it, despite
the echo of her parent's voice in her mind.

There were always more tasks to accomplish, more problems to take
care of, more humans to placate and marbendlar to pacify.

The marbendlar bakery had been Lilja's lifelong dream and, secretly,
Adla's as well. Adla had been raised learning to bake at Lilja's side, to
prepare dough and pack it into the volcanic sands, to test the temperature of the ground and determine the length of time it would bake, the
way her family had done for generations. The best memories of Adla's
childhood couldn't be disentangled from the flavor of freshly baked fish
tarts and seaweed pastries, the scent of bread mixed with volcanic sulfur.
So, when the time came to name it, Adla's Bakery it became, informally
sealing her fate as its successor—to the eternal disappointment of her

other parent, who thought Adla's future lay in politics instead. As many marbendlar children left for other waters, shrinking the community, the bakery almost failed, but a decision made shortly before Lilja's death saved it.

They opened to humans.

Now, business boomed, and a steady flow of customers—human and marbendlar—made the trek to try the famous black bread and pastries.

Marbendlar came to see humans up close, many for the first time, gawking at how they awkwardly folded their legs under the stone tables. The humans gawked back, trying to touch the smooth, bald heads of the marbendlar, shocked when the stereotypical image they knew of mermaids with long, wavy hair proved false. They also invariably perceived marbendlar as female; Adla didn't understand gender, no matter how many times her human business partner, Saeunn, explained it. Nonetheless, she spent so much time around humans that she had come to think of herself in gendered terms when speaking their tongue. It was always something of a relief to return to marbendlar surroundings where she did not have to exist as something she was not.

Adla never felt that way with Saeunn, though. Saeunn was the only one, human or marbendlar, at ease navigating between the two disparate worlds. Adla's Bakery wouldn't have found success without her, and Adla dreaded telling her about the council summons.

Adla eyed the familiar signature mark on the stone message before flipping it over, her shimmering tail swishing through the water in displeasure at the sight of her parent's name, indicating Hekla's authorship of the summons. Unlike Lilja, Hekla's life had been consumed by maintaining human-marbendlar separation in the waters around what the humans now called Iceland. Every night as a child, Adla had fallen asleep to fairy tales describing the long-ago arrival of humans and the ensuing wreckage of the lands and sea: the capture of innocent marbendlar, the mutant half-children that were born, and the curses those children wrought. Every flood, earthquake, and volcanic eruption was somehow the result of their horrific existence, though no children had been documented in living memory. The stories always included the brave marbendlar fighting back, running the humans out, preserving the purity of the species, and prospering.

Lilja had served as a counterbalance, whispering anecdotes about the goodness of humans in Adla's ear when Hekla wasn't looking. But once

Hekla found out what Lilja was doing, and to whom the bakery was opening, it damaged their relationship beyond repair—and Hekla's rigidity only grew worse once Lilja was gone.

Adla sighed. It was time to go to work.

The swim to the bakery always felt long when she was running late. Adla broke to the surface of the water, scanning the shoreline. The serving counter, built from dark ocean stone, jutted out of the sand, oddly tall, with rows and rows of drawers and serving displays to keep the baked goods protected depending on the varying tides. Tables for patrons dotted the shoreline. On calm days, water lapped at their feet, nicely warmed by the volcanic gasses burbling up through the sands. But, on days like today, water crashed over the tables, leaving only the bravest humans to laugh and shriek as they attempted to eat their bread and scones. The rest complained, having driven hours to experience the marbendlar bakery yet too scared to enjoy the bread how it was meant to be enjoyed—damp with salt water. It was fine dry, Adla supposed, but if the point of visiting was to experience life like a marbendlar, she didn't understand why they clung so strongly to their own cultural norms.

A high, clear laugh skimmed over the surface of the water, drawing Adla's eyes. There Saeunn stood on the black sand shore in the shadow of the nearby volcano, her skin glacier-pale, with a long shock of dark hair and legs that went on and on. Adla was accustomed to seeing legs, now, but she always needed an extra moment when it came to Saeunn's, to ponder how someone could possibly move with such graceful ease despite such disproportionate anatomy.

Just as Saeunn's laugh reached Adla, Adla's gaze reached Saeunn. She found Adla out in the ocean, tossing her a wink and a smile while carrying on whatever nonsense conversation she was having with the idiotic tourists that seemed to require such massive gesticulations. It didn't matter who Saeunn was talking to or what about; she always seemed *happy*.

Adla might be jealous if she didn't have so many other issues to concern herself with.

Adla approached once the angry humans were out of sight. As soon as Saeunn noticed her swimming up to the shore, her eyes grew soft. Adla experienced a squirming sensation somewhere in her long torso at the sight of it, not uncommon when she was greeting Saeunn for the first time each day. It was perplexing how Saeunn appeared unceasingly delighted to see her. She must have long since gotten used to the sight of the marbendlar; she'd worked around them for over two years. But every time she spotted Adla, her eyes lit up like it was the first time.

Saeunn waded into the water to greet her; a shelf break enabled Adla to stay mostly underwater while Saeunn remained onshore. Adla tried to return Saeunn's smile, but her chest tightened as she remembered the summons, preventing her from making her expression convincing.

"I know it's choppy today, but I think you'll still have plenty of business. There's some adventure tour coming up, and I've already talked a few people into giving it a try. It's the same old song and— Oh." Saeunn paused, squinting down. "That's not what's upsetting you, is it?"

"I am concerned about the patrons, of course," Adla replied, uneasy. She had thus far managed to avoid involving Saeunn in marbendlar politics, but it was harder and harder every time something surfaced that threatened the bakery. "Among other things."

Saeunn's gaze was heavy upon her; Adla was drawn to meet it, something magnetic about the icy blue depths of Saeunn's eyes. Sometimes, they looked so incredibly similar to marbendlar eyes that Adla found a strange comfort in them. Like coming home.

Adla shook off the thought. Humans could not be farther from the reality of her home, no matter how familiar she and Saeunn had become to each other.

Saeunn studied her, then shifted her gaze up over the water. She often did this, leaving Adla unsure whether she had gone off into a daydream. Everything about her was ethereal and dreamlike, as though she'd simply appeared one day from some magical, faraway land, and sometimes still got lost there in her head. Adla waited more breathlessly than she cared to admit.

"Should I let the volcano take the bakery so we can finally run off and elope?"

The unexpected question pulled a helpless huff of laughter from Adla's lungs, relaxing the muscles of her face into something of a smile.

"Are you seriously implying you're the sole reason the volcano hasn't erupted on us yet?"

"Are you seriously ignoring my proposal? It took a lot of courage for me to ask you that." Saeunn's smirk contrasted with her pouty tone.

"Just wait, now you've probably activated some generations-long curse with your impertinence. By tomorrow we'll be lost to the lava."

"No, Adla, *they'll* be lost," Saeunn replied with a sweeping gesture around the bakery, one eyebrow flicking up, "but *we'll* be married and drinking cocktails in the Caribbean."

"The water in the Caribbean is much too warm. I'd melt. At least here, I can return home offshore, where it's cool."

"I've been trying to make you melt all these years, and only now you tell me you'd prefer freezing? You're impossible."

Adla was definitely smiling now, her cheeks warm and tail glowing, an involuntary response to the nonsense Saeunn loved spouting. She was trying to come up with a good return jab when Saeunn added, her voice gentler, "Tell me what's troubling you, love."

Adla bit her lip, wondering briefly if Saeunn called their other colleagues such affectionate names. "I don't want to worry you."

Saeunn barked out a laugh. "That you're concerned about that only worries me more."

Adla ran a hand over her head, then heaved a sigh. "I've received a summons to appear before the marbendlar Council of Elders."

Saeunn's lips pinched. "To commend you on your impressive business acumen, I presume? To recognize you for the wealth you've brought to your community?"

A sad laugh escaped Adla. "It's my last chance to testify in defense of the bakery before it's deemed forbidden. The Elders have been trying to reverse our work since the moment you, Lilja, and I began, and it seems as though they might finally succeed."

Saeunn was studying her again. "I'm sorry, Adla."

"I didn't want to tell you, but I suppose you should know you might need to start looking for new work soon."

"When's the meeting?"

"Next week."

"I should say, what is the exact time, date, and location?"

Adla furrowed her brow, dubious. "Why would those details matter to you? It's not as though you can attend an underwater marbendlar Council meeting."

"I may have an idea, but I'll need the details first."

"Humans are forbidden, Saeunn. Even if you were somehow able to breathe underwater, you'd be run out on sight."

"Adla." Saeunn glared at her; Adla glared back, but relented.

"It's next Saturday at one in the marbendlar Chamber of Commerce."

"Thank you." Saeunn's face softened. "Would you like any assistance preparing your testimony?"

The days continued to pass as they always did, though Saeunn stuck even closer to Adla's side than usual. They normally checked in with each other before opening, after closing, and throughout the day, but for a human who had to remain on land, Saeunn was oddly present in Adla's periphery. It was becoming…distracting.

"You're cute when you're concentrating," Saeunn commented, completely derailing Adla's calculations. It was only then Adla realized she had the tip of her tongue stuck out between her teeth as she added up their weekly profits.

"Must you interrupt me when I'm working on something?"

"Interrupting you is the most fun I get to have all day! Are you really going to take that away from me?"

"You're going to run this bakery into the ground."

"It already is in the ground. It's practically underwater, thanks to you."

It was a running joke of theirs, and entirely too stupid to justify the enormity of the smile on Adla's face.

"Is any of our traditional bread available for marbendlar guests," a low, haughty voice interjected, "or is it only for humans, now?"

The smile vanished.

"Hekla." Adla had not seen her parent in fourteen months. "I'm surprised you would debase yourself by coming this close to shore."

"I needed to speak with you," Hekla said. Hekla's eyes slid up to Saeunn, thigh-deep in the water. "And I can never find you at your home. Shall I follow you to the marbendlar-only area?"

Without waiting for a reply, Hekla turned and swam away.

"Holy shit," Saeunn mouthed at her. "Your mom?"

Adla grimaced and nodded, then waved as she followed Hekla into the water and around to the cove. Neither spoke again until no humans were in sight.

"Look at you, even performing human gestures now," Hekla said, somehow managing to sneer in voice alone. It felt like swimming into a lair of jellyfish. "You've changed so much, Adla."

"I've done what I needed to in order to keep Lilja's dream alive."

"I never see you anymore."

"Yet, somehow, you still manage to get your messages to me." Adla's jaw twitched. "I shouldn't have been surprised by the summons, but I was. How could you do this to me?"

"I didn't become the head of the Council of Elders by encouraging intermingling with humans. I have to do what's best for our people. I wish you wouldn't put me in this position."

"*I* put *you* in this position?" Adla's voice shook. She hated that her emotion rose to the surface so easily, like a piece of coral detached from its reef and carried away by the tide. "What about the fact that you're going to destroy my entire life?"

"You'll move on. Hopefully to a more acceptable line of work."

"No," Adla said. It was getting more and more difficult to pull enough oxygen from the water around her; she felt the sudden urge to surface, to break free from the weight of its depths. "It doesn't matter what I do. I'll always be a disappointment to you."

"You could still turn yourself around," Hekla said, "but I doubt it."

"Why are you here?" Adla asked abruptly. She'd grown accustomed to this kind of talk from Hekla throughout her life, but, after months of distance, it stung.

"I wanted to give you the opportunity to resolve this without the public humiliation of a Council summons. Although the Council insisted on sending the message, I believe I could convince them to work with you on reverting the bakery to marbendlar-only, if you're willing to be reasonable."

Adla stared, disgust curling up her throat. "Separation is no longer an option for the marbendlar. I would see the bakery destroyed before I would close it to humans."

"You sound like Lilja."

"I hope it was worth it," Adla spat out, no longer able to hold her fury in, "to lose your partner and your child in exchange for tenuous power over a dying community."

"Everything I've ever done has been to save our community and our people. I hoped one day you would see that."

"The opportunity to take over as head of the Council had nothing to do with it, I'm sure." Adla was so heated, she was surprised the water around her didn't boil. "The world has changed, and we're better for it."

Hekla's face strained. Adla yearned not to see herself so clearly in the familiar expression.

"I look forward to nothing more than seeing this bakery razed to the ground."

And you along with it, Hekla didn't have to add.

The night before the Council meeting, Adla found herself scrapping another bad version of the speech she had already tried writing countless times. There was no way she'd be able to pull this off. She'd never been good with words; her thoughts moved too fast for her to slow them down into oration.

Her mind worked well for dreaming up recipes, for writing business plans, for building and creating and enacting. It worked less well for…relating to others. And now, her bakery—possibly even her people's survival—depended on it.

Adla was more certain than ever that the future of the marbendlar lay in cooperation with humanity, but that didn't make her task at all easier for her. She wore the strict lessons of her childhood like a second skin. The very notion of humans still brought a chill of danger, as though she'd swum into deeper, darker waters without realizing it. But Adla was fighting that chill, and it grew less intense every day.

Saeunn, Adla knew, played a large role in that. She was the polar opposite of dangerous: bright, cheerful, kind, optimistic. And her eyes were so, so blue. It was hard not to trust those eyes.

Adla blew out a stream of bubbles. Spouting poetry about Saeunn's eyes wouldn't convince the Elders to allow the bakery to stay open. There was a bigger purpose to Adla's Bakery; it needed to be preserved, and not merely so she could continue working with Saeunn. What they had accomplished was historic—truly groundbreaking. Saeunn had understood that from the beginning. But it didn't matter how many times Adla tried to start the speech; the words simply wouldn't come. Hekla's doubt and disappointment lingered in every one.

How would she convince the Council of Elders when she couldn't even convince herself?

Adla arrived at the Council chambers aglow with trepidation, every muscle in her body fused with tension. A pause outside the entrance turned into a minute, and one minute into several—but putting off entering wouldn't make the meeting any easier, nor would delay save the bakery. Taking a deep breath, she swept through the entrance into the cavernous, rounded room framed by bright, multicolored coral. Fish swam happily in and out, ignorant of their surroundings.

The Council of Elders floated in their seats, each of them wearing a grim expression. Hekla barely acknowledged Adla as she entered the public area.

"Attention," Hekla commanded. "We call this meeting to order."

Adla barely heard a word as the meeting's business started, her mind occupied with her still-undecided testimony. The more time she'd tried to decide what to say, the more fighting the Council had felt like a lost cause. That felt even more true here and now, facing the Council of Elders and knowing her own parent was set to make a case against her.

"The main order of business today is Adla's Bakery, located on the sundown shore of the island. For two years, this business has wreaked havoc on marbendlar culture and privacy by exposing us, our people, and our ways to humans. It's only a matter of time before the issue becomes more serious and history repeats itself. Adla has come to speak on behalf of the bakery. Adla, you may take the stand."

"I wish to testify first." A high, clear voice rang out, as familiar below water as it was above. Adla swung around, her already-rapid heartbeat growing faster, battering her chest.

Saeunn entered the Council chambers, her dark hair streaming behind her and a long, orange marbendlar tail in place of her long, pale legs. Adla was frozen. It was impossible. Saeunn was human. Saeunn couldn't be here—least of all with a *tail*.

"I am Saeunn, Adla's business partner in the bakery. I've dealt with human relations since the bakery's inception. Those who know me have only ever known me as human. But the truth is, I'm the child of a forbidden human-marbendlar relationship, and I am both."

An audible reaction rose from the Council; Adla was stunned. There had been no record of human-marbendlar relations as long as Adla had been alive. Saeunn ignored the tittering and plowed on with the easy determination she had in everything she did.

"I've lived all my life in secret, unable to tell anyone the truth about who I am. Hearing the call of the water and putting on my scales at night to swim when no one is around. Am I such an abomination? What, exactly, is so horrifying about my existence? What harm have I done in being who I am? What harm did my *parents* do in falling in love?"

Adla was speechless, watching Saeunn gesticulating in that wildly human way, but *here*. Underwater, in the Council chambers, the very place where Adla had grown up, swimming around and hiding behind seaweed, blind to the damage caused by legends of unspeakable dangers and the isolationist policies and separation of their peoples. The reality of how harmful it was had felt hypothetical until this very moment—until Saeunn, with her marbendlar eyes and her long human hair, with her scales shimmering and her tail twitching with emotion. She was lit up, a flame in her eye that couldn't be doused despite the water surrounding them.

Adla's heart clenched.

"It was your *partner*, Hekla, who first told me that not all marbendlar believe the tales that have long been told about me and those like me." A collective release of bubbles went up from the marbendlar present as Saeunn addressed the head Council Elder. "Lilja helped my mother figure out how to raise a half-marbendlar child, because she knew there was nothing *wrong* with us. She had such high hopes that you would come to understand and use the power you wield in the community for good, the way she said you had done when you were young. She taught me the language and the ways of the marbendlar out of the simple belief that, one day, I would find a place with you. And I have."

Saeunn's gaze turned to Adla. Adla felt the other marbendlar eyes follow, electric, but was unable to look anywhere but at Saeunn.

"Adla's Bakery—*Adla*—gave me my first opportunity to move between the two worlds I've always been caught between. I was never fully able to exist in one or the other because I'm *not* just one or the other. But Adla's is the space between, and it's the only place where I've ever felt at home, because it's where I can be who I am. Not human, not marbendlar, but both. And who knows how many more like me might be out there? Forced to act like something they're not, to remain hidden? It doesn't have to be this way. Adla has proven that."

Adla finally tore her eyes away from Saeunn and looked to the Council—to Hekla. The parent she had spent her life battling, resisting, emulating, craving the approval of and always disappointing. Hekla's expression was inscrutable, as usual, but Adla saw a glimmer of something moving behind Hekla's eyes—something she didn't dare hope for. Not yet.

"Adla's Bakery will leave a legacy on Iceland, and on this earth, as the place where we finally made peace between two seemingly disparate worlds. If we let that peace come to be. If not, the generations of secrets and lies will continue, and those like me will be left again without a place. I'm begging you to permit Adla to continue her revolutionary work. And I will be right alongside her, helping to usher in a new time of change and cooperation using the simplest but most meaningful means possible: by breaking bread together."

Saeunn swam down from the platform. No one seemed to want to fill the space she left behind, as though her words still stood there, piling on top of one another, expanding to fill the chamber and crowd out the doubt. The only thing that could pull Adla from her reverie was Saeunn herself swimming over, her hair trailing behind her. It was the oddest sight, and it brought Adla back to reality.

She had a million questions, but she said, simply, "Saeunn."

"Adla," Saeunn returned, her smile tinged with nerves.

Hekla called the session back to order.

After the meeting ended, with a Council decision to come the following day, Adla returned to the bakery with Saeunn.

"Adla, I—"

"Fish tart?" Adla interrupted, swimming up to the drawers that held the day's baked goods.

Saeunn laughed, her tail sparkling underwater, and nodded. Adla took two and led them to a deserted table in the cove, water lapping gently across it in the high tide. They floated into their seats and inhaled the flaky pastries, not speaking until they were done. Then, Saeunn reached out and took Adla's hand in both of hers.

Adla's pulse spiked.

"I wanted to tell you. So often, I imagined telling you. I almost couldn't hold it in. But I was scared."

"Because you thought I'd break our work contract?" Adla said, blinking.

Saeunn shook her head with an urgency Adla didn't understand. "No. I wasn't—I mean, maybe I was worried about losing the contract. But mostly I was worried about losing *you*." Saeunn inhaled deeply. "Because I knew when you found out about me, I'd have to tell you the truth about everything."

"There's something *else*?" Adla wasn't sure she could take any more surprises.

"Yes. I couldn't say anything before. I feared you would be...disgusted. I know what you've been taught. But now that you know who—what—I am, I can't live with myself without you knowing." Saeunn's gaze was pleading, her dark eyebrows knitting up together.

"Knowing *what*?"

"That—I've fallen for you."

The oxygen in the air was no longer serving the purpose Adla needed. She dove underwater, sucking it out of the droplets instead, letting the ocean revive her. When she resurfaced, Saeunn looked comically terrified, eyes wide and mouth dropped open. Before Adla could respond, she continued, "I thought you might suspect. Because of the way I was with you. I couldn't help—"

"I wouldn't—I wouldn't even let myself think it," Adla said, trying to knock the dazed quality out of her voice. "Because I didn't think we could ever— I thought you just liked messing with me."

"I know," Saeunn said. Her lips twitched. "I mean, I do like messing with you. But I've always been in awe of you, Adla. Every second we spend together makes my life so much brighter. Being with you always feels like being home." Saeunn paused, casting her eyes down. "But I didn't want to put you in that position—"

"Saeunn," Adla interjected. Her heart was in her throat, threatening to spill out along with her words. Everything was binding together inside her, the way it felt to knead dough to the smoothest texture, the perfect elasticity, until she knew it would come out of the dark sand soft and toothsome with the crispest crust. "I know. I—I wouldn't let myself think it, but I think I always *knew*. Because I fell for you too. A long time ago. And the fact that you're part marbendlar—it makes things easier, but it doesn't change anything. You're still *you*, and I'd want you either way. Any way I can have you, and no matter what happens now with the bakery...I want to face it by your side."

Saeunn's smile was so bright it drowned out the sun.

"Will you—stay still—I need you to try this!"

"Catch me!" Saeunn flew by in a blur of orange tail and tinkling laughter. Adla managed to stretch out her hand and wrap her fingers around long strands of hair, effectively stopping her with a yelp. "That's cheating!"

"I knew that hair had to be good for something," Adla said. Saeunn closed the distance between them with a knowing smirk.

"I *know* that's not the only thing you like about it." Saeunn's eyebrow quirked. Adla's tail glowed.

"Try this." Adla shoved a piece of eel croissant in her mouth.

Saeunn chewed, tilting her head slightly to the side. "Can I get it a little less wet?"

"The fact that you prefer your bread dry is truly the most abominably human characteristic about you." Undermining her words, Adla slipped an arm around Saeunn's waist, pulling her closer.

"You have to take the good with the bad when you're mixing with humans and the human-adjacent." Saeunn's nose wrinkled. "Which you're going to be doing for a long time, now."

"I still can't believe it," Adla said, shaking her head.

Hekla had come to her the night after the meeting, looking smaller and more tired than Adla had ever seen before, and finally prepared to talk. Hekla had always been ambitious; Lilja had loved that, at first. The drive, the passion, how Hekla was always ready to do whatever was necessary to make a difference. As a couple, in their youth, they'd gotten involved in an underground human cooperation group, but Hekla became so afraid it would sour any chance at a political career that Hekla swung in the opposite direction and never looked back.

"It was purely ideological," Hekla had said, voice trembling. "I didn't realize there were real lives affected, lives that Lilja had helped. I didn't realize, until Saeunn."

The bakery would be safe.

"You're stuck with me." Saeunn sighed, releasing a stream of bubbles.

"It is a daily struggle." Adla tucked Saeunn's hair behind her ear.

"Your sacrifice is noble." Saeunn's palms on her scales felt hot, even in the cold water.

"Shut up," Adla said, then kissed her.

BREAKING BREAD
PREQUEL
BETH LUMEN

Adla hadn't been prepared for the legs that approached her at the shelf break that day. Long, pale, and bare, nothing but a small pair of shorts covering the tops of them. Adla had seen legs before; she had even met a couple of humans. But *Saeunn's* legs were something else entirely.

"Hi! Oh my God, it's so nice to meet you." Saeunn crouched down and held out her hand. Adla was momentarily distracted by the gesture, then returned her attention to examining the way the legs folded up to become smaller.

"I'm Adla," she said.

"I know. Your mom told me. I'm really excited about this idea." Saeunn sat right down in the water in her shorts.

"You'll get wet!" Adla warned.

"Who cares?" Saeunn's lips curved into a wry grin. "It's only water."

Adla knew then that Saeunn wasn't like other humans. With the legs submerged, she was marginally more able to focus. "Why did you hold your hand out to me?"

"Oh, it's a human greeting to shake someone's hand when you meet them! Sorry, I didn't even think about it." Her voice lilted with an unfamiliar accent, full of infectious enthusiasm.

Adla's gaze followed Saeunn's hands to her long, dark hair, which she was gathering up. In seconds, it went from flowing around her, the tips dragging in the water, into a small knot atop her head.

Saeunn must have caught her staring. She laughed. "You're cute. Have you met a human before?"

RAIN AND MOONLIGHT

LEX T. LINDSAY

baker, bakery, bipoc, bisexual, f/f, fat, magic use, past tense, pining (mutual),
reunion, second chances, witch

Sun. There'd been sun five minutes ago with nary a cloud in the sky.

Daisy's coven mother used to tell her the rain goddess favored her
more than most of her chosen. Iris's alleged favor was good for the
plants Daisy coaxed to life with her magic, but it was horrible when she
was already running late to work only to have the sky open up the moment she walked outside.

She'd need to order a broomshare. It couldn't be helped. Beneath her
apartment building's excuse for an awning, she dug through her bag,
pushing aside old receipts and keys. Beneath mail she'd been meaning to
sort through for at least a week, she found the small, branded crystal for
the Swyft-n-Lite service and gave it a squeeze, holding it until it pulsed
in her hand to let her know she'd joined the queue.

Pressing her back against the brick as much as she could, Daisy
sighed deeply and wished—for not the first time—that she was a different type of witch, the kind who could turn a small clutch purse into an
umbrella or a gutter into an awning. Or an awning into an even bigger
awning. The kind who could fly her own broom instead of relying on
Swyft-n-Lite. She pulled out the crystal again, the surface of it shifting
the moment it encountered her skin. Two small dots carved themselves
into the sapphire.

Two minutes. Two minutes, and she'd be secure on a broom equipped with a water-repelling charm. She'd tip an exorbitant amount if the witch flying it could charm her dry as well.

Raindrops marked the seconds, slanting sideways and soaking her to the bone. When the standard electric-blue shaft of a broom appeared, Daisy nearly sagged with relief.

"Well, well, well. Daisy Guthrie."

On the back of the broom, a witch pushed back the hood of her cloak to reveal a tangle of hair colored every hue of the rainbow.

Helix Andromeda patted the handle of her broom in invitation. Daisy swallowed hard.

Helix looked…well, she looked even better than she had when they went to college together, back when Daisy had harbored a massive crush on the girl who sat two seats down from her in Magical Ethics. The hair was different but not unexpected. Helix had always liked to play with magical body modification. Daisy had seen her hair sea-green and caution-yellow and—one summer session during Pride month—pink, purple, and blue all together. The Helix grinning at her from the back of a broom, both of her dark brown cheeks dimpled, had charmed her eyes today as well. In the natural near-black of her irises swam a cosmos of stars and comets that glittered and winked.

"You getting on?" Helix asked.

Daisy blinked at Helix from where she'd been frozen to the sidewalk, no longer concerned with the rain beating down on her favorite lilac sundress—homemade on her coven mother's vintage sewing machine because Daisy was sick and tired of fast-fashion plus-sized clothes that never accounted for fat arms. Laughing awkwardly, she clambered onto the back of the broom.

"I can dry you off, if that's okay with you?" Helix offered, already kicking off of the pavement.

"Please."

In one big rush, all the water fell from the hem of Daisy's dress. She supposed Helix could've muttered the proper spell beneath her breath, but some part of Daisy knew better. Helix had mastered silent casting in the years since graduation, and no, this utter display of competency in her field of magic was not going to drag Daisy's old crush up out of the soil like an old bulb bursting back to life. It wasn't.

"So, how long have you been doing this?" Daisy asked, intently focusing on the way the raindrops seemed to blur past them from within the cocoon of magic surrounding Helix's broom. It was that, or she might notice the way Helix's thighs looked when they flexed around the handle to turn this way and that. She'd rather walk to work in the downpour than take that dangerous road.

"A few years. Just off and on around holidays and special occasions. Gift giving as a love language, you know? What are you gonna do?" Helix shrugged in front of her and expertly maneuvered the broom between two buses, ignoring the way both drivers honked at her.

"What's the occasion?"

"Double full moon this month. Celeste is one of my patrons."

Daisy didn't ask any more on that. Relationships between a witch and a deity were sacred, the details of any rituals or requests often kept secret from everyone but their most trusted friends and family members. Daisy never talked about Persephone and Iris, either, and as much as she might have wanted to be that close to Helix many full moons ago, she wasn't.

With that sobering thought, the broom pulled to a gentle stop in front of Daisy's Delectable Desserts.

"I've seen this place a few times," Helix said, offering Daisy her hand to help her off the broom. "It always made me think of you, but I didn't realize it actually *was* you."

"Well…" Daisy did a little point-and-dance that she definitely would not lie awake thinking about for days on end. "Now you know."

Helix grinned at her and then got a faraway look in her cosmic eyes. "I still remember that one equinox bonfire. You brought…" Helix held up two fingers in the universal symbol for "very small."

"Pomegranate tartlets?"

"Yes! Perfect balance of tart and sweet, melt-in-your-mouth crust. I didn't know what fruit was in them, but I still dream about those tarts."

Daisy felt her cheeks warming. "Oh. Uh, yeah. Thank you." Smooth. "I have them. Inside, I mean. Well, not right now. But at spring equinox. And I have…I could make you some. Sometime. You know, before then. If you wanted."

Very, very smooth. Daisy wasn't going to get a full eight hours for days at this rate.

But if Helix thought she was being strange, she didn't show it. Instead, she gave Daisy a slight smile, warm as the reemerging sun kissing

Daisy's arms.

"I'll hold you to that, Daisy Guthrie." With that, Helix gave her a small salute and took off. A few seconds later, it started raining again; Daisy hastily retreated inside with at least two customers on her heels.

A week passed, giving Daisy just long enough to only barely obsess about how ridiculously she'd spiraled into a sapphic panic at seeing Helix again. She tried out a new recipe for a lemon-and-violet Danish. She tacked a new positive article about her bakery to the corkboard behind the register. And she worked on an elaborate three-tiered wedding cake, replete with two magical wizard statuettes the customers had provided, both of whom refused to stop kissing and dancing together long enough for her to actually place them.

She was halfway through pouring them a dance floor out of chocolate so they'd stop ruining her chai buttercream when the bell on the front door jingled.

"I'll be right there," Daisy called from the kitchen.

"No rush." Helix's voice floated back to her from the main space in the bakery, making Daisy fumble and spill half the chocolate on her stainless-steel work table instead of in the mold. A good portion of it dripped over the side and onto her dress and shoes.

"Oh no, oh no, oh no, oh gods."

"Hey, are you…oh."

Why?

Daisy turned toward Helix and did her best to shrug, like this was no big deal, happened all the time. She meant to do this, actually. Chocolate is very, very "in" this season. All the rage in Paris and Milan.

"I've got you, Spring Daisy," Helix said. And, just like that, Daisy watched all the chocolate arc through the air and back into the pot, leaving not even a drop behind. This time, she knew it was wordless casting. Helix's mouth hadn't even moved. Daisy put the pot down and did her best to stammer out a "thank you," a task that got harder the longer she looked at the woman across from her—hair a bright ombre of aquamarine giving way to deep teal, eyes still glittering with all the vastness of the universe.

But that smile that Helix never altered was the real killer—a 6.0 on the Dimple Scale.

Daisy was *not* going to fall for her again. Except…

"I was hoping I might take you up on those tarts, but you seem to have your hands full." Helix moved closer and bent down to watch the two figurines in starry cloaks twirling on Daisy's work table. She laughed when one of them dipped the other low and then had the gesture returned in kind. A kiss followed soon after, giving way to their foreheads resting together while they swayed to music only they could hear. Helix watched them for another moment and then turned her bright eyes on Daisy. "Hope I'm so in love one day that mere Imprints of the two of us are this sickeningly sweet."

"Is that what they are?" Daisy asked.

"Yeah." Helix playfully nudged one of them just enough to make them swat at her with a soundless laugh. "They animate with an impression of you. It's like magical memory foam. They aren't you, but they're the vibe you put out into the universe."

Daisy watched the two miniatures laugh at a joke no one else could hear. "Deities above and below, if that's just their *vibe*."

"Exactly. They must be, just, Darcy and Liz '05 happy."

"Achilles and Patroclus in Elysium."

"Jane and August."

"Kelly and Yorkie."

"Yusuf and Nicolo."

With every passing name, Helix and Daisy smiled at each other a little more. Daisy turned her attention back on the figurines, now sitting with their backs against a mixing bowl, one tucked under the other's arm.

"I'm glad we both acknowledge Darcy and Liz as the only acceptable het couple," Daisy said.

Helix scoffed. "Daisy, did you even pay attention in English Lit? As if either of those absolute bisexual disasters were straight."

"Okay, you've got me there." Daisy laughed. "Darcy was at least a little into Bingley."

"And Liz and Charlotte were *really good friends*."

"Just a couple of gals being pals."

"Girls were just more affectionate with each other back then." Helix leaned against the work table with her back to the cake, palms on either side of her wide hips, fingers curling over the rounded edge. She'd charmed her nails a bright blue that matched the lightest parts of her hair, but they didn't stay that way for long—the color faded darker and darker into a deep ocean-green. Daisy stared at them for a beat too long, until they started lightening again, and then she looked up at Helix, who raised one thick eyebrow.

"Brought you something, by the way," Helix said, tossing a book at her. It was a journal bound in thick leather, embossed with ivy. "For recipes, notes to your patrons, your beautiful thoughts. Whatever. It's charmed so no one else can read it. I just vaguely know you're in it with Persephone, too, and ivy is a thing for her, right? Either way, plant witch. I thought of you." Helix shrugged and licked her lips.

"Th-Thank you." Daisy cleared her throat, running her fingers over the cover. "If...if you, uh, can come back after three, I'll have tarts for you."

Helix lit up like a sacred hearth. Dimple Scale: 10.0. Alert, alert. Situation critical!

"Yeah?"

"Sure. And a fresh pot of homegrown herbal tea to pair with them."

"Daisy Guthrie, you sure know how to show a gal a good time," Helix said in a mock old-timey Hollywood accent.

Daisy pretended to rub at an itch on her neck for fear that Helix might see her pulse point jumping beneath her skin. "Well, toots, you know me." And, wow, okay, not the worst reply, actually.

"I'll go put on my best dress then, sugar." Helix did a silly little curtsy and headed out of the kitchen.

"It's a date then, doll."

At the swinging door that led back out into the small dining room, Helix turned back and locked eyes with Daisy. Supernovas exploded in both irises. "Gods, I sure hope so."

When the door swung shut behind her, Daisy immediately needed to sit down. She had to take several breaths before she was able to make herself get up and start tempering another batch of chocolate to finish the wedding cake.

At ten minutes before three, Daisy found herself in the kitchen of the bakery, covered in flour and with her fingers stained pink-red by pomegranate. She'd meant to make a full batch of two dozen tarts, with a handful plated and looking pretty next to steaming cups of tea, the rest packed up in one of her signature white-and-green boxes. She'd have had the fruit juice stains scrubbed away with Mitsi's Magical Mess Remover, her dress dusted clean and hair fixed into something respectable.

She'd be sitting casually in the cozy dining room of her bakery, sipping her tea and waiting while reading her almanac or one of the magazines sitting in her mail stack. There'd be an empty planter on the table and when Helix walked in, she'd push a flower up through the soil just for her.

Instead, she had managed to assemble exactly six tarts so far—unbaked and sitting in the pan. The kettle wasn't even on. Her hair frizzed more and more from the humidity of her own nervous sweat.

Why hadn't she said four o'clock? Or seven? Or next Wednesday?

Logically, she knew it didn't matter. This wasn't a work deadline or an appointment. This was just a friend coming to get some tarts with another friend. Maybe a date, but had they been serious about that part? Daisy genuinely wasn't sure, but she…

"Oh, gods," Daisy cringed, her hand accidentally slipping into the mixing bowl of pomegranate filling, half-tipping it, goop dripping sadly over the side when she righted it. It was at that precise moment that she heard someone come into the shop. Daisy looked at the door to the kitchen and saw Helix peering through the little window before pushing inside.

Helix looked at her hand and then stopped at the end of the work table, several feet away. A small smile played at her lips—blue, now, to match her hair and nails. "Hey again, Daisy."

"I swear I'm not usually this much of a mess all at once on a single day."

Helix kept looking at her. Her dimples slowly appeared, hovering at a quiet 2.0. "Really? Because I seem to remember a fire in the twelfth-floor kitchen of Jupiter Hall."

"It wasn't a fire! Some frat boy or other absolute heathen had left an entire puddle of melted plastic on the bottom of the oven."

Helix's dimples briefly deepened to a 6.0. "I remember the fire alarm going off, and walking outside, and there you were, already dripping wet from the sprinklers. You were in those pajamas you had—the green ones with the little succulents in teacups. For a second, Celeste threw light on your hair, and then…"

Daisy sighed. "And then it started raining."

Helix stepped closer, pulling a clean kitchen towel from a shelf on the way. It was that, instead of magic, that she used on Daisy's hand, wiping away most of the pomegranate filling with gentle swipes of terry cloth.

"You looked really pretty, you know," Helix said softly, "with Her light in your hair."

Goosebumps tracked down Daisy's arms, her throat feeling a little tighter than it was supposed to. Helix dropped the towel on the counter and glanced at the mess around the kitchen and on Daisy's clothes.

"Please," Daisy whispered, and without so much as a twitch from Helix, the entire kitchen seemed to leap into the air. Helix kept her eyes on Daisy's even while flour swirled around them in clouds reminiscent of cosmic dust. Red joined the white—specks of stray filling forming the nebulae of this galaxy that circled around them. It seemed like eons that they stood there in the center of this hurricane, but it was likely only seconds, the mess sorting itself and quietly streaming into the trash, laundry, compost, and recycling.

"There," Helix said hoarsely, and Daisy looked down to find that even the pink on her fingers was gone.

"Sorry I'm terrible at timing."

"Don't be. I'm not." Helix turned toward the worktable, clean now except for the half-made tarts and ingredients. She picked up the tiny round cutter Daisy used to cut her dough and started pressing out rounds. Daisy watched her for several seconds before Helix glanced her way and gave her an amused look that seemed to say, *Well, are you coming over here or not?*

"Oh, uh…" Daisy started picking up the dough rounds and pressing them into the tin, rinsing and repeating and instructing Helix on how to re-roll the dough (with a little magical chill added in to keep it from getting too warm) until the tin was full.

"Would it be against your morals as a baker to let me fill these?" Helix asked. "I'm faster than a spoon."

"Be my guest," Daisy said, and pomegranate filling leapt into each of the miniature shells. She let Helix at her tea leaves while the tartlets baked, using that time to put the extra dough and filling away in the walk-in and to make sure she didn't miss any of the orders she needed to have done for pickup the following morning.

By the time the tarts were ready, Helix had a pot of tea and two cups set on a table out in the dining room, right next to the empty pot Daisy had placed there several hours ago.

"I'm doing a really bad job hosting this date, if we were serious about that," Daisy said, sliding a plate of tarts onto the table. Normally, she would've let them cool more before serving them, but when she'd said that aloud, Helix had given her a look and, right, of course. Helix was the right kind of witch to speed up that process.

Helix didn't answer the "date" comment at first, choosing instead to take a tart and pop it into her mouth. She chewed on it for what felt like decades, eyes closing like she needed to shut off one sense just to better appreciate every note of flavor. When she finally swallowed, she reached for a cup of tea brimming with cream and took a sip.

"No one believes in fate more than a witch, Daisy Guthrie." Helix sat back in her chair and folded her hands on the table. Her nails continued cycling through hues of blue.

"I don't understand."

"Once upon a time, I saw a girl with moonlight in her hair, and I fell a little in love," Helix pulled another tart onto her own little plate, but she left it there. "Once upon a time, I listened to a girl go on a rant about consent in Magical Ethics, and the way she got so passionate about it and about all the other things she cared about...I wanted her, and I wondered if Celeste hadn't put me onto her on purpose—if my goddess hadn't known something I didn't. And then I proceeded to finish college and never do anything about it. Even when my heart did a little involuntary magic every time I saw her."

"I..." Daisy slumped in her chair. "But I just grow plants, and you can move mountains, and I was the one with the crush who never did anything."

"Like I said, no one believes in fate more than a witch. When the girl you never fessed up to comes back into your life seemingly out of no-where, maybe you need to pay attention." Helix finally ate the other tart, much faster this time. "And as beautiful as you were with moonlight in your hair, and as much as you hate the fact that Iris loves to drench you, you look absolutely stunning covered in rain."

"I..."

"And I've seen what plant witches can do, Daisy. Plant witches can reforest entire areas destroyed by arson or wildfires. They can remove invasive species that are choking out native plants or waterways. Don't act like you couldn't move mountains, too, if you had enough vines to work with." Helix took another sip of tea. "But also, the size of the things we do with our magic—or even without it—aren't what make us worthy of life and love. You love to bake, right? So you use your magic for that, and you make yourself and others happy. It's enough for you. Why wouldn't it be enough for me?"

Daisy took a swallow of her own tea, mostly to keep the ache in the back of her throat from spilling out of her eyes. Slowly, she reached for the empty pot, wrapping her hand around it and coaxing a lily up out of the soil, petals an unnatural hue of blue to match Helix's…everything. The galaxies in Helix's eyes died out while she watched it grow, leaving behind only the soft deep, deep brown.

"Why didn't you ever say anything?" Daisy asked.

"Because"—Helix smiled, reaching out to gently touch a petal—"I'm a hopeless bisexual."

"Maybe not so hopeless now, huh?"

"And, also, because half of the stuff I just said is stuff I learned from you. Isn't that the way of girls who like girls? To be so intimidated by each other for different reasons?" Helix shook her head.

"Gods above and below," Daisy whispered into her teacup. Because it was true. Helix had worded it differently, but she'd gone on that same rant more than once in Magical Ethics class for a myriad of reasons. That it didn't matter if someone's magic was capable of rewriting the universe or only rewriting a grocery list. What mattered was that they were a living, breathing being who the gods chose to bring into existence for one purpose or another. Their value was that, and so was everyone else's. She looked at Helix. "It's amazing sometimes how we forget to grant ourselves the grace we give to everyone else."

Helix smiled her quiet 2.0 dimple smile. She shifted and laid her hand on the table within easy reach of Daisy's. It rested between the tarts and the teapot like a quiet invitation—there, if Daisy wanted to take it.

"For the record," Daisy said, putting down her teacup, "I remember you having plenty of passionate opinions of your own, a lot of them great, a lot of them a part of who I am even after all this time."

On the tabletop, she found Helix's hand and covered it with hers, her fingers curling around one side toward her palm.

Across from her, Helix picked up a tartlet with her free hand and held it up like a glass of champagne at a queer wizard wedding.

"To fate," Helix said.

With a grin and a fluttering heartbeat, Daisy reached for the plate.

RAIN AND MOONLIGHT
CODA

LEX T. LINDSAY

From just inside the door of the greenhouse, Helix Andromeda watched Daisy Guthrie work. Daisy was in her element here, a priestess in a cathedral of green.

"You can do this. I know you can." Daisy's thick fingers wound their way into rich, dark soil. The hair on the back of Helix's neck prickled at the magic in the air.

"Come on," Daisy whispered. The other plants in the room answered that call in their own ways. In the corner a rosebud slowly unfurled, revealing spirals of red and white. Herbs in the window grew taller and thicker. A Venus flytrap opened and shut as though to speak.

And whatever sat beneath the soil and Daisy's fingers?

"There you are." Green shoots peeked up beneath the surface, one tendril growing long enough to weave its way around one of Daisy's

wrists. Daisy let it, tiny blooms appearing against her skin like a living bracelet.

"Oh." Helix's soft voice finally caught Daisy's attention. Daisy glanced back at her and then at a clock on the wall.

"You're early."

Helix cleared her throat then shrugged. "Not by much."

Gently, Daisy coaxed her wrist free of the flowers, softly encouraging the vine onto a little trellis. She made her way to Helix with a smile, carrying with her the scents of lavender and jasmine and earth.

"I missed you, Hellie."

A kiss soft as petals in the moonlight. Helix savored it and stole another. "I missed you more."

ℭ**T**OMB **M**ANY CO**O**KS

EM ROWNTREE

angst (minor), baker, bakery, customer/employee, deity, existential crises, first kiss, humor, interspecies relationship, m/nb, mythology (greek), mythology retelling, nonbinary, past tense, pining (mutual), third person point of view

At the heart of a bright city was a place where the shadows lived. In just one room, on the ground floor of a building that was otherwise sundrenched, there were well-fed, glossy shadows that spooled out over the floor, over chairs and tables and countertops. All the floors above had wide glass windows and smiling neighbours—but downstairs, little nicks of purple and blue promised teeth in the dark. The blackness clung to the walls in spiders' leg patterns, and it moved slowly, creepingly. There was a hum in the air—something deep, too low for human ears to hear, low enough that only the heart could heed it.

At the centre of it all was always a lone figure. He was tall, with skin that had the ashen-pale undertone of death, and he wore a long robe, its silken folds catching the shadows in small screaming pools of darkness that shifted and cried harder when he moved. He was gaunt, with dark hair and heavy brows. His eyes were raven's-wing-black and lost in a thousand-yard stare. And his every movement, from the curve of one finger to the tilt of his sharp jaw, was in the shape of tragedy. His gaze never lingered; every time it moved on was the end of another story, the snap of another thread, the withering of another life. He was demise. He was ruin. He was Hades, Lord of the Underworld.

Today, he turned around and said, "Sorry, did you want those cupcakes to go?"

The customer on the other side of the counter stared at him for a long moment, a middle-aged woman with several plastic shopping bags on her arms. Faint strains of Beethoven's Fifth wafted from wall-mounted speakers, filling the silence.

"Um," she said, staring up at Hades with wide eyes. "Yes, could I get a box?"

"Absolutely." Hades turned his attention back to the four cupcakes sitting on his counter—black velvet, with blackberry icing—and set them neatly into a coffin-shaped box. He sealed the lid with a sticker that read, in swirling purple letters, "Tomb Many Cooks." With a flourish, he slid the finished product towards the waiting customer. "Here you are. Careful not to tip the box. But feel free to tip the baker!"

He gestured a little hopefully towards an urn on the counter with a sign reading "Tips" that stuck out at a jaunty angle. The customer stared at it for a silent second then fumbled for her wallet.

"Thank you! And if you'd like to taste one of our samples, go ahead! We're testing a new recipe this week." Hades indicated a tray that had several bite-size squares of brownie arranged neatly on top.

With a slightly fearful glance at Hades, the customer picked up one of them and put it into her mouth.

"Oh," she said, "it's so…"

The colour drained from her face. Hades watched as her expression fell from surprise to sudden terror, and onward to sadness, and then downward to a deeper terror. Her hands trembled. Her eyes met Hades's, full of despair.

"Oh, god," the customer said.

"Yes," Hades said, a little wearily. "That's me." He bent down, crow-like, to look under the counter. His fingers drifted over paper bags, stickers, pens, a pair of scissors, and settled on a copy of a book of quotes from Nietzsche, one of a small stack. With a sigh, Hades straightened up and set the book down on top of the customer's cupcake box. "No extra charge," he said. "I hope it helps. Thank you for coming to Tomb Many Cooks. Don't forget to rate us online?"

His tone held an uncertain note, as though wondering if he wanted this particular customer experience to be rated. The customer, with the fear of mortality sharp in her eyes, picked up her cupcakes and her book and left the shop. Hades watched after her for a long moment and then glared at the brownies.

He stalked through a black, gauzy curtain to the kitchen; picking up a marker, he wrote "buy more Nietzsche" on the whiteboard by the door, underneath "new bread roll recipe by Friday" and "look up what 'foreclosure' means."

The pile of letters on the desk to the left of the whiteboard, with their red stamps and threats, demanded to be opened. Hades, though, stood still by the door, surveying the chrome-and-velvet cleanliness of his kitchen with something bordering on despair.

He let out a sigh that held the doomed screams of millions along its edges.

There came a sound of bells tolling—mournful, full of menace; at the noise, Hades pulled out his phone. Tapping on the notification, he saw an email about a new review online. With a wince, he clicked the link.

"Great cupcakes. Free book. We all die anyway. Four stars."

Hades breathed out. His thumb gently touched the yellow stars on the screen.

He lifted his chin. With a small nod to himself, he put his phone away and got back to work.

"…it's inevitable," said the teenager with six piercings and dyed black hair, staring into nothingness with a light dusting of powdered sugar on his lips. "Every life is nothing more than a promise to death. Even as we begin, entropy takes hold."

"Mmhmm," Hades said, reaching across the counter and gently taking the sample spoon out of his hand. "So, did you want the jam or custard doughnuts?"

"What's the point?" The teenager looked down at his hands. "What's it all for?"

Hades looked at the kid's pale, abject expression, and reached absently for Nietzsche. Behind the teenager, there was another customer; Hades glanced briefly towards them as though worrying they'd leave before fixing his attention back on the existential crisis before him.

"You wanted to buy doughnuts for your mother," Hades said. The natural cadence of his voice turned it into a tragedy, as though he were certain the doughnuts would be her last.

"I…" The teenager looked wildly around the whispering shadows of the bakery, desperate eyes seeming to see almost through the veil to what awaited on the other side. He met Hades's gaze. "Custard," he whispered.

"Excellent choice." Hades used tongs to slip two custard doughnuts into a paper bag. "That's eight-fifty."

The teenager held his card to the machine until it beeped, and Hades handed him his receipt.

"Have a grave day," Hades said. "A great—sorry, a *great* day."

Without another word, the teenager grabbed his doughnuts and left the shop. Hades turned his attention to the next customer.

"Hi!" they said brightly, stepping forward.

They were short—at least a foot shorter than Hades himself, though they looked to be about the same age, minus the eternity of loss and torment. They wore a pink rabbit onesie with the hood pulled up so that the ears flopped on either side of their face and a smile that widened when they met Hades's gaze. Their almond-shaped eyes crinkled at the corners.

They intercepted Hades's full sweep of their outfit. "You don't want to know," they said.

"Oh."

"Wait, well—That makes it sound bad, doesn't it? Like I'm in some kind of crime ring or something. A rabbit onesie gang."

"I, um." Hades stared at them. "Are you?"

"I wish." The customer peered down at the cupcakes absently. "It's way more boring. I work at a preschool, and one of the kids spilled juice on my jeans, and this was the only thing I had in my car. So…" They looked back up to Hades and held their hands out to the sides, striking a pose for his inspection.

"It's, um. Nice," Hades said.

"Wait until you see my fluffy tail." They grinned, and Hades blinked again, three times, very fast.

"Oh. Yes. Well." He cleared his throat. "What were you looking for today?"

"Nothing specific," the customer said brightly. "I just had to come in and take a look, and can I just say…wow. This place, it's really…" They looked around the room, eyes catching on the sharpened shadows and the casket-shaped blackboard advertising the cupcake flavour of the day.

"Really different to anything I've ever seen. And—"

"Thank you?" Hades hazarded, interrupting without meaning to.

"Yeah! No, but really," the customer went on. "Like, I've seen my share of gimmicky pop-up bakeries, let me tell you. Takes a lot to surprise me these days."

Hades glanced at the twisting darkness looming around them and back to the customer, but they just smiled at him, apparently unbothered. The pink of their onesie was so bright it practically glowed. It looked so soft. Hades's fingers curled up by his sides.

"Thank you," he said more quietly.

"There's a real…commitment to this place," they went on. "I mean, you look amazing, for a start."

Hades brushed down his robe, self-conscious, as they turned their attention to the array of cakes and buns on display. One of their rabbit ears fell into their face, and they attempted to blow it back away with a sharp breath; when that didn't work, they swatted it with a hand.

"Anyway, I saw the sign. I had to come in. What should I try? Any recommendations?"

"Oh." Hades cleared his throat. "Well…the bread rolls are freshly made every morning. The jam in the doughnuts and the Victoria sponge cake is made from locally sourced fruit. And, um, the cupcakes are popular. We have black velvet, red velvet, lemon…"

"Wow! They look incredible." The customer peered closer through the glass. "Who decorates them?"

Hades looked down at the array of cupcakes, which had an assortment of delicate skulls and bones painted across the frosting. A few had gravestone-shaped cookies sticking out the top.

"Um. Me," he said. "I'm the owner. And the only employee. I'm…yes." He swallowed.

The customer looked up at him, eyes going round.

"You made these?" they asked, a note of gentle awe in their voice. "They're so beautiful!"

"Thank you," Hades said, and his tone sounded less doom-laden and more quietly flustered than usual.

"Do you think I could try one?"

"Oh. Um…" Hades glanced down at the Nietzsche under the counter and then back up to the onesie-wearing customer. Their smile was hopeful, and they looked very small against the shadowy backdrop of the high-ceilinged bakery. "Well—I mean, yes, if you really want to."

"I'll pay for it," the customer said. "Don't worry."

"Oh, no, it's not—not that," Hades said, plucking a cupcake out of the cabinet—the one with the lightest frosting, dismal lilac rather than doom-laden ebony. He held it for a second and then put it on the countertop, quickly, as if fighting the urge to snatch it back. "It's just, they're a bit…potent. Some people don't—"

"Yum," the customer said as they picked up the cupcake, peeled back the case, and took a big bite.

Hades watched, the tips of the fingers of one hand pressed to his mouth as though he'd had to stop himself from calling out for them to stop. He watched, eyes anticipating the worst—as they always did, but perhaps even more so than usual.

"Oh, god," the customer said. Hades closed his eyes, his shoulders hunching.

"Yes," he said, "that's—"

"Oh, wow. This is *delicious*. I mean, really."

Hades's eyes snapped open. The customer was chewing through a mouthful, looking at the cupcake rapturously. Their face wasn't ashen; their eyes weren't leaking existential despair.

"Excuse me?" Hades said.

"Like, holy *wow*. That frosting, is it blueberry?"

"Um. Blackberry," Hades said.

"It's literally incredible. I seriously don't think this can be real."

"It's…" Hades stared at them as they peeled back a little more of the cupcake case and took another bite. "You don't…do you feel all right?"

The customer snorted.

"Why?" they said lightly. "Are they poisoned? Arsenic in the frosting? Oh…my god." They swiped a little frosting off their lip with their thumb and licked it. "I wouldn't even care. I'd finish this anyway."

Hades blinked hard and shook his head as though to clear it.

"No," Hades said. "It's just that, after eating my cakes, people sometimes feel just a bit too…um. Mortal?"

The customer looked at him with frank, levelheaded confusion. They flipped the ear of their onesie back again.

"Mortal?"

"Yes. Well…you saw, earlier…"

"Oh, the kid who was right before me? Yeah, he was a bit intense, wasn't he?" The customer took another giant bite, rolling their eyes up and lifting the cupcake higher as though in praise of its existence. "Mmm. So good."

"It's not just him. Everyone's like that, actually," Hades said, a note of careful misery in his voice, beyond the usual underlying endless tragedy. "What I bake, it makes people sad. I keep trying to change my recipes. But I...I always make people sad." He held out his hands for a moment, at a loss.

"Not me," the customer said stoutly, and took the last bite of cupcake.

"No," said Hades, "not you." He stared at them, dark, thoughtful eyes taking in their full-lipped smile and dimples. Almost to himself, he said, "My first happy customer, and it's right before I'm about to shut down."

"Mmhmm. Wait. Wait, what?" they said. "No!"

The corners of Hades's mouth almost turned up at their sudden vehemence, but he re-gathered himself.

"I keep on upsetting people," he said. "It isn't right."

"But—"

"And it isn't a good business model. I spend so much money on philosophical literature."

"You didn't upset me," the customer pointed out with a touch of indignation. "Anyway, what do you even mean, you make people sad by baking? Because, one, that sounds kind of bananas. No offence. And two, even if it's not bananas, you're, you know, taking a lot on yourself there. Maybe these people are already in a bad mood when they come in here? I mean, the decor really lends itself to a certain kind of person, that's all I'm saying."

Hades looked into their eyes and saw a lightness that refused to believe what he'd said. He hunched his shoulders self-consciously.

"I don't think it's that," he said. "I think it's me."

"Well." The customer finished licking frosting off their fingertips and adjusted their fluffy hood. "Either way. You can't close down now. I *need* to be able to come back here."

"You..." Hades's head whipped back up, his robe of mortal darkness swishing around him, the whisper of its passing like the last gasp of a damned man. "You want to come back to my bakery?"

"Don't tell me that's never happened before."

"It...well, no," Hades said. "People don't usually like to have their sense of reality broken twice."

Across from him, the customer put their hands on their hips, dimpling the folds of their onesie.

"Okay," they said. "That can't be right. Your food is amazing; there must be something else going on. Maybe we just need to…do some surveys. See how people feel when they come in versus when they leave. That could clear up the whole 'this is all my fault' thing, right?"

"Um," Hades said.

"I mean, look, I'm not saying that I just lost sixteen of my hours at the preschool to Deborah, and so I'm gonna be at a loose end two days a week and could really use the distraction, but what I *am* saying is, I'm great at surveys. I love a clipboard. We could make this happen."

They raised an eyebrow at Hades, who looked back down at them with an expression that mingled the usual awareness of infinite universal destruction with confusion and a little shyness. His mouth opened and closed as though he didn't know what to say, but his head gave a shake— preparing to reject the offer.

The customer's smile dimmed, and they tilted their head to one side. In a lower and quieter voice, with a clearer note of sincerity, they said, "Maybe you just need some help? I've got the time. And I'm not kidding. I'd do anything to save these cupcakes."

The hard and sharp lines of Hades's face softened. He pressed his lips together, and then, very slowly, he nodded.

They turned their grin up to full power and stuck out their hand.

"All right, then," they said. "I'll come back tomorrow. Oh—and my name's Seph, by the way."

On the first day working with Seph, Hades handed a customer a small bit of brownie, watched him take a bite, and saw his face fall.

Seph, standing next to Hades and watching the customer, too, said, "Interesting."

"Oh, no," the customer said.

"I don't underst—" Seph started.

"Oh, *no*. Everything comes to an end, doesn't it? Everything— Even— Oh, god, even the people I love the most—it's all going to end one day, and…" He trailed off, one hand clammily gripping the counter.

Hades opened his mouth to reply, but Seph leaned forward, pen in one hand and clipboard in another.

"Mmhmm," they said. "So, out of curiosity, how would you rate your mood on a scale of one to ten?"

"Rate?" The customer looked at Seph as though they'd lost their mind, as though they were blithely roasting marshmallows over the cold fires of hell. "My mood?" He shook his head. "It all ends," he said faintly. "All of it."

"Uh-huh," Seph said. "I'm going to mark that down as a two. Okay, well—taking another bite, so that's a two-point-five."

On the seventh day working with Seph, Hades found himself in his kitchen late in the evening, staring at a whiteboard covered in figures.

"Right," Seph said. "I'm saying, people were returning ratings up to three percent higher when they ate the cookie samples instead of the brownies, so maybe you should lean into that. Pelt them with chocolate chips and see if we can bump the numbers any higher."

Hades had one finger thoughtfully pressed to his chin. Seph, in front of him, stuck their blue marker into their mouth and grabbed an orange one, which they used to circle the word "cookie" several times.

"You don't think that…" Hades cleared his throat. "You don't think the numbers might be slightly off since you have to make up all of the ratings after they've eaten the samples? Because they're too busy having a crisis to give you a number?"

"Huh?" Seph turned to look at him, indignant behind their mouthful of marker. They made some more noises that could have been words; Hades reached forward and unobtrusively took the pen out of their mouth by one end. "—and that's why my ratings are completely unimpeachable, and you should do what I said."

They caught Hades's eye with a little knowing smile, which he returned.

"Okay," Hades said.

On the eighth day working with Seph, Hades cooked with someone else in the kitchen for the first time.

"More chocolate chips," Seph said.

"I've put all of them—"

"I know you've got another bag. I saw it last week in the cupboard in the corner."

"I don't know how extra chocolate chips are going to stop people from realising their inextricable bond to mortality…"

"Are you kidding? I forgot my own name the other day when I ate that doughnut where you put orange zest in the filling." Seph, sitting on a counter in the kitchen, pointed a finger-gun at Hades and twisted their accent into something out of a Western. "Add the chips, kid."

Hades used one hand to lower their weapon and went to fetch the chocolate chips.

On the fifteenth day working with Seph, Hades threw a mini-cupcake across the shop, and Seph caught it neatly in their mouth. They lifted their arms up, eyes sparkling, chewing triumphantly.

"You're concerningly good at that," Hades said.

"It's a gift," Seph answered before they'd finished their mouthful.

"Maybe we should take it on the road."

Seph's eyes went wide as they swallowed. "*Yes*. You make the cupcakes. You throw the cupcakes. I catch the cupcakes. I eat the cupcakes." They checked each item off the list on their fingers, and when they held up their thumb, they turned it into a thumbs-up. "We profit."

"Profit does sound good," Hades said. He reached down and picked up the last copy of Nietzsche that he had, setting it on the counter as would a widow lay flowers on her beloved's grave. "I need to restock on these, but I blew the budget this week on Earl Grey for those scones I wanted to try."

Seph wandered over to the counter. Hades tensed as they came closer, shoulders hunching, a hint of colour appearing in his ashen cheeks. Seph smiled at him and slid the Nietzsche off the counter to look at it.

"Um," Hades said. He swallowed as Seph stared down at the book. "I was wondering. Tonight, if you're…if you wanted to, I mean…"

"Wait. This is what you've been giving everyone to try to, you know, help with their crises?" Seph said, holding it up.

Hades blinked.

"Um. Yes?"

Seph slapped him lightly on the shoulder with the book.

"No! Really?"

"…yes?"

"Don't buy any more of these, okay? We need something new. Like…a Paddington book, or something." They rolled their eyes. "They need reminding that life matters, that it's good sometimes, not…whatever that's meant to be."

"Paddington?"

"Trust me. Anyway, sorry." They tossed the book back down onto the counter. "You were saying?"

"Um…just…" Hades sighed and it rang with the grief of a thousand lost loves. "I was saying that I was going to cook tonight. That's all."

"Well," Seph said after a little pause, "I was going to go home and nurse a box of cupcakes. But, I mean…"

"Stay," Hades said, and then added, "if you want to."

Seph looked at him quietly for just a moment, and then smiled.

That evening, Hades stirred a bowl of cake batter while Seph sat on the part of the kitchen counter that had become their personal spot. It was close to the heater but also near enough to the cooking that they could swipe any spoons-coated-in-something-sweet that Hades left unattended for too long.

"So then Deborah says," Seph said, swinging their feet, "that she doesn't *care* if my gerbil's ill, she won't cover for me."

"That's rude."

"I *know*. It's almost like she doesn't like me," Seph said.

"She doesn't?" Hades asked.

"Are you kidding? She can't stand me."

"Why?" Hades said, setting down his mixing spoon with a little less doom-filled finality than usual. He had his eyes on Seph, and there was something approaching lightness in his expression. Seph grinned.

"Probably the same reasons a lot of people can't. I don't know."

"A *lot* of people don't like you?" Hades's voice shifted to outright astonishment. He stood up tall, a raven with its feathers indignantly puffed up.

"You've got to be joking," Seph said, half laughing. "With the amount I talk? And these cutesy clothes? And the way I've always got my nose in someone else's business?" They gestured to themselves and then around the kitchen as if making their point.

"But those are good things," Hades said.

"To you, maybe," Seph said.

"Yes," Hades said. "To me."

The two of them tilted, abruptly, into silence. Neither of them seemed to know where to look, glancing at each other and then away, cheeks reddening.

Seph leaned over. Hades went still—and then Seph reached out, swiped the mixing spoon, and licked off a bit of batter.

"Well," Seph said, "thank you."

Hades sighed, and what could have passed for a rueful smile crossed his face.

"You're welcome," he said.

On the thirtieth day of working with Seph, a customer came in who looked messy-haired and a little unwashed, her clothes mismatched and rumpled as though dragged, still dirty, back out of the laundry basket.

"Welcome to Tomb Many Cooks," Hades said. The imposing note in his voice made a fair attempt to compensate for the crumbs strewn down his robe by the cookie that Seph had been balancing on his nose two minutes before. "How can I help you?"

"And how would you rate your mood on a scale from one to ten?" Seph added.

"Um," the customer said, her eyes trying to take in the two of them as well as the baking on offer. "I…an Earl Grey scone, I think, and…erm…maybe…a four?"

"Four," Seph echoed as they made a note, while Hades reached for his tongs.

"Well, four sounds a bit dramatic, doesn't it?" the customer said. "A five? Thank you." They accepted the scone in its paper bag from Hades and then glanced over the samples. "May I…?"

"Please," Hades said, though his eyes betrayed concern. The customer reached out, took a cookie, and bit into it. Watched by Seph and Hades together, her face shifted as she chewed.

Her eyes filled with tears.

"Oh," she said. And her shoulders relaxed.

"Are you all right?" Seph asked, while Hades reached for a Paddington book from under the counter. The customer looked down at the cookie and then up at Seph.

When she spoke, her voice was clearer than before.

"You know, everyone keeps telling me I am," she said. "Or I will be. And that it'll get easier. But to be honest, it's really bad, and I'm not— I'm not— Everyone just wants me to feel better, but this…" She took another small bite. "This is…this is what it feels like all the time. I didn't think anyone else knew what it's like." She blinked, and a tear dropped, heavy, down her cheek. She swiped at it. "Oh my god. I'm sorry. It's just a cookie. What am I even saying? This is so embarrassing. God, I'm sorry."

Hades set down the Paddington book on the counter and then looked her in the eye with all his understanding of endless loss. She breathed out and took another bite of the cookie.

Seph was quiet for a moment, and then they said, "And how would you rate your mood now?"

Hades nudged them in the ribs with an elbow as sharp as a grave-digging shovel, but the customer looked over at them, unfussed, and said, "I think…a two." And their expression lightened, just a bit. "But it was a one before."

On the fifty-first day of working with Seph, Hades heard them say thoughtfully from across the kitchen, "Something's changing."

Hades looked up at them, away from the tray of coffin-shaped pome-granate-and-white-chocolate cookies he'd been decorating with small pink hearts. Seph was staring thoughtfully at the whiteboard, tapping on their chin with the nib of their marker pen, leaving little spots of ink. Hades smiled to himself and picked up a damp cloth as he moved towards them.

"What do you mean?" he asked as he went.

"The ratings," Seph said.

"What about them?"

"They're different. You've noticed it too, right?"

Hades reached them, gently took the marker out of their hand, and replaced it with the cloth. They let him do it without asking questions, seemingly too deep in statistical analysis to notice, and the ink started to come off as they kept tapping their chin.

"I mean," Seph went on, "it's like a hundred-and-twelve-percent increase in customer satisfaction. Was it just the extra chocolate chips? Or Paddington? Did anything else change?"

Hades looked down at their thoughtful face, the way the lines at the corners of their eyes got deeper as they narrowed them. He didn't answer.

"Plus, the amount of customers we're getting every day is up." They grinned at Hades, who smiled back—not the worn, accepting smile of eternal mourning, but just a smile. Warm and sincere. "We're making it work, aren't we? You're going to need someone in here full-time with you, soon."

"You," Hades said, far too quickly.

"Ha," Seph said. "Wait. What?" They turned to look at him, and their eyes widened when they saw no trace of humour on his face.

Hades's shoulders hunched. He looked away, searching for words; when the silence stretched, he turned and disappeared out of the kitchen and back into the main shop, where he began tidying his counter with hands that weren't quite steady.

After a few moments, he heard a voice say, "Do you mean it? You want me here full-time?"

Hades stopped rearranging the Paddington books. He looked at Seph. As they always had, they glowed against the backdrop of the bakery—the shadows deeper and more lovely behind them, the look in their eyes so gentle and bright. They were watching Hades as though waiting for him to laugh, with several splodges of ink still on their chin.

Straightening up, Hades met their gaze. For a second, it seemed as though his courage would fail him—then, quite suddenly, he reached out and took Seph's hand.

"Stay," he said. "For as long as we have."

In his voice was the knowledge that it would not be forever. In Seph's eyes, as they looked back at him, was the certainty that it was—without doubt—worth it, all the same. They came closer still. Hades cupped one hand under their chin, and they closed their eyes.

Only the shadows saw the rest. The shadows that pooled across the floor, still full of wails and murmurs, coating the inside of Hades's building at the heart of the bright city.

But shadows can live well within bright hearts, as it happens. So long as the hearts are true.

DREAMING OF PINES

TRIS LAWRENCE

bipoc, bisexual, coffee shop, creature transformation (dog), customer/employee, first
kiss, f/m, f/f/m, immortal, interspecies relationship, magic use, memory loss, past
tense, polyamorous relationship negotiation, polyamory, reunion, second chances, third
person limited point of view, twosome to threesome

A new door blew wide with a biting, chill wind and a woman stumbling
through. She turned to close her door and planted both hands against
the plain, dark wood, holding on as if it might burst open again as soon
as she let go.

The shop was quiet, only one of the many small tables occupied by a
group of women having coffee and muffins while their own door stubbornly lingered, set into the wall behind the quietest of the group.

Mel smoothed her apron down, readying herself to greet the newcomer; the hound at her feet stood and shook himself off before padding over to greet her himself.

Josh rarely paid attention to those who came and went. That he re-
acted to this new arrival was enough to capture Mel's attention.

He whined and pawed at the newcomer's ripped jeans until she turned
away from her door and sank down to her knees. Her black hood fell
forward, obscuring her features as she reached for Josh's ruff, scratching
him behind his ears.

"Hello there," she murmured. "What's your name?" She reached for
his collar, a small huff escaping as she read the tarnished silver tag that
hung from the worn leather. " 'Hello, my name is Josh.' Well, my name

is Britt. Do you live here?"

Behind them, her door faded into the weathered pine of the interior walls.

Mel exhaled. She was staring; she blamed Josh for that. She needed to remember her job: feed the people who came into the café—whether they could afford it or not—and give them whatever it was they needed most.

"Welcome to the Cloverleaf Café," she called out. "I'll have your order up in a moment."

Britt looked up, her hood falling back and long, curly hair spilling out. It was thick, mostly dark against the olive undertone of her features, but with russet highlights and faded pink at the very ends. Her features had no lines, but her eyes seemed old, with dark shading beneath them. "I haven't ordered anything yet."

"You don't need to." Mel smiled; no one ever took her explanation seriously. "The Cloverleaf Café is magic. Find a place and settle in, and I'll bring you out the chef's special of the day."

"I don't have a lot of money." Britt unzipped her hoodie as she moved slowly toward the couch by the fireplace, Josh nudging her with his nose to herd her there. Her high-top sneakers scuffed against the old wooden planks of the floor with every step.

"Pay what you can, if you can," Mel said. "No one is ever turned away." She made her way behind the counter into the small kitchenette, watching as Josh ensured that Britt made herself comfortable.

He sighed, stretching as only a hound could, and lay down on the warm hearth.

She's a college student, Mel thought. She mixed cocoa and espresso in equal parts with a large shot of almond milk. Caramel foam topped the drink; her hands moved without her directing them, etching the foam into the shape of a small forest of pines.

She brought the large mug to where Britt had sunk into the couch, her knees spiked up and shoulders hunched. Josh had moved from the hearth to the couch beside her, his nose resting on her leg. Britt's fingers tangled in the fur atop his head, clutching him like a favorite stuffed animal.

As soon as Mel set the mug on the oak coffee table, Britt shot upright, reaching for it. She hesitated with her fingertips just shy of touching.

"I really don't have any money," Britt said, her gaze dropping.

"And I meant it when I said you don't have to pay." Mel stood, half-tempted to sit when Josh whuffed at her. "Give me a minute, and I'll fetch you something to eat, too."

Britt lifted the mug, cradling it in both hands as she inhaled the steam. "God, this smells so good. When I was little, my grandmother would sneak me coffee because I wanted to be big, like her. She made it so sweet and chocolatey, and I loved every bitter sip." She inhaled again, then took a cautious taste. Her eyes widened. "How did you—?"

"That's the magic of the café," Mel said, pinned by the weight of Britt's regard. Josh snorted. "Whatever you need," Mel continued. "We have it for you."

"Whatever I need." Britt laughed sourly. "Right."

There was pain in Britt's words. Anger, too, and resentment, but it was the pained resignation that her wishes were beyond fulfillment that called to Mel. She should say something, but she could find no easy words. She took a step backward as Britt took another sip, and when Britt's focus turned to the coffee, Mel felt as if she were released. Hurrying into the kitchen, she reached for the ingredients that felt right. She finely chopped cornichons, sweet gherkins, pickled ginger, fresh radish, and a small amount of onion. The scent was briny and bright as she added the vegetables to rough-chopped eggs and blended it all together with both mustard and mayonnaise. She slathered it thickly on fresh rye, baked before the first customer arrived that morning, and realized she'd made enough for two sandwiches. She considered the two plates, then added a large snickerdoodle to each one, uncertain whether that choice was for Britt or herself. The burst of spice and sugar always reminded her of childhood; they were the first thing her mother taught her to bake, and held a part of her heart.

When she returned to the main room, the women in the corner got up with a burst of noise. "I've left money on the table!" one of them said. Their door faded in the wake of their passing, leaving behind a smooth expanse of wood. There were no other doors; other than herself, Josh, and Britt, the café was empty.

Britt had finished her mocha, the mug abandoned on the coffee table, and retreated into a corner of the couch. Her feet were drawn up, and her arms were around her knees as she curled into herself. Josh sat next to her, his body pressed against her shoulder, his head tilted against hers. Britt unfolded slowly, her hand sliding through Josh's fur, the tension of her shoulders easing when he leaned closer.

Mel placed both plates on the table, sliding one in front of Britt along with a napkin. One hand still resting atop Josh's head, idly combing through the short fur, Britt leaned to look at the plate. Josh's presence had relieved most of her tension, and interest lit her expression.

The third place on the couch remained unoccupied. Mel sat on the edge, her body angled toward Britt and Josh, and drew her own plate and napkin closer; he stretched and one foot bumped against her hip as his head remained close to Britt's arm.

"Don't you have to work?" Britt asked.

"No one else is here," Mel replied. "Until there's another door, I can rest."

Britt picked up the plate, lifting it to peer at the sandwich, her brow furrowed. "Another door?" she asked.

Josh barked; Mel clearly heard the *go on* in his tone.

It didn't matter. Customers never remembered, or if they did, they never returned. Whether they believed or not, the café would send them to where they needed to be.

"I told you: the Cloverleaf Café is magic." She lifted her own sandwich and took a small bite: she wanted to know what food lived in Britt's heart. It wasn't a combination she would have considered, but the bright flavor burst over her tongue as she took another, larger, bite. "Wherever you found us—we're not there. We're not anywhere, really, yet we're everywhere at once. When you're ready to leave, a door will be here to take you to wherever you need to go. This is—" She cut off, lifting the sandwich. A chunk of egg salad tumbled from between the bread slices onto the plate. "This is amazing."

"You sound surprised." Half of Britt's sandwich was already gone, and she spoke around a mouthful. "You made it. I didn't know anyone else knew how to make egg salad like my grandmother."

Josh whined. Mel plucked a bit from her plate and held it out so he could try it.

"I made what you needed. She must mean a lot to you." Mel wiped her fingers delicately on her napkin, then returned to her food as Josh pivoted so he could nose her knee and beg for more.

"She did." Britt shoved the rest of the sandwich in her mouth, closing her eyes as she chewed. She set the plate down, capturing the snickerdoodle before she returned to her corner of the couch, feet on the cushions and knees drawn up once more. She nibbled at the cookie, laughing when Josh begged a bite from her. "Can I?"

"He can eat anything we can," Mel said dryly. "Do you—Do you want to talk about her?"

She wasn't used to sitting and chatting. It had been ages since she took time out of her day to talk to a patron. There were still no new doors. It seemed almost as if the café was keeping others out, giving them the time to connect.

Britt broke off a piece of the cookie, holding it down for Josh without looking. "She meant a lot to me," she said. "She was almost a hundred when she died, and I'd just started high school. I lost the only person who truly understood me. We were generations apart, but we spent so much time together. There were things I didn't know how to say yet, but she got me; my parents and my siblings never did. Without her—I feel like I've lost my only ally. I can't find anywhere else to fit in."

Her gaze drifted away. "I dream of her sometimes. More than just 'sometimes.' I dream of her a lot. I dream of fields of thick blue-green grass. I dream of eating these sandwiches for the rest of my life, and knowing that it means someone loves me. I dream of giant sunflowers that tower taller than I'll ever be." She dropped her gaze to look at the empty mug on the table. "Over and over, I dream of forests full of pines."

"What do you think it means?"

Britt laughed, dry and cynical. "I'm a girl from a small town that's made out of more pavement than greenery. I think it means I'll always be dreaming of something that I'll never find."

There was a door by the fireplace, made of rough-hewn wood with a wrought iron frame where a window ought to be. Mel didn't want to call attention to it; she curled her hands in her lap. It might be someone new arriving to interrupt them. It might be meant for Britt.

Josh barked sharply, and Britt glanced up. Eyes wide, she said, "That wasn't there before."

"I keep saying it's magic, yet no one pays attention long enough to believe me."

Britt licked her lips. "I believe you."

She stood slowly, leaving the rest of the cookie on the plate. Mel wasn't sure she'd eaten much of it and was surprised by the twist of disappointment in her gut. The snickerdoodle must have been only a memory from Mel's heart, not a part of Britt's, and Britt hadn't wanted it.

"Where does it go?" Britt asked.

"You'll have to open it and find out," Mel told her. "If I had to guess? It involves giant sunflowers and forests full of pines."

Britt's expression lit up, eyes crinkling when she smiled. "And maybe the rest of my dreams too. If you say it's magic…" She stepped over Josh to get to the door and paused with her hand on the knob. "Thank you. For feeding me, and for listening."

"Any time," Mel said, even though she knew it would be the only time.

She caught a glimpse of pines, tall and swaying in the breeze, as Britt stepped through and pulled the door closed behind her.

"You could have saved me more than a bite." Josh was human again, dark eyes crinkled in the corners as he grinned. His human form was familiar after all their time together—familiar and well-loved. She knew the feel of his close-cropped, light-brown curls beneath her fingers; she took comfort in how the same arm muscles that held her with care also kneaded dough without tiring.

Picking the last bit of crust off her plate, he popped it in his mouth. "That was good."

It *had* been a good sandwich. Britt held good things in her heart, alongside her sorrow.

His hand covered hers, threading their fingers together. His skin was dark, his hand large and strong as he held her. Her skin was lighter, and held more wrinkles and spots.

That one point of contact, palm to palm, was enough to tether her here in their café.

"What are you thinking?" he asked.

She was thinking that something was missing now, and she longed for the food in their hearts. She should make a strawberry-rhubarb pie, like she had the first time Josh came to the café—something that reminded him of home and childhood, and of an older brother who was also a best friend. She was thinking that he could work beside her, rolling balls of dough into sugar and spice, because they could always use more snickerdoodles. Perhaps then, they could heal.

She pressed their joined hands over her heart. "I was thinking about the first time I saw you," she murmured. "And about the last time I saw my mom."

Josh's nod said he understood, that he too recognized that this moment felt like those moments had. Mel could almost taste the importance, even though nothing had changed. From now on, she'd always think of egg salad this way.

"Everyone gets what they need most," he reminded her gently. He gathered her into his arms as they both stood. The café supplied music, and he danced slowly with her in the emptiness as the lights dimmed. "I think our day is done, Mel. Come to bed?"

She shook her head, holding on as they swayed in the near-darkness. As long as the music played, she wanted to stay here—to linger, like doors sometimes did. She wasn't ready to let go quite yet.

Britt returned with a rush of frozen air, snow swirling in around her. She pushed the door shut and pressed her hands against it, as if the wind might blow it open again. Mel barely caught a glance of her face, shrouded by a fur-lined hood, but recognition pulled in her gut, confirmed when Britt pushed her hood back and turned to lean against the door, head tipped back, long grey-brown braids peeking out from the coat.

There were more lines on her face, but Mel knew her. Knew her, and knew that the pesto she'd been grinding in the mortar was for her.

Mel smiled and called out loud enough that Josh would hear her in the kitchen. "Welcome to the Cloverleaf Café. Your order will be up in a minute." She added, a little more quietly, "Welcome back."

Britt stayed where she was, eyes still closed as she peeled thick leather gloves from her hands and undid the double panel of buttons from her coat. "I've been looking for this café for more than a year," she said. "You said that it was everywhere and nowhere, but, for the longest time, it was definitely nowhere at all."

"Why?" Mel sank into Josh's touch to her shoulder, looking up to receive the soft kiss he pressed to her forehead as he set a serving bowl laden with penne on the counter. She scraped the pesto into the bowl and tossed it with the hot pasta; the fragrant scents of garlic, basil, and pignole rose. She inhaled, closing her eyes.

Pine trees, swaying in the breeze.

She swayed with the image for a moment; her breath caught, and her hand pressed to her chest.

Josh anchored her with a hand on her back. "Mel."

Oh.

She opened her eyes again, looking to where Britt remained by her door. Britt's coat was half-off, her hands clutching it rather than letting it slip loose as she stared at them. As Mel met her gaze, Britt's expression shuttered, her eyes skittering away to survey the empty café.

"It's quiet here today," she murmured.

Mel reached beneath the counter for three bowls, setting them out on the wooden surface.

"Eat," she said.

Britt stayed, unmoving, as her door faded behind her. She let Josh take her coat to hang on the rack along the wall. Mel served up pasta for three, garnishing the bowls with chopped-and-toasted sunflower seeds.

"Eat," she repeated when Britt was free. "Warm up by the fire. You've come in from the cold, and we have what you need most."

Britt's gaze was fixed on Josh, narrowed and thoughtful. "I didn't know you were in a—" She stopped as he turned to face her, close enough that if she reached out she could touch him. When he tilted his head back, her gaze fell to the worn collar that graced his throat no matter his form. She stopped short of grasping the tarnished silver disk.

"Oh," she whispered. " 'Hello, my name is Josh.' You're magic."

"Most things in the café are," Josh agreed. He bridged the distance between them, hand falling on the top of Britt's head with a gentle pat. "Hello, Britt. We remember you."

They'd spoken of her over the years when memories intruded into their daily life. Mel couldn't quite say why, but there were times when she'd wake with Britt's name on her lips until Josh stole it from her with a kiss. It was just another thing—another memory from the past—the one time when they had shared the experience, rather than gifting it to one another with stories and food.

Mel still loved the egg salad she had made for Britt that first time; she and Josh had shared sandwiches almost as often as snickerdoodles or strawberry-rhubarb pie.

Britt exhaled roughly, unfreezing to take one bowl from Mel and cradle it carefully in her hands. "Thank you."

It seemed the café would give them privacy once more, though Mel watched the walls, expecting doors to appear before they all settled by the fire. Britt took the middle of the couch; Mel took one side, and Josh took the other after he brought out a platter of snickerdoodle cookies and individual-sized pies.

Britt took a bite and made a noise low in her throat that wrapped warmly around Mel's heart. She didn't speak, simply eating and making happy little sounds while the meal disappeared bite by bite. Josh ate while he watched, but Mel held her fork and did nothing, unable to look away from them.

The bright garlic-and-basil scent rose in the air. Josh gestured with his fork, and Mel stabbed a piece of pasta and raised it to her lips. The earthen scent of pine underlay the brighter flavors, grounding the taste in her heart. It was delicious and drew her in, her stomach rumbling with sudden hunger.

This was Britt now, she realized. The egg salad embodied the person she had been. It would always live in Britt's heart, but the pesto embodied the woman she had become. Within the Cloverleaf Café, everything was timeless. Snickerdoodles would always be Mel's heart. The sweet-and-sour of strawberry-rhubarb lived within Josh. But the world outside the café was full of change.

Britt brought that change into the café, to Mel and Josh.

Britt finished the bowl and set it on the coffee table. She surveyed the waiting platter, then carefully selected a cookie.

Mel feared that Britt would tear her heart apart again; she hoped that this time, Britt might embrace it, keeping it safe within her own heart.

"I never stopped dreaming of forests full of pines," Britt said quietly. She sat back, the cookie held loosely between her hands. "Or fields of towering sunflowers. I thought I'd found them at first, because where I went—it was absolutely different than where I'd been. Rougher. For a girl who'd never lived outside a small town that thrived on technology, it was definitely an experience. I learned how to hunt and how to fight. I learned to live outdoors, within the forests. I carved out a space and built a home." She paused, gaze fixed on the cookie. "I fell in love."

Stomach twisting with anxiety, Mel set the bowl down on the table and pushed it away.

Britt broke off a piece of snickerdoodle, releasing sweet spice into the air. She snapped it again, splitting the single cookie into three pieces. "I fell in love more than once," Britt continued. "It's easy, when you're accepted—when you feel like you might have finally found a place you fit in."

Mel couldn't stop looking at the pieces of snickerdoodle in Britt's hand: her heart, broken in three.

She rose on instinct, gaze darting across the wooden walls, seeking a new door, an interruption, anything to take her attention away. It hurt to hear that Britt had fallen in love. Her feet wanted her to move, yet she was rooted to the floor, heart racing uncomfortably over things she didn't understand.

Josh half-stood, but Britt got to Mel first. She didn't stand, but she leaned toward Mel, holding out one of the three snickerdoodle pieces in silent offering.

Mel took it with her fingertips, inching closer but not sitting down again.

When Britt offered it, Josh took the third piece. Britt raised hers like a glass in toast. "To finding home," she said.

Glancing to where Mel hesitated, Josh raised an eyebrow, and Mel felt his silent admonishment. She sat slowly, her piece of cookie reaching out to touch the one Britt held as Josh met them from the other side.

"To finding home," Britt said again. She took a bite. "*Oh...*" she exhaled. "This is bliss."

Tension slipped from Mel's bones. She glanced at Josh, catching his approval and gentle understanding. He knew Mel better than she knew herself, and he had a way of knowing what people felt, the way she knew what food held their heart.

It will be okay, his soft smile seemed to say. She should reach out. Britt might accept her heart.

"When I was a little girl—" Mel cut off at Britt's amused look. "Do you think I was born old?"

"You look exactly the same as you did when I came through a lifetime ago," Britt pointed out. "For all I know, you've always been the same." She nibbled around the edge of the cookie, reminding Mel of the girl she had first met. Now, however, Britt focused intently, savoring every sweet, spicy bite. On her other side, Josh devoured his piece, chewing with a happy smile.

Mel savored each morsel of her own, wanting to taste what they tasted. She paused when Britt touched her to secure a stray lock behind her ear.

"You have the same salt-and-pepper hair," Britt said. "The same whiskey eyes, surrounded by tiny laugh lines, and the same clothes. It's as if no time passed here."

"Magic," Josh reminded her. He glanced away, gaze falling to the table where the strawberry-rhubarb pies sat, untouched.

"I was born here," Mel said quietly, "to a mother who left when I was old enough to handle things on my own. She taught me how to listen to the whispers of the café and how to bake snickerdoodles. They were the first thing I ever baked with her, and the last thing we made together on the day she left."

"Where did she go?" Britt asked. When Mel faltered for an explanation, Britt looked to Josh, as if he might know the answer, her gaze narrowing. "You're part of the café's magic too?"

Josh picked up one of the small pies, raised it, and gestured at Mel to encourage her to explain.

"My mother left because she found her door, and it was time for her to go," Mel said. "I don't know where she went, but it was where she needed to be, more than she needed to be here. Josh walked in one day while I was making pie, and he…" She wasn't sure how to explain how right it had felt when he made his way into the kitchen and worked with her, his strong hands rolling out the dough while she finished the filling. She didn't know how to explain how long it had been before she trusted that he truly was going to stay.

"I won't have a door." Josh's words fell firmly into the air, surrounded by the scent of strawberries and rhubarb as he bit into the pie. "With Mel is where I need to be."

Britt licked her lips, watching him. "Would it be rude to eat two desserts?"

There was another question in her words; Mel tasted it on the air. It hung between the three of them, wrapping slowly around them and tugging them closer together. Mel slid along the couch, and her knee pressed against Britt's as she leaned past her to lift a pie, splitting it carefully so the filling wouldn't spill out.

She held out half to Britt. "We offered. These are yours for the taking."

Britt touched her tongue to the filling first, her nose wrinkling at the sharp, sour bite of the rhubarb until the strawberry chased that away with its sweetness. When she finished the piece in her hand, Josh held a bite out, and Britt captured it in her teeth, swallowing his offering with closed eyes.

"Stay," Mel whispered. This was a new memory, wrapped in savory, spicy, sharp, and sour sweetness. She wanted to capture it as it was, and to have it again, over and over.

But it wouldn't be the same without the whole meal. The desserts alone were sweetly delicious, but the lingering flavor of the pesto in her mouth grounded the fruity flavors in a way that Mel hadn't realized was missing until they combined perfectly.

She could see it now, and as she met Josh's eyes he nodded at her. He slid his hand across the back of the couch, behind Britt's back, and Mel grasped it, tangling their fingers together.

"My dreams never changed," Britt said. "I wanted to know what they meant. I obsessed over them for so long that I drove one lover away. After that, I tried to forget them, but years later, when I lost another lover, the dreams came back. So I went searching, seeking answers."

Britt placed her empty hands on her knees, palms up. Josh covered one with his free hand, and, after a moment, Mel did the same. Britt squeezed gently. "I learned that sunflowers mean loyalty and new beginnings. They mean the joy and light of life, along with longevity, and things that are meant to last forever. And pines? Pines are immortal. They grow, and they grow, and they bend in the wind, but they don't break like hardwoods do. And neither sunflowers nor pines are meant to grow alone. They're part of a forest or a field. A copse, maybe. But always more than one or two."

"Timeless," Josh said, his thumb sliding over the skin of Britt's hand. "And maybe a little bit magical."

She grinned. "Yes, exactly. And I think—when I was here before, I knew who I was, but I hadn't had a chance to just be *me*—to live and experience life. I needed that door, back then, but now…now I know what I'm looking for."

Mel couldn't find the words. Her throat was tight, her heart beating rabbit-fast in her chest. She was thankful when Josh spoke for both of them.

"Will you stay?" he asked.

Mel tightened her grip on both of them. "Please," she whispered.

Britt closed her eyes, her smile growing soft and sweet. "If you'll have me," she murmured, her hands tangled with theirs, holding on tight. She brought both their hands to her mouth, kissing them as Mel's and Josh's knuckles brushed across her lips. "I'd like to stay. It took a long time for me to realize where I needed to be, but once I knew…I had to find my way back."

The café was magic. People entered through one door and often left through another, led by their heart.

But this time, the door led Britt to them, as had the door that brought Josh to the café long ago.

"I'll make your grandmother's egg salad whenever you want." Mel released Britt's hand so she could touch her cheek, turning Britt to look at her as Britt's eyes blinked open. "If you want to stay with us, we'd be happy to have you."

"I'd be happy to be had." Britt beamed, her eyes crinkling with pleasure as giggles bubbled up.

Josh slid closer, and they wrapped Britt in their arms as she laughed. She settled her head back against Josh's shoulder, resting her cheek against his, then leaned forward to press a kiss to Mel's cheek. Their lips met and flavor suffused Mel's mouth.

The woodsy resin of the pignole.

Luscious strawberry and sour rhubarb.

Spicy-sweet cinnamon.

She stroked Britt's hair as Britt turned from her to press a kiss to Josh's lips, sealing their promises with that quiet, shared taste. They were each so different, but their hearts blended in such a delicious way.

"You are home," Mel assured her, and Josh's voice joined hers as she added with a small smile, "Welcome to the café."

"I've got everything I wanted right here," Britt assured them, and her kisses left Mel dreaming of pines, and of the sweetnesses to come.

Sustenance

TRIS LAWRENCE

Time was an illusion in the Cloverleaf Café. Mel used words like "morning," "afternoon," and "night," but there were no clocks and no set schedules. Time was ordered around when she woke before the first customer and when she slept once the light dimmed after the last one left.

No days were the same. Sometimes, she'd rush out of bed, down the stairs, and into the kitchen, knowing she needed to get bread rising or coffee brewing before a door appeared to herald a customer's arrival. Other mornings were slow and soft, spent in quiet companionship with Josh. There were days when the café bustled with a constant flow of doors and people, and days where Mel and Josh toiled side by side in the kitchens, making food without learning whose heart hungered for it.

No matter the day, at the end she and Josh worked together to package any remaining food that had been prepared and take it to the door that waited. There was always someone just outside.

The food would always get to where it needed to go, bringing sustenance to hearts that needed it the most.

WAITING TO BREATHE

TRIS LAWRENCE

Mel felt the days pass, empty in a way she hadn't known since before Josh came to the café. She found herself counting each new start to the morning, seeking something forgotten.

Josh found her as she made the four-hundredth mark on a small piece of paper that sat on a table in the kitchen. He brought her hand to his lips, kissing her knuckles. "Talk to me."

She cast a glance at the open archway leading to the counter and the quiet space beyond. The café waited, silent and empty of the people who would later come. She met his gaze as if she might find the right words in the way he looked at her.

He leaned in and licked her lip teasingly, then pressed slow kisses to her mouth, to her jaw, to her throat.

She smiled and held him close. "I love you," she murmured. "Do you ever feel as if the air itself is waiting to take another breath?"

Josh stilled, one hand lingering at the small of her back. "Sometimes. Before I found the café—before I found you—I knew there was something else out there. Something I needed to do."

"Then you found your door."

"Then I found my door," Josh echoed. "I've been here ever since."

"I think there's a door—"

"Yours?"

She heard worry and pain in his voice. "No. I'm not going to leave. I feel as if we're waiting for someone to arrive."

SOMETHING IN THE WATER

WILLA BLYTHE

angst (minor), bipoc, coffee shop, customer service representative, death of a parent (off-screen), depression, elemental (water), emotional hurt/comfort, f/f, fat, humor, love at first sight, magic use, memory loss, past tense, third person limited point of view

Having a job with a halfway decent schedule, a livable wage, health insurance, and no terrible coworkers was the kind of magic most of Merrily's friends from undergrad had longed for while they were in classes. Here Merrily was, three years after graduation, working at the family coffee shop, and she wondered if maybe it was actually a curse.

Hobb Hill Beans and Leaves had been in the Shire family for generations, and when Merrily had come looking for a job after college, Aunt Trish had welcomed her with open arms. Merrily had been grateful.

She *was* grateful.

It might not seem like she was grateful, but only because Hobb Hill was about the most boring place someone could possibly live, and bemoaning this fact was one of Merrily's most beloved pastimes—one she often had time to indulge, since there was nothing else to do.

It was dull. It was stagnant. It was depressing in the extreme to be here while most of her friends were finishing Master's degrees or getting married or going on exotic vacations. They were doing things, and Merrily was stuck here...doing *nothing*.

But it wasn't such a bad life, really. At least she still got to Practice.

"Here's your half-caff vanilla latte with that good luck charm,

Portia," she said, passing the cup across the counter to a willowy woman in a gray suit. "You're going to rock this interview. I believe in you."

Portia smiled as she took the cup, drank without hesitation, and calmed. "Thanks, Merrily. I know it's going to be okay. I just have to…"

"You've just gotta be you," Merrily finished for her. "The Universe will do the rest."

Portia looked down at her watch, blanched, and headed for the door without even saying goodbye.

Please let that charm work. Portia deserves her break, Merrily thought as she picked up a rag and began wiping down the counters. Time to lean, time to clean.

The bright chime of the front door signaled another customer, and Merrily looked up only to freeze, breath caught in her chest, stunned like a fawn in the headlights.

This woman, she thought, *might be the most beautiful woman on the entire planet.*

And then she thought, *Oh god, I smell like a sweaty coffee bean!*

She flushed brilliantly as the customer—a plush, curvaceous woman, a little shorter than Merrily herself, with dark-brown skin, big brown eyes, and long brown hair that cascaded down her back and shoulders in a riot of curls—rushed toward the counter, looking relieved and distressed.

"Welcome to Beans and Leaves, can I—?"

"It's *you*, isn't it? Please tell me it's you. I really, *really* need it to be you." Her voice was sweet and melodic. Merrily could have listened to her babble all day.

"It's absolutely me," Merrily agreed instantly, dazed. "Um. What am I?"

"A witch," the woman said. "The only unregistered witch in the tri-county area—and, possibly, the only one not in the pocket of the Cherry Grove Homeowner's Association. Please, I need your help. It's urgent."

Merrily straightened, nodding more to herself than the woman. "Yeah— I—I do magic, yes. I guess you could call me a witch. And I don't…work with an HOA. So. I might be able to help."

"Oh, thank the Source. I'm Thea," the woman said, holding out a small, expertly manicured hand. Merrily took it on instinct. "And I need you to break a curse."

Merrily winced. "Ah, okay, well— That's—That's super unfortunate,

I really do feel for you, Thea, but—"

"But what?"

Merrily tried to pull her hand away, gently.

Thea did not let it go.

Oh, no.

"Well…" Merrily shrugged, trying to let her down easy. "I do small magic? The Little Practice, we call it. Good luck charms, help with intentions, dream-reading, stuff like that. Curses, that's…"

"That's…?" Thea kept hold of her hand, a prisoner caught in the limbo of the over-the-counter area that was normally reserved for the passing of currency and drinks.

"Well, that's Big Magic," Merrily said. "I don't do that. I'm sorry. You'll have to find someone else."

Thea looked at her. And blinked. And then—to Merrily's horror—began to *cry*.

"No no no, don't do that, please don't do that," Merrily begged, trying to pull away to find her a tissue, but Thea held tight to her hand.

"There—*is*—no—one—else," Thea said in a thin, shaking voice on the edge of disaster.

Merrily just couldn't let this happen. Not with tears. Not if she was never going to get her hand back.

And definitely not to the prettiest girl she'd ever seen.

"Okay, all right, I can at least take a look," Merrily said. "Let's have a seat, and you can tell me everything. Would you like some tea?"

"Yes, please," Thea said, sniffling.

Merrily waited, her hand still warm in Thea's steadfast embrace, and then—when it became obvious she wasn't going to get it back—she said, "Well…I'll…need both hands to brew it."

"You can't do it one-handed?" Thea asked, looking uncertain.

"I really need both hands." Merrily gave her a smile. She couldn't help it.

"If you think it's necessary…"

Thea dropped her hand, and Merrily turned to look through the box of tea blends, thoughts racing. Big Magic? Breaking curses? She couldn't do this; she'd be in way over her head.

She still remembered well what happened the only other time she'd tried Big Magic. She could hear Aunt Trish's voice over the phone even now, years later, crackling and horrible with sadness: *"I need you to give me a call as soon as you get this…"*

But as she turned, her hand prickled with the awareness that it was no longer in Thea's, and that…meant something.

It meant she had to try.

The Paradise Park gate was big, wrought iron, and looked like it had stood for centuries. Merrily waited in the pool of light cast by a streetlamp and looked at her watch—three minutes past their meeting time—and then up and down the deserted street. No Thea—and no anyone else either, not this close to the edge of the forest this late at night.

More time to examine the gate without any…distractions.

Merrily bowed her head and sank deep inside herself. At her core there was a well, deep and ancient, filled to the brim with a soft golden light. She stood next to it and swirled her fingers through the radiance, feeling the warmth, the glow of it.

She didn't *do* this. Ever. Even just coming here, to the wellspring, felt like asking for trouble. But Thea had been so desperate that she felt like she had to try.

The fact that Thea's gorgeous doesn't hurt either, Merrily thought, resenting her own weakness. *Just can't say no to a pretty face.*

She pulled a handful of light out of the well, watching as it sank, glowing, into her skin like water into soil. She shifted her perspective outside herself and placed her glowing hand on the fence. The light slid over the iron posts with their shiny black paint and their sharply pointed finials. It sank between the bars, feeling out all the edges, down to the concrete where the sidewalk met the grass. It pooled and spun up again, illuminating her face as it surged up the big double gate, searching for the mechanism, the lock, the *magic*—

And abruptly stopped, because *whoa, what the hell was* that?

Merrily staggered back, tripping over her own feet and falling into a soft, warm body that wrapped protectively around her.

"Sorry I'm late," Thea said cheerfully. "Though it seems like I arrived just in time."

Dazed, Merrily regained her footing and turned to greet her. "Um, yeah, I guess you did. Thea, what did you say was the reason you can't get inside this park again?"

"They banned me because I haven't paid my HOA fines," Thea said, tossing her curls defiantly. "If you don't pay them on time they add *fees*. Why anyone thinks adding an extra fine to a fine you already couldn't pay is the appropriate solution, I couldn't tell you!"

"And…the HOA fines are for…?" Merrily asked, trying to make sense of the magic on the gate, the strange conjunction of power, like a wall made up of a thousand bricks all carved from different kinds of stone. She peered at it, looking for some physical manifestation of the layers of magic there.

"My window blinds are three-quarters of an inch too wide."

Merrily stopped, turning back toward Thea.

"You've got to be joking."

Thea raised her hands in an eloquent shrug. "If I was, I wouldn't be barred from the park, and we wouldn't be out at eleven at night trying to fix it."

Merrily snorted. "That's ridiculous. That's the most ridiculous thing I've ever heard. That's so—"

"Trust me, Merry-girl, nothin' can kill your magic faster than bureaucracy," Dad said, rifling through a stack of envelopes. Merrily stirred the soup on the stove, swaying to a vinyl on the record player. "It sucks the life out of everything it touches."

"Never mind that, Dad," Merrily said, leaning down to sip the soup from a spoon. "Come taste—what does it need?"

She held the spoon out for him, one hand cupped underneath, and he blew gently on the steaming liquid before taking a sip. He looked thoughtful for a moment, then nodded. "Needs cumin. And intention. Don't forget about it, or it'll turn out weak and flimsy, like the excuses Mayor Dorchester makes every time somebody asks why management of Paradise Park is transitioning to one of those damned HOAs. It's highway robbery—"

"Here, how much cumin?"

"As much as your heart tells you. Feel it with your innermost self. And then taste it, and if it's not quite enough, add a little more."

"…Merrily?" Thea's voice sounded like it was coming from very far away. "Are you all right? You look…like something's wrong. Do you need a tissue? Are you going to—"

"I'm fine," Merrily said, forcing the memory away. She swallowed the lump in her throat, shook off the taste of cumin on her tongue. "There's…a lot of magic on this gate, Thea. Are you sure you can't live without getting into this park? What's keeping you from just…I dunno, going to a different one?"

Thea shook her head. "It's not that easy. My stream is in this park. I can't just go to another."

"Your stream?" Merrily looked at her, confused, before the pieces slotted into place. The cascading hair. The fluid grace of her movement. The *babbling*. "Goddess, you're a water spirit, aren't you?"

"And you're as smart as you are pretty," Thea said with a grin which faded immediately. "I need to get back to my stream to replenish myself, recharge, but the only parts I can access are in this park."

"And...if you don't get in?" Merrily ventured hesitantly.

"I've...already begun to forget things," Thea admitted. "If we stay away long enough, we forget who we are, where we're from, that we're magic at all. I don't even remember which river I came from, which lake or ocean—the memory of this little stream is all that's left."

Merrily frowned but nodded. "There's so many layers of spellwork in this wall, figuring out which curse applies to you would take weeks, maybe months, and I don't think we have that kind of time. I'm going to just...bull my way through and see if I can blast a hole big enough that the whole thing fails." Thea looked concerned and opened her mouth as if to protest, but Merrily cut her off. "I'm the witch, right? You asked for my help. So let me help."

"If...you think that's what's best," Thea said uncertainly, stepping back.

Merrily nodded again, gathering her strength. It should be relatively straightforward: pull as much power as she could, shove it at the lock until it broke, and then the integrity of the wall would fall—including the spell keeping Thea from her stream. It wasn't the kind of Big Magic she'd done before, but that was a good thing. The less complex it was, the less power she'd be drawing on from outside herself, the less she'd be asking for from the Universe—the less it would want in return. This would work. It would be fine. Nothing terrible was going to happen.

Hopefully.

Merrily positioned herself in front of the gate and pulled her power up from the wellspring inside her, glowing golden and brilliant as it shone from her hands. It poured over the sidewalk, the fence, the gate. It lit the night with the radiance of dawn, glazing everything with a luminescence that pulsed in time with her heart. She stared at the big lock at the center of the gate, looked past it to the wall of magic, the curses, the layers of power that hundreds of witches had laid here to try to enforce these stupid rules.

"Don't ever forget about the Little Practice, Merry-girl. It lets us do the unimaginable. When it's time to break down your own barriers, you'll know."

Dad's voice echoed in her head, making Merrily's breath catch, but she pushed it away, pulling light into her hands until they were blinding with power. She stepped forward, grabbed the lock, and *pushed.*

A metallic *screech* broke the quiet of the night as Merrily was thrown backward onto the pavement. She blinked up at the moon before Thea's anxious face blocked out everything else.

"Oh, Merrily, I knew that was a bad idea—are you okay?" Thea offered her a hand to help her up, but Merrily waved it away. She felt fine—except she didn't.

She'd failed. She'd known she would.

"Bad luck," she said quietly, pushing up on her elbows, then sitting, then standing. She dusted herself off. "Sorry."

"Are you hurt?" Thea repeated, not seeming to understand.

"Not really," Merrily said, hearing the dullness in her own voice. "But I'm pretty tired. Gonna go ahead and get home before it gets any later. Sorry, Thea. I'm sure you'll figure something out, though."

"Wait!" Thea said as Merrily turned to go, grabbing her hand once more. Merrily pulled it away. She wasn't going to let Thea trap her. "Merrily, wait, please—I'm sorry it didn't work, but can't you find another way? Perhaps a different method? Maybe with some research, or—"

"Bye, Thea," Merrily said, stuffing her hands in her pockets, turning away. "I hope you find someone who can help."

"Merrily," Thea whispered, so soft, so broken she almost didn't hear it. "You were my last hope."

But that wasn't true. Because Merrily wasn't anybody's hope—not really—not anymore.

BEFORE

Merrily yawned as she pulled her shawl tighter around her shoulders, watching the horizon as the first rays of sunlight peeked gently over it. She went over the steps of the spell again in her mind, closing her eyes to listen to the sound of the river behind her as it flowed sluggish and powerful in its bed. She knew the steps to the dance by heart, of course—she'd been practicing for almost a year, ever since she realized there was a blight on this river. While she had taken her survey samples for Hydrology II, done dissections for Anatomy and Physiology, studied tissue under the microscope in Biology III, and even fought through Organic Chemistry, she was also doing this: committing each step, each flourish, each intention, to memory, so it could be repeated as easy as breathing.

One, two, three, four—

Merrily swayed to the rhythm of the river's song, the melody it sang to her when she touched it, as she let the shawl slip from her shoulders and began the dance—moving into the water's shallows and through the steps with powerful intent. It was so cold, but she felt exhilarated by the chill. The current tugged at her ankles, trying to pull her deeper in as the music swelled in her mind. An orchestra of strings, winds, and percussion cascaded over her as she twirled and stepped, clapped and dipped, tracing out the pattern of the spell in the water.

—five, six, seven, eight—

The worn-smooth rocks covered in moss under her feet made it easy to slip out into deeper water, until she was in the river up to her waist. Reaching her arms overhead, she called down the purification of the sun, inviting it to cleanse the river of the poison. As the music began to swell toward a crescendo, she headed toward the final steps of the spell.

One, two, three, four—

She spun and spun and spun, arms starting out at her sides and then slowly pulling in toward her torso, and with them, pulling the poison in and up through her, out of the river. This was the part she'd been afraid of, the part she knew was dangerous. This was the part that made this dance Big Magic. It hurt, prickling at her insides, stinging and burning her throat, eyes, nose, and palms. She turned, stepping and swaying, spinning and sweeping, water dancing and singing all around her.

—five, six, seven, eight.

Her feet touched the ground in front of an urn she'd placed earlier, and she bowed over it, pouring the poison out of herself and into the vessel to be carried away somewhere else. Feeling it leave her was a relief, and she laughed out of sheer joy to have finished.

She'd done it.

Big Magic.

For the first time ever, Merrily Shire pulled off a *real* spell, and in two weeks she was going to graduate from college, and everything would be smooth sailing from here.

That's the way Dad always said it'd be. *"Work hard up front, then it's just smooth sailing, Merry."*

He was going to be so proud. She grabbed her phone to call him, unable to wait despite the fact that her wet clothes were freezing. A text message on the home screen from Aunt Trish just said, "Call me." The voicemail indicator blinked.

The thing about Big Magic is that it never, ever turned out the way you planned. He'd always told her that.

Why hadn't she listened?

"Merrily, honey? It's Aunt Trish— I—I need you to give me a call as soon as you get this. It's…honey, it's…it's about your dad."

Beans and Leaves was silent as Merrily sat on the counter, sipping steamed milk with caramel syrup—a comforting favorite. She looked up as the bell sounded over the door, unsurprised. She hadn't locked it. Thea's steps were light and slow.

"Merrily?" she called. "Are you okay?"

"Yes," Merrily said, and sipped her drink. "I wasn't really hurt."

"So what happened?" Thea stepped into the small pool of dim lamplight, looking confused and a bit forlorn.

"You saw. I tried to open it. It didn't work."

"I saw something," Thea agreed. "I'm not sure what it was. It looked like you were making yourself a battering ram."

"That's a way of opening it," Merrily huffed.

"It is, I guess," Thea said. "But…is it the best way?"

Merrily was silent, sipping her milk. She didn't know what to say.

"Though sometimes a wall of water can break down a floodgate, most of the time it won't," Thea said softly. "Most of the time, a dam will stop the river, and there's only one way to get through it: find a weakness and wear it out. That's my power."

"You wear things out?" Merrily asked, laughing.

Thea waggled her eyebrows, teasing, and said, "I do." Then she grew more serious. "I thought perhaps we could try again—together—my way. Just try to…wear out the lock."

"Thea, I…" Merrily swallowed, shaking her head. "I want to help, but…"

"But what?"

Thea looked at her, soft, open, so sweet and so kind and in so much need, and Merrily couldn't help but spill the truth.

"I don't do Big Magic because I can't pay the price. Not again."

"What kind of price is there?" Thea asked, quiet.

"It's always different. It—It isn't something you choose. The magic takes something from you. And last time, it—" Merrily hesitated, breathing in deep through her nose and out through her mouth. "It took my Dad. He died in a car wreck. I got the news right after I finished the only Big Magic I ever tried."

"Oh, Merrily…" Thea looked stricken. She reached out to take Merrily's hand, holding it in both of her own. She brought it to her lips to kiss, and for a moment Merrily let herself think about kissing those lips with hers, how soft they'd be, how sweet. But she couldn't ask for that when she'd failed so thoroughly. When she had nothing to offer.

"You see now," Merrily whispered, "why I can't try again."

"I see why you would struggle with it, yes," Thea said, still holding her hand. "But—you know, don't you, that the Source doesn't take that way? It keeps the Universe in balance, yes, but it wouldn't punish you for using the power it gave you."

"It did, though," Merrily argued. "I did the spell and—"

"And something terrible happened," Thea agreed. "But that had nothing to do with your magic, Merrily, and everything to do with the choices of others—of the other drivers on the road, of the city managers, of the car manufacturers, of your father himself—but not of you. It wasn't your fault."

Merrily had seen thousands of people walk into Beans and Leaves, and none of them—not the pretty ones, not the nice ones, not even the insistent ones—had gotten as close to her in three years as Thea had in one day. With every word Thea spoke, it was as if she had worked her way into all the weaknesses inside Merrily's armor of boredom and disinterest. Merrily had barely put her mug down before the tears started coming, and then she was wrapped in Thea's warm embrace as a torrent swept through her.

Years, she'd waited. Years, she'd wasted.

Thea's hand on her hair brought her back to herself; Merrily raised her splotchy, tearstained face to look at Thea. "I'm—I'm sorry—"

"Don't be." Thea leaned forward. Merrily wasn't sure what was going to happen—but then she felt the press of Thea's lips to hers, soft and sweet as she'd imagined. When Thea pulled back, she whispered, "You're all right. You know, now, don't you? It was never your doing."

Merrily nodded, sniffling.

"Do you think you could kiss me again?" Merrily asked, laughing a little. "I didn't do my best the first time."

Thea laughed, too, and peppered her face with kisses, gentle, cleansing, until meeting Merrily's lips with her own again. This time, Merrily kissed back in earnest, opening to Thea with all the promise of spring, all the hope that had been dormant for so long.

"Will you try again?" Thea asked when she pulled away, not far, forehead pressed to Merrily's.

"Yes," Merrily agreed, tears still leaking from her eyes. "Yes. If you'll help me, I'll try again."

The gate stood as solid as before, but Merrily looked at it with less fear now. There was no way she could do worse than she'd done earlier. And Thea was going to help.

"How do you want to do this?" Merrily asked. Thea's fingers tangled with hers, her palm warm.

"Well—blasting it isn't going to work," Thea said. "You can see it, right? What does it look like?"

"Like a wall made up of lots of different kinds of bricks," Merrily said, looking at it with her Sight again. "Very tall, and deep—like they've been laying bricks here for years, and never taken them off."

" 'Course they have," Thea grumbled. "If I had been to my stream recently, I could be of more help—but my magic is so quiet right now…"

"It's okay," Merrily assured her. "We can do this. We'll figure it out."

Thea smiled and squeezed her hand, and that was a kind of magic all its own, the power in that little squeeze. It made something in her flutter to life, like flame on a wick. Merrily reached out with her other hand and touched the gate, saw past it to the wall beyond as she lay her hand against the bricks. Her light began to cover the wall, spilling over the different sizes and colors of bricks, highlighting each of them one at a time. She didn't direct it beyond saying, *Find the weaknesses.*

The light flowed over and to the other side. She could feel it moving along the length of the wall, but she couldn't see it—blocked by the magic of the gate. She watched, waited, for some sort of sign—and then Thea gasped and squeezed her hand again.

"Merrily—is that yours?"

She turned to look, and a light—a brilliant beam about the size of an ink pen—shone into the darkness like a spotlight from the other side of the wall.

"I think we found our gateway," Merrily said with a grin, and tugged Thea down the sidewalk toward that section of the fence. They stopped in front of it, and she readied herself for the spell—the Big Magic—to sink into the crevice and make it hers, to wear it out the way water would.

"Can I help?" Thea asked, and Merrily knew, in her heart, how she could.

"Dance with me?"

Under the stars, Merrily felt Thea's hand on her shoulder, and her own found Thea's waist. Together, they began to dance—to nothing, at first, no sound at all but their shared breaths, until a soft melody sprung up from all the places they touched, just the barest hint of the flute in Merrily's head. Merrily led the dance, leaning into it, into her power, into *Thea*, and as they danced, the song grew louder, stronger. The beam of light expanded, the crack in the barrier growing with every turn they took around the sidewalk.

One, two, three, one, two, three—it had been a long time since she'd danced at all, much less like this, and the feel of the magic flowing through her was like nothing else. It was like seeing the world for the first time—and also like coming home. She laughed, unable to help herself or look away. The light kept growing, shining brighter over them as new cracks in the wall began to form, branching out from the first as their dance began to wear down the magic.

"It's working," Thea said, grinning so hard it must hurt.

"We're doing it," Merrily agreed. She pressed her forehead to Thea's, rubbed their noses together, and the song grew, a tune that echoed in her mind, sounding very familiar as it crashed joyously over her. "Thea—?"

Just then, behind Thea's head, light poured in like a sunrise over the horizon as the wall came down all at once, crumbling to dust. Thea shuddered and something in her seemed to break as well. She turned from the dance and ran, past the unlocked iron gate and straight for the stream in the back corner of the park. Merrily followed, watching as

Thea leaped from the little footbridge into the stream, fully clothed, and something—happened.

Merrily had thought she'd seen Big Magic before. She'd thought she'd done Big Magic before.

There was Big Magic.

And then there was this.

Before her, Thea seemed simultaneously the same and wholly different, transformed by her contact with the water. The song that had played in Merrily's head as they had danced swept through the boughs of the trees overhead, joyous and bubbling, and Merrily remembered where she'd heard it before. She rushed forward and knelt by the bank.

"It was you, the river near the woods—the one I danced in—"

"It was *you* who healed me," Thea said, smiling widely, tears gathering in her big brown eyes. "I felt so good after being sick for so long, I got right up and left—but I forgot to come back, and I kept forgetting, until suddenly I couldn't remember even when I tried to. All I remembered was this little stream, and I knew I had to get here, and that I should go to you for help. Now I know why."

Merrily swallowed around a lump in her throat. She threw her arms around Thea's waist. "You have to know you helped me just as much," she whispered. "I couldn't have done it—any of this—without you."

"No," Thea agreed, and tipped Merrily's face up to her own with gentle fingers under her chin. "And now it's done. What would you like to do next?"

"Well...I...think I'd like to take you on a date, if you'll have me," Merrily laughed, and Thea laughed too.

"Yes, Merrily, I'll have you," Thea whispered, and for a moment Merrily closed her eyes, listening to the river song, feeling Thea's presence wash over her. Then, Thea pulled her up, up, into a kiss, sweet and searing with the force of life that Merrily had been missing. Pure and golden and powerful: the kind of kiss that knocked the world a little off its axis, that shifted the ground under one's feet, that slid everything just enough out of place that it fell into something so much better.

The kind of kiss that you could build an empire around.

The kind of kiss that wore down all defenses.

"I'll pick you up at eight, then?" Merrily asked, breathless, lips still brushing Thea's.

"Bold of you to assume I'm letting you leave."

HOMECOMING DANCE
WILLA BLYTHE

"Dance with me?"

Merrily looked far more beautiful than she had any right to, soft and hopeful in the golden light of her own power. As if Thea could refuse her. She fit just right in Thea's arms, like they'd danced together before, like they were designed for it.

Something whispered in her ear, pure and sweet, enticing her to come close. It sounded familiar. It sounded forgotten.

It sounded like something that would have to wait. She clung to Merrily as they twirled around the sidewalk, the pool of light surrounding them growing brighter, larger. She had thought having Merrily in her arms would settle something inside her, but it didn't. She wanted *more*—more time, more touch, more of the magic of that smile on her face.

Come back.

"It's working," Thea said, ignoring the call—the pull—that gripped something deep inside her.

Come home.

"We're doing it," Merrily said, and she laughed, and Thea nearly died from joy at hearing it.

You're so close.

The touch of Merrily's face against hers made her ache for something—something on the edge of knowing, something within reach—

"Thea—?"

The brilliance of Merrily's light poured over her dear face like dawn, and, in seeing it, in seeing her in all of her glory, Thea knew.

She remembered.

And she was home.

ᎧHE BAᴫᴫAD OF ᎩGGDRASIL

KRISTI MAE

anti-soulmates, aphobia (internalized), aromantic, classism (mentions of), coffee shop, customer service representative, f/f, friends, mythology (norse), norway, queerplatonic relationship, soulmates, third person limited point of view

On the day when the world celebrates the union of the two mages, the cumulonimbus clouds unfurl over the ridge of the mountains. The mist whispers over the vaulted arches of the cathedral, singing a lullaby that no one hears over the rustle of wedding guests turning up the collars of trench coats against the wind. The stained glass inside the rose window—*the pride of Ålesund*, they say—tells of an ancient ash tree, one who sees all and knows all.

Under the cover of the dusty grey sky, unseen gardenias bloom at the foot of the stairs and stretch to the burbling river. They're all pristine, shivering in the breeze, except for one: its stem is ragged, lonely; its petals and pistil are missing among a sea of white. Yggdrasil knows, and hopes for, this flower—and so does she wait.

Inside the cathedral, Alina stands near the altar. Her arms cradle a sprawling bouquet, but she curls the fingers of one hand around a single white bloom. Her sister stands in front of her in lace of the finest flowing alabaster, so Alina can't see her smile, but it's reflected on her partner's face, lopsided with the uncertainty of this new world into which they embark. They're no longer halves, but instead are united as one

218

whole. His smile stretches from cheek, to jaw, to that invisible space where joy catches fire and spreads, unfettered, to all who witness it.

To all but Alina.

Her smile is pasted on her cramped cheeks. Twenty-seven years of grass-stained knees, of laughter alone in the garden, of falling behind her baby sister in all that mattered, culminates in *this moment.*

"Now, you are prepared," the priest says, standing between Elisabeth and her intended, Åse. He lifts his hands, palms up, to invite them to follow.

"With the removal of this ring," the priest continues, "we honour the entrance of these soulmates into magical society. In so doing, we pay heed to Holy Yggdrasil and our untenable connection with her branches and roots."

Elisabeth and Åse raise their hands. Matching thin, pure-silver rings around their index fingers respond to their closeness—to the proximity of their soulmate. Two bands of light, tethered together like chains, emerge from each of their hands.

"With the removal of this ring," the priest repeats, "we honour the entrance of these soulmates into magical society. In so doing, we pay heed to Holy Yggdrasil and our untenable connection with her branches and roots."

A smile blazing on his face, Åse slides Elisabeth's ring off with a tender touch. The light crackles as Elisabeth does the same with his. Their palms press together, and the bright bands sizzle and multiply around them, fuse into a single opalescent beam, and rise above them for a single moment that suspends the cathedral in breathless anticipation.

Then, it shatters.

Finally released, the light spreads like fire over the congregation, high up to the flying buttresses, low down underneath the toes of the watching souls. Alina breathes in, the air suffused with colour and magic that she will only ever be able to witness, never experience. In seconds, the light fades, but the energy remains.

The priest's voice is soft when he speaks once more. "May Elisabeth and Åse love each other forevermore, as Yggdrasil loves us."

Alina crushes the bloom in her hand.

The next morning at Baker Hansen, Alina puts on her favourite scowl and dismisses the wedding from her mind. Time to return to real life: research, work, and solitude. Things familiar and safe.

The musky scent of rising yeast welcomes her first steps into the small corner shop. The sun pours into the room's corners and reflects off cozy tables made of painted oak. Alina settles at one, tuning out the murmurs of the other customers as they speak in mixed Norwegian and English. She opens her notebook to work, and the relief that escapes her lips when her fingers wrap around the fountain pen is more acute than any bullshit Yggdrasil supposedly offered.

In non-magical society, the ring is a symbol of commitment, joy, and love, which is a sharp contrast to its role as a shackle in magical society, Alina writes. *All mages should strive for such a transition. Someday, we shall not be bound.*

Alina takes a satisfied sip of her coffee. A stunning paper, truly. Remarkable as they come.

The coffee burns her tongue.

She leans over to write more, but a whispered giggle nearby makes her turn.

"Skatten min," the girl says in a light, warning tone. *My treasure.*

The tealight in front of them is lit, its flame too large for its small body; it flickers and dances under the hand of the person who sits across from the girl. His eyes aren't on the flame but on the girl, brighter than a thousand candles and more adoring.

Despite his distracted gaze, the flame grows under his hand, sputtering in weblike tendrils above the edge of the tealight, reaching with greedy fingers toward the open window.

Alina turns away with effort; something about the creak of her chair sounds defiant, and that heartens her. Their laughter seems to rise up in mockery around her, just as the smoke does.

"I'd appreciate if you didn't burn down the establishment." The voice comes from behind her, lilting with a foreign accent and an air of uncalled-for command. As quickly as she'd turned away, her gaze is tugged to the speaker—a woman with chestnut-red hair that cascades down her shoulders. She appears to work here, dressed in a forest-green apron with the name "Sjöfn" embroidered on the front with a tiny heart over the "n."

"Sorry," the boy mutters, reducing the flame with a wave.

The woman—Sjöfn—glares at the couple and walks off, a plate of rye bread and cheese in one hand and a kokekaffe in the other.

Warmth pulsates around the knuckles of Alina's left hand; there's a tiny amber glow around the band on her left index finger. Alina looks up once more, her heart clawing for a way out of her chest, but Sjöfn is gone. When she looks back at her hand, the glow has disappeared.

Alina tucks her books against her chest and flees outside. Breathing heavily, she leans against the wall beside the bakery's back door, gazing blankly over the tables and umbrellas scattered about the tiled patio before her. She ignores the curious gazes that other customers send her way and settles down at the table nearest to her.

Surely, she'd imagined it. Surely, it was a cruel trick of the light, a delusion spurred by shadows from the wedding the day before.

I don't have a soulmate, her brain repeats wildly, in opposition to the rhythm of her heart. *I've never felt the pull. I've never felt— That's not who I am—*

The glow had been weak, the feeling warm instead of searing hot. What did it *mean*? Where were her books on this when she needed them?

But there are no books here, only memories of days when she'd tried and failed to summon the same enthusiasm her friends had for when they'd find their soulmates, when they'd finally be able to harness the true magic of Yggdrasil. There were so many days when she'd sat alone, waiting for it to hit her—waiting for the moment she would *want* it to hit her.

"Sorry about those kids," says that voice she'd just tried to convince herself she'd imagined.

Alina jumps. Sjöfn's eyes are startlingly blue, like a quiet shade of the sea at low tide. Absently, Alina hides her hand behind her back, craving and dreading that receded flicker of warmth.

"They weren't bothering me," Alina says.

Sjöfn leans against the wall beside her, planting one foot against it in a supercilious display and pulling a cigarette and a lighter from her pocket. Setting the cigarette aflame, she lifts it casually to her lips. "It was written on your face, darling."

Alina recoils and digs her nails into her palm. This can't be her soulmate—someone who so blithely sullies the air? Yggdrasil has got something wrong. As Sjöfn exhales, smoke twines around her in ribbons of shining slate.

"Do you have to do that?"

It's so long before Sjöfn responds that Alina isn't sure she heard. Sjöfn taps her fingers over the cigarette, watching the ash as it flutters into the dirt. "It helps me commune with the spirits."

"You're still wearing your ring."

"Why should I need a partner to commune with the spirits?"

Alina wants to laugh in bafflement. "That's kind of how it works." She's not sure how this whole *soulmate* thing goes—is she supposed to ask a total stranger on a date? One who doesn't even strike her as particularly lovely?

Sjöfn shrugs. "It is if you buy into the propaganda."

She twists the smoke; the ribbons coil into a bow. Alina stares at it, spellbound, until it's drawn toward the forest and dissipates into the wind.

"Love isn't propaganda," Alina says. "I saw it happen just yesterday."

"Did you?"

"At the wedding. Surely you've felt what happens when the rings come off." Warmth nudges at Alina's hand once more. She doesn't dare peek down as it spreads through her fingers and palm like lava in her blood. Stubbornly, Alina props her chin in her hand and stares at Sjöfn's face, pale save for where a faint blush obscures the freckles dotted over her nose and cheeks.

"Maybe that part is real," Sjöfn says.

Her statement has a mild air of sarcasm, but the shine in her eyes gives Alina hope. Over the years, her soul has frayed into a whispered shadow of what she once was promised, but maybe Yggdrasil hasn't lied. Maybe Sjöfn is the person she's been waiting for her entire life. Maybe Alina's time has finally come.

They talk briefly about nothing, dancing around a flimsy, fake connection that neither of them seems willing to acknowledge.

"I have to get back inside," Sjöfn says, snuffing the cigarette against the wall. "But would you tell me your name?"

"It's Alina."

"Hyggelig å møtes, Alina." Sjöfn holds out her hand, and Alina takes it. She barely holds back a gasp when the warmth that had flirted about her hands throughout the conversation takes root in her skin and spreads like fire through a perpetual winter's night.

And then she knows: Yggdrasil never lies.

The next morning, Alina wakes to a stomach in knots and eyes puffy from lack of sleep. The warmth is long gone from her hands, but lingers around her, slipping under the duvet to nestle between her outstretched arms. She spent all night researching sjelevenner in hopes of finding *something* new, something she'd somehow missed during her years of research. Sjöfn had seemed so sure of herself. Was it possible to have magic without a partner? Wasn't acquiring the magic the only reason anyone tried to find a partner anyway? She can't find anyone answering these questions. It can't be that easy.

Her feet carry her back to the bakery; she's drawn there as if beckoned by the sea itself.

From the moment the aroma of bread and roasted coffee beans tugs her into another world, her eyes are on Sjöfn. Her unruly hair is tossed into a bun, her gaze focused on the milk that she's frothing for a latte as if it's of paramount importance. Alina trades her weight between her feet, heart in her throat. She isn't used to *caring* about being more important than someone's coffee.

She steps up and orders from a girl who she forgets instantly, shoving fifty kroner across the counter like a teenager on her first trip away from home.

And that's when she catches Sjöfn's bright-blue eyes, and Sjöfn smiles.

Alina tries to smile back, but she's not sure she manages it before her traitorous feet launch her outside. To safety. To the table she'd been sitting at yesterday when they first spoke.

Not that she's hoping for Sjöfn to follow.

A few minutes later, the door opens with the chime of a bell, and Sjöfn *does* follow her, and Alina might collapse.

"God morgen, Alina," Sjöfn says cheerily. "You came at a good time. Your kokekaffe?"

"Takk," is all she trusts herself to reply, wrapping her hands around the steaming mug. She inhales the smoky, bitter scent, utterly lost for what to say. Sjöfn seems unconcerned, drawing out another cigarette. She conveniently seems to be able to take a break each time Alina shows up at the café.

The anxiety that had been rising in Alina's stomach all morning takes hold of her throat. Her frantic searching returned little, but she had learned that it was risky to acknowledge the connection with a soulmate. Many relationships started aflame, then went south because of the intensity of early passions—and when the nascent bond shattered, with it went their chances of ever being mature mages.

Alina certainly doesn't want *that*.

"Do you believe in Fossegrim?" Sjöfn asks over a plume of smoke.

Getting the deal-breakers out of the way? Alina is tempted to reply, but she worries what such an answer would imply. Instead, she shifts in her seat, thinking of her school friends cooing over celebrities on TV and fussing over their nail polish before dates, as if such frivolity was worth something. Is this bumbling uncertainty what they had felt? It couldn't have been.

"Why would I need folktales when I can have the real thing once I have a partner?" She means it to sound flirtatious, but it comes out far too genuine.

Sjöfn crosses her arms. A smile plays at the corner of her lips. "I happen to think it's good to be part of something bigger than yourself."

Isn't that the whole point of having a partner?

Alina holds her tongue. She crosses her arms across her chest, pretending her eyes aren't drawn to the sliver of Sjöfn's ring that peeks out from between her chest and arm. If only she could see if it was glowing; if only she could see if Sjöfn was the key to the freedom she craves.

"Shouldn't we be talking about the weather?" Alina says. "Or your favourite colour, maybe?"

Sjöfn puffs out a curl of smoke as if that's an answer. It twists through the air like a serpent, its raised head peering into Alina's soul, and she simultaneously wants to lean in and run away. "Partners don't approach that level of communion with the world, Alina. Magic can't fix what's broken. It can only pretend."

Alina exhales, trying to subdue her irritation. She's learned a lot about soulmates, but this is *not* in the rule book. Maybe Sjöfn feels nothing for her. Maybe she's expecting too much from this complete stranger. Maybe one-sided soulmates are a thing. With her luck, that's exactly what Yggdrasil would deliver to her after decades of loneliness.

"Next Thursday, take fenalår for Fossegrim," Sjöfn says. As if Alina looks like she would ever steal smoked mutton from someone, much less offer it to a water spirit, *especially* as an unpartnered mage. "You have to keep going back for him to teach you, but you should be able to feel him there, watching you."

"Your favourite colour is purple?" Alina says, winded by the effort it takes to hide her interest. "That's lovely. I'm partial to green, myself."

A grin spreads wide across Sjöfn's face. She snubs out her cigarette against the brick wall. "Du er søt. But it's blue."

Like your eyes, Alina doesn't say.

"I should get back," Sjöfn says as she straightens. "You might dismiss Fossegrim, but I think if Yggdrasil made us soulmates, it will have been for a reason."

"What do you think the reason is?"

Sjöfn just smiles and turns away.

"So, what do you do when you're off work? Adventure through the forests?" Alina asks. With all Sjöfn knows about the creatures of legend, she's probably traipsing around with fairies or elves on any given evening.

Sjöfn's eyes twinkle as she takes a sip of her coffee. "Well, Asgard gets lonely."

Asgard. The name is familiar, reminiscent of a grand kingdom in the air connected to the rest of the world by a rainbow bridge.

"Who's Asgard? Your pet dragon?" She knows they don't exist, but the fantasy is pleasant, and she can't help but smile.

Sjöfn blinks, but recovers quickly. She leans forward as if to tell Alina a secret. "Yes. I like to fly on his back over the fjords. But only at dawn, to avoid traffic in the skies."

"I hear it's unbearable at twilight," Alina says sagely. "All the youths coming in, pretending like they understand anything about how to respect the earth."

"You get me!"

"Mmhmm. Dragon-riding etiquette is serious business."

Sjöfn's bright smile softens as she looks down, mixing the froth in her coffee. "He's my calico cat. I read him poetry."

Alina bursts into laughter. Flying with dragons is one thing, but thinking about Sjöfn cozying up in her recliner with a cat nestled in her lap makes Alina flush with warmth. And not in her fingers this time, but in her cheeks; a feeling that, just for a moment, exists outside Yggdrasil's influence.

Alina returns to the bakery six times over the next seven days. Talking with Sjöfn doesn't feel quite like she's used to hearing about—it's comfortable and friendly, not like buzzing sparks—but that doesn't mean they couldn't be soulmates. There's magic hidden there. There must be. But while Sjöfn will joke about her cat or share her favourite colour, getting more information about anything that actually *matters* proves impossible. Finally, desperate to hear more about the magic, Alina returns to the one topic that might provide the answers she seeks.

"What happens if I bring fenalår for Fossegrim?"

It's only a folktale, and as much as she loves to indulge the idea, she can't pin her hopes on it. Besides, if she embarks alone on such an endeavour, everyone she knows will gossip about her even more than they already do. Their whispers always lurk in her consciousness:

"Alina's a weirdo."

"She doesn't even have a soulmate. She's not a mage if she can never do magic."

"She just thinks she's better than us."

But Sjöfn hears none of those insidious whispers. Instead, she pokes at the dessert Alina has convinced her to share. "You know the story. He'll connect you with nature."

"Do you think it's true?"

"It was for me."

"Will you go with me, then?" Alina asks. "You know, as my soulmate?"

Sjöfn makes an impatient noise. "You have to go alone. Soulmates are Yggdrasil's nonsense. They don't cut it there, not for Fossegrim."

Alone, to the edge of the forest! A place kept sacred for couples! As if she can just ogle the magic that isn't hers and scurry away like a mouse. It goes against everything she'd been taught.

"It's just that…Fossegrim is shy," Sjöfn says quietly.

Alina laughs. According to the legends, Fossegrim is a massive water spirit who lures in unsuspecting innocents. He's not afraid.

"Alina, usually only couples go there. If you're single, you go in secret, by cover of night. Why do you think he's never seen?"

It's certainly one explanation. And she'd be lying if she claimed she didn't yearn for the clatter of branches overhead and the rush of water between her toes.

"Okay," Alina says. "I'll go."

Sjöfn's eyes light up with pleasure. She reaches her hand out to Alina, palm up, silver band glinting in the sun. The air whistles around her in an invisible embrace as their fingers twine together, warmth kissing warmth, and the glow engulfs them.

She may not understand the secrets—of soulmates, of love, of Sjöfn, or of the earth—but she can't deny the feeling that this is exactly where she is supposed to be.

Alina twirls in front of the mirror, her red, pleated dress flowing about her legs. She grins, but the smile in the mirror looks smaller than it should. She stretches her cheeks wide, coaxing her face to match the picture in her head. Sjöfn is stubborn, insistent that having a soulmate is valueless, but it's only a matter of time before she sees all that she's missing. It's up to Alina to show her how beautiful love is.

She gazes at the reflection of pale, slender fingers that don't feel like hers. The band around her index finger emits a constant glow, more gold now than silver. Has Sjöfn felt the same emotions as she has? The little catch in her throat when she tries to speak, the prickling desire to touch—the *butterflies*! They must be real. Sjöfn must have felt them too.

Her expression in the mirror eases into a smile that crinkles around her eyes. She raises her hand to hover just short of touching the glass, and joy sparks a bright glow through the ring. In truth, meeting Sjöfn is the best thing that's ever happened to her. To no longer be forced to pretend! To be allowed to sink into a world that's never been hers! How could this be anything but the realization of Yggdrasil's sacred promise?

When her hand finally touches the mirror, the glass splinters.

Alina inhales sharply. She runs her fingers down the broken web of shards, trying to summon energy that she doesn't know how to control. But nothing moves; the glow around her ring disappears, like it's whispering that she will be shackled forever.

Alina closes her eyes. It doesn't matter. Soon—Soon, she will be united with Sjöfn in the way they were always meant to be.

She can no longer wait.

At the bakery, Alina waits outside at their normal table until Sjöfn joins her, setting down a plate of kvæfjordkake for them to share.

"Would you like to go out sometime?" Alina says, tapping her feet underneath the table. "On a proper date?"

Sjöfn stares at her, her spoon suspended in midair. Alina swallows. The silence that stretches between them is unbearable. Why is it so difficult to ask out one's soulmate?

Finally, Sjöfn laughs. It's almost a cruel sound.

"That's not something I *do*, Alina," she says, then adds, as if in apology, "and, frankly, it doesn't seem like something you do, either."

The words slam into her with more force than Sjöfn delivers them with. "What do you mean?"

Sjöfn sighs. "You know how I feel about soulmates."

Alina does—of *course* she does—but she wants to cling to that feeling that coursed through her in front of the mirror: that sense of inevitability, of sureness, of the world and Yggdrasil's magic. She craves the butterflies that flutter between her ribs and murmur a story that is easy to tell.

"Don't you want the magic?" Alina whispers.

Sjöfn looks baffled, and Alina's cheeks burn. "Is that what this is about? You don't need that."

"Of course I do," Alina protests. "It's...it's the only way your life can have any...*status.*"

Frowning, Sjöfn puts down her spoonful of cake. "What, exactly, do you think I do? Sit around all day serving coffee, then go back to my pathetic, no-magic life at the end of the day?"

"It's not...you." It's the clearest way Alina can say, *I wish I was like you.* "I'm just—I'm sick of feeling like this, Sjöfn."

"I've already told you that you don't need a partner to have what you want. Why don't you believe me?"

"If it was that easy to just *learn* magic, why would anyone bother trying to find a partner?" Alina asks. She can't back down about this.

"It's not as powerful as partnered magic. But that doesn't mean you can't—"

"Then why are you so resistant to having a soulmate, when you could have it all? You could have me! You could have love! You could have more than just these...*stories* that people tell to make themselves feel better about not having a soulmate!"

Sjöfn is quiet, her gaze intense, but she leans forward. Alina sucks in a deep breath.

"I want you to look at me, and tell me you want that," Sjöfn says.

Breath lodges in Alina's throat. It steals the words from her mouth.

"Look at me, and tell me you're in love with me, Alina."

The words don't come, though she tries to summon them. How easy they should be to say!

Sjöfn leans back once more, apparently satisfied with herself. "That's what I thought."

Baffled, Alina flounders, afloat at sea with no raft. Without the certainty of love...what's left?

"There's a place I know," Sjöfn says. "A place you'll like."

"Take me there," Alina whispers, and unlike her past feelings, this conviction feels like maybe it could be her own.

They meet the next morning at the burning edge of dawn. Alina doesn't bother with a dress, and Sjöfn doesn't bother to tell her where they're going, instead tying a midnight-blue cloth over Alina's eyes as casually as if she's asking about the weather. Sjöfn refuses to answer any questions, instead coaxing her to "pay attention to how the earth feels," as if that's easy with her vision restricted, as if that means anything.

The trill of blackbirds celebrates morning; their song floats over crackling branches as squirrels chase each other through the brush. Alina longs to shed everything *dating* and *soulmates* and run into the arms of the sea, but she has no idea how far from home they are. She shuffles forward, unsteady on her feet, the whispers of yesterday's conversation keeping her uneasy.

"Can't you feel it, Alina? The wind calling for you?"

"Maybe," Alina says.

The grip around her shoulders tightens. "Tell me something. Do you believe that everyone who gets married actually loves their partner?"

"I don't know, Sjöfn."

"Well, maybe you should *ask*."

"Maybe you should let me have what I want!"

Alina tugs forward harder than necessary and loses her balance—though whether she's unbalanced by the root underfoot or by the weight of her frustration and longing, she doesn't know. She barely catches her footing in time to press into the sandy sludge that forms the edge of the fjord. The sound of rushing water fills her eardrums; she somehow hadn't heard it previously, but now it's everything, has been there all along, since long before she and Sjöfn forged a connection.

She needs to be free.

She needs to *see*.

Alina tears the blindfold off.

Before her stands a grove of knotted yew trees that protect the water's narrow shore, their branches spread toward the sea's tender cerulean heart. The mountains crest high above them on both sides, the morning mist now cleared from their peaks. Power oozes from limb to limb of the ancient wood, seizing her soul and heaving her into the depths of the fjord. Yet, despite the might before her, the water is gentle as it kisses the grass, and the leaves above them knit a canopy that houses them alone.

"Where are we?" Alina breathes.

"In the place that has been waiting for you," Sjöfn says softly.

Alina turns to her, but Sjöfn is focused on pulling something small from the folds of her coat. It's long and thin, with evenly spaced holes and intricate patterns carved into antique rosewood.

A flute.

Alina watches with bated breath as Sjöfn brings the instrument to her lips and begins to play.

As the notes sing upon the breeze, the stream seems to redirect, straining toward their herald. The wind strikes an anthem, calling them into a harmony that Alina has never bothered to hear. The clattering of branches, the shivering blades of grass, the rattling of granite pebbles along the shore: all coalesce into an effortless symphony.

The water joins too: first in a rushing hiss, then in rising waves that glisten in the sunlight as if sharing a whispered secret among raucous joy.

The water sings, and it calls Alina to dance.

Without care for her clothing, she leaps, first at a wade and then in a hungry dive.

Weight barrels into her—Sjöfn enveloping her, warm and constant. The water takes them up, and up, and breathtakingly *up*, until they're flying on the current. They're soaked, cresting high over the earth for exhilarating seconds that stretch and fold into eternity. Alina tries to breathe; the water plunges into her nose and throat, but she doesn't choke. Instead, it flows hot through her like she's inhaled pure mountain air, warmed by the relentless shining of the sun.

And then the music fades.

The water slows and washes them ashore.

Alina lies, splayed on the ground and panting.

"You said you couldn't do magic," she rasps.

Sjöfn's panting, too, lying beside her, drenched hair clinging to her neck, water dripping from her skin. "It wasn't mine," Sjöfn says. "I listened to the call of the forest, and Fossegrim taught me. I learned, Alina."

Alina rolls to Sjöfn's side, closes her eyes, and presses their foreheads together. She feels like she's standing on the precipice of the rest of her life.

"Welcome to the magic of the earth," Sjöfn murmurs.

Sjöfn takes Alina's hand, lifts it to her mouth, and places a tender kiss on each of her fingers before settling on the silver ring on her index finger. "There's something I've been thinking about…something else I want to try. But I don't know what will happen."

"What is it?" Alina says, her voice nothing more than an exhale.

"Let's throw them away."

The rings?

Of course, the rings. *Someday we shall not be bound*, she had written, and the idea that *someday* could be now—that all along, Yggdrasil *had* never lied—takes her breath away.

Alina nods. They each pry the rings from soaking fingers with held breaths as the quiet burble of water laps at their ankles. And then, simultaneously, they cast their rings into the unfathomable depths of the sea.

IN LIKE FLYNN

JO MATHIESON

academia, bookstore, coffee shop, dragon, first kiss, genderfluid, getting together, m/nb, magic use, meet cute, non-binary, past tense, pining (mutual), professor, student (college), third person limited point of view

As he was about to quit his search of Buy Books and Brews, a title caught Crispin's interest: *Theories of Advanced Displacement*. The book had a plain cream-colored binding and was sturdy-looking, like a textbook, though a very old one. It was exactly the kind of tome he spent his Saturday mornings looking for, visiting used bookshops that sold both mundane and magical texts. Crispin reached for the book and bashed his knuckles against those of another patron; he pulled his hand away in surprise and pain, and they grabbed the book off the shelf.

"Excuse me," Crispin said in a polite, but firm, tone, "I was looking at that book."

"Yeah, well, so was I." The speaker was younger than Crispin by a few years, and, given their age and apparent interest in advanced magical theory, he was surprised that they weren't wearing the indigo robes of a student Mage, but rather plain grey trousers with a pale-yellow shirt.

"I'm writing a historical account of theories of magical displacement, you see," Crispin said in what he thought was a perfectly reasonable tone.

"Yeah, well, I'm studying to do actual displacement, and I saw it first, so tough luck." The other customer stared down at Crispin with large green eyes that were partially obscured by an unruly mop of medium-length dark hair, then turned on a heel and stalked away.

Arguing further about which of them had spotted the book first would be pointless, but Crispin followed the retreating figure toward the checkout counter out of curiosity. Advanced displacement wasn't a popular topic of study, even among Mages.

"That will be thirty-two dollars, please," Danai said, smiling at the customer and ringing up the sale on the antique mechanical cash register. The book sat on the counter with its front cover open so that Danai could check the price that was pencilled onto the flyleaf. *A Complete Manual for the Advancement of the Art of Displacement*, read the book's subtitle in a blocky, no-nonsense font. It really was exactly the kind of research material he needed, Crispin realized, growing more annoyed as the other patron pulled crumpled bills and a handful of coins from their pockets.

"Will you sell it to me for…twenty-seven dollars and sixty-five cents?"

Crispin's hopes soared. He got out his wallet and extracted two twenty-dollar bills, ready to swoop in and claim his prize. As a regular at Buy Books and Brews, he knew that the shop's owners, Lucy and Danai, were strict about their price policy. Sure enough, Danai said—

"I'm sorry, but the marked prices are non-negotiable," and inclined her head toward the large sign behind the checkout that outlined the price policy and warned patrons that there were magical items on the premises. "I'll hold it for you for five minutes, if you want to go across the street to the bank machine."

Crispin frowned. Was he going to lose the book after all?

"I can't use an ATM. I'm a Mage," said the other patron, sounding frustrated and disheartened. Crispin almost felt bad for them. Almost.

"Sorry, then," Danai said. She noticed Crispin hovering near the counter. "Hello, Crispin. Nice to see you."

"I'd like to buy that book, please." Crispin tried not to gloat as he handed Danai the bills.

Danai nodded and took Crispin's money, punching in the amount and hitting a big button that made the register *ding* and the heavy cash drawer shoot open. While she counted out his change, Crispin pulled the book toward himself. He didn't think the other patron would try to steal it, but…a wave of shame washed through Crispin at the very thought.

"Where are you studying?" Crispin asked, trying to make amends with pleasant conversation.

"What's it to you?" There was a challenge in the person's voice and in the expression they directed toward him.

"I was just thinking that perhaps we could study the book together?" The words were out of Crispin's mouth before he knew he was going to say them.

"What do you mean?" the other patron asked cautiously.

"Since we're both interested in displacement, maybe we could meet here for coffee once a week and, ah, read the book? Together?" Crispin hated that he had started to stammer as the offer tumbled out of his mouth, like an awkward puppy negotiating a staircase for the first time. He felt a blush creeping up his neck to his cheeks; asking this person for coffee made it sound like he was inviting them on a date. That wasn't Crispin's intention—he just felt bad for them. But, before he could correct the misconception, a small, hopeful smile replaced the guarded expression on their face.

"That's…that's a very generous offer…" They trailed off, but their smile widened, highlighting their rosy lips, which were bracketed by high cheekbones and a narrow chin.

"Crispin," Crispin said, tucking the book under his arm so he could extend his hand to shake. "It's nice to meet you."

"I'm Nyle." Their handshake was firm and warmer than Crispin had expected. "I work during the week, so weekends would be best for me. When would be good for you?"

"How about next Saturday? Around"—Crispin pulled out his pocket watch to check the time—"is ten too early?" Spending the next few Saturday mornings studying *Theories of Advanced Displacement* with Nyle would be at least as productive as his usual habit of prowling second-hand bookshops for such books.

"Ten should be fine. I'll see you next week?"

"Sounds good!"

"Cool." Nyle gave Crispin a cheerful wave and smiled at Danai before leaving the shop.

"That was very thoughtful," Danai said.

Crispin shrugged, already second-guessing his offer. What had he been thinking? *I wasn't thinking at all, that's the problem. Well, if it doesn't work out next Saturday, I can always make up some excuse to cancel after that,* he told himself as he headed to the coffee counter to order a caramel macchiato.

Heading into the bookshop one week later, Crispin was unaccountably nervous. He hefted his leather satchel to feel its reassuring weight. He'd checked three times before leaving his apartment to make sure he'd packed *Theories of Advanced Displacement*, a notebook, a half-dozen pens and pencils, even his slide rule and a small abacus, though he was unlikely to need either. The bell above the door jingled as Crispin entered Buy Books and Brews, and he glanced toward the café area, unsure if he wanted to find Nyle there or not.

And there they were, sitting at a table by the window with a teacup and a notebook in front of them, reading a paperback novel. Nyle glanced up at the sound of the bell and raised a hand in a half-wave. Crispin pasted what he hoped was a friendly smile on his face and headed over.

"I hope this table is okay; there's better light here by the window," Nyle said.

"It's fine. I'll get myself a drink, then we can start." Crispin put his satchel on the floor by the unoccupied chair and went to the counter.

"Your usual?" asked Lucy, manning the "Brews" part of the shop while Danai handled the "Books" part.

"Just the coffee today." Crispin didn't want to talk through a mouthful of pastry or risk getting crumbs stuck between the book's pages. Besides, his stomach was still a little jumpy with nerves. Meeting a stranger to discuss magical theory wasn't the kind of thing Crispin usually did. He had always been more comfortable with books than with people. Though this particular book might change his mind about that, considering what he'd learned about it in the past week…

"Go sit down. I'll bring it over to you."

"Thank you," Crispin said, and handed over a five. Once Lucy had made change, he dropped a dollar into the tip jar and went back to the table where Nyle was watching him from over the rim of their steaming teacup.

Crispin sat down and got out *Theories of Advanced Displacement*, his notebook, and a pencil.

"I guess we'll start at the beginning, yes?"

"Sure."

Crispin opened the book and held his breath, waiting to see if…

Sure enough, a small cloud of pinkish-gold smoke billowed out and coalesced into the unmistakable shape of a dragon.

Crispin sighed.

"What the heck is that?" Nyle said, starting backward.

"Name's Flynn, and who might you be?" asked the dragon, peering at Nyle as it stepped out of the book and onto the table.

"Flynn seems to…live in the book, and absolutely refuses to explain anything about how or why."

"I think she just likes to annoy people," said Lucy as she came over with Crispin's coffee. "And cause mischief, and eat sweets."

"Not 'she' nowadays. 'It' will do fine," the dragon said imperiously, drawing itself up to its full eight-inch height and putting its hands on its hips, which, considering how short its arms were, looked quite comical. Crispin had learned better than to laugh. "Dragons only have gender when they choose to, and currently I do not."

"Yeah! Nonbinary solidarity," said Nyle with a grin, and held out their hand for a high-five. "I'm Nyle. It's nice to meet you." Flynn blew an amused puff of smoke in lieu of smacking hands; it curled around Nyle's fingers before dissipating slowly.

"We'll see about that once you've gotten to know it better," Crispin muttered under his breath.

"Lucy, dear," Flynn said, turning to her with a slight bow, "I would like a spicy mocha latte in the largest cup you have and a sweet roll of some kind."

"We have cinnamon buns, apricot Danishes, and chocolatines. Which would you like?"

Flynn considered briefly. "The cinnamon bun, I think. Thank you kindly."

Crispin sighed and pulled out his wallet.

"I can, uh…" Nyle said, reaching into their pocket.

"Nope." Flynn grinned at Nyle, showing rows of sharp teeth. "He"— Flynn jerked its chin at Crispin—"bought the book, so he's responsible."

"It's okay," Crispin said. "Flynn started eating me out of house and home as soon as it appeared. I should have anticipated this." Crispin handed the money to a very amused Lucy, who promised to be back with Flynn's order soon. "So, maybe we can get to work?"

Nyle looked like they had a number of questions they'd like to ask Flynn, but they nodded and turned their attention to *Theories of Advanced Displacement.*

Crispin and Nyle worked their way through the first three pages of the prologue, taking turns reading softly aloud until Lucy came back with Flynn's order.

"I'll just put this here," Lucy said, setting the latte and cinnamon bun in the center of the table.

"Perfect, thank you again," Flynn said with a deep bow that looked elegant despite it being performed by a stout miniature dragon with pink-and-gold scales. Flynn dragged the cinnamon bun, which was almost as big as itself, over to the latte bowl, maneuvered it onto the saucer, and propped it up so it was leaning against the cup's rim. Then, the dragon scrambled over the side of the cup, stubby wings frantically flapping. Nyle watched, bug-eyed, as Flynn settled into the bowl of latte as if it were a bathtub and sighed an exaggerated, contented sigh.

"Lovely—just lovely," Flynn said, and leaned over to take a bite of the cinnamon bun. "And delicious. Thank you, Crispin."

"You're welcome," Crispin said dryly. "Now, if you're all set, perhaps Nyle and I could get back to studying?"

Flynn airily waved one arm, splashing some coffee over the side of the cup. "Don't let me stop you."

Crispin sighed, picked up his pencil, and turned to Nyle. "Where were we?"

"Your hair looks fine," Flynn said from where it was perched on Crispin's dining room table.

"What?" Crispin stared moodily at his reflection in the hallway mirror, trying to decide if he should wear a different shirt. "Does this color make me look sallow?" he asked, glancing at Flynn.

"The shirt is fine; it brings out the amber in your eyes, and your hair is also fine."

"My hair?" Crispin said distractedly.

"You've been fussing with it for five minutes. If you don't leave right now, we're going to be late!"

Crispin pulled out his pocket watch and checked the time. Flynn was being overly dramatic, as usual. He couldn't possibly have spent more than a minute in front of the mirror. Besides, he had a full seven minutes before the bus came, and it was only a two-minute walk to the bus stop from his apartment. It was, however, time to pack up and leave.

"Well, then, you'd better hop back into the book so that I can pack my satchel, hadn't you?"

Flynn disappeared in a puff of smoke that seemed somehow cranky, and Crispin packed the book, double-checking that he had his notebook and pencils. He strode briskly out of his apartment, full of excited anticipation.

Half an hour later, he was sweaty, puffing, and cursing under his breath as he dashed into Buy Books and Brews, hoping Nyle was still there despite Crispin being a full fifteen minutes late. His heart soared when he spotted the familiar figure at what had become their usual table.

"I'm so sorry. Some idiot student Mage didn't move to the back of the bus quickly enough, so the electronics in the dashboard died. I had to walk ten blocks." Crispin had actually jogged most of it, worried Nyle would think he wasn't coming.

"It's fine. Don't worry about it," Nyle said with a warm smile.

The wave of relief that washed through Crispin was disproportionate to the circumstances. He smoothed his hand through his hair, hoping it didn't look too unruly, and felt abruptly self-conscious as he remembered Flynn teasing him about fussing with it. And speaking of Flynn…

Crispin took *Theories of Advanced Displacement* out of his satchel and slid it across the table. "Here, say 'hi' to Flynn—it's in a particularly snarky mood today. I'll go order."

Standing in line for his coffee and Flynn's latte and cinnamon bun, Crispin hoped the dragon wouldn't say anything embarrassing to Nyle in his absence. So what if he wanted his hair to look decent before going out? That was perfectly normal! Flynn was just trying to get a rise out of him.

Glancing at their table, Crispin wished Nyle didn't always arrive before him and buy their own tea. *Maybe next week, I'll get here extra early, and I can buy drinks for all of us. I can say Flynn was impatient for his latte*, he thought, grinning.

"You're in a good mood today," Lucy said as she handed him his receipt.

"I guess I am," Crispin said, and wondered what change Lucy had noticed. He was certainly eager to get back to the table and start discussing chapter four with Nyle, but that couldn't be what Lucy was talking about. Or perhaps it was. Crispin hadn't been this engaged by his research in years, and he knew it was because of his study partner. Working through complex magical theories with Nyle had become the highlight of Crispin's week, and so he hurried back to their table.

"I've been thinking about liminal dispersal. Do you think the author means that you need to relocate your perception to the unidimensional plane—energetically speaking, that is?" Nyle's face shone with excitement, and they talked animatedly.

Crispin thought it over, then shook his head slowly. Nyle was brilliant, and working hard to understand the material, but they didn't yet have a senior Mage's foundational understanding of liminal physics. "That doesn't make sense, unfortunately," Crispin said, trying to disagree as kindly as he could. "You can't relocate the projection without the force horizon dispersing."

"Oh yeah? Watch this!" Nyle's eyes flashed with challenge as they shoved up their sleeves and extended their hands over the table. With barely a clatter, the bowl of spicy mocha latte in which Flynn reclined rose until it floated six inches above its saucer. The cinnamon bun which had been propped against the cup's side fell over with a quiet *thump*—proving Nyle hadn't merely cast an illusion. From the table next to them came the desolate *bleep* of someone's phone dying. The cup drifted left and landed gently next to Crispin's.

Crispin's mouth hung open in astonishment; he closed it and swallowed. "That was a third-level displacement! I can't even do that! How did *you*?"

Nyle looked quite pleased with themself.

"Like it says in the book—unidimensional relocation. I just pushed against the plane to keep the dispersal focussed."

"You…just pushed…against the plane," said Crispin, so astounded that he couldn't keep the incredulity out of his voice. "It takes years of practice to achieve that kind of control! Or it usually does…how…?"

Nyle sighed and looked down at their hands. "I work as an animator. In a factory. I spend seven and a half hours a day, five days a week, directing magical energy, so I can practically do it in my sleep. In fact, I'm sure I *have* done it in my sleep on a few Monday mornings. That part is easy. Once this"—Nyle pointed at the book—"explained that all I had to do was oppose the energy dispersal by using the Earth's plane as a counterbalance, it was simple."

Crispin gaped again then consciously shut his mouth. "You're a factory animator?" he said, shocked. Animators were drawn from the lowest ranks of magic users, those who didn't have enough power or control to create even the simplest of illusions. Animators only needed to be able to sense magical energy and push it into the toy, or rich person's gadget, or magically enabled microwave oven, or whatever, that was being animated. "But you're a talented Mage!"

Nyle set their jaw and said tightly, "Talented but poor. Couldn't afford to go to university, so I got a job that at least allowed me to practice magic, and…" Nyle waved at the book and notepads spread out on the table between them. "I study on my own."

Things that had been niggling at Crispin finally clicked in his brain. Why Nyle was studying advanced theory, but wasn't a student; that all they ever bought at the coffee shop was a single cup of tea; and how, on the first day they had met, Nyle hadn't had enough money to buy the book.

"I'm…I'm sorry."

"I don't need your pity," Nyle said sharply and pushed back their chair as if they might leave.

Crispin put a hand out and had to stop himself from grabbing Nyle's arm. "No, I just meant that I'm sorry you didn't get the chance to study magic in a more…structured way. You obviously have a great deal of aptitude for it."

Nyle looked at Crispin for a long moment; Crispin held his breath, wondering if they were going to walk away. But Nyle settled back into the chair and smiled crookedly. "Sorry. I get a little touchy about…things."

"That's, ah, that's perfectly understandable, of course." Crispin was so relieved that Nyle wasn't upset with him, he couldn't think of what else to say.

Into the awkward silence, Flynn said, "Excuse me!" Nyle and Crispin stopped staring down at their notebooks and looked at it, still lounging in the bowl of latte with its stubby little arms spread out on the top rim of the bowl like a frat boy in a hot tub.

"Great little demo, Nyle, but I can't reach my cinnamon bun from here." Flynn's imperious manner broke the tension. Nyle grinned and apologized, picked up Flynn's cup (not using magic this time), and put it back on its saucer. Crispin retrieved Flynn's cinnamon bun and propped it back against the rim where Flynn could reach it. Flynn blew a puff of smoke in Crispin's direction, then munched on a raisin.

"So, I'd really appreciate it if you'd explain to me again about how to relocate your perception to the unidimensional plane," Crispin said with a sheepish smile that grew wide and happy as Nyle launched into an animated explanation.

Flynn finished munching on the toast with raspberry jam that Crispin had provided, burped loudly, and waddled over to where Crispin had forms, catalogs, and pamphlets spread out on the table. Flynn sat on the edge of a thick course catalog and peered at the papers Crispin was studying.

" 'Western Technical College Scholarship Application,' " Flynn read from the top one. "What's this all about?" Flynn blew a puff of smoke that swirled around Crispin's hand, obscuring the form he was trying to fill in.

Crispin sighed, knowing that the crotchety little dragon wouldn't be ignored or put off.

"I'm starting a scholarship application for Nyle," he said, even though that was patently obvious.

"And why, exactly, are you doing that?"

"Because Nyle is a gifted Mage who deserves the chance at a decent education and a respected career as a magic user!" Crispin said, his ears turning pink.

"I see."

Crispin expected more commentary from Flynn—a sarcastic remark, at least—but the dragon looked at the form moodily, little wisps of smoke trailing out its nostrils and curling around Crispin's pen.

Crispin wondered if Flynn would miss their weekly coffee shop meetings with Nyle as much as he would. Would Nyle miss them at all? They'd reached the end of *Theories of Advanced Displacement* two weeks ago and had exhausted their options for further discussion on the topic last Saturday. Crispin was sure that, this week, Nyle would suggest they stop meeting.

He'd even taken a day off work and scoured his usual used bookshops—and some specialty magical bookshops as well—searching for another book on a related topic that he could "happen to find" in order to have an excuse to keep meeting with Nyle. Having failed in that endeavour, he hit upon the idea of gifting *Theories of Advanced Displacement* to them, and also had researched scholarships and put together the beginnings of an application package, including a glowing letter of reference in which Crispin described Nyle as his "research associate."

Crispin put the application forms, his letter, and some pamphlets about Western Technical College into a large manila envelope. Then, he carefully wrote his full name and address on the flyleaf of *Theories of Advanced Displacement*, under where "$32.00" was still written in Danai's fluid handwriting. If, for some reason, Nyle wanted to contact him, they could. Crispin blew on the ink to dry it and pushed the book toward Flynn.

"Time to go."

Flynn gave him an indecipherable stare, then disappeared in a puff of smoke.

When Crispin arrived at Buy Books and Brews, Nyle was sitting at their table. Crispin felt an anticipatory surge of loneliness, imagining visiting the shop the next Saturday and finding that corner devoid of the familiar figure. He pasted on a smile as he sat down and took the book out of his satchel. He left the envelope where it was, suddenly overcome with doubt. What if Nyle was insulted by his offer? What if they applied, but didn't get the scholarship—or worse, didn't pass the entrance exam? That was unlikely, though. Nyle was intelligent and hardworking. They would no doubt pass with flying colors.

Nonetheless, Crispin's stomach clenched with nerves, and when Lucy came over with his usual order of coffee and Flynn's latte and cinnamon bun, he was so anxious that he dropped the money he was trying to hand her. She gave him a kind smile that bolstered his courage enough for him to clear his throat and say, "Ah, I want you to have this." He slid the book to Nyle's side of the table.

"Oh," Nyle said. "Are you sure? Um, wow!"

Nyle looked so pleased; Crispin's heart swelled. "Completely sure. I have all the notes I need for my research paper. You'll get more use out of it than I will, especially if you look this over and decide to do something with it." Crispin took the manila envelope from his satchel and laid it on top of the book.

"What's this?"

"Open it," Crispin said, and clasped his hands tightly together under the table to stop them from shaking with nerves.

Nyle opened the flap of the envelope and peered inside. Their expression grew confused as they slid the contents onto the table and looked through them.

"What? Oh, I see. Western Technical College? That's…that's not where you work."

"No, I'm a researcher at St. Bartholomew's. But WTC is an excellent school. It may not have the history or the prestige of St. Bart's, but it has much more comprehensive scholarship packages, and the student body is more diverse. You won't be the only student your age at WTC— you probably would be at St. Bart's, you see—and there's more, ah, economic diversity as well." Crispin had considered trying to get Nyle a place at St. Bart's, but, as tempting as that was, he knew Nyle would fit in much better at the more modern, less stuffy school. "I know a few of the instructors at WTC, and they're top-notch. And I think they'll be more open to your, ah, less conventional approach to magic."

"You mean they won't tell me I'm doing it all wrong," Nyle said sourly.

"I don't think they will, no."

As they talked, Nyle shuffled through the forms and papers, and they went still when they found Crispin's letter of recommendation. Crispin's stomach clenched again, and he held his breath as Nyle read it. Finally, they looked up and held Crispin's gaze.

"Why are you doing this for me?" Nyle asked softly.

"Because." It came out as a croak. Crispin cleared his throat and swallowed. "Because you're a talented Mage, and you deserve a chance at a good education."

Flynn snorted, breaking the tension. "He's doing it because he likes you, but he doesn't have the guts to ask you out on a date. He's been all sad and mopey for the last week because you've finished studying the book and won't be seeing each other anymore."

Surprised, Nyle turned to Crispin. "Is that true?"

A blush crept up Crispin's neck; he swallowed again and said, "I, ah, I do like you. I like you a lot, and I hate the idea of not seeing you again. But this"—Crispin gestured at the scholarship application papers— "was honestly just because I wanted to help." Gathering his courage, Crispin said in a rush, "What Flynn said is true, though. I would like to keep seeing you. If that's something you—"

"Oh, for pity's sake! Nyle, please put us all out of our misery and tell Crispin that you like him, too, and you want to date him!"

"Thank you, Flynn. We can manage from here," Nyle said. They reached out and covered Crispin's hand with their own. "I like you, too, and Flynn is right: I would very much like to date you."

Jo Mathieson

Crispin's hand was warm and tingly under Nyle's; the feeling spread throughout his body, and he wondered if he was allowed to kiss Nyle yet, or if he should wait until their first "official" date. Before he could decide, the matter was taken out of his hands.

"I've been wanting to kiss you for weeks," Nyle said. "May I?"

Crispin nodded, and then found his voice. "Yes, please."

Nyle leaned in slowly, kissing Crispin gently. The soft sweetness of Nyle's lips was so captivating that it took Crispin a second to realize that he should respond, rather than just bask in the delicious sensations, but then he reciprocated with what he hoped was appropriate enthusiasm.

Finally, they parted, grinning stupidly at each other. "Where would you like to go for our first date?" Crispin asked.

"I don't care where we go. I am, however, looking forward to talking about something other than magical displacement. I've enjoyed our studies, but I want to get to know you better," Nyle said with a wide, warm smile that made Crispin's heart melt.

"Anywhere that has nice, big latte bowls and good pastries is fine with me," Flynn said. The dragon had its elbows on the edge of the cup, watching them with its chin propped up on its hands.

"What makes you think you're invited?" Crispin said, and Nyle laughed at Flynn's put-out expression.

"You'd think there'd be some gratitude for—"

Crispin reached out and gently pinched Flynn's snout shut with his forefinger and thumb. "Shh," he said, and went back to kissing Nyle.

ꙮN LIKE FLYNN
PREQUEL
JO MATHIESON

Danai pulled a book out of an old crate, examining it closely to determine its condition. Its embossed title read "Spells and Enchantments for the Art of Love." Danai rolled her eyes but continued to inspect the book—it would bring a very good price. The binding was intact, and there was no buckling from dampness. She riffled the pages, scanning for marks or damage, then almost dropped it when a cloud of smoke billowed out. When she had finished blinking, a small, stout dragon with pink–and-gold scales was standing on the bookshop counter, staring up at her.

"Well, it's about time! I've been trapped in that book for an age! Now, my dear, what matter of the heart can I help you with?" asked the dragon. Before Danai could answer, the dragon's snout tilted up into the air and sniffed. "Is that coffee? And chocolate, and…raspberries! I haven't had a raspberry in…I don't suppose I could impose upon your kind heart to provide me with a snack?"

"I've met the likes of you before, so there will be some ground rules: I'll only feed you for free this once. You're welcome to inhabit any of the books, and to interact with my customers, as long as you promise not to drive them away," Danai said.

"You drive a hard bargain, my dear, but a wise one. I'll have a latte and whatever that delightful-smelling chocolate-and-raspberry confection is."

Danai waited.

"Please," the dragon finally added.

A LEAP WORTH TAKING

T. S. KNIGHT

age difference, bisexual, coffee shop, f/f, f/m (past), found family, getting together, minor character death (past), past tense, reincarnation, restaurant, second chances, third person limited point of view, united states of america

"I've been reincarnated," Shiloh said in lieu of her name or any proper introduction. She picked at the heat shield on her coffee cup, staring at it instead of at the two women across the table. Away from the bustling noise of the espresso machine, the steady rain pelting against the window behind her was an unexpected comfort.

Shiloh held her breath and looked up.

"It's a rather yellow feeling, isn't it?" the woman to her left mused, stirring her mug of green tea.

"Yellow?" Shiloh asked, distracted by her vibrant eyeshadow and copious jewelry.

"Yes, yellow. Positively, if you ask me. Not that you did."

"Er," Shiloh started, but the second woman interrupted.

"Don't mind Amethyst's colors," she murmured. Setting down her steaming mug of Earl Grey, the scent of bergamot curling off the surface, she leaned forward. She had a voice like the tea, rich and warm and oddly soothing.

Amethyst stirred her tea, seemingly enamored with the rippling surface. "It's not only about the colors," she complained.

"I assume, then," the second woman smiled gently, "that you're here for the group? My name is Elsa."

Shiloh shook her extended hand, her palm sweaty against the woman's, cheeks burning.

"Yes, I am," Shiloh said haltingly. "Like I said, I've—I've been reincarnated."

"Right," Elsa nodded. "Sure, reincarnated. Why don't we start with your name? Are you from the city too?"

She gave her name, distracted by the buzz and hubbub of the shop around them. "I'm from here now, but my past self—he lived in San Francisco most of his life—or, *my* life? What's the preferred way to say it?"

Elsa and Amethyst exchanged a look, speaking in a language of blinks. Elsa wore at least three differently patterned shirts, one atop the other, in almost-clashing shades of yellow and green. They were an unusual pair—Amethyst covered in gemlike sparkles and Elsa in gauzy layers—but they moved and spoke like members of the same family.

"Am I in the right place?" Shiloh stared between them, fingers falling back to pick at the coffee sleeve again. "I saw the flyer at the library, and it said this day, this time, and this shop, and you two...you looked the part, but maybe I've gotten something wrong...?"

"No, no," Elsa said, reaching across the table to calm Shiloh's anxious hands. "This *is* the Reincarnation Support Group. We don't get many new faces—despite the name, the flyers are more a promotion for the café than for us."

"We're just a bit violet, you see," Amethyst flicked a hand as though her meaning was perfectly clear. "And you're early. There are two more on the way."

"I didn't mean to intrude or anything," Shiloh went on, speaking faster the longer she talked. "I've just been having these experiences, and I'm sure you know what I mean if you've been through it. All my friends say I'm losing it, but I think it could be real. I hope it's real."

Amethyst took a long drink of her tea, watching Shiloh with a cheery expression. "We won't think you're losing your mind."

"You're early, is all," added Elsa, "and it's no bother. We don't always know what to expect from new folks, but I'm sure everyone will be glad to meet you."

"We are." Amethyst nodded sagely.

Shiloh shivered, leaning away from the cold window, and pressed her hands around her quickly cooling cup. It stuck to the linoleum table as she lifted it for a drink, but the coffee was rich on her tongue. Drinking bought her a moment before she'd have to tell her story. It had been easier to convince herself of the truth of her reincarnation when it was only in her head.

"I didn't believe it at first," said Shiloh. "But now I'm sure. There's no other explanation for everything I've been through and for all the memories I've got."

"Certainly," Elsa agreed.

Shiloh began to explain, at first slowly, and then all at once, carefully sifting through the memories for those appropriate to share.

She could say this much out loud: the dreams began nearly two years prior, a recurring story that wove in and out of reality. Through it all, a mysterious and intimately familiar woman with short hair and bright eyes followed Shiloh's every footstep.

Shiloh came to know this woman better than she knew herself. She could predict her responses to jokes that Shiloh's dream-self told, as if they'd known each other for a thousand lifetimes before. Dreams of kissing her felt more like memories, her skin tangible, warm, and soft. Shiloh could smell her honey-and-strawberry shampoo on the empty pillow in bleary morning moments.

Even as Shiloh described the face in her dreams, flushed pink with the relief at finally sharing her story, she could hear the tone of the dream-woman's voice echoing in her ears. She could feel the edge of a familiar scar on that other shoulder as she traced fingers down bare skin in a montage of someone else's memories.

"Then, it was the man in the mirror, the—me," Shiloh said, clearing her throat and trying to shake off the sense of heaviness around her shoulders. Amethyst and Elsa leaned forward, rapt. "I'm not superstitious. I'm really not."

Before she could continue—in the middle of her story about realizing that her hand felt wrong without a wedding ring—the bell at the door rang. Two people who couldn't be more different from each other stepped inside, all bright smiles and laughter, mid-conversation. Amethyst gave a loose wave, glitter bangles jangling on her wrist. It was odd to imagine the four women together even though these were clearly the rest of the group: Amethyst, like a firework in human form; Elsa with her gauzy chamomile personality; and these two, a teenager with bright-blue hair and brighter-red lipstick and a suburban matriarch with a pastel-pink cardigan buttoned up to the neck.

They ordered and walked over to the table, each with a mug in hand.

The teenager introduced herself as Emily as she set the massive cup of black coffee on the table, the mug bigger than her face. The woman—Claudette—assured Shiloh that she wasn't Emily's mother and sipped from a blue mug piled high with whipped cream, marshmallows, and sprinkles. Looking at it, Shiloh's teeth ached.

"A newbie! Sick," Emily crooned, reaching across the table to poke at Shiloh's coat. She shrugged it off in embarrassment, pulling it over the back of the chair.

"Give her some space," Claudette admonished in an unmistakably motherly tone.

Emily rolled her eyes and took a great swallow of coffee. Shiloh gulped. That coffee had to be scalding.

"So, out with it. You got a story?" Emily asked, tilting her chair backward on two legs.

Shiloh hesitated, looking at each of them in turn.

"I've been reincarnated," Shiloh said with new confidence. "I was married to a wonderful woman in a past life, and I died. She's still alive, and here in this city, and I want to talk to her, but I don't know what I'm doing or how I should go about it."

"Right, sure. But, like, what's your story?"

Shiloh stared at her. "What do you mean? That is my story."

Claudette raised a hand, and Emily fell unexpectedly silent at the gesture. Though she looked like a modern-day Stepford wife, complete with highlighted and cropped hair, she had kind, genuine eyes.

"We all have our stories," Claudette said, as though explaining to a child. "We've got our reasons, shall I say, for needing a special kind of community."

"Isn't that supposed to be the whole…reincarnation thing?"

Across the shop, the espresso machine hissed. Shiloh stared around the circle. None of them would meet her eyes. Confusion, tinged with the bitter twist of embarrassment, settled on her shoulders.

"You do believe me, don't you? I was reincarnated. It happened."

"Of course that's how you feel," Amethyst nodded, raising both hands as though blessing the table.

"Reincarnation—or the idea of it—brought us together. Each of us experienced something—a dream, perhaps, or bad déjà vu—that made us reconsider something in our lives," explained Elsa as the whirring of the coffee in the background slowed to a quiet hum. "But really, thinking about reincarnation—and the possibilities of it—was more the indicator we needed that something was missing in *this* life."

" 's nothing missing in my life," Emily muttered, snapping her chair forward so the front legs smacked against the ground. "But someone's got to keep these old biddies feeling young."

"But—" Shiloh stammered. "But it's a support group. For reincarnation. That's what the flyer said."

"And we get the support we need."

"What Emily means to say—" Claudette began.

"What I mean to say is that we're all a little lonely, or whatever, and getting to have this group to, I don't know, talk about what the fuck our worlds could look like if we led a different life makes things easier. Not that I care."

It was quiet for a moment. However bitter Emily's tone was, the group seemed to agree, and Shiloh slipped into the weight of loneliness. If they didn't believe her—if they met only due to their care for each other and not to discuss the reality of reincarnation—then she was back where she started.

Amethyst leaned across the table and said in a quiet, conspiratorial tone, "I think she does care."

"But," Elsa said, then looked at each of them in turn, "I'd like to think we're decent listeners."

"You don't believe me."

"Now, there's no need to get like that," Amethyst hummed, "all blue-green and sour. We don't have to believe you to be willing to listen and care. This is what we do for each other."

Shiloh considered this, balancing the feeling of isolation—of madness—with her impressions of this little family in their corner of the busy shop. There was something warm and reflective in Amethyst's smile, something gentle in the way that Elsa looked at her. Those Shiloh had told before had dismissed her story without listening to each detail haunting Shiloh's days and nights. But, at this table, with the rainy window at her back and coffee in her hands and four new confidantes before her, Shiloh found new courage.

And so she told them everything.

She told them about the restaurant in the alley off Spruce Street where the food tasted exactly like home, exactly like her wife. She told them about how her arms felt a little too short, like she used to be able to reach the top shelves. Amid her recounting of the road trip to the Grand Canyon, Claudette pulled out her phone, showing photos of places far from the regular trails, validating Shiloh's memory of a place she had never been in this lifetime.

Shiloh told them about the name she'd once called her own, and about what Joel used to look like and how he lived.

She told them about Aline. She told them about the quartz-crystal pendant she always wore and how she'd twirl it in her fingers when she was happy, like on those nights when they both laughed so hard they couldn't breathe.

The coffee shop filled and emptied and filled again, and Shiloh couldn't stop the words from coming. Once she'd started believing in Joel, the memories filled every empty gap in her mind.

"And I love her, and I'd love her in every form, even if that love wasn't romantic. I don't think that this body is any different from Joel's, or from any body before that. And I don't know if she'll feel the same way, but…" Shiloh trailed off. "Maybe I ought to try?"

She finally looked up, expressive hands falling to the table with the sense of defeat, but four pairs of eager eyes stared at her.

"Of course you've got to try," Emily snapped, and everyone relaxed, tittering at her outburst.

"I want to talk to her," Shiloh said. "I think—I *hope* that she'll see Joel in me, the way I know him and the way that I know her."

"What are we waiting for?" snapped Emily. "You said she's got a restaurant, right? Bet we could get in there."

"I might have…" Shiloh said and hesitated. "I might have done something a bit impulsive."

The group waited.

"I don't know," Shiloh said. "I didn't want to scare her away. I can't try to talk to her during dinner, that would be a madhouse. And if some random person sent a note claiming to be Joel, I wouldn't blame her for throwing it out."

Emily stared at her. "What did you do?"

"I called the restaurant a few days ago, er…didn't really say what it was about, just that I needed to speak with her, and was there a time I could come? She said I could have fifteen minutes."

"More than I'd give," Claudette muttered.

"I think she thinks I'm a food blogger or something?" She looked down at her hands, warm shame in her cheeks. "I didn't lie, not exactly."

"When are you meeting with her?" Elsa cut in before Claudette could add whatever she was about to say.

Shiloh pulled out her phone, clicked the power button.

"Uh. About…half an hour from now. Shit." She rubbed a hand over her face. "I was so panicked about what to do and what to say, if she'd think I was completely mad. The flyer for this group was the only thing that stopped me from calling the restaurant back to cancel. But I should cancel, right? This is crazy."

"Absolutely fucking not," Emily said.

"I don't believe in reincarnation, not at all," Claudette said, but the corner of her mouth twitched up, ready to smile given an opportunity. "But, I must say, better to try and get rejected than not try at all."

"It doesn't have to be romantic love, after all," added Elsa breezily.

"What exactly are we waiting for?" Emily said. "The love of your past life is waiting."

"I—" Shiloh stared at them. "I don't have the bus schedule from here."

"Silly girl," Amethyst hummed, reaching for her arm across the table. "You're part of the group now, real reincarnation and all. We wouldn't let you go it alone. That'd be horribly purple of us."

"Purple!" Emily echoed. "Horribly so. Unfortunately for you, you're stuck with us now."

"I'm driving," added Claudette, and no one argued.

As they broke into a bustle of dishes to return and coats to put on, Shiloh couldn't help but get swept up in it. It wasn't until they were slipping out the door that she realized they no longer felt like strangers.

"This is crazy, right?" she asked as she slid into Claudette's car between Emily and Amethyst.

"Bonkers," Emily agreed. "And you're doing it."

The corner restaurant that smelled like home and Aline was only five miles away, but the drive felt like it took five years. Each red light lasted three times longer than it should, even with Amethyst giving airy directions from the passenger seat, offering ridiculous anecdotes about her younger self and the stores that used to be there. Shiloh wasn't sure she ought to believe the stories, so she only half-listened, her mind racing toward the end of the drive and their looming destination.

And then they were there, and Shiloh was terrified all over again.

In the minivan outside the restaurant, Shiloh could imagine the gentle brush of familiar hands over broader shoulders than her own, easing the stress of a long workday. Aline felt closer and farther away than she had since the day Shiloh decided the dreams were real.

"I can do this," she said. It was going to work. Aline would recognize her, would see Joel's echo in every inch of her. She imagined reaching for Aline, full of hope, but doubt clouded the image. What if Aline couldn't—or wouldn't—see it?

"No…no, I can't do this."

"We'll just take a breath of fresh air," Emily said, and opened the door. The rush of cool breeze into the car was choked with Shiloh's fear. Emily tugged her out, and Shiloh stumbled as her feet hit the asphalt.

"She's going to think I'm insane."

Amethyst stepped over and wrapped her in a tight hug. "It'll be all yellow," Amethyst murmured into her hair.

Even so, Shiloh couldn't relax, thrumming with nervous energy.

"Oh, God. We should just go back now."

Emily looped an arm through Shiloh's and tugged her forward one step at a time, hands gentle but firm.

"Hey," Emily said, in a voice pitched just for the two of them, though the others lingered on the sidewalk close behind. "Tell me about that meal? The one that helped you realize this woman was your Aline."

Shiloh breathed. Swallowed. Stepped forward. Leaned on Emily, just enough to keep from stumbling. Finally, almost inaudibly, Shiloh said, "It was silly, really. Just a simple dish with chicken and potatoes."

Emily nodded, and they moved a little closer. The door wasn't far, and the street was mostly empty.

"Chicken and potatoes," Emily prompted.

"She's got this way with seasoning," Shiloh murmured, losing herself in memories of the rich scents of dinner on the stove and of stealing a bite of potato when Aline's back was turned. It always ended in the snap of a dish towel or the gentle rap of a wooden spoon on her—on Joel's—knuckles. The smell of garlic and rosemary on the stove, with carrots and potatoes steaming rich and sweet, was heady, erasing the blur of the parking lot and the smell of rain. "And when she cooks, I can taste how much she loves me. You know?" she rambled, barely conscious of her speech or her progress toward the door. "You'll taste it. You'll all taste it, maybe, someday."

They reached the door too soon, bright glass and a gleaming handle in bronze. Shiloh reached for it with shaking hands. At least if Aline sent her running, she would have people to run back to.

"We'll wait for you," Elsa said, in her gentle way.

Shiloh turned back toward her, and she smiled, and somehow Shiloh felt more confident.

"It'll be bright baby blue," added Amethyst.

Claudette tidied Shiloh's coat, brushing a hand over her hair.

And then Shiloh was tripping ahead, Emily shoving her forward, and she let the faith of the group carry her through the vestibule.

She was inside.

The restaurant smelled like lingering garlic and herbs and a home she remembered from another lifetime. The walls had the woven gold decoration from an artist they'd both fallen in love with many years before at a big craft fair. Drinks in hand, they'd wandered through stand after stand until they had stopped and stared at these beautiful pieces. It had been nearly thirty years ago, and neither of them could have dreamed of affording them then. But here they were, adorning the walls of this quiet restaurant.

It was early, and there was a waitress in the corner folding napkins, music blasting from her headphones so loud Shiloh could hear it. The waitress jumped when she noticed Shiloh, and pulled an earbud out.

"Can I help you?" she asked sharply. "We're not open yet."

"I'm expecting her," Aline interrupted, stepping through the double kitchen doors. "I left the front unlocked."

The waitress looked between them and slipped the earbud back in her ear, turning her back to keep folding.

Aline's hair was pulled up, tucked into a tight bun at the back of her head, and far longer than Shiloh remembered. She wore a chef's coat, crisp and still mostly unstained so early in the afternoon. Aline's expression was painfully neutral. She wore glasses with stylish frames, perfectly cut to suit her face and absolutely out of place for the image Shiloh had in mind.

"Could we speak for a moment?" Shiloh asked, searching for her voice.

"Isn't that why you're here?" Aline raised one eyebrow, neutrality quickly turning to something between annoyance and apprehension. Aline must have realized she was no food blogger; she crossed her arms, eyes closed off. "Do I know you? Are you writing something?"

"I'm not writing something, but I do want to talk," Shiloh answered. "This would all be a lot easier if I could just explain it."

"Look, are you all right? You don't look so great, and I really don't have time for any…" She waved a hand at Shiloh. "For any oddness. I've got staff to oversee and dinner to finish preparing."

Shiloh swallowed hard and stepped forward. There were three tables between them, and she wasn't blocking Aline from leaving, but there was electricity in the empty space. The distance pulled at Shiloh's chest. The truth of her reincarnation was confirmed by every plane of Aline's face, as certain as the tile floor beneath her feet. Could Aline feel it too?

"You don't have to sit with me," Shiloh said quietly. "You don't know me, and you don't have any real reason to think I'm not completely crazy, but…" The words came to her, sharp as memory, familiar on her tongue. "Does the phrase, 'every leap might let you fall, but it'll get you to the next step' ring a bell?"

Aline stared at her, a single curl slipping out from her bun.

"What did you say?"

" 'Every leap might let you fall, but it'll get you to the next step,' " Shiloh repeated more confidently. She raised her chin and met Aline's eyes and said the words she knew from Joel's voice—her voice—two decades past.

"What is this?" Aline asked, heavy with an aged sadness.

"Can we talk?" Shiloh asked again.

Whether it was Joel's adage, the feeling of something between them, or Aline's endless kindness, she acquiesced. They settled into wooden chairs on either side of a table for two, half-set plates and an unlit candle between them.

"You had a husband," Shiloh offered carefully. "Many years ago, you had a husband."

"That information isn't difficult to find."

"Joel Weiss. You lived together for three years in that tiny San Francisco flat before his accident."

Aline sighed. She made a show of checking her watch, running her thumb over the face of it and staring for longer than she needed to if she was merely checking the time. Shiloh was too far in to stop now, though apprehension nearly consumed her words.

"He gave you that watch, didn't he?" Shiloh asked, jutting her chin at it. "There's an inscription on the reverse." She waited, watching for the subtle twitch in the corner of Aline's mouth: her tell. "JW and AC. There was meant to be a full quote, but Joel couldn't afford it. I—" She caught herself. "He didn't tell you that for two years."

"Right," Aline snapped. "Right." She stood up, shoving back the formal chair.

Shiloh copied her, hands on the table. A thousand possible responses passed through her, but none of them were right. This wasn't how she'd played out this meeting. Aline was supposed to feel that same electric charge, vibrant and real between them, and yet it seemed like she felt nothing. Was Shiloh a stranger to her? Could she feel nothing when Shiloh felt so much?

Aline wouldn't look at her, but she hadn't left, either, and Shiloh couldn't breathe.

"I don't know what exactly possessed you to contact me," Aline said. "What kind of a sick asshole comes into my restaurant and my life to say these kinds of things? Are you some sort of stalker?" She raised a hand, dismissive, sharp. "I don't care. Don't contact me again."

"Please," Shiloh begged, the only word she could think to say. "Wait. I'm sorry. I didn't mean to invade your privacy. I know this is hard."

"You don't know."

"I know who Joel is, or who he was. I know this sounds crazy. This is a different city, a different lifetime."

"Completely crazy," Aline cut in. "You've interrupted my workday to excavate old grief, for what? Some ridiculous pleasure?"

"No," Shiloh said quickly. "I swear it, Aly. I'm not trying to hurt you."

"You have sixty seconds." Aline's voice quivered, but she held onto the back of her chair. "Tell me why you're here—why you're *really* here—or I'll have you back out the door before you can blink."

"Do you still believe in reincarnation?"

"What?"

"Do you think that people, when they die, can be born again? With their old memories in tow, all of it, all over again?" She could scarcely breathe, heart in her throat. In another lifetime, they had spent a summer night speaking across the pillows about the possibilities of life and afterlife.

"I'd have to think about it." It was the answer Aline had given then, too.

"And if you thought about it?"

Aline hesitated. Shiloh knew that she'd thought about it, back then. She'd thought about it for nearly twenty minutes while Joel had stared at the whorls on the ceiling and tried not to fall asleep. In their bedroom, Aline had said she'd do anything to find Joel.

They'd never considered the other possibility.

Shiloh stared at the loose folds of Aline's chef's uniform, that crisp white against her brown skin. She was older now, hair lighter at the temples. She had tiny crow's feet that crinkled as she peered at Shiloh, and her high cheekbones made her jaw more distinct. Meeting Aline's eyes always felt like baring a part of her soul, and that was even truer in this lifetime. Shiloh couldn't look away.

It took less than twenty minutes this time.

"It could be possible," Aline said finally. "We don't know what happens after death."

Shiloh pressed into the space left open by her words. "If someone you loved had passed away, could you believe that someone new could be a reincarnation of that person?"

Aline did not break eye contact. "I don't know." She knew. She had to know, had to feel this taut rope between them as fiercely as Shiloh felt it.

"You've lost someone. Do you ever wish he would come back?"

Aline's intake of breath was too sharp, too sudden, too angry. Shiloh regretted hurting her instantly.

"Yes," Aline said, and Shiloh could breathe again. "I wish it even still, some days more than others."

Shiloh leaned across the table and touched one of Aline's knuckles, still white on the back of the chair, with the tip of her finger. Aline blinked, then looked down at their hands before Shiloh withdrew, afraid.

She asked, in a voice almost too quiet to hear, "If he were standing right in front of you, would you be happy to see him?"

"I would be happy."

"Even if he looked different?"

"Even then."

"Even if he were a young woman?"

Aline sat down in the empty chair with a soft *thump*, and Shiloh followed suit. Shiloh put one hand out on the table, palm up.

She had woken up one morning, half-delirious with sleep, lost in another half-memory, half-dream. Aline had run her hands over every line on her palm, tracing them as if memorializing every shape, every meaning hidden in the whorls of her fingerprint. When she woke, the image of Joel's palm still in her mind's eye, she stared down at her own hand. Each fingerprint and whorl on her palm was precisely the same.

"I know it sounds impossible," Shiloh said. "But I think I might be Joel all over again. I think we might have a second chance."

Neither of them said anything.

Aline reached across the table and let her hand fall just beside Shiloh's, so that their pinky fingers touched. They sat like that for what felt like hours, but must have been only minutes, heat and stillness all at once.

"Can it be possible?" Aline asked, though it was clear that she was asking herself more than Shiloh. "It can't be."

Aline pulled her hand away.

"But"—Aline shook her head, jaw set—"it doesn't matter. It doesn't matter if it's true."

Shiloh stared. And stared. She stared at the frown threatening the corner of Aline's mouth. She stared at the age spot on the arch of her thumb.

"Maybe I don't get it," Shiloh said suddenly, meeting Aline's eyes again. " 'Cause I think it matters an awful lot. There's history here." She gestured between them. "Years and years of history. That's supposed to matter. We have a story that spans two lifetimes. Isn't that enough?"

Aline was already speaking before Shiloh could finish. "That's exactly the problem. You might be a wonderful person, maybe even a friend, but there are so many years we haven't lived together. I'm a different person from the Aline of twenty-five years ago, with a different life and different wants."

"But that's just it. I'm different, too, this body, this lifetime, and yet: here we are."

"Here we are."

An alarm on Aline's watch began to beep, and she turned it off without looking.

"Maybe this is a start," said Shiloh. "If we can't pick up where we left off, maybe we can start here?"

Around them, the restaurant was still, the waitress gone and the subtle clinking of the kitchen staff at work ignorable. Outside, Shiloh was sure that the group was still waiting, would wait for her whatever answer she received at this table. What mattered wasn't them, nor the quiet patience of the restaurant prepared for dinner guests, nor the time they had spent together and apart. What mattered was this moment, and Aline sitting there, considering Shiloh fully for the first time since they'd laid eyes on each other.

"It won't be easy, you know," Aline said. "It's been a long twenty-five years."

"Well then," said Shiloh, taking her hand. "We'd better get started."

MAGICAL MORSELS

ANGEL

NINA WATERS

I always knew she was an angel.
Crazy, they said.
She couldn't be an angel, they said,
There's no such thing.
I greeted her daily.
I made her coffee.
I baked her scones.
She had no halo,
No wings,
No alabaster robes,
But she had a heavenly smile
And eyes that shone like stars.
"What can I get you today?"
"Oh, you know what I like."
And I did.
I knew she liked hazelnut
And strawberries
And croissants.
I knew she never smiled at anyone else
Like she smiled at me.

I fell in love
In dribs and drabs,
In pinches and dashes,
In morsels and sips.
And I knew my heart would never heal
After the day she came in and said,
"I've been reassigned.

I'm leaving."
I never felt so lonely
As the first morning she didn't come
At her regular time.
And I never felt so adored
As when I checked my phone post-shift.
She'd messaged me to complain
About her new barista.

We fell in love—
In emojis and lolspeak,
In memes and retweets,
In texts and livechats.

"I'm flying back," she promised,
And I didn't ask where to meet her.
I didn't ask which plane she took.
I didn't try to meet her at the airport.
Because I'd always known she was an angel,
And when she appeared in my bedroom,
Wings aflutter,
Halo shining like the stars,
I knew
I was right,
And I knew
I was loved.

Ten Minutes to Closing

T. S. KNIGHT

"You'll meet your soulmate and be able to read it one day," her mother said as she brushed a reverent hand across the cookbook's page. It was supposedly open to a pumpkin muffin recipe, but Vaughn saw nothing.

Vaughn learned the book by her mother's words anyway, reciting the recipes as she worked the oven. She curled her magic into the center of each cinnamon bun, pressed love into the layered croissants.

One day.

"They're very handsome," her mother hinted, nodding to the person reading a tattered novel in the corner.

Vaughn pulled down the cookbook. Blank. "Not them," she sighed. "But I don't mind."

She was sweeping the shop at ten minutes to closing when the bell above the door jingled.

Vaughn looked up. There were two beautiful women standing in the entry, looking as surprised as she felt.

"Oh," she said.

"We heard you've got the best pastries around."

"It's love magic," Vaughn said, breathless. "It's in the recipes, in everything I make."

The second woman smiled radiantly. "How wonderful."

Vaughn served them fresh pain au chocolat and her best cocoa, setting it out at a table with three chairs.

"Forgive me if this is odd," the first woman murmured. "I feel like I've been waiting all my life to sit here in this café with you both."

The second woman's face was blissful as she took the first bite of flaky pastry.

Vaughn didn't need to look at the cookbook to know. "I think it's been worth waiting for."

In Favor of Tomorrow

T. S. KNIGHT

Usually, the little shop on the corner of Flick Street was brimming with people and noisy with music, but as Etienne entered it was silent but for the wisp of a man in the corner, a coffee-stained apron in his lap.

Etienne slid into the chair opposite.

"You came," Loren said. "I wasn't sure you should."

Loren's voice was as frail as the rest of him, his fingers like bones tapping on the table. He was so much worse.

"Of course I came," Etienne said. "I've done it."

He pulled the ring from his pocket with a handkerchief and set it down between them. The pewter band's simplicity disguised its power.

"Take it back," Loren said. "Put the ring on, take your magic back, and leave."

"I won't."

Etienne reached for Loren's hand and brought it to the table, close to the ring. Loren's hand shook; whether from weakness or worry, Etienne wasn't sure.

"Let me take care of you," Etienne murmured.

The ring glowed with the proximity of Loren's fingers. One touch, and he would take every drop of Etienne's magic. One touch, and he'd live.

Loren reached for the ring.

The shop and Loren buzzed to life at once. Dreary gray faded into incandescent orange, customers filled the seats, and the sweet smell of coffee poured back into the air.

"You're safe now," Etienne said, more to reassure himself.

His chest ached where his power had once rested, but Loren's hand was strong and alive under his. That was magic enough.

INDEX

BACKERS

OUR PREMIUM PATREON SUPPORTERS

Anonymous
A Taylor
Sam Brown
Tina Houck
Aria L
Karen Welborn

ABOUT THE AUTHORS

I. A. ASHCROFT

A writer and programmer, I. A. Ashcroft lives a happy life alongside his constant feline companion, Potato. Ashcroft has published two original sci-fi/fantasy novels, is hard at work on the third in the series, and has been writing for fandoms for over a decade, loving stories that emphasize unlikely bonds, mythology, magic, and hope in the darkness. In between storytelling efforts, he enjoys cooking, fiddling with technology projects, and rolling dice with friends while wearing funny hats.

JESSICA BLACK

Jessie, pen name Jessica Black, fandom name alocalband, decided she wanted to be a writer at the age of seven and hasn't looked back since. With a degree in screenwriting, she spent the majority of her career working on assorted projects in Hollywood, New York, and Puerto Rico. Lately, however, she's settled down to a quieter life with her cat, her library, and a constantly filling notebook of new ideas. Hobbies include reading, hiking, gaming, knitting, and going to hockey games.

WILLA BLYTHE

Willa Blythe made her storytelling debut at age 4 with indie smash "Sam the Stinky Skunk," and she hasn't stopped writing since. Her first audience—her grandparents—shared a love of art and craft with her that remains central to Willa's writing practice over thirty years later. Today, she lives in New York with her family and primarily writes queer romance and speculative fiction.

SCARLETT GALE

Scarlett Gale is the author of *His Secret Illuminations* and *His Sacred Incantations*. Long ago, under another name, she was the co-author of *Needles and Artifice* (Cooperative Press; 2012), featuring a rollicking romantic steampunk adventure novella and associated knitting patterns, of which she also designed several. She writes and produces fringe theatre plays based on B-movies, such as "Bodacious Barbarian Babes vs. The Indigo Empress" and "Showgirls of Beast Island." She is a co-producer of the Alison-Bechdel-approved Bechdel Test Burlesque, which in 2017 was included in the Women and Gender Studies curriculum at the University of Oregon. She lives in Seattle with her wife where she gardens, knits, reads, and drinks warm beverages. Unsurprisingly, she also has cats.

A. L. HEARD

A. L. Heard is an aspiring writer from Pittsburgh. She's been writing fanworks for over a decade and self-published her first novel, *Hockey Bois*, in 2021. Some of her short stories have been published through the indie press Duck Prints Press, where she also contributes as an editor. Ultimately, though, she spends her free time writing about characters she adores in worlds she'd like to explore: contemporary romance, historical fiction, science fiction, and fantasy. In between writing projects, she works as a language teacher, plays hockey, tours breweries with her boyfriend, and spends her evenings playing dinosaurs with her two sons.

T. S. KNIGHT

T.S. Knight is a US-based writer and an avid reader. *Add Magic to Taste* was her first published short story. When not writing or beta reading, she spends time diving into history, wandering through museums, and cooking food for the people she loves. A kayaker, knitter, and cat mom, she loves to create and read queer stories most of all.

TRIS LAWRENCE

Tris Lawrence has been writing since she was a child, filling notebooks with the worlds, dreams, and voices from inside her head. She declared in sixth grade that she wanted to be a writer, promptly started drafting her first novel in seventh grade, and never looked back.

Tris has always been fascinated by the way people work: how their relationships fit together, how they interact socially, how they learn and discover. She has read avidly her entire life, devouring mysteries, romances, science fiction, and fantasy novels, and as an adult still loves all of these genres, as well as reading YA constantly. Her favorite stories center on people who are learning or discovering new things, and coming-of-age stories top that list, which is how the school of Pine Hills University came to be. She wants to share stories of people who are learning how to relate to each other, how to adult, how to college, and how to just be. She hopes to share stories about diverse characters with representation of everything she wishes she could have read growing up, and she hopes that these stories will touch the lives and hearts of those who read them.

When not writing, Tris is a wife, a mother (to two children, a cat, and a dog), a knitter, a system administrator, a black belt in taekwondo, an avid reader, and a music aficionado. Sleep, she claims, is optional.

LEX T. LINDSAY

Lex T. Lindsay likes cats, tats, and cool hats. When she isn't shaking words loose or yelling about Captain America, she can often be found lurking in the woods. Find other sapphic love stories in *Add Magic to Taste* (also from Duck Prints Press); *Upon a Twice Time* (Air and Nothingness Press); and *Clockwork, Curses and Coal* (World Weaver Press). Occasional Tweets @LexTLindsay.

BETH LUMEN

Beth Lumen (she/her/hers) has been writing both fan fiction and original fiction forever, and she is thrilled to have the opportunity to contribute to this anthology as her first published work. She's written in various book and TV fandoms since the mid-2000s, most recently for queer contemporary novels. In addition to reading and writing happy gay love stories, Beth loves volleyball, traveling, hiking, and making a mess in the kitchen. She lives in St. Paul, MN, with her lovely partner and the two best dogs.

KRISTI MAE

Kristi Mae is a STEM doctoral student in Canada who holds degrees in music, psychology, and (unofficially) napping. She is asexual and aromantic and enjoys creating queer fiction that subverts expectations for what relationships should look like. In her free time, she loves to do bookbinding projects and write stories for her friends in fandom.

PUCK MALAMUD

Puck Malamud (pronouns: ve/ver/vis/verself or they/them/theirs/themself) is a librarian, writer, and poet who has lived in a variety of large East Coast US cities since immigrating from Ukraine in the 1990s. Ve is co-author of a chapter on being LGBTQ in the library profession, and author and co-author of multiple fanfics in various fandoms, though primarily *The Untamed* and *Mo Dao Zu Shi*. When not desperately trying to keep up with vis Libby holds, Puck can be found building community and engaging in a rotating (and ever increasing) collection of hobbies.

JO MATHIESON

Jo Mathieson is a prolific writer of queer romance stories. Jo lives with her spouse (also a writer) on a small farm in in Eastern Ontario, Canada, where they grow vegetables and raise heritage-breed chickens.

OWL OUTERBRIDGE

Owl Outerbridge is a disabled author and editor living in the Pacific Northwest with her wife, child, and menagerie of small animals. Fueled by over twenty years of writing experience, ADHD, and a passion for the English language, she writes sapphic science fiction and fantasy stories about love, life, hope in dark times, and sometimes motherhood. When she isn't writing, she advocates for universal preschool, special education, and LGBTQ rights and representation. She can often be found out in nature with pen and knitting needles in hand, and stomping through wet places in search of pretty rocks with her beautiful family.

MAGGIE PAGE

Maggie Page lives in Texas with family, including her incorrigibly clumsy mom with a green thumb, two silly dogs who are also mother and daughter, and a fierce feline hunter. Maggie has previously published several poems and a piece of flash fiction with collegiate and independent journals.

When not indulging the urge to write, Maggie enjoys music, traveling, camping, dabbling in various art forms, principally watercolor and graphic making, and torturing her loved ones with her ruthless board game victories.

EM ROWNTREE

Em Rowntree's first foray into the world of writing was with a story called *The Magic Land* that featured a unicorn and a flying carpet the size of a country, and they've been chasing that high ever since. They've been sharing their writing online for almost seven years and have had poems and short stories published in anthologies. They live in the UK.

SHEA SULLIVAN

Shea Sullivan is a life-long writer living in upstate New York. As a late-blooming queer person, she enjoys writing about complex characters coming into themselves and finding comfort in being exactly who they are.

Shea's day jobs in computer programming and middle management have molded her into the patient, sarcastic, big-hearted, frustrated human she is today, but it's what she does outside the 9–5 that really excites her. When she's not writing, she can be found painting, napping, making quilts, watching documentaries, and trying not to adopt more animals, usually with a cup of tea in hand.

FLORENCE VALE

Florence is a Norwegian picture book author and fanfic enthusiast. Her current obsessions include Star Trek: Deep Space Nine, The Magnus Archives, and just about any actual play podcast she can get her hands on. In addition to *Add Magic to Taste* and her Archive of Our Own account, you can find her writing in the original zines *Mansion of Fears* and *Carpe Noctem*.

NINA WATERS

Claire Houck (she/they/he), pen name Nina Waters, fandom name unforth, is queer, married to the lovely Lisa, and a mother of two. Claire has been writing fanfiction since the young age of seven, when she penned (well, two-finger typed and printed dot matrix) the timeless classic "the story of my littl ponies and the glob." Since then, her spelling, grammar, and prose have improved immensely. She has written over four hundred short stories, a number of novellas, and 16 novels—some original, some fanfiction—including *A Glimmer of Hope*, which was successfully Kickstarted and self-published in fall, 2016.

ABOUT DUCK PRINTS PRESS LLC

Duck Prints Press LLC is an independent publisher based in New York State. Our founding vision is to help fanfiction authors navigate the complex process of bringing their original works from first draft to print, culminating in publishing their work under our imprint. We are particularly dedicated to working with queer authors and publishing stories featuring characters from across the LGBTQIA+ spectrum.

Back us on Patreon to get a bonus, brand-new *Add Magic to Taste* story by Willa Blythe!

Find us online at our website, **duckprintspress.com**, or on social media:
Bluesky: duckprintspress
Dreamwidth: duckprintspress.dreamwidth.org
Facebook: duckprintspress
Instagram: duckprintspress
Mastodon: @dppunforth
Patreon: duckprintspress
Pillowfort: duckprintspress
Pinterest: duckprintspress
TikTok: @duckprintspress
Tumblr: duckprintspress

Goodreads: https://www.goodreads.com/user/show/129902473-duck-prints-press-llc
Storygraph: https://app.thestorygraph.com/profile/unforth